ABOUT THE AUTHOR

Over ten years ago, Jo moved from suburban Brisbane to rural Tasmania. Since then, she's been wrangling an ever-growing collection of animals, bringing up two sons, and attempting to transform blackberry-infested paddocks into beautiful gardens. Now, she also writes full-time, creating twisty, suspenseful stories that feature flawed characters who've made mistakes, but who turn out to be stronger than they think.

Jo has been a dental assistant, an event co-ordinator, a travel agent, and has run an online shop—never really believing her passion for writing could lead to anything. In 2015, while living in Bangkok with her husband and kids, she completed an MA in writing—realising along the way that she had to stop procrastinating and just write (and finish) at least one book.

So with the mantra 'if not now, when?' stuck to her computer, she did. *The House of Now and Then* is her debut novel. She is now working on her second book.

You can find Jo on Instagram at @jo.dixon.writes; on Facebook at Jo Dixon, Writer; or on her website jo-dixon.com.

THE HOUSE OF NOW AND THEN

JO DIXON

FICTION
HQ

First Published 2023
First Australian Paperback Edition 2023
ISBN 9781867250302

THE HOUSE OF NOW AND THEN
© 2023 by Jo Dixon
Australian Copyright 2023
New Zealand Copyright 2023

This is a work of fiction. Names, characters, places, and incidents are either the product of the author's imagination or are used fictitiously, and any resemblance to actual persons, living or dead, business establishments, events, or locales is entirely coincidental.

Published by
HQ Fiction
An imprint of Harlequin Enterprises (Australia) Pty Limited (ABN 47 001 180 918), a subsidiary of HarperCollins Publishers Australia Pty Limited (ABN 36 009 913 517)
Level 13, 201 Elizabeth St
SYDNEY NSW 2000
AUSTRALIA

® and TM (apart from those relating to FSC®) are trademarks of Harlequin Enterprises (Australia) Pty Limited or its corporate affiliates. Trademarks indicated with ® are registered in Australia, New Zealand and in other countries.

A catalogue record for this book is available from the National Library of Australia www.librariesaustralia.nla.gov.au

Printed and bound in Australia by McPherson's Printing Group

To my partner in crime.
Together we can do anything.
Shall we make some more crazy plans?

Thirty years.
I've lived a life between then and now.
It has passed with fleeting moments of joy and happiness,
and long, long days when the guilt and regret have been
suffocating. Always I have missed you. Missed us.
You saved me and, in turn, I gave you pain and loss. I lie
awake dreaming that your life has been the spectacular,
exhilarating adventure you deserve. That your spirit wasn't
crushed beyond repair.
I know you must want answers, but I'm too much a coward.
I don't have the courage to face you—I can't be the one to
give you the truth.
I have done my best.
It was not enough.
I am sorry, my love.

CHAPTER ONE

Tuesday, 10 December 1985

Pippa climbed from the back seat, the dust from the drive-way immediately settling inside her sandals and sticking to her sweaty feet. The shoes had been a bad choice. Rebecca had insisted these orange chunks of plastic were better than a worn pair of Volleys, and in an attempt at friendship Pippa had gone along. Now she had only herself to blame for the bandaid-covered blisters on her heels. She lifted an arm, shielding her eyes from the glare of the Tasmanian summer sun, and squinted at a house that defied all her expectations.

She laughed incredulously as the challenges of four days on the road and one night on the heaving *Abel Tasman* ferry were immediately forgotten. 'Holy shit, Jeremy, you and Eloise didn't give anything away, did you?'

Jeremy turned and grinned back at her. 'Better than you thought it would be?'

'Absolutely.' She went to stand beside him, knocking him with her shoulder. 'Man, I was expecting some cute little cottage with a permanent lean and possums in the roof. And *that* would've been okay.' Instead, this building was sleek and white, a stark contrast to the muted greens and browns of the dry bush. There were simple, long lines and stone features, and the angled roof rose from this side to the other like a ramp. Jeremy's godmother Eloise might live in the middle of nowhere, but this modern masterpiece was very in keeping with her style: elegant, artistic and worldly.

'I wanted it to be a surprise,' Jeremy said.

'Nicely done, my friend.'

Jeremy swung his keys around his finger, the metallic jangle and the tick of the Laser's cooling engine loud against the quiet of the day. Pippa glanced across at Rebecca, who was busy smoothing out her knee-length pink shorts and fussing with the banana-coloured bandana that held back her hair. She tugged at the ends of the knot, making cotton rabbit ears stick up from her freshly permed curls. Preening complete, she came around the car to take her usual position, glued against Jeremy's hip. He lifted an arm and draped it across her shoulders.

'Must be worth a fortune,' Rebecca said.

'Probably,' Jeremy replied. 'I think Eloise was romantically involved with an architect when she was younger.'

'What? He gave her *this*?' Pippa asked. Eloise's life was fascinating.

'Not quite. I think he gave her his skill … you know, designed it for her, drew up the plans. Anyway, it's about fifteen years old now, I guess.'

Pippa admired the building and its position high on the hill. The bush ran up to the peak behind them, and from the other side of the house was a wide view down and out to the water. 'No neighbours,' she noted.

'No anything.' Rebecca sounded unimpressed.

Jeremy, on the other hand, looked thrilled. 'We'll have to do a drive up to Hobart for shopping. Stock up on everything. Don't want to get caught short on supplies.'

'Like toilet paper?' Pippa suggested.

'Oh god, not the toilet paper.' Jeremy knew exactly what she was talking about. It was a shared tale of misadventure that was funnier in the retelling than it had been to experience. 'Who could forget Phuket!' He snorted.

'We thought we were so organised.'

He shook his head. 'We had no idea.'

'And you got the runs.'

'No, *you* got the runs. I was fine … for the first night.'

They grinned at each other, remembering the disaster those few days had been. They'd been almost strangers before that trip, but by the time they'd returned home to Brisbane they were destined to be lifelong mates.

Rebecca didn't laugh. 'Sounds hideous,' she said.

Sometimes Pippa felt sorry for her. It couldn't be easy when your boyfriend had a girl friend. A friend who had, until last week, also been a housemate. A friend he had travelled with, partied with, and slept with once … or twice … or so. And a friend who had saved his life. It made for a unique connection. It must be hard to be with Jeremy when Pippa came as part of the package. But then Rebecca would direct one of her snide comments towards Pippa, subtle and careful, draped in fraudulent concern and good intentions. 'Oh, Pippa, I love your style—I never get tired of seeing that skirt.' 'Pippa, I'd have invited you, but I thought my colleagues would bore you.' 'Gosh, I envy you, Pippa—it must be so nice not having to get up every day for work, but I do love my job so I guess

I'm lucky.' Pippa would stop with the pity and feel something a little more vindictive. She wasn't jealous. She didn't want Jeremy for herself. She simply didn't like his girlfriend.

'Is your godmother here?' Rebecca asked him.

'Should be. She's expecting us, and that's hers.' He pointed towards the small carport where a red Triumph sat with its roof down.

Pippa followed the others to the front door. While Jeremy knocked, she peered inside, a glass panel beside the door providing a view across a foyer, down to a split-level open living area, and through to a wall of windows and French doors. The ceiling and floors were lined with a gleaming golden wood, the walls were white, and artworks and bookshelves were on display. It was spacious and light and incredibly stylish. Oh yes, living here for the next ten weeks was not going to be hard at all, even if she had to put up with Rebecca for the first five.

'The door's unlocked,' said Jeremy when Eloise failed to appear. 'Should we go in?'

'No, we can't do that.' Rebecca was a stickler for rules, and proper etiquette, and appropriate behaviour. There was no way *she* would have lost her job under suspicion of theft. But then she would also never have backpacked through a developing country, played strip poker, or danced drunkenly around a beach bonfire with total strangers. Jeremy would have. In fact, he had—with Pippa right by his side. These days he was more restrained, although his adventurous spirit was still there. If he'd been completely tamed, he wouldn't have packed up his life, ready to relocate to London in two months. Even with a potential job in place, it was a big move.

'No, you're right,' he said. 'Let's have a look around. She's probably out walking somewhere.'

The three of them traipsed around the house to where a paved terrace extended out from the closed French doors. While Rebecca and Jeremy did a full lap, Pippa put on her sunglasses, flopped into one of the cushioned cane chairs and admired the view. A cloudless sky. A steep expanse of cleared grass running a hundred metres or so down to an edge of bush. A stretch of dark water separating them from an undulating length of land in the distance. It was truly spectacular.

'There she is,' Jeremy called, pointing and waving.

Towards the bottom of the hill, Eloise stepped out from beneath the trees. A small shaggy dog trotted at her side.

Pippa jumped up, leaving the others standing where they were, and galloped down to meet their hostess. The last time Eloise had visited Jeremy and his mum in Brisbane, Pippa had hung out with her and thoroughly enjoyed her company. They were kindred spirits, Pippa liked to think, even though Eloise was as old as her parents.

'Welcome.' Eloise opened her arms and wrapped Pippa in a long hug. 'I'm so glad you could come.'

'I'm so glad you asked us.' Pippa gave the dog an enthusiastic scratch behind the ears. 'Who's this?'

'Honey.'

'Hello, Honey.' The dog dropped to the ground and offered her pale belly for Pippa to rub. 'You're lovely, aren't you? What sort of dog are you?'

'She's a special blend of unknowns, and she'll love you forever if you keep doing that.'

Pippa spoke to the happy dog and gave her a final pat. 'I promise there'll be plenty of cuddles for you, Honey. But let's head up, shall we?' She stood and linked arms with Eloise as they climbed back towards the house. 'This place is amazing.

When you said "come and house-sit my Tassie cottage", this—'
she waved an arm to encompass not only the house but also its
beautiful surroundings '—is not what I pictured.'

'It's rather gorgeous, isn't it?' Eloise smiled. 'I love living
here.'

'Are you sure you want to leave this place in our hands?'

'Oh, I doubt you could get up to more mischief than me.' She
glanced up to where Rebecca and Jeremy stood side by side,
then whispered, 'Looks like my darling godson will be behaving himself.'

'And to think he was such a wild boy,' Pippa murmured
back, shaking her head in mock dismay.

'Maybe she's wicked in bed.'

'Nope.'

'And you know this because …?'

'Share house. Thin walls. Not much goes unnoticed.'

Eloise squeezed her arm and laughed. 'Let's get you settled.
Then drinks before dinner. I have all the ingredients for sangria. What do you think?'

'Brilliant idea.'

As they reached the terrace, Eloise gave an effusive welcome
to the others before flinging open the doors and inviting them
into her home.

This summer was going to be spectacular.

CHAPTER TWO

Monday, 12 June 2017

Gin suited Olivia perfectly. Legend declared it the drink of dejected, fallen women. Women like her. She was—according to a million outraged folk on social media—a truly wicked woman, and much of the time she tended to agree. But on good days, she tried to think of herself as someone who'd made some really bad choices ... and quite a few stupid mistakes.

Either way, the gin helped. The cap on the new bottle gave a satisfying snap as she twisted it open. She poured for a slow count of four, added a splash of tonic water, then went back down the wide steps to the living area. Brian was on the sofa, curled into her favourite blanket, the one made from the fleece of sacred alpacas and woven by the light of a blue moon, or something like that. The one that cost stupid money. The one that could, for a moment, make her think she was cherished. If her silence was going to be bought, then she could allow herself a few luxuries. She told herself this every time she hit *Add to Cart* and *Checkout Now*.

She bent over and whispered in his ear, 'Love you, Brian. But that's my seat.'

He lifted his head to give a sleepy mew but didn't move, and she didn't have the heart to push him out. He deserved alpaca more than she did—the raggedy ears and missing eye showed his life had been tougher than hers. She'd adopted him from a Hobart rescue centre three months ago, a week after her arrival in Tasmania, and they made a good pair. One flawed, emotionally battered twenty-nine-year-old and her fearless, slightly broken buddy, both of them unwanted. Having a companion had made her self-pity and loneliness slightly less crushing.

She sat cross-legged next to him, pulled a cushion into her lap, and took a long drink of her G & T. The house had come fully furnished, and the modular L-shaped sofa was large and comfortable. The blanket and cushions were her own touches, as was the portable bluetooth speaker through which a mellow mix of Sufjan Stevens and Nick Drake was playing. When Brian rolled onto his back, she pulled out her phone and snapped a few photos. The light was soft, the fire flickering in the background, his front paws reaching out. She uploaded the best shot to Brian's Instagram account with the comment 'Living the life' and a slew of hashtags, then scrolled for a few minutes through her carefully curated feed. Cats. Cats. Stationery. Cats. Journalling. Beautiful hotels. Cats.

Her finger hovered over the search icon. The urge to check in on Hayden flowed through her, shrinking her best intentions, like a gambling addict faced with a row of sparkly, tinkling pokies. She no longer followed him and would have to tap in his name to see what he was doing. Chances were, despite everything, things were perfectly fine in his world.

'Step away from the pain machine,' she said to herself fiercely. She dropped the phone onto the couch and lifted her glass, drinking till the gin softened her edges.

If she was going to get drunk, she needed to eat. To heat something up. Especially since she now had options. For the past few days her fridge and freezer had been empty, but the night before, as the last sheets of toilet paper had spun free from the roll, necessity had won. She had made the forty-five-minute trip to the nearest supermarket, entering the white fluorescent glare with her beanie pulled low and her eyes averted, just another late-night shuffler doing their shop in a near-empty store. With the focus of a seasoned doomsday prepper she'd catered for her hibernation, filling her trolley with frozen meals (the calorie-rich comfort kind), chips, dips, cheese, chocolate, tonic water, several bottles of gin, and the toilet paper.

She sipped again, then set the glass on the sublime mid-century coffee table, the one she didn't own, and nudged the small pile of mail. The yellow redirection stickers were a reminder to change her postal address. But what was the point? She didn't even know if she'd be staying here much longer, and none of this stuff was vital.

Except the redirection service would soon expire, and then her personalised junk mail would land at her old apartment. The new owners knew they'd bought it from *the* Olivia Haymers, because her name was on the contract. Getting her mail would add extra titillation. *Wow, look at this, she shops at Zara and L'Occitane and once supported the RSPCA. Ooh, a lingerie catalogue! Well, well, that's not a surprise, is it? Does she fancy the tacky crotchless red knickers or the glamorous black corset?*

Olivia flicked through the pile. The square pink envelope was last. It was sweet lolly-pink, the pink of ballet tights and bubble-gum and little girls' pencil cases. The handwritten address was partly visible under the printed yellow sticker, written in vivid red and embellished with swirls and flourishes.

Her heart lurched, thudding hard and fast at the base of her throat.

She'd erased her social media, changed her email address and her number, cut all association with her old life and moved to the middle of nowhere in Tasmania, the arse end of Australia. She was hidden from the world, her life small and quiet. For months there had been nothing from Leena. No angry messages, no veiled threats, no strange, gushing recollections of their exploits. The silence had been serene, and Olivia had relaxed a little, become complacent. She had begun to believe it had stopped, that her refusal to respond any further had finally sent a clear message.

She'd been so stupid. Of course it wasn't over. It would never be over.

Olivia dropped the letter back on the table and escaped to the huge windows, still clutching her glass. Over the past hour the view had become ominous, and in the descending darkness Bruny Island hulked long and low on the horizon. The water of the D'Entrecasteaux channel, normally shel-tered and calm, was being swept into a wild dance by the brutish force of the wind. The sky was heavy with clouds. Not for the first time, she wished the room had curtains so she could close out the night and create a cocoon. Eloise—the landlady Olivia had yet to meet—must have deemed them unnecessary, happy to be high on the side of a hill with-out a neighbour or a road in sight. But Olivia knew better than to presume she was hidden. There was always someone watching. Just because you couldn't see them didn't mean they couldn't see you.

She crossed to the floor lamp and switched it off, the room now lit only by firelight. Picking up the envelope, she moved to the glass-enclosed fireplace and rested a hand against the surrounding stacked stone wall. She hesitated. It wasn't the guilt that stopped her from throwing it on the flames. It was more a need to know—to peel back a bandage, to examine a wound and see if there was still a festering mess of infection. Because maybe, just maybe, Leena was making amends. Maybe the wound had healed.

Olivia ripped it open.

On the front of the card was a mouse, her arms full of brightly coloured flowers, *I Miss You* in flowing cursive font beneath her feet. The letter was folded inside.

5 June 2017

My dearest Olly-Indy,

Where are you? I'm finally free and breathing real air—and the first thing I wanted to do was see you! I can't believe you sold the apartment I found for you. I'm hurt. Disappointed. It is not okay. You put me in that place, took your hush money and ran away. You should be ashamed.

We need to talk, don't you think, sweetie?

Knowing how efficient you are, I'm confident this letter will reach you. What a pity I can't follow it to where you are hiding. I'll have to think of some other way. It can't be that hard. No one can truly disappear.

Think of me, my dear friend. I am going to find you. Because, really, you owe me. And debts need to be paid. Don't you agree?

Leena xx

Olivia folded the pink paper, pressed it back inside the card and put her head in her hands, the alcohol now acid at the back of her mouth. What did Leena want? Revenge? They both had to live with the consequences of their actions. For Leena, that had meant jail. For Olivia, it had meant the loss of her job and the respect of the industry she loved. It had meant being criticised in the media, eviscerated online, and abused in the streets. It had meant shame and humiliation. Moments of fear. And now, isolation and crushing loneliness. Surely that was enough?

Obviously, Leena didn't think so.

CHAPTER THREE

Tuesday, 20 June 2017

The need for water dragged Olivia out of an uncomfortable sleep. Her bladder ached and her stomach heaved. She swallowed, her tongue lumpish and sticky, and a needle of pain twisted behind her right eye. After hauling herself closer to the edge of the bed, she groped for the glass on the bedside table. It was dirty, smeared with fingerprints, with smudges of lip balm around the rim. She gagged at the faint taste of gin in the water.

In the week since Leena's letter had arrived, Olivia had been existing in a rut of inactivity and slobbish living, unable to leave the house—unable to do anything. It was as though the tiny ember of motivation and hope she had gently been nurturing had been thoroughly doused. Over the past few days, she had taken four novels from the floor-to-ceiling wall of books left by Eloise but had got no further than the third chapter in any of them. She'd wandered slowly from one end of the long house to the other, from the bedroom she'd made her own, through the lounge, up the five steps to the foyer, past the dining area, and along the short hall to the spare bedroom. Then she'd retraced her steps, aimlessly moving cushions, reshelving the unread books, plucking cat hair from the sofa. She'd spent hours in a black hole of online shopping and lost track of what she'd bought: another throw rug, a set of French linen sheets, scented candles, bath oil, a pair of red gumboots. She'd vaguely justified her purchases as self-care, then realised she didn't have to justify anything to anyone. And that none of these things would make her feel better anyway.

Yesterday she opened a new notebook and wrote *Five Year Plan*. Underlined it, then crossed it out. Wrote *Goals*, thinking it would be better to start with a general sense of what she was working towards. Underlined that too. Sat staring out the window for an hour. Scribbled out the word. Goals had to be achievable and measurable and have deadlines. Her world was too small, too restricted. Time meant nothing. There were too many things beyond her control. She wrote, *What do I want my life to look like?* Then started crying, because the question hurt too much. She ripped out the page, burned it, closed the notebook and threw it in a drawer.

After that she dragged rugs and pillows to the floor, making a nest in front of the tall windows. She counted the blue wrens flitting over the huge old-fashioned brick barbecue, and the eagles soaring against the pale blue sky. Looking down on the water, she watched the ferry moving back and forth across the channel, and the occasional boat motoring one way or the other. She couldn't see people, but she imagined them out there, living their lives.

As night fell she decided to move her atrophying body and had the brilliant idea that a few drinks and some loud music would ease her misery. The first few glasses did their job. She switched to an oldies playlist, to avoid any reminders of nights in clubs, and turned up the volume. D:Ream promised her that things could only get better, and she believed it, singing along loudly and badly. The Spice Girls and Jennifer Lopez had her dancing, and it all felt great, or at least numbingly better, until at some point the alcohol stopped lifting her up. Then there was a rapid plummet to sobs and snot, with Bonnie Tyler's 'Total Eclipse of the Heart' perfectly summing up the state of her life. She *had* fallen apart.

Her life was ugly and unfair. No one would ever love her. No one would ever even have sex with her—not unless shagging a film star's leftovers was a turn-on. Everything she had worked for was lost. She could never get a job in hotels again. Her stash of money wouldn't last forever. Leena would always want revenge.

And ultimately it was Olivia's fault.

Sitting on the edge of her bed, she groaned and set the water glass down. She had to get over this pathetic self-pity. Maybe it was time to stop hiding and do something a bit more proactive … like leave the country. Sure, it hadn't worked the first time, but a popular luxury resort in Ubud, Bali, had been a bad choice. It had been too soon after the trial, and there had been too many Australians with their cameras. This time she could do it differently. She could live a simple, anonymous life off the beaten track in Thailand, or Iceland, or New York. What was stopping her? She might as well take the money and start again somewhere new.

Brian rose from his spot at the end of the bed, arched his spine, stretched out one back leg then the other, and then stalked through the valleys of her doona to smoosh his shabby head against hers. He was her one responsibility. Her only anchor.

'Okay, I know,' she moaned. 'I have to stop wallowing.'

The unavoidable fact was, life went on, whether you were an active participant or a barely conscious objector. The days turned, the weeks passed, and sometimes things happened around you or to you. And the cat needed to be fed.

She heaved herself upright. 'Don't think, move,' she muttered. She had to try.

*

It took her two hours, a long shower, several Panadol, and some strong coffee to leave the house. Her body was craving proper sustenance, the sort of nourishment that couldn't be delivered by a processed meal that came sealed in plastic.

Unable to face the long drive to the supermarket, she headed to the nearby village, bumping over potholes in the dirt verge as she pulled up outside the Devils Bay general store. This far south of Hobart, the Channel Highway was little more than a country road: seven big steps would take you from one side to the other, and there were no gutters or even footpaths. The speed limit was fifty, and the volume of traffic ranged from non-existent in the evenings to a slow stream of hire cars and campervans in the summer holiday rush. On this sullen day the village was empty. The only traffic was in the channel, a tin dinghy putt-putting across the flat water near the jetty.

From the outside the store looked like it hadn't been touched in half a century. There were large multipaned windows, weatherboard walls with flaking paint, and a corrugated-iron awning. A noticeboard was next to the front door, notes and flyers flapping. Yoga, film nights, the monthly market at the village hall, a bonfire evening at a local farm, hay for sale, offers to house-sit, a workshop on spinning and weaving, and a house for rent. There was nothing here that she wanted or needed. The village was a magazine-worthy lifestyle location, but she wasn't interested in joining the community.

Even though her trips to the village had been incident free, Olivia instinctively braced herself as she pushed open the door. Perhaps the locals weren't all that concerned about scandals happening outside their bubble, or maybe her moment of notoriety was passing. Perhaps she was unrecognisable in her dull, practical clothes and shorter hair. But she couldn't be sure, and whatever the case, she hadn't yet got to the point of venturing out without anticipating confrontation. Stares and words and sneering laughter could come at any time.

The store had a high rafted ceiling and well-stocked shelves. Olivia picked out vegetables, local smoked salmon and a heavy loaf of sourdough. The woman at the counter was friendly and spent several minutes making small talk. Olivia managed a smile and a few seconds of eye contact, disproportionately buoyed by the interaction.

The post office was next and felt easier, since she had become something of a regular. She'd first met the postmistress, Wendy, two weeks after her arrival, after she'd finally realised there was no letterbox at her gate. Turned out she didn't need a letterbox because, incredibly, there was no delivery. Everyone in the area had to trek to the village to get their mail, making the tiny post office the centre of activity. It was like living in one of those quaint, predictable British TV villages where murders happened every other week. Olivia had taken a post office box, accessible at any time, so she could pull up in the dark and retrieve her mail without being observed. This had worked until she'd started with the online shopping binges. Parcels didn't fit in the box. Now she'd learnt to time her visits for late afternoon.

'Hello there, love, how're you going?' Wendy called out as soon as she entered. 'Bit of a glum day, isn't it?'

Olivia held the door for the boy who was leaving, then moved to the counter. 'Hi, Wendy.' It was impossible not to smile at the woman's warm greeting.

Wendy piled Olivia's packages on the counter and scanned the delivery barcode of each one. 'Not too many today. Some books, by the look of them.'

Olivia glanced at the labels. 'Notebooks and journals.' Old habits were hard to break and she still salivated over beautiful stationery, the sort that promised to improve her life. It didn't matter that she had a dozen equally lovely notebooks at home.

'Nice,' said Wendy. 'Love a good notepad. So, not finding it too cold then? Have you got enough wood stacked and ready?'

An old guy with gnarled hands and a battered truck had delivered the firewood. Happy to chat, he'd reassured Olivia that down here the one antivenom saved you from all three deadly snakes. He'd told her to avoid the big ants with bright orange legs and pincers—jack jumpers, they were called. People died from those suckers, he'd said. Olivia couldn't tell whether he thought he was being helpful or if he enjoyed scaring the hell out of fresh-on-the-ground mainlanders.

'I think I'm all set,' she told Wendy. 'It did take me a while to get the hang of lighting a fire, though.' She was rather proud of the fact she now knew her kindling from her logs and could coax a smouldering, smoking fire back to flames.

'Well done! Everyone thinks it's as easy as striking a match, but making a good fire is a real skill, I say. Here you go, love.' Wendy pulled envelopes from her side of Olivia's box and set them on top of her parcels.

Olivia looked at the mail. An oily dread slid over her, smothering the thin pleasure she'd taken from the chat. 'Thank you,' she said, needing to leave. The redirection stickers were glaring at her, warning there could be a danger in the pile far worse than deadly ants.

'Need a hand to the car?'

'No thanks, I'm right.' Olivia picked up the packages and tucked the brochures, magazines and bills under one arm, avoiding the urge to check for hate mail. 'See you soon!' She had to get to the car, to see what she was holding.

She was at the door when Wendy called out, 'Oh, I nearly forgot.'

Olivia lifted her head and smiled vaguely, desperate to leave.

'Someone was here yesterday, asking about you.'

CHAPTER FOUR

Olivia stopped, one hand against the post office door. Her mind was stuck, her body immobile. 'Who ...?' She sucked in a breath and tried again, fighting to speak in a tone of everyday curiosity rather than fear. 'Who was looking for me?' She took a few steps back into the room.

Wendy quickly assessed her, then gave a reassuring smile. 'A man. Youngish, kinda good-looking, but not too pretty if you know what I mean. I didn't get his name, but definitely not a local. He had a Pommie accent.' She leant forward and rested her folded arms on the high wooden counter. 'And—I should've said—from the way he was asking, he was more interested in the house, Eloise's house. Wanted to know who was living there now. And he wanted to know about Eloise—if I knew where she'd moved or had any contact details, that sort of thing. Of course, even if I did know, I couldn't give out that sort of information. Privacy and all that.'

'This person didn't ask for me by name?' The surge of panic was yet to retreat.

'Oh no, not at all. Sorry, did I give that impression?'

Olivia tried to smile, to show she wasn't concerned. 'Um, a little.'

'Oh love, no, no, no. And when he asked about who was in the house now, I just said it was rented out privately and left it at that. Anyway, wanted to give you the heads up. Some people are way too curious about that house.'

'Oh, okay then. Thanks.' Relief doused her anxiety, leaving her light and woozy.

'If people come in here asking after locals—where they live, how to find them, that kind of thing—I pull out the actual phone book, take a look to see if they have a public listing. If they don't, I say I can't remember.'

Olivia shook her head. 'I imagine you remember everyone.'

'Of course, I've been here fifteen years. I know who's who alright, and where they are. Who's shacked up with who. Who's separated. Whose mail should never be given to their spouse. But that's not knowledge to be handed out willy-nilly. Like I say, privacy is important.' She gave Olivia a direct, knowing look, making it clear her message was personal.

'So, if someone rocked up wanting to find a particular person?'

'They wouldn't find out from me.'

'No matter the reason they gave?' Olivia shifted the parcels in her arms.

Wendy shook her head. 'I know what you're asking. And, don't worry, if someone came looking for you, they'd get the same response. You may only have been here a wee bit, but if you're living here, you're a local.'

Olivia's nose prickled painfully as a wave of emotion caught her off guard. Although Wendy knew exactly who she was, her inclination was to protect not criticise. Olivia took a breath. 'That's good to know. Thank you. I appreciate it.'

'Don't worry. Down here, it's not like in the city.' Wendy put a fist on her hip as though she was facing down all the vices of Sydney. 'We love gossip as much as the next gaggle of geese, but we know the value of privacy too. The village learnt that years ago. This place is too small for us to start exposing each other. So don't fret, love.'

Olivia let out a long breath, the tension completely flowing out of her. But something Wendy had said stopped her from leaving. 'What did you mean by people being curious about the house?' Eloise's place was lovely and a classic example of a particular style, but was it of any architectural significance?

'Oh, right. I presumed you knew. About the disappearance? No? Of course not. Okay, well basically, some kids were staying at Eloise's house—this is back in the eighties—and one of them disappeared. He was about eighteen or nineteen, I think, maybe older. And that house was the last place he was seen. His car turned up in the carpark at the yacht club in the city, but he was never found.'

'Gosh.' Goosebumps flitted up her arms. 'What do they think happened?'

'Oh, you know, there's a bunch of theories. Even though the coroner ruled him deceased years later, there were never any real answers. Now, what happens is, we get the occasional true-crime nut turning up thinking they can solve the mystery.' Wendy threw up her hands. 'God knows what they reckon they're going to achieve. So far they haven't been able to get much info out of the locals, so there's barely anything about the case online. I suspect this Pommie bloke is another one of them.'

That made sense. True-crime mysteries were addictive. Even hearing this brief outline of the story had tickled Olivia's curiosity.

'Anyway, if this guy hassles you, tell him to sod off. And then come and tell me. You don't need people like that bothering you.'

Olivia had an urge to wrap her arms around her postmistress. Despite Wendy's diminutive size, she had a combination of warmth and tough pragmatism that made her seem like the sort of woman who would dispense wonderful hugs. And Olivia could definitely have done with one—it had been so long since she'd made physical contact with anyone.

She was saved from making a fool of herself by the arrival of a man in well-worn overalls and a shabby akubra. No doubt he was one of the born-and-bred local farmers and not a cashed-up mainlander who'd moved here with dreams of growing their own vegetables, having a few chickens and breathing fresh air.

'Hello, love,' said Wendy, reaching for the man's mail. 'How are you today?'

'Good. You?' The man put a hand on the counter, settling in for a chat.

'I'll see you later,' Olivia called as she headed for the door again.

Wendy gave her a look that was both warm and embracing. 'Take care, sweetie! See you soon.'

*

That night Olivia slept badly. When she'd been standing in the post office, Wendy's explanation had been reassuring. The man looking for Eloise's house was an amateur sleuth, maybe a true-crime podcaster, nothing to do with Olivia. But when she woke in the middle of the night, when the world was at its darkest, dread won out. Someone wanted to know who was living here. The story the man had given was probably a cover. He could be a journalist motivated by Leena's release or an investigator hired by Leena to track Olivia down.

Or maybe Hayden had hired him. For a delicious moment, her thoughts veered into more fantastical options. Maybe Hayden missed her, he regretted everything, and he wanted to find her, reach out to her. He wanted to love her again—or apologise for abandoning her to the vengeance of his fans. But even at 3 am that fantasy was too crazy. Hayden may not have voiced his contempt, but she knew he was done with her. He blamed her for the disaster that had followed the end of their affair. Most likely he despised her.

Leena had made it clear she was determined to find Olivia and make her pay. Now, days later, a guy had turned up asking questions. Surely that was no coincidence.

The light of morning pushed the paranoia back a little, taking Olivia from panic to wariness. Watching the glow of the pink and orange sunrise, she reminded herself the man had only asked Wendy about contacting Eloise.

Olivia had stumbled across a private listing for the house online, and its classic lines and isolated location had made her yearn for the simple peace it seemed to offer. By then she knew there was nothing left for her in Sydney. It had been sixteen months since she'd ended the affair. Nearly a year since Hayden's pre-emptive mea culpa video and the great wailing of the masses. Eleven months since the gossip press named her as his lover. Ten months and three weeks since the first ten-second clip was anonymously posted online, revealing Olivia naked and astride Australia's favourite actor. Ten months and twenty days since she was fired. And nine months since Leena's trial. Olivia hadn't worked since, and she had been photographed, verbally abused and written about more times than she could ever count. When she realised Leena would soon transition to the suspended part of her jail sentence, the need to get away became overwhelming.

Her apartment sold quickly, and after clearing her whopping mortgage, she stashed the rest in the bank. She answered the ad for the house with an offer of six months' rent in advance and sold herself as the perfect tenant. Nothing said *responsible* like being the former assistant manager of a hip boutique hotel.

A day later the landlady rang. 'Are you the girl caught up in that horrid sex-tape blackmail case, with that actor?' Eloise asked, skipping small talk and striding straight into the muck.

Olivia's heart fell. 'Yes,' she said. It was tempting to laugh about how she was cursed with the same name as that hussy, but what was the point? 'Unfortunately, I am.'

Eloise made a contemplative noise. 'I imagine it must be a diabolical state of affairs.'

'It certainly is.'

There was a pause, and Olivia braced herself for rejection.

'I can see why you want to get away to Devils Bay. You'll want to lay low and be inconspicuous for a while, I should think. Let all those ghastly gutter dwellers find something new to focus on.'

Empathy from a stranger? It happened, but not often enough to outweigh the abuse.

'That's my intention,' said Olivia. 'To live a very quiet life.'

'Well, quiet you shall certainly have. But please, no cameras in the bedroom.'

'The camera wasn't me—' she protested, then realised she was being teased when Eloise chuckled.

'Dear girl, the sooner you learn to laugh this all off, the better it will be.'

'I can't imagine ever seeing the funny side,' she said with a small, polite laugh.

'I'm sure. But it could be something to aim for.'

There was no chance Olivia would ever find humour in this chapter in her life, but she didn't say so. She moved in two weeks later, and the house turned out to be everything she had hoped: isolated but not too remote, and beautiful in a retro way, with an amazing view.

Making herself toast and coffee, she found herself wondering again about the connection between the house and the teenage boy who had disappeared. Taking her plate and mug, she crossed the foyer to the small round dining table on the opposite side. The dining area was separated from the entrance by a wooden divide of open shelving, and a half wall gave the area a mezzanine feel, opening it to the lounge below and allowing views through the French doors. Olivia sat in one of the upholstered chairs and set her coffee on the table, careful to slip a coaster underneath. She did a quick keyword search on her phone: *Missing boy. Devils Bay. Unsolved.*

She was immersed in her reading when a car pulled up outside. The sound of its engine was unexpected, confusing. She didn't get visitors. From her position the glass panels either side of the solid door gave her a clear view of the vehicle. A man emerged, stretching, looking around as though assessing the lay of the land. Her instinct was to hide from the uninvited stranger, to drop to the floor and scurry to the furthest corner and wait till he left. She edged off her seat, her hands gripping the table, her stomach knotted so tight it hurt. Then he looked towards the door and saw her.

He moved forward, his knock unnecessarily loud, making her flinch. She stood up, trying to reassure herself that he was only looking for Eloise, that this had nothing to do with her. She slipped her phone into her back pocket and went over. With her hand on the doorknob she looked at him through the glass. She guessed he was her age. Tallish and lean, he was dressed in the sort of city-hip casual that cost more than it should have. He was looking away, taking in the view.

She eased the door halfway open. 'Yes?'

He turned to her and pulled off a pair of sunglasses, holding them in both hands. 'Hello. Um, look, sorry to disturb you, but I was wondering if you could help me?' His accent was English. He needed a shave, and he had bags under his bloodshot blue eyes. His dark blond hair was pulled back into an untidy man bun. The t-shirt beneath his hip-length, high-collared jacket was wrinkled. He looked tired. His smile was endearingly awkward, and as he talked he stood straighter, like a kid who had been told to make a good impression.

She didn't answer but gave him a look and a quick nod, permitting him to continue.

'Right. Yes. Right.' He cleared his throat. Shifted his weight. Ran a hand over his hair, but failed to smooth the errant strands. 'Well, my name is Tom Kearsley, and I'm trying to find someone who used to live in this house.'

'I can't help you.' It came out snappier than she had intended.

He blinked a few times. His hands were turning his sunglasses over and over. 'Um. Right. Okay. It's just that it's for my father. I'm trying to track down a girl he used to know.'

A girl? So this wasn't about the boy who had vanished. But that didn't change anything. 'I can't help, I'm new to the area.' This time she was a little less abrupt. 'Sorry.' Olivia began to close the door. He didn't seem like a threat, but she'd been fooled before.

'No! Please, wait.' His arm shot out as he took a step forward, his palm connecting with the wooden door, his sunglasses dropping to the ground.

For a second she was too shocked to react. Had he really stopped her from closing her door? Then the trepidation that had been curled tight and low in her body surged upwards, tipping her into a panicked fury. 'Don't you dare. Go away.' Her voice was loud, her anger raw.

'God. Shit. I'm sorry.' He dropped his hand. 'I shouldn't have …'

She slammed the door and fumbled for the lock, then took two steps back, her heart beating hard and fast. He wasn't leaving, just standing there, his head down, shoulders bowed, hands hanging limply by his sides. He looked up, meeting her eyes. She pulled her phone out and held it up. 'Fuck off or I'm calling the police!'

He flinched. As he mouthed, 'I'm sorry,' he looked like a dog that had been kicked, now contrite and begging for a gentle hand. It was a great performance, but if he was so innocent, why had he tried to force his way into her home? No, he was pure bullshit, and she had finally learnt not to buy into other people's lies.

CHAPTER FIVE

He'd well and truly fucked it up.

Tom bent to retrieve his sunglasses and then quickly turned away, aware he was freaking out the poor woman on the other side of the door. Christ almighty, what the hell had possessed him? He'd seen the door closing and panicked, desperate to keep the conversation going.

'Bloody idiot,' he mumbled, furious at himself.

He walked to the hire car and climbed in, glancing back at the house as he pulled the door shut. She was still watching through the glass, one hand clutching her phone against her chest, the other arm wrapped tight around her waist. She was maybe a bit younger than him, attractive in a fresh, unadorned way. Her eyes had been wary beneath a messy fringe of dark hair, her worried face swamped by the rollneck of her oversized grey jumper. Shit. He'd really scared her. For a moment, he considered trying again. Maybe he could put right his complete cock-up of the situation and reassure her he wasn't a threat, only a sleep-deprived regular bloke who was way out of his comfort zone. He didn't, though. He wasn't an arrogant dickhead.

He pushed the heel of his hands into his aching eye sockets, then started the car, managing a humiliating six-point turn before starting down the long dirt driveway.

None of this was going according to plan. On the flight out he'd pictured himself being ushered into living rooms or kitchens by nice middle-aged ladies who'd offer him tea and cake before they happily answered all his questions. The biggest problem would be extracting himself from rambling recollections of their lives thirty years earlier. He couldn't have been more wrong.

No one wanted to help or even hear him out. The lady at the village shop hadn't been living here back then. The couple of people he'd approached on his walks had insisted they'd never heard of Jeremy Kearsley and had no contact details for Eloise, and the postmistress had fobbed him off, giving him only the tidbit that Eloise no longer lived in Devils Bay. He'd hung all his hope on whoever was staying in the house, because surely they would have her contact details.

At this stage, his plan was based entirely on him finding Eloise. Because there was only one detail he was reasonably confident of, that Eloise Fowler had owned the house in 1986, and she still owned it now. Poking around online he'd discovered that Australian real estate sites listed the sales histories of most properties—not the personal details of the owners, but sale prices and when they had sold. For this house there was 'No Sales History', meaning it had never changed hands.

Eloise had been here that year. She had known the girl called Pippa, and presumably his father too, so she might know where Pippa was now. It was a long shot, but he had to start somewhere. Except he'd crashed and burned at the first level.

He shut his eyes. God, he was tired. He shouldn't be driving, and he should have got some real sleep before he'd started in with his questions.

Without any solid plan he drove back to Devils Bay, parking once again outside the post office. What next? He'd managed to prove himself completely useless with people, which wasn't a complete surprise. Maybe he should give up. Go home. Pay a professional to do the job.

He groaned at the thought of the thirty hours of travel between him and his flat—and of admitting failure. He was doing this for his dad and couldn't hand it over to a stranger, not yet. This place offered the only thread he could grasp, so he had to grip it tight, let it unwind, and follow.

He flipped down the visor and checked himself in the mirror. Bloody hell, he looked like a kid who'd been at a two-day music festival and hadn't slept or showered. No wonder he'd freaked that woman out. He sighed, got out of the car and crossed the road to the shop. Coffee first. He'd pull himself together. Recalibrate. Try again. In fact, try harder and smarter. And, yeah, be less creepy. Game definitely not over.

CHAPTER SIX

Tuesday, 10 December 1985

The last whispers of daylight were fading into the mellow black of night as they carried their empty plates to the kitchen and returned to the terrace. It was after nine, and the warmth of the day had been pushed aside by a fresh breeze. Eloise had come out with a bundle of light blankets, and Pippa now had one wrapped around her shoulders, a glass of sweet white wine in hand. The sangria had long since been drunk, and no one could quite gather the energy to make more, so Eloise had pulled a cask from the fridge. Jeremy had his arm around the back of Rebecca's chair, his body leaning into hers.

They had just finished having a lengthy, polite, and boring conversation centred around Rebecca's work. She sold cinema advertising but considered herself a marketing executive. If she stuck to her career plan, she should be an account manager in a few years, but apparently it would take commitment and hard work and a willingness to be proactive. Pippa had watched Jeremy as his girlfriend talked, pride and admiration written over his face, his attention utterly focused on the girl he'd fallen for. Her friend was happy. He was in love. And for that she was glad. Who was she to criticise and judge? He was a big boy who could make big boy decisions about his relationships. In a moment of heart-swelling goodwill she resolved that while they were here, she would put in more effort with Rebecca. They'd never be close, but they were bound by Jeremy, and there was no need for animosity.

'Are you still writing?' Eloise asked Pippa.

Pippa grinned at her, buoyed by her magnanimous state of mind, the buzz of the wine, and the soaring sense of possibility she always had in a new place. 'Not much writing in the last few months. But, bloody hell, it's time I did.'

'Perfect place for it,' said Eloise. 'Did you bring your typewriter?'

'I did.'

'We'll have to tie you to a chair,' said Jeremy with glee. 'Make sure you stay in one place long enough to get something on paper.'

'Pippa is a bit easily distracted.' Rebecca explained this to Eloise in the voice of someone confident in their superiority, and Pippa's benevolence dispersed like mist on a hot day. Whoosh, gone, just like that.

'The bane of creativity.' Eloise cocked an eyebrow. 'Always needing to engage with the world.'

'At least I'm out of Brisbane,' Pippa said. 'I was definitely getting restless. There's so much more to see and experience. If I'm stuck somewhere too long, I start to think I'm missing out. Technically I'm now homeless, with no commitments beyond looking after this incredible house. When you get back in February, Eloise, it might be a good time for me to head off again.'

'Yes, but if you keep travelling, then you really will miss out.' Rebecca probably thought she was being wise and helpful. 'Everyone else is getting on with life, and you'll be left behind. It's a competitive world—you have to make your mark as early as you can.'

'Oh, I don't know,' mused Eloise. 'That straight and narrow life isn't for everyone. I didn't follow that path, and I think we can safely say I've done alright.'

'If only you could make a career out of travelling on the cheap and writing,' Jeremy told Pippa. 'You'd be a huge success if that were the case.'

Pippa smiled at her friend. He really was a good guy.

'What a fabulous idea.' Eloise's fervour made Pippa laugh.

'I'm just not too sure how I go about making that a reality.'

'Why didn't I think of this before?' Eloise leant closer to Pippa, a shrewd look on her face. 'Write me a few travel pieces, and I'll take them with me to London, where I will hand them to a guy I know—with a solid recommendation.'

'A guy you know?'

'Not just any guy, but a publisher who is wanting to get behind a new series of travel guidebooks. From what I've heard these books will be targeted at people like you: young, adventurous, doing it on the cheap, getting off the well-trodden travel path.'

'Yes, that's you, Pippa,' Jeremy said, joining in eagerly. 'When we were in Thailand you were always finding the best places to stay, the best beaches, the best bars, and you could somehow figure out how to get around when the rest of us were a bit lost.' Pippa had run into Jeremy on Khao San Road in Bangkok. She'd been travelling for about six months by then and had been excited to see a familiar face, even though they only knew each other vaguely. Jeremy had been only too happy to join her. He'd been new to the whole backpacking gig and, despite being a couple of years older than her, was somewhat overwhelmed. 'I wouldn't have had such an amazing time if it weren't for you.'

'You wouldn't be *alive* if it weren't for her,' Eloise called out with a laugh.

'Yeah. Yeah. That too.' He gave Pippa the look he always had when reminded of his near-death adventure. His smile was tender, his eyes soft with gratitude and humility.

The beach had been remote, the drinks strong, and Jeremy's ability on the little scooter severely impaired. Pippa had been the one to wake at 3 am and realise he hadn't returned. She found him in a putrid ditch and somehow managed to wake some locals and, with her limited Thai, make them understand. They loaded him onto the back of a truck and drove an hour to the nearest—very basic—medical centre. She stayed with him and, when she realised how serious the situation was, wrangled transport to a better, more well-equipped hospital. He was unconscious for nine days. They'd been best friends ever since.

Jeremy shook his head a little. 'Imagine if other travellers had a book they could use, something with all that word-of-mouth, feet-on-the-ground advice to make their trips really amazing. Wouldn't you like to write something like that?'

'Sure.' Pippa looked at Eloise and Jeremy's animated faces. It was a great dream. But she was a mostly unemployed waitress with less than half a degree and a sideline in clomping down the runway in shopping-centre fashion parades—hardly a top contender.

'You have nothing to lose,' said Eloise. 'You've got three days to write me three articles. Write about where you've been— Thailand, Indonesia, Malaysia.'

'Brisbane?' Pippa laughed.

'Sure, why not? From the other side of the world it could look exotic. Find an angle.'

Why not give it a go? There was no harm in investing a little time and imagination, even if the chance was slim. Because, if she couldn't push herself to make an effort when an opportunity was dangled right in front of her, then she might as well give up on dreaming, follow Rebecca's advice and get stuck into living an ordinary life.

Pippa raised her glass. 'Thank you, Eloise. I'll start tomorrow.'

*

The next three days passed in an easy flow as Pippa settled into Eloise's house. The three guests quickly learnt the ropes: Honey's routine, when and how to feed the small flock of chickens, what to do if the power cut out, and how to get to the nearest shops and pub. Away from the constraints of their regular lives, the awkward dynamic between Pippa, Jeremy and Rebecca seemed less fraught, less likely to result in sharp words or barely covered barbs. Pippa even found herself laughing with Rebecca as they ran screaming from the overprotective rooster. The property gave them all the space they needed. Jeremy and Rebecca took Honey for long walks down to the water or over the hill, while Pippa sat at her typewriter or found a comfortable spot to sprawl with a book. She helped Eloise with her packing, happily working through the clothes and accoutrements the older woman would need for an English winter. The evenings saw the four of them come together on the large uncovered terrace, usually with wine, sangria or beer.

On Eloise's last night, Pippa handed over her pages. There were four pieces intended to excite those who dreamed of running away to wilder shores. Pippa vacillated between confidence and scathing self-criticism. She was too young, too naive, not a good enough writer to be paid for such amateur rubbish. But Eloise deemed the work worthy of being pushed before her contact. Jeremy cheered Pippa on, and even Rebecca seemed pleased on her behalf. Not that any of it meant anything—not yet.

Pippa shrugged at their enthusiasm and made self-deprecating remarks before changing the subject. 'So, two months on our own! We promise, Eloise, not to throw too many parties or sell your silverware.'

'Well, I don't have any silverware. And who would you invite to a party? I think your circle of friends is a bit limited down here.'

'Give us a week,' said Pippa. 'We'll soon know everyone in the area and half of Hobart. We've got two weeks until Christmas, three until New Year's, and I'm sure we can round up a ragtag assortment of local lovelies by then.' She was joking, of course—she had no intention of taking advantage of Eloise's home—but the thought of the party season had been on her mind.

'Of course it's going to be a quiet Christmas,' said Rebecca, 'but I think we can make it special.'

Pippa had been unconcerned about not being in Brisbane over the festive period. She'd missed a couple of family Christmas lunches recently, and although her parents expressed disappointment at her absence, they weren't overly concerned. There was a six-year age gap between Pippa and the eldest of her two younger sisters, and their relationship was affectionate but not close. Maybe one day that would change, but while Pippa had been drinking rum in a shack bar on a Thai beach, her sisters had been eating packed lunches and worrying about schoolwork and pimples. While Pippa was having her fill of intoxicating short-lived flings, her sisters were dreaming about Rob Lowe and imagining their first kisses. And of course her parents' focus was on getting the two younger girls through school unscathed.

The idea of spending Christmas with only Jeremy and Rebecca wasn't exciting, but it wasn't a worry. On the other hand, Pippa did want to celebrate New Year's.

Eloise seemed to read her mind. 'I'd suggest you head into town for New Year's Eve. The yachts will be in from the Sydney to Hobart race, and there's always a pretty raucous atmosphere down around the waterfront.'

'Now that sounds like somewhere I'd like to be.' Pippa scooped her hair off her neck, then rested her head in her hands and smiled up at the night sky. As much as she was enjoying the quiet, she would need a hit of excitement before too long.

CHAPTER SEVEN

Thursday, 22 June 2017

Wendy handed Olivia the letter with a smile stuck somewhere between bemusement and a grimace. 'I said I'd pass it on to you. But I don't want you to feel obliged to, you know, communicate with him or anything.'

Olivia looked at the blank manila envelope in her hand. 'Sorry, who is this from?'

'That English bloke—he came back yesterday, said something about wanting to apologise. I'm guessing he took it upon himself to just rock up at your door, did he?'

Olivia nodded. 'He was asking about a girl who once stayed in the house. Something to do with his father.'

'Was he now?' Wendy didn't sound impressed. 'A girl? That's a different approach.'

'I couldn't help him, obviously.'

'So what's *he* apologising for?' She squinted her eyes and crossed her arms. 'What did he do, love?'

Olivia gave a small shrug. After she'd spent a good part of the past twenty-four hours replaying the encounter, she had come to the tentative conclusion that while his hand on her door had been vastly inappropriate and her reaction not unjustified, she didn't believe he had intended her harm.

'He wanted to talk. I didn't.'

Wendy made a sceptical sound. 'Well, don't let him bully you into anything. He obviously doesn't know Eloise, and goodness knows what he wants with her—or with you. If he doesn't take no for an answer, tell me. I'll get on to the local copper.'

Olivia found herself smiling. Having someone stand firmly behind her, especially in this place where she didn't belong, was enough to give her a delightful rush of gratitude.

*

Olivia waited till she got home to read the letter. She sat at the table with the coffee and carrot cake she'd picked up from the shop, and Brian curled up on her lap. The room was warm, Nina Simone was playing, and the view out the windows was magnificent. Olivia was safe, almost happy. Wendy's support, the peaceful surroundings, and the absence of any further communication from Leena were all helping to soothe her. She felt like she had the mental resources to deal with this latest intrusion.

Inside the envelope there were three A4 pages torn from a spiral notebook. The writing was big and messy.

I am so very, very sorry for my terrible behaviour yesterday. I don't know what came over me. Well, I do, sort of.

I could blame the jet lag, and lack of sleep, and my general state of desperation. But it's no excuse. I scared you. And that makes me feel utterly awful.

I'm sorry. Really sorry. I'm going to try to start again, but I understand if you don't want to engage with me.

Olivia set down the first page. As far as apologies went, it was a good one. But would he have gone to the trouble if he didn't want something from her? Still, her curiosity had increased from couldn't-care to prepared-to-listen. She picked up the second page.

My story is quite simple. I am trying to find a girl who stayed in Eloise Fowler's house—your home—about thirty years ago. I am looking for her on behalf of my father, and I've flown out from London in the hope that by being here in person I will have more success than I've had online. I have very little information to go on:

- *Her name is Pippa.*
- *She and my father, Jeremy Kearsley, stayed in Eloise's house one summer in the eighties.*
- *He loved her.*
- *Eloise knew her.*

I'm hoping that if I can contact Eloise she might know where Pippa is now. I can't find any details for Eloise online, but I believe she still owns the house. Maybe you have a number or email for her?

If you can help me, I would be extremely grateful. On the next page I've provided details about myself, so please feel free

to check up on me. And if you're comfortable, you might be able to help me move forward with my search.
Sincerely,
Tom Kearsley

The third page started with a list of his social media accounts, including LinkedIn, Instagram and Twitter, and then had notes pointing her to online articles. Olivia began with his LinkedIn. She'd long since wiped her own account but could see his basic details: his name, a headshot, the fact that he was *Co-founder and Producer at Iconic Digital*, and a brief blurb about how he'd founded the company with a mate and come from a digital gaming background. She couldn't grasp exactly what it was he did, so she looked through his Insta grid. He had 55k followers, and 585 posts, most of which focused on tech expos and gaming. There were also candid shots from what appeared to be his workplace, with banks of monitors, bright colours, people in casual wear, a dispro-portionate number of beards, an abundance of t-shirts and hoodies. And among them, Tom. Smiling. Being a likeable, attractive goof.

Yeah, but how many nice guys ended up doing shitty things?

All Olivia could say for certain was that he appeared to be who he said he was, and the articles she scanned backed this up. It seemed he was a bit of a success in the world of gaming—everything she read made him look good.

She googled his name, looking for details he hadn't pointed her towards. Her reaction shifted first to surprise, then quickly to empathy. The *Daily Mail* had obviously loved the story of a self-made geek and his glamorous reality TV star wife. There were lots of references to their love affair being mismatched, and oodles of images of Tom standing beside a heavily made-up woman with red hair to her waist and a preference for dresses that were either tight or startlingly low-cut, sometimes both. In these pictures he wasn't mucking about. Gone were the t-shirts. He was stiff, his clothes more stylish, and he had a look on his face as though someone was screaming at him to smile—'Smile! Come on, sweetie, give us a smile!'—and all he wanted to do was hide. Or maybe Olivia was projecting—maybe he revelled in the attention.

She turned back to the third page of his notes. He'd included a local mobile number, along with the name of his Hobart hotel, an email address, and an international number for his WhatsApp. There was a final message.

I won't come uninvited to the house again, but if you have any questions or feel you could help, please do make contact. Thank you.

She flipped to his explanation and read it again. She *did* have questions. Like, why was he even looking for this Pippa person? And why did he have so little information to go on? Why was he doing this for his father? And what did a 'game producer' or 'game director' actually do?

Brian climbed off her lap and started demanding his dinner, so she closed her laptop. The online sinkhole had claimed nearly three hours of her life. She'd wandered down digital dirt tracks that had taken her far from her starting point. It had been the first time she'd dared link through to the *Daily Mail* in over a year. She now knew Tom's wife had been on *Big Brother* UK, and had come fourth on *I'm a Celebrity ... Get Me Out of Here*. She'd learnt they were no longer together, and that Tom's company was scoring wins doing whatever it was it did, thanks to the huge sales of a videogame called *Fallen from Hell*.

What she hadn't found was anything about a Jeremy Kearsley who could be Tom's father, or about Eloise. Olivia had searched for her landlady to see if Tom's story rang true, and sure enough—other than a few pics that appeared to have been taken at a Hobart art gallery and at a theatre—she too had come away with no personal information. Even the rental ad hadn't come up, probably because Eloise had kept her details out of the listing.

'Okay, Brian.' Olivia stood and stretched, hoisted up her sagging trackpants, pulled her hair into a stubby ponytail, then popped the lid on an individual serve of cat food that promised *fine dining for the most refined feline*. Yep, that was her Brian. A reformed stray moggy who was now a prince.

She watched him eat for a moment, then went to build up the fire. Coming back to the kitchen, she opened the fridge and then the freezer. She settled on toasted sourdough, which she slathered with Duck River butter, one of her favourite Tasmanian discoveries. These days she didn't fuss about calories, instead enjoying the delicious, decadent freedom of not needing to impress anyone. Her size had gone up, but her care factor had gone down.

She settled into the sofa, feet on the coffee table, toast in her lap, phone beside her. She was licking the butter off her fingers when she reached a conclusion. She would listen to this Tom guy. And she would do it on her terms, keeping her personal details and her own humiliating tale of woe a secret. Sure, this was a turnaround from slamming the door and screaming at him to leave, but for a few hours she'd been fully immersed in someone else's story. Her brain had been focused on something beyond the ache of her own life, which could only be a good thing. The fact that Tom Kearsley was interesting—and yes, good-looking—and she was miserable and lonely had only a teeny bit to do with her decision.

CHAPTER EIGHT

New Year's Eve, 1985

Pippa fidgeted with the cutlery on her plate, then dunked one more chip into the sauce. She checked the time on the yellow Swatch that Jeremy had given her for Christmas. Good, it wasn't even half eight. Plenty of time to find some action.

They'd made the one-hour trip to the city and had chosen to have dinner at the Drunken Admiral on Hobart's waterfront—at the opposite end to the pubs of Salamanca Place. The restaurant was in a tight row of hefty stone buildings that had been built in the early days of the city, when using convicts for free labour was the accepted way to get ahead. The furniture was chunky yellow-toned wood and the decor was all things nautical. Thick ropes looped from the ceiling, and there was a ship's wheel alongside dented brass lanterns. The food was good, but the view through the old paned window was limited.

'So, anyway, this kid I was reading about is, like, eighteen or nineteen or something,' Jeremy rambled on. 'And he's crewing on one of the boats in the race—*Insurrection*, I think it's called. A local boat, not one of the super big ones, but it still looks decent. Might go and look at it later. And this kid is one of the youngest crew members ever. Pretty big thing to take on. Must be a tough character.'

'Good on him,' Pippa said. 'We should all have adventures when we're young. Why wait?'

Rebecca shrugged dismissively. 'Bit riskier than taking a holiday, though, don't you think?' She was still eating her fish after carefully peeling off the crumbed outer layer and setting it atop the untouched pile of chips. She cut a small piece of the white flesh and speared a tomato wedge from her salad.

Pippa leant across and seized one of the unwanted chips, causing a frown to flit across Rebecca's face.

'Definitely risky.' Jeremy signalled the waiter for another round of drinks. 'Last year, over half the boats had to turn back, the weather was so bad.'

'Well, I'm sure he wouldn't be on board if he wasn't competent.' Pippa craned her neck to peer out the window in the solid stone wall. A group of young women strode past, their laughter loud. She wondered if she should rush out and ask them where they were going. Where was the best place to hang out tonight?

'Of course he is,' Jeremy said, failing to sense her boredom with this topic. 'The owner of the boat wouldn't take him on as crew if he was going to be a liability. The article said his father started him sailing at five or something like that. Wonder what he's like? Must make for a fun childhood.'

Pippa tuned out the rest of what he said, focusing on what little she could see of the waterfront. The building they were in faced the length of the docks, rather than looking out at the harbour, and she could see that the marina was crowded with boats that had finished the race. Crowds milled about, watching the stragglers of the fleet arrive, or wandering the boardwalks and service roads of the docks. The energy was building, even though it was still light. They needed to make a move, to get in amongst it.

'Guys,' she said, 'let's go and find the party.'

*

Pippa plonked her empty glass on the sticky bar table. The pub was packed, and she had to yell her goodbyes to the girls she'd met only an hour earlier before elbowing her way through the crowd. The Customs House Hotel was a classic corner pub, with large windows and floors of basic accommodation. Situated across the road from one of the piers and close to Salamanca, it had, according to photos on the walls, been serving sailors since the turn of the century. There were plenty of them there tonight. The surging roar of joyful shouts and raucous laughter was a balm to her soul, and she played along when a scruffy, half-sozzled guy put an arm around her waist. As he pulled her close, she executed a well-practised slide and turn, slipping out of his grip and away from his reach. Laughing, she blew him a kiss as she made her escape, leaving him with his hands clutched over his heart while his mates mocked his failure with howls of amusement and slaps on the back. She still had almost two hours until the old year rolled into the new, and she was in no hurry to line up the traditional midnight snog.

She was grinning as she stepped onto the street. It was dark now, streetlights and well-lit windows bright against the night. Drinkers stood around outdoor tables, and traffic moved slowly, avoiding the pedestrians who were wandering either in the direction of the boats or one of the pubs. She thrived on this atmosphere. The good-natured fun and flirting, the waves of happy noise rising around her, the hint of promise and potential that she always felt when she was out among like-minded people. She'd abandoned Jeremy and Rebecca an hour or so earlier and had agreed if she hadn't stumbled across them by midnight, they'd meet at the car at one. Jeremy had looked a little wistful as she'd left, anchored as he was by his more cautious girlfriend. For Pippa—and for the Jeremy of old—being immersed in the flow of people was far more intoxicating than sitting and watching a procession of partygoers.

Jeremy had said they were going to look at the boats, so she wandered in that direction. The racing fleet had left Sydney on Boxing Day, and the maxi-yacht *Apollo* had arrived in Hobart three days later, after the run down the coast and across Bass Strait. Yachts of all sizes were moored within metres of the pubs on the waterfront. People who loved the water and all things sailing milled about, admiring the boats, alongside those whose knowledge of open water racing extended no further than this one famous event.

The yachties were obvious. Those crews lucky enough to have corporate sponsors wore matching jackets and caps, while the less well-financed teams had a uniform look of deck shoes, shorts and all-weather jackets. Mostly men, these sailors had tanned faces with creases and cracks, their tousled hair still stiff with salt. This was their time to celebrate. Pippa had seen several groups encamped at the pub she'd just left with jugs of rum and Coke crowding the tables, a competitive running jug tally being kept on a blackboard. A yacht might not have won line honours, but the crew could still claim fame in the pub.

Pippa followed the crowd, taking her time along the rough wooden docks. There were boats with owners and crew onboard, drinks in hand, music playing. She had no particular interest in sailing, although the idea of cruising the tropical Whitsundays or drifting around the Greek islands had a certain appeal. But the boats were interesting enough to look at, and the festive atmosphere was intoxicating. She wandered up and down the lines of boats, reading the names. What boat had Jeremy been yabbering about? A one-word name, nothing flowery. Something with a bit of fighting spirit.

Towards the end of a dock, she watched a yacht slide neatly into position, its crew returning from a night cruise on the river. *Insurrection*—yes, that was it. She looked around, half expecting to see Jeremy and Rebecca, but they weren't here. She turned back. The guy at the wheel showed deft control while another man swung a rope around a post and then stepped onto the jetty to secure them. The low throb of the motor cut out, and he worked a neat, elaborate knot. 'Good job, Leo,' he called to the guy doing the driving.

No, that wasn't the right word, Pippa thought. Was he steering? Or at the helm?

On receiving the praise, Leo gave a thumbs-up and grinned. He was no older than her. The tall lights lining the dock cast irregular, shifting shadows, but Pippa could make out his smile, wide and bright and infectious. The particular combination of lips, chin and cheeks was strangely familiar. Jeremy's face worked much the same way. A crease in one cheek, the full mouth, the slight tilt to the line of the lips. It was a face and smile she'd seen nearly every day for the past two years—or a very good copy.

The man on the dock tied off the boat and jumped back onboard, and the small crew milled about, gathering their gear as they got ready to go ashore. Jeremy's look-alike, very obviously the youngest, was surely the young sailor in his story over dinner. Had the article included a photo? Had that been part of Jeremy's interest in this guy?

As she moved a little closer, she overheard the older men teasing Leo, urging him to go and have some fun. One of them caught her watching and grinned. 'Hey, love, do you want a date?' he yelled. 'This handsome young man needs someone to take him to the pub.' He lassoed the poor guy with an arm around his neck and offered him to her. 'You up for it?'

She joined in the banter with the ease of someone who had years of practice. 'I don't know, does he come with a good recommendation?'

'Absolutely! He's just done the race. Excellent little sailor. Not bad looking, either.'

The poor guy looked mortified. He caught her eye for a split second, then tried to extract himself.

'I *am* all on my own,' she called out with a laugh. 'In fact, he'd be doing me a favour. There are some really drunk yobbos around here.'

That was all the encouragement they needed. They bundled him off the boat, giving him no choice but to walk towards Pippa. He stopped right in front of her, uncrossing his arms and shoving his hands deep in the pockets of his shorts. His eyes were familiar too, the same pale blue with a darker ring around the iris—like Jeremy's. But there were also differences. Hair that was lighter, curlier, longer. His greater height. A lean strength to his body. He seemed capable and self-possessed.

'Sorry about them. You don't have to do this.' He spoke quietly and frowned a little, as if annoyed by the well-intentioned interference of his mates. 'Maybe if we walk in the general direction of the pub, they'll leave us alone.'

She could do that, but perhaps something more would be better. 'Don't apologise,' she said. 'I meant it. I am on my own, and you look like you could be good company.'

He nearly smiled. 'I could be a complete tosser.'

'If you are, I'll make a quick escape.'

He shrugged. 'Well, if you're up for it.' He smiled then, Pippa watching his mouth as it moved in that familiar way—like Jeremy's, but not.

'I'd love to have a drink with you,' she said.

After a brief hesitation, he held out his hand for her to shake. 'I'm Leo.'

The roughened skin of his fingers closed around her own. 'Hi, Leo. I'm Pippa.'

*

The countdown to midnight was deafening. A hundred happy people were calling the numbers as though their lives—or drinks—depended on it. 'Ten! Nine! Eight!' Pippa and Leo's voices added to the cacophony, their glasses raised, hauling the New Year into existence through sheer willpower and the strength of their shouts.

Leo's body was hard against Pippa's side, one arm around her waist, the two of them crammed into a nook of Customs House. Tucked away, they'd avoided most of the jostles and bumps of the crowd, and Leo had been a perfect gentleman. He'd repeatedly made the perilous journey to the bar, returning each time with clean glasses and a jug of rum and Coke. After one trip he'd had to ease aside a slightly slobbery Lothario who had been doing his best to make a move on Pippa. Leo slapped the older man on the shoulder, saying, 'Sorry, mate, she's with me,' which had delighted Pippa.

There had been several interruptions from yachties who knew Leo, and at one stage he was accosted by a couple of girls. Very drunk, they'd grasped his arm, giggling and shrieking, and asked him about people he might know, friends they had in common, what it had been like on the boat. One of them had tried to put her arms around his neck, and he grimaced. Pippa had stepped in. 'Sorry, do you mind? Leo is with me.' Pleased to be returning the favour, she'd put her arms around his waist and leant her head against his shoulder, making such an obvious display of possession that the girls had to retreat.

Leo had returned the hug, holding her tight. When they were alone again, he looked down at her, their faces close. 'Thanks,' he said.

It was one of those moments when the zing of attraction reduced the world to no more than the space between them. Pippa had waited for the kiss. Their bodies were pressed together, their eyes locked. His focus dropped to her mouth, and her body tightened in response. His lips met hers, the kiss cautious then deepening. Then not. He pulled away, still watching her, but a wry smile now in place. His grip loosened, a shift in his weight so that a gap was created between them, the moment slipping away.

She knew he was interested in her. Well, she was pretty sure. Maybe he was less of a floozy than she was. Maybe he didn't want to rush, which was fair enough.

Mostly they talked. The conversation wasn't always easy over the noise, but with their heads bent together, mouths close to ears, they had managed to have a laugh and share details. Leo was younger than Pippa, nineteen to her twenty-two, and fresh out of school. But he didn't come across as a kid. He was deliberate and intense, and when he smiled it was like a reward. He was nothing like Jeremy, who was light and charming and had the gift of pointless chatter. Within a short time, Pippa had lost sight of any physical similarities she thought she'd seen.

She liked this guy. Liked his steady strength. Liked the way he shielded her by putting his back to the crowd. Liked the way he listened.

She was drunk, but she trusted her instincts even when she was starting to sway and her words were slurring. Right now, those instincts told her Leo was lovely—lovely and sexy and capable, and definitely one of the good guys. And bloody gorgeous. Kissing him again was going to be delicious.

'Seven! Six! Five! Four!' The crowd chanted, reaching a crescendo. 'Three! Two! One!'

Pippa loved this bit. In the second when the old year fell away and the new year threw itself open, anything seemed possible.

'Happy New Year!' Euphoria erupted around them. Whistles, shouts and cheers rose in a thunderous roar.

Pippa joined in, her arms raised, then spun to face Leo, stumbling, grasping at his shirt to steady herself. She looked up at him, laughing, exultant, ready and willing to claim her midnight gift. He was clasping her by the hips, his face calm, the slightest twitch of a smile on his lips. She went up on tiptoes, wobbling, leaning against his chest. Her arms went around his neck. 'Happy New Year,' she murmured as she kissed him.

It wasn't the passionate kiss she had expected and craved. He responded, but his hands stayed planted, holding her still, keeping a space between them. She wriggled, trying to crush her whole body against his. He held firm, then eased his mouth away. Where was the hip-to-hip grind, the hands clamped on her arse or sliding over her back? Where was the lust?

She pouted up at him, her hands clasping the back of his neck and head, urging him to keep going. He didn't relent. 'Let's get out of here,' he said. 'Get some fresh air.'

It seemed he wanted to find a more secluded spot, maybe down on the docks, in the shadow of one of the warehouses or on the yacht. That would work. She nuzzled his neck and giggled. 'Sure.'

He gripped her hand and led her through the crowd. People were spilling into the street, nobody in a hurry, everyone happy to stroll unsteadily, to call out to friends or strangers, or to sing loudly. Leo guided her away, finding a low wall near the water. He jumped up and sat while Pippa stepped into the space between his legs. She ran her palms up and down his thighs, distracted by the thought of sliding her hands beneath the fabric of his shorts.

'How are you feeling?' he asked.

She laughed. 'Great!' Although, if she was honest, her stomach was starting to swish. Nothing she couldn't handle; she'd certainly felt worse.

'How are you getting back to the house?' he asked.

'The house?'

'Where you're staying with your friends.'

That was right. She'd told him about Eloise's place, and about Jeremy and Rebecca.

'Hmmm.' She took a deep, steadying breath. 'I should find them. Rebecca's driving us back.' She swallowed against the pressure building at the back of her throat. *Shit.* If she didn't move too much and kept breathing, she'd be alright. 'Maybe

I could stay at yours?' She wasn't ready to say goodbye. The night was young, her body unsatisfied … and a little queasy.

He gave a tight smile. 'I live with my folks, so that wouldn't work.'

'Oh.'

Her hair blew into her face, and he gently pushed it back. 'You're beautiful.' He said it quietly, as though talking to himself. He considered her face and ran the tip of his finger down her cheek. 'I don't suppose you'd want to catch up again, would you?'

She hadn't thought that far ahead. 'Yes, I'd like that.'

She was having trouble focusing on him, her gaze sliding when she tried to concentrate on his face. She frowned, blinked, took a breath, then said, 'I think I need to sit down,' before slowly sinking to the ground, his arms supporting her as he positioned her back against the wall.

*

They stayed there for an hour, side by side on the footpath, looking out at the water as Pippa did her best not to puke. 'Tell me about your future?' she said at one point, and Leo quietly talked about his parents' expectations and the law degree he was due to start in February. He described the sailing he hoped to do with his mates, as well as his dreams of becoming good enough to be taken on as a professional crew member. Pippa was happy to listen, her head against his shoulder, their joined hands in her lap.

By the time she had to go she was feeling a bit better, and they walked hand in hand towards Salamanca Place. They'd made plans to meet the day after next, Pippa having invited him down to the house and given him directions.

'Pippa!' Jeremy was waving at her from across the street. 'We've been looking for you.'

Leo and Pippa stopped and waited as her friends crossed the road.

'Happy New Year, guys,' she said. 'Did you have a good night?'

'Yeah, it was great,' Jeremy answered. He was looking at Leo strangely. 'Hi, I'm Jeremy.' He stuck out his hand. 'I'm Pippa's friend. This is my girlfriend, Rebecca.'

'Leo.'

They shook hands in the way of two men sizing each other up. Rebecca fluttered her fingers in a silly wave, her head tilted in serious consideration as she looked Leo over.

'Leo?' The look Jeremy was giving him was one of surprise and agitation. 'Leo who?'

Pippa had been thinking about how much she wanted to kiss Leo again, but Jeremy's tone drew her attention. It wasn't like him to be overly critical about her love life. In their share house there had been a morning or two when he'd been forced to make conversation with a guy he barely knew. He'd certainly never acted jealous about the boys she had in her room. He liked to give his opinion and inevitably would tell her she could do better, but he was never openly rude to anyone she brought home, so his slightly aggressive question seemed out of character.

'Clifford,' Leo said in his measured voice, not appearing concerned by the question.

Jeremy exhaled a grunt of shocked laughter. 'You're the kid from the *Insurrection*.'

'Yes.'

'I read about you. You're, what, nineteen?'

'Yep.'

'Bit young, don't you think, Pip?' He directed this at her, his tone accusatory. 'How did you find him, anyway?'

She glared at her friend. 'I was looking for you—and stop being weird!' She said it with a laugh, even though she wanted to smack him. 'Now, go away. I'll meet you at the car, alright?'

Jeremy didn't move. He was tense and seemed to be debating whether to say more.

Rebecca tugged on his arm. 'Let's go,' she said, pulling him away.

He took a few steps, then shrugged her off, turning back to Pippa. 'Did you pick him up, or did he come on to you?'

'*What?* Why the hell are you asking that?' Pippa snapped. She didn't want to end the night like this, but anger was beginning to override the joy. 'Take a hike, Jeremy.'

He shook his head and scowled before retreating. Rebecca looked back at Pippa and mouthed *sorry*.

'Well,' said Pippa, wanting to make light of the interaction. 'That was bizarre.' Jeremy was not going to ruin what had been a thoroughly excellent night. She moved to stand in front of Leo.

'He's the guy you live with?'

'Yep. One of my best and truest friends ... who tonight is behaving like a complete wanker. He isn't usually like that.'

Leo put his arms around her, pulling her close but still not groping or grabbing. He was so restrained, thought Pippa. Careful and deliberate in the way he spoke and acted, which was the complete opposite to her own impulsive behaviour. It was nice. Somehow more sincere than a quick pash-and-dash. She gently kissed him, keeping her urge to ravish under control.

'I'll see you on Thursday?' she asked softly. 'You'll still come down?'

He nodded. 'Yeah. I'd like that.'

She stole one last kiss, then stepped back. 'Thank you for a great night.'

As she walked to the car, she looked back over her shoulder. He was right where she'd left him, watching her, a smile on his face.

CHAPTER NINE

Friday, 23 June 2017

Olivia sat in her car outside the post office and swallowed hard against the urge to scream. She'd been feeling better. The endless cycling of her fears and failings had slowed, even paused for lengths of time. She'd slept well the night before, comfortable with her decision to meet with Tom. She had drunk only one glass of red wine and taken a long bath. It had been almost two weeks since Leena's letter had arrived, and Olivia had started to think of it as simply another burst of fetid hot air from her toxic ex-friend. Nothing to worry about.

The two postcards had caught her off-guard. The first one would have snagged the attention of anyone who handled it. The picture was sleazy and sexist, with a woman in a minuscule bikini, her artificially enhanced breasts escaping from a smidgen of fabric and floss, her long tanned legs emphasised by her tiptoe pose and cocked hip.

On the back was the redirection sticker and a message written in black.

Taken any good pictures recently?
Maybe it's time the public saw you from a new angle.

What exactly did Leena mean? The threat was apparent, even though the how and when were less obvious.

The second card was a promotion piece for one of Sydney's most prestigious hotels, with the two images on the front showing the harbour location and discreet opulence. On the back Leena continued her taunts.

I'm living the best life.
I'm going to make sure you get the miserable life you've earned.

How? What did she have planned?

Olivia pushed her head back against the car seat. The cards were so revolting, so sordid. Wendy had handed over the mail with a friendly smile and some cheerful banter, but she would have seen the messages. How could the kind-hearted postmistress not be disgusted? Surely that was what Leena had intended. Sending postcards was a tactic, a way to point a finger at Olivia: *Look at her. She's bad. She's a slut.*

She thumped her head back again and again. She wanted to explain everything to Wendy, to defend herself, but talking about her past was inconceivable. Instead, she would do what she did best. She would run away and hide. Retreat to her bunker and hope Leena couldn't track her down.

Olivia drove with exaggerated care, forcing herself to concentrate on the curves and bends of the road, aware that her mind was skidding, her hands shaking. Behind her, an oversized ute came up fast. It had glinting chrome bars and glossy paintwork. The dickhead driver was sitting hard on her bumper, trying to bully her out of his way. Her hands prickled sharply with the adrenaline of fear and anger. She pulled over, flicking him the finger and yelling, '*Wanker!*' at the top of her voice as he accelerated past. Tears slid down her face.

It took her five minutes to calm down enough to continue driving. By the time she arrived home a raw sadness had seeped in to dilute the distress. Leena had been her friend—a great friend, Olivia had thought. She had glossy memories of fun and laughter and the sharing of intimate details, especially about Hayden. From her first giddy meeting with the celebrity to the protracted decision to end things, Olivia had shared everything, and Leena had supported and encouraged her— had been excited for her. Had helped staunch her guilt. How had it gone so spectacularly wrong?

In early 2014 Olivia had been looking for an apartment to buy. She'd turned twenty-five the year before, and after she'd spent five years proving she could go without and save money, her father had given her a lump sum to put towards her deposit. She was, after all, Olivia Indigo Haymers, daughter of the developer Eric Haymers, and while he'd been a supportive—if distant—father, he didn't believe in making things too easy. He hadn't been handed his success, and in his opinion she needed to develop some grit. She knew she was extremely fortunate and had been determined to impress him. Listening to his lectures and advice on building success and wealth hadn't been too arduous.

That Saturday morning she had three apartments on her list and barely a breath of optimism after going through the cycle—love, hope, auction, despair—four times in six months. Her financial position was better than that of most people her age, but what she could afford was still severely limited. She arrived late to the last viewing and jogged up the stairs against the flow of other home hunters, all clutching their brochures and notebooks. As she wrote her name and phone number on the sign-in sheet, an agent with a gleaming salesperson's smile approached, holding out a brochure. 'Hello, I'm Leena.' She was wearing a tailored navy dress that stopped a centimetre above her knees and was both perfectly professional and body-hugging sexy. Her stilettos made precise clicks on the timber floor, and her blonde hair was in the sort of immaculate, clever ponytail requiring a styling wand and several hair ties that Olivia never attempted before a work shift. Olivia immediately felt drab. Leena glanced at the list. 'Nice to meet you, Olivia. Any relation to Eric Haymers?'

It wasn't the first time Olivia had been asked, and she saw no problem with being honest. Although her father was intimidating and known for a degree of ruthlessness, she was proud of him—in fact, she idolised him and the world in which he lived. The holidays she had spent with him were some of her happiest memories.

'He's my father.'

Leena raised her groomed eyebrows, her smile becoming even warmer. 'This place is a little downmarket for a Haymers, isn't it?'

'Dad is a big believer in making your own way.' She wasn't going to go into more detail on their family dynamic, or the amount of cash he had given her. 'Which I understand completely.'

'Oh, totally. I get that. He is self-made, and I imagine he respects and encourages that ethos in others.'

'He does.'

'He's an inspiring man.' Leena's face lit up, and she tilted her head. 'Well, let me give you some details on this place.' She waved a hand to take in the boxy room. 'For a start, the price guide is well under the expected sale price, but there's nothing new about that. Of more concern are the neighbours. Across the hall live two brothers with seriously questionable hygiene, which they cover with clouds of Lynx. They have a preference for pizzas and all-night sessions with bongs, booze and bad music. They are, however, very friendly, especially to attractive women. You should be a hit. They will, I'm sure, knock on your door on a regular basis and invite you to join them. But, hey, that might tickle your fancy. And,' her voice swung into the singsong pitch of a true saleswoman, 'don't forget you *are* walking distance to Bondi Beach and all that it has to offer. So, this is a very desirable property.'

Olivia peered around the generically styled apartment and decided not to waste her time. 'Thanks for the honesty,' she said as she went to leave. 'I don't think this is for me.'

'You know, I have something coming up that might suit you. It's not on the market yet, but I could wrangle an inspection for you if you think it might tick some boxes.'

'Sure. Where is it?'

Leena was collecting her brochures and closing up behind them. 'Tell you what, I'm starving, and this was my last open for today. Want to join me for a late lunch? Then we can chat about what you're looking for and your budget.'

Olivia hesitated. Did she want to sit down with this woman to discuss property? She didn't feel like nodding and smiling to a sales pitch over a quinoa salad. But then Leena didn't appear to be quite like other agents she'd met. The woman was funny and a bit irreverent. And besides, getting an inside scoop on the property hunt couldn't be a bad thing.

'Sounds great,' Olivia said.

At the cafe, she watched Leena charm the harried waiter, displaying sympathy for the stress he was obviously under and flirting just enough to make the poor guy besotted with her. When he left Leena rolled her eyes. 'What a sad little hipster. Probably hasn't been laid in years.'

Leena wasn't beautiful, but that didn't seem to matter. She took her long legs, awesome cleavage, perfect hair, and winning smile and worked it to perfection. She was one of those people who could completely focus on someone, making them feel special. That first lunch had extended into the afternoon as a bottle of bubbles was easily emptied and a second procured.

Although Leena was a few years older than Olivia, they quickly discovered they were well aligned. Both were driven to achieve in their careers, both had five-year and ten-year plans, both had an appreciation for self-help books. They believed in chasing big dreams but agreed that 'doing' was as important as the 'dreaming'.

Later that week, Leena showed Olivia an off-market apartment in Coogee that was nearly perfect. Olivia made an offer that was accepted, and that afternoon Leena rang and persuaded her to go out and celebrate.

They started with drinks at a popular bar. 'Here's to your upcoming acquisition,' Leena said, raising her Aperol spritz.

'Thanks.' Olivia grinned. 'You've been amazing. I can't believe how easy you made it.'

Leena lifted a shoulder and waved a hand. 'Oh, you know, what can I say? I am brilliant at what I do. Maybe one day you'll do something special for me.'

Olivia laughed. 'Maybe. I'll have to think of something suitably impressive.'

'I'm sure we'll think of something,' Leena said.

After a few more drinks, she led them to the dark throbbing space of a restricted-access club Olivia hadn't even heard of. This was the sort of socialising she mostly avoided. It was too expensive, too detrimental to her schedule and work performance.

'It's not every day you buy your first piece of property,' Leena cajoled, her arm threaded through Olivia's, her head close to her ear. 'You've earned this little celebration. Besides, if you look over there—' she nodded towards a group of guys standing nearby '—those fine specimens are showing considerable interest.'

Leena led the way by teasing and flirting with the immaculate, openly available men, knocking them back when they started to bore her or became too cocky. After so many years of restraint—of being sensible and committed to her carefully constructed plans—Olivia found the night exhilarating.

She hadn't intended for it to be the first of many. She did try to resist Leena when she rang to propose other nights out. Sometimes Olivia even said *no*. She always put her job first, knowing she couldn't maintain the hotel's standards if she was hungover or sleep deprived.

As their friendship evolved, Leena asked to meet Eric. Eventually, Olivia brought her to one of the scheduled lunches she had with her father. These were a permanent diary entry for the first Friday of every month, provided Eric was in town. Her relationship with him had always been strictly managed. When she was eight, her mother had run from the bright lights and high-society life of Sydney, taking Olivia to the earthy authenticity of northern New South Wales. After that, Olivia had been delivered back to the city for twice-yearly visits with her father. She'd loved those fortnights at his pristine, perfect house. His current home was even more spectacular. An architectural stack of black glass-fronted boxes, with polished concrete throughout, and a perfectly edited interior over five levels. All of it facing Sydney Harbour.

Leena had been in raptures. She'd asked for a tour, then talked real estate with Eric until he'd finally changed the subject. It hadn't been overt, but her body language had made it clear she was quite interested in Eric too. For the first time in their friendship Olivia had been irritated by Leena. She needn't have worried, as the arrival of Janice at the lunch immediately changed the dynamic. Eric's current wife was intimidating in all areas. Her appearance, business success, and personal wealth were astonishing. Besides, he wasn't the sort of man to be lured by youth alone.

Later Leena shrugged off Olivia's careful criticism. 'Olly-Indy—' she'd taken to using abbreviated versions of Olivia's names '—your father is an amazing man. What's wrong with me learning from him? One day I'll have a house like that. All it takes is focus, intelligence, hard work, a well-defined plan, and a willingness to do whatever it takes. And I have all those things—and more. I don't apologise for wanting that and for making the most of every opportunity that comes my way.'

'Like a chance to meet my father?'

Leena's smile was enormous, her eyes excited. 'He's going to meet with me again. I'm going to pitch to be the agent for that boutique development of his, the one in Rose Bay. Not one apartment under two-point-five! He was very open to hearing my proposal. Working with your dad will take my career to the next level.'

Olivia didn't doubt her, but she was wary of how her father perceived this forced interaction. When she spoke to him she was relieved to hear he had been genuinely open to dealing with her friend.

Then things got complicated. In November 2014, Hayden Carlyle checked in to the Supreme Suite at Olivia's hotel. She'd dealt with plenty of celebrities by then, and her warm but professional demeanour didn't waver. Even when the affable film star shook her hand, flashed his famous dimpled smile, and then repeatedly asked for her assistance. He was handsome, with messy dark hair and a face that was perfect for hardened hero or wounded lover. His body was frequently seen shirtless on screen. The public adored him for being down-to-earth, funny, and committed to his wife of seven years and their two young children. On this trip he was travelling alone—for meetings, he said. Mostly he seemed content to hang in his suite, calling on Olivia to personally deliver a bottle of his favourite wine or six bottles of a locally produced kombucha, or to source a PlayStation. Or to discuss his needs. Or to stop a moment and have a drink with him. He talked to her as though he'd been starved of regular conversation. He flattered her, focused on her, then kissed her. Whispered to her about how wonderful she was. How real. How beautiful. How he needed to see her again.

It was surreal, exhilarating and terrifying, all at the same time.

Leena was her confidante and a source of encouragement. 'He obviously likes you, Olly-Indy. Go with it. You never know where this will lead. See it as an opportunity.'

They were sitting in a bar, Olivia desperate to be given clear direction. 'But he's married.'

Leena leant forward and clasped her hands. 'You're not the one doing the wrong thing. You can't be his conscience. If his relationship really is as great as they make out, he wouldn't be showing interest in you, would he?'

'I don't know.'

'Darling, you need to have more confidence in yourself—and be prepared to take risks.'

'You think this is risky?'

Her friend sighed. 'Doing something new and exciting always carries an element of risk. But it's how we move forward, on to bigger and better things. How we make more of our lives. You'll never know where this could lead if you don't give it a go. This could be the best thing to ever happen to you. I mean, he's Hayden Carlyle, but you're Eric Haymers' daughter. This could be huge.'

'Or it could be no more than a fling.'

'In which case you enjoy every second, make some fabulous memories, and get a few goodies out of it. After all, he's not short on money.'

Olivia had taken the advice. Gone with it. Lived in a dream for most of 2015. Only to wake in a nightmare. When she looked back now, those days seemed vivid, intoxicating and unreal—and a long, long way from her present life.

She stepped into the house, hung her coat on its hook, and dropped the postcards on the table. There was no one except Brian to witness her descent into midmorning drinking, so she poured a gin big enough to smooth out the anxiety and drown out the nastiness of Leena's latest intrusion. She was also mourning everything she'd lost because of the crap choices she had made. Immersed in Leena's friendship, she'd gone from a ten-year plan, self-imposed rules and bullet journals to a much wilder life, and the excitement had been addictive. Dressing up and being provocative had been addictive. Crazy sex with crazy sexy guys had definitely been addictive. The relationship with Hayden had been thrilling. Her moral compass had been trashed.

Leena may have convinced Olivia to sleep with Hayden the first time, but she had eagerly taken on the role of mistress. Olivia was the one guilty of pretending his wife didn't exist and of thinking that the sleazy, selfish affair was something special because of its veneer of glamour. What she wasn't guilty of, though, was secretly filming the two of them in bed and trying to extort money in exchange for silence—that was all Leena. Her so-called friend had manipulated, lied, and black-mailed. Olivia had done something morally wrong, but Leena had broken the law.

Enough! Olivia stood up, carried the drink to the kitchen and poured it down the sink. Leena was a nasty schemer who refused to admit her own culpability, and Olivia intended never to see her again, ever. As the peppy affirmations declared—she couldn't change the circumstances, but she could control how she responded. She didn't have to cower. She picked up the postcards, held them high and tore them in half, dropping the pieces on the table.

Lifting her jacket from the hook, she pulled it back on. A bushwalk would have to be better than indulging in another bout of drunken wallowing. She pushed her feet into her runners and bent to tie the laces.

Tom would come over in a couple of hours, so she needed to pull herself together. She considered cancelling—but that would be letting Leena continue to define her life. The bitch wasn't here. She didn't know Olivia's location. That meant she couldn't do anything but stomp and snarl and push her poison into a mailbox. Tom would be a welcome distraction.

'Sorry, Brian, you'll have to stay here,' Olivia said when the cat rubbed against her legs. He stood at the door as she pulled on her beanie, and she had to nudge him with her foot to get past, promising to give him plenty of attention when she returned.

Trekking over the hill and down the other side to the road was more challenging than just wandering down to the water. The steep, narrow path was little more than a roo track, and she had only walked it once—and then only halfway. If she made it to the top today, she'd do the full circuit, all the way down, and then loop back around to the water's edge. That should wake up her near-dead endorphins.

Her mother would have been delighted to see her embracing the great outdoors as a solution to her stress. She'd always been perplexed, even disappointed, that Olivia had shunned her love of nature and of simplistic, grounded living. They'd both had a desire for self-improvement, but where her mother had been all about Mother Earth, well-being, meditation and serenity, Olivia had yearned for the shimmering success she'd seen in her father's world. Now here she was, hauling herself through the bush—despite her fear of spiders, snakes and killer ants— in the hope of making her pain go away.

Within ten minutes she was breathing hard. By the time she'd reached the top her thighs were a quivering, burning mess. But her fear and anxiety had been replaced by anger. Leena could take her dirty little messages and implied threats and shove them up her Pilates-toned arse.

CHAPTER TEN

Tom tentatively knocked on the door for the third time. The only response came from a tatty-looking cat who stood at the sidelight, peering at him through one large eye. He pulled out his phone and opened the email he'd received yesterday, checking the date, the day, the time, suddenly worried he had somehow lost or gained a day. No, he was here when she'd said.

She was Olivia, no last name. Her email address gave no hints to anything more.

A silver Honda CRV was parked under cover, suggesting she must be on the property somewhere. But from what he could see, this was a huge parcel of land—the driveway alone had to be a mile long.

He walked the length of the rather nice house, taking a crazy-paved path that led to the far side. An expansive terrace extended out from glass doors and huge windows that gave him a glimpse of the interior. He had an urge to peer in, then remembered his vow to be less creepy. If she turned up and found him with his face smooshed against her windows, she would not be impressed.

Instead, he turned to look out at the breathtaking view again. He was still admiring it when she emerged from the tree line at the bottom of the hill. She looked up, and he lifted his hand high, trying for a friendly gesture that wouldn't be misconstrued.

She stopped. Hesitated. Raised a hand in response, which was enough for him to start towards her.

About halfway down, his strides began to gather speed. He realised the slope was deceptive and was, in fact, quite steep, and that his leather runners, perfect for the office in London, weren't exactly suitable for the wilds of Tasmania. His front foot slipped forward, and his arms flew up to maintain his balance. 'Shit. Fuck! Bugger.' He stumbled, just managing to stay upright. 'Hi. Hello.' He was breathing harder than a simple walk should have demanded—really impressive. 'Thank you for asking me here. I appreciate it. Olivia, is it? I'm Tom Kearsley.' He stuck out his hand and tried not to puff. 'Can I say again how very sorry I am about the other day. It was awful of me to do that. You know, to push on your door. I'm not a thug. I promise.'

She was below him on the slope and had to reach up to give his hand a brief shake. Her eyes were darkest brown, defined by black lashes that weren't glued on or thick and sticky with mascara. There was a flush of red in the pale skin of her cheeks and at the end of her nose. A vivid green beanie hid all but a few wisps of her hair, and she was rugged up in a large, practical weather-proof jacket over pink trackpants. She was very pretty, which was not going to help matters. Realising he was towering over her, he stepped down and sideways.

And slipped, again. 'Fuck. Christ.' His left leg went out from under him, and his hands hit the ground as he stopped himself from tumbling even further.

Olivia gave a choked laugh.

Kill me now. Could he be any more of an idiot? He could feel the burn of embarrassment.

'Come on,' she said as he got to his feet, 'we can talk down on the beach.'

Before he could reply she'd started back the way she'd come. He followed cautiously, taking timid steps and clutching at branches as they worked their way around the larger trees and pushed through close-growing scrappy undergrowth. Two minutes later they reached the water. 'Nice place,' he said. The tiny bay was about fifty feet from end to end and curved slightly, the rocky ground strewn with heavy, weathered branches. It wasn't much of a beach, more a narrow edge with stringy trees leaning forward over the clear ground towards the quietly lapping water. Olivia took a seat on a large flat rock at one end. 'May I? Do you mind if …?' He nodded towards the space next to her.

She shifted over slightly, indicating he could sit. He left as much space between them as he could, glancing at her as he sat. She was studying him. 'You're really on a mission.' He had a sneaking suspicion she was trying not to laugh at him. He'd gone from being a threat to a joke, which he guessed was an improvement.

He smiled, nodding a little too enthusiastically. 'Exactly! That's exactly what this is. Although, you know what, it's more of a quest. A mission tends to involve a range of tasks to achieve—things to be ticked off. A quest is an arduous journey towards an end goal. So I'd describe this as a quest. It's certainly arduous.' He laughed awkwardly and glanced down at his feet as he kicked a small stone. 'The things we do for our parents.' He looked up.

She was gazing at him with amused disbelief. 'Right, a quest then.'

He shrugged. 'Yes. To deliver a document.'

'To Pippa?'

'Yes.' He was delighted to know she'd paid attention to his story. 'A letter from my father to the girl he loved.'

'And you've come from England?'

'Yes. Christ, it's a long way to get here, isn't it?' He looked around. He'd travelled from London to the southernmost end of the southernmost part of Australia. It was no surprise he had got off to such a bad start. 'I only arrived three—' He stopped, doing a quick check in his head. 'No, four days ago. I think I'm still jet-lagged. You'd think going business would make a difference, but it was still a bloody squeeze on those lay-out seats. It's so long to be stuck in a plane—economy must be hell.' What the hell was he babbling about now? He sounded like such a tosser. 'Shit. That's a stupid thing to say. What I mean is, I'm lucky, really lucky. I'm not actually an entitled twat. I appreciate being up the front. It was fine, absolutely fine. Great service and everything.' He had to shut up.

A short snort-laugh burst out of Olivia. 'It's a hideous trip.'

'Anyway, I'm not having much luck,' he mumbled, mortified. He closed his mouth and tried to arrange his thoughts so he could manage a rational, succinct conversation.

'Can I ask,' Olivia said, 'why your father hasn't given you more information? Do you have Pippa's surname or even her full first name—isn't Pippa short for Philippa—or where she lived, details of her family, that sort of thing?'

'Her surname is "French". I don't know about her full first name, and I don't have anything else.' Tom leant forward to rest his forearms on his thighs, his hands clasped between his knees. Took a few seconds. This was the hard part. 'My dad passed away about eighteen months ago.'

'Oh. Gosh. I'm sorry.' He could hear the sincerity in the softness of her voice.

'It's fine.' He knew he had to explain the situation, but it was hard. The breeze picked up, scuffing the surface of the water. A bird began to warble, something deep and melodic with the occasional whistle. He listened for a few moments before speaking. 'It's a bit of a story, but I'll try to keep it short.' He took a breath and let it out. 'My dad is ... or, I guess, *was* Australian. His name was Jeremy Kearsley, and he grew up in Brisbane. He never talked about his childhood. He only had his mother, and she died before he left Australia. But he spoke about this place, this house, a few times over the years. I believe he spent one summer here when he was twenty-four.'

The bird stopped singing, the bush now strangely quiet. He waited a moment, then pushed on. 'Anyway, he didn't give me many details, more like wistful moments of happy memories. I know that he arrived in England in the late eighties. Found work, met my mum a couple of years later, had me. The marriage only lasted about five years, but Mum and Dad stayed on good terms, he did quite well for himself, all the usual details. And he stayed.'

'Did he ever come back?' She turned towards him, and he could feel her eyes fixed on him.

'Here? No, never.'

'What about Brissie?'

'Brisbane? Not as far as I know.'

She seemed to consider this for a bit. 'Aussies moving to the UK isn't uncommon. But to cut all ties ... that seems odd.'

'Does it?' He glanced at her, drawn into her gaze for a second, before looking back out at the water. 'Yeah, I guess it is. Although, he didn't have that many ties to cut.'

'So why are you here now?'

He sat up straighter, stretching out his legs. 'About three months ago I finally got around to clearing out some of Dad's stuff. I needed to get his house ready to go on the market. Anyway, I came across a leather folder, one of those zip-up compendium things. You know the ones, about so big.' He motioned with his hands and stopped when she nodded, realising it wasn't an important detail. 'Inside there was some old paperwork, including a printed itinerary from his trip from Hobart through to London in 1986, and an old driver's licence from back when they were still paper. There were also five photos. Some of them had writing on the back. In one picture there's the house—your house—and two women named as Eloise and Pippa. Another one of just Eloise, and three of Pippa. Some of the photos of Pippa make it very obvious she and Dad were a happy couple. There were other people here too, I think.'

'Okay. And you got curious and wanted to meet her?' She sounded doubtful, as though questioning why this would entice him to travel so far.

He cleared his throat. 'There's also a large envelope, heavy with a thick letter or document or something. The envelope has *Pippa French* written on the front, in my dad's handwriting.' Tom paused. He'd been both surprised and curious when he found it. His father had been enigmatic and private, but the discovery had immediately felt significant. 'And it has instructions to hand it to her.' He didn't mention the bold lettering added underneath: *Private, for Pippa only.* Or how he'd weighed up what to do, fighting the urge to read the contents. A thousand dramatic scenarios had run through his head. In the end, though, his conscience had stopped him from lifting the sealed flap and he'd begun to get excited about the challenge laid down for him. It was his job to find Pippa and deliver the package. If he achieved the goal, maybe he would have earned those answers.

Olivia had drawn up her feet to the edge of the rock and was hugging her knees. 'What do you think it's about?'

'At a guess, I think Pippa was the love of my dad's life. Or maybe the memories of that summer—and whatever lovely things happened between them—turned her into his one great regret.'

'Regrets, I have many,' she murmured.

'Don't we all.'

Their eyes met again, fleetingly, before they both looked away.

'Haven't you been tempted to open it?' she asked.

Only every other day. He studied his hands, the tiny waves cresting across the water, and then the sky. 'Well. Maybe. But it wouldn't be right—I have to at least try to honour my dad's wishes. I mean, make a real concerted effort to achieve the outcome he wanted.'

She rested her chin on her knees. 'Yeah. I get that.' A gust of wind pushed at their backs, and she turned to look at the sky behind them. 'We'd better go.'

He glanced over his shoulder to where a heavy mass of slate-grey clouds were rolling forward. 'Wow, where did that come from?'

'Things can change quickly around here. It's sunny, then stormy, then back to sunny, all in an afternoon.' She jumped off the rock and moved towards the path. 'You don't want to be caught down here.' He followed, nearly colliding with her when she suddenly stopped. 'Would you like a cup of tea? Come in out of the weather for a bit.'

'That would be nice, thank you.' Brilliant! He was getting somewhere.

Their pace was slow as they climbed the steep hill and he had to concentrate on not slipping. By the time they were at the house, the first of the stinging, cold rain had reached them. She walked him around to where his car was parked, bypassing the terrace and the wide French doors to enter through the front. He followed her lead, taking off his useless runners and hanging his soggy jacket beside hers on a hook inside the door. She dropped her beanie on the table, shaking out shoulder-length brown hair that curled at the ends and fell over her face. She scooped up some rubbish from the table and scrunched it into her fist. 'I'll grab us some towels,' she said, leaving him standing at the top of the wide stairs that led down to the open, uncluttered space of the lounge.

He thanked her when she returned, the two of them quickly drying off. 'Great house,' he said. 'This is what you call mid-century modern, right?'

'I think so?' she replied without confidence.

He looked across to the wall of glass and the view down over the wind-tossed trees to the water. The sky was an expanse of rushing black clouds, the rain hitting the windows hard. The room, on the other hand, was warm and inviting, embers glowing in the glass-fronted fireplace where a fire had burned low. She moved into the small kitchen next to the entrance, and he followed.

'I'm lucky to live here,' she said.

'Do you like feeling so removed from the rest of the world?' As someone who lived in a tightly packed city, with everything available at any time, he was genuinely curious.

She didn't answer straight away. 'I like the quiet,' she said at last.

'Are you working from here?'

'No. Not working.'

'Taking it easy?'

'Something like that.' It seemed she didn't want to elaborate.

'Are you here alone?' He regretted the question the second it left his mouth.

She flicked him a look and shrugged. 'Mostly.'

He needed to stop the inquisition. 'Strange to think of my father having been right here. I don't imagine the house has changed much.' He pictured Pippa and a younger version of his dad in these rooms, kicking back and drinking beers with music playing, the doors flung open to the summer heat. The house would have been a dream come true for kids on the cusp of their adult lives. They would've had no responsibilities, complete freedom, and plenty of space. What a summer it would have been.

Olivia was pulling out large mugs and a blue box of Lady Grey tea bags, and he had to shift to the other end of the bench so as not to crowd her. She paused, a tea bag swinging from her fingers. 'You said your father's photos were all taken when he was here?' Her face had lost some of its wariness, shifting into a puzzled frown.

'Yes. I even recognise that big barbecue out there.' Tom nodded towards the terrace. 'Although two of them were taken in a bedroom, so I guess they could've been taken elsewhere.'

She dropped the tea bag into a mug. 'Oh. And there were names on them?'

'Yeah, Eloise and Pippa.'

'But you said there were others in the photos.'

'Sort of in the background in one photo, just their outlines.'

She rested a hip against the bench and folded her arms, her head angled. Those dark eyes watched him as though she was waiting for him to say something profound. He looked away, feeling awkward under her scrutiny.

'No mention of anyone called Leo Clifford?' she asked. 'No one in the pictures who might have had that name?'

'Leo Clifford?'

She nodded. Waited.

The photos were in his hotel room, but he had studied them so many times he didn't need to look at them to know the answer. There was no clear picture of a man or any mention of one.

CHAPTER ELEVEN

The kettle clicked off, and Olivia concentrated on pouring the water into two cups. 'Milk, sugar?' she asked. She kept her eyes on her task rather than on the man who was now in her house. The galley kitchen was narrow, with less than two metres between the cabinetry running along each side. Tom stood perched against a bench and seemed to fill the space. She stepped around him, trying not to get too close.

'Milk, no sugar,' he answered.

She jiggled the tea bags, suddenly worried about her casual tea-making skills. Didn't the English take their tea very seriously? Did he expect a pot and leaves, the pot warmed, a strainer over a cup, not a mug—and was the milk supposed to go in first? She couldn't remember. Her years of hospitality work had apparently been forgotten. 'Sorry, not very fancy, and I'll let you add the milk.'

'I don't need fancy, that's fine. Thank you. Do you take milk too?'

She shook her head as she grabbed the milk carton from the fridge and handed it to him. Then she took out a half-eaten packet of caramel Tim Tams and thought about putting them on a plate before deciding it was pointless. She could improve the presentation, but it wouldn't redeem her skills as a hostess. He brought the milk and his tea to the table, and she brought the Tim Tams along with her mug. 'It's all I've got,' she said, offering the biscuits to him as they pulled out chairs.

He took one and bit into it. 'Nice.'

For a couple of minutes they sipped the tea without speaking, the silence filled by the howl of the wind and the heavy rain on the roof.

'You were asking about someone called Leo,' he finally prompted. 'Why's that?'

She set down her cup and looked at him. This was a safe subject and better than talking about herself. 'There's a story about this house, about something that happened here in the eighties. I wondered if your dad and Pippa might've been here at that time.'

He tapped at the crumbs he'd left on the table. 'And there's a Leo Clifford in this story?'

'Yes. He was here, in this house, in February 1986.' The couple of brief news articles she'd seen hadn't given the address, but one page had a photo taken from the gate looking up the drive, the house hidden behind the hill, which confirmed what Wendy had told her. 'Then he disappeared.'

'Disappeared?'

She nodded as she reached for a second biscuit. 'He was from Hobart, from a good family. He'd finished high school the year before and was set to head to uni. And he'd recently done the Sydney to Hobart yacht race. Have you heard of that?'

'My dad and I watched the start of the race every time I spent Christmas with him. Starts on Boxing Day, right?'

'Right. Well, apparently Leo was a really competent young sailor. Anyway, he was last seen by his girlfriend—I don't know her name—who was staying with him in this house at the time. She said goodbye to him in the middle of the night. He drove off and was never seen again. His car was found in Hobart, at the yacht club, with the keys under the seat, but there was no trace of him. It was considered extremely unlikely that he took himself off somewhere or died by suicide. His disappearance has been filed away as a missing person cold case, one of many, with a verdict of presumed dead.' She leaned forward a little. 'It's possible your dad and Pippa could have been staying here at the same time.'

Tom leant back in the chair, thoughtful. 'They might have been. The dates are almost a match.'

'They are?'

'Three of the photos have months written on them—December 1985 for one and January 1986 for two.' He was watching her intently, as though waiting for her to explain what this all meant. She felt her cheeks grow warm. He wasn't a pretty boy like Hayden. His face was stronger and more interesting, and his eyes crinkled up when he smiled. She was becoming increasingly aware of the gentle tug of attraction.

She looked down to hide what she was feeling. 'I've only read a little bit online—well, there isn't much available—and nothing mentioned the names of anyone else who was here.'

'But you think it's a possibility? That Dad, Pippa and this Leo guy might have been connected, might even have been friends?'

'Sure.' As Olivia finished her tea, it occurred to her that this might not be a good thing. No other names had been given, nor suspects listed, but perhaps that was for legal reasons.

A smile pulled at Tom's mouth and crept into a full-blown grin. 'Maybe that was why my father moved away—because of the dark cloud of suspicion after Leo's disappearance. And he never got over the loss of his friend, and that's why he never talked about life here.'

Tom was taking a very positive view of all this. 'Sure, that's one possible scenario,' she said. 'When did your dad head off for the UK?'

'Early February 1986. When did Leo go missing?'

She racked her brain. 'Sometime around then. I don't remember the dates, but a quick Google search will tell you.'

'What's a quest without mystery and intrigue, and discoveries along the way?' Tom leant forward on the table, nearly closing the distance between them, and Olivia pulled back. 'I wonder if Eloise would remember the details?' he asked with a cheeky tilt of his head. He had a piece of hair sticking up, and she had a ridiculous urge to reach out and smooth it down.

'She might.' Olivia gave a small laugh—he was certainly persistent.

'It sounds like there must have been a few of them staying here over that summer. And I suppose Eloise was here too.'

'Actually, no, I don't think she was, not in February. Leo and his girlfriend were house-sitting—that's what one article said.'

'That's interesting. But she was here in December 1985 with Pippa and presumably Dad, according to the photos. I'm sure if I had a quick chat with her, she'd be able to give us more information, maybe put me in touch with Pippa ...'

Oh, what the hell. Olivia stood and crossed to where her jacket was hanging. She dug in the pockets until she found her phone, then returned to the table, flicking through her scant contact list. 'I feel very strongly about people's right to privacy. We should all be careful about giving out private information.' She needed to make her position clear.

'I understand, and I absolutely agree. I know all about what it feels like to lose your privacy. But I promise I'm not intending to intrude on Eloise. And if she's very annoyed, she can just block my number.'

Olivia held her thumb over the screen and met his gaze. 'I'll ring her, ask if she'd like to be put in contact with you.'

'That would be great, thanks.' He managed to sound both thankful and a little disappointed. Perhaps patience wasn't one of his virtues, but he did have the decency and manners not to push any harder.

She tapped the phone and lifted it to her ear. 'I'll explain why you'd like to speak to her.'

'Okay.'

Eloise could decide for herself if she wanted to chat with Tom. Surely she would—she'd given every indication of being a friendly and generous person.

Olivia herself was now even more curious about what happened here all those years ago. Who wouldn't want to know more? Like, why hadn't Jeremy returned for Pippa, or why hadn't she joined him in England? Was there a connection with Leo? What had happened to him? And what was in the letter Tom was so determined to deliver? Was this a love story, or something else?

A series of fast angry beeps made her pull the phone from her ear. 'Damn. No reception.'

'No bars?'

'No, worse than that. There's no service at all. The tower must've gone down in the winds.'

'Really? That's something that happens?'

'Apparently. I have been warned about the perils of living out here.'

Now his disappointment was obvious. 'I don't suppose you could give me the number?'

She shook her head. 'I promise I'll ring her as soon as I can.'

'Thank you.' He carried their mugs through to the sink and returned the milk to the fridge. 'Sorry if I sound demanding. I do understand your position.'

There had been many times at her hotel job when Olivia had needed to withhold information. She'd learnt to gently but firmly refuse to hand out details when, say, a woman rang to ask what her husband had ordered for room service. Or when the press were trying to track down a guest staying under a false name. Or if an entitled guy wanted a woman's room number. Olivia had come across juicy tales and salacious tidbits, the sort of gossip that could have earned her a small fee. But she'd always been professionally tight-lipped—and that was before *she* had become the tidbit of gossip. Keeping hold of Eloise's information was no different.

She went down to the fireplace in the lounge and raked together what was left of the glowing embers, then put on a few small logs and made sure they caught. The weather was still vile, so keeping the fire going was necessary not simply for warmth but also to maintain a sense of cosy, safe containment.

'I should head off, I suppose,' Tom said, coming down to look out the windows. The view to the water was now obliterated by bucketing rain.

She hesitated, nervous about the suggestion she was about to make. 'It's not good weather to be driving in,' she said, trying to sound nothing more than practical. 'Branches and even trees often come down across the road when the weather's like this.'

He considered her warning. 'I don't want to impose on you.'

'It's okay. Brian and I don't have anything planned.'

'Brian?' He looked at her questioningly. 'Boyfriend? Husband? Son?'

She pointed to a corner of the sofa where Brian was buried, unmoving, in the folds of the alpaca blanket. 'Cat.'

Tom stepped closer and peered down before he reached out to scratch Brian's head. 'He's got bits missing.'

'Yes, but we try not to make a big deal of it. He's a tad sensitive.'

Tom laughed. 'Fair enough. Brian, you are one handsome fellow.'

A day that had started out appallingly now had the chance of being rated mostly good, verging on great. She tried and failed to dampen a huge smile. 'Since you could be stuck here with Brian and me for a little bit, would you like a glass of wine?'

'Sure.' His smile matched hers. 'Why not?'

*

The storm continued through the late afternoon and into the evening, darkness descending before it was even five. The power went off about the same time the sunlight was completely obliterated. Olivia set fat scented soy candles on the coffee table, pleased that one of her online shopping binges had proven to not only be indulgent but highly practical.

'Just a word of warning,' she said to Tom, 'no power means no water.'

'Honestly?'

'The house is on tank water, and without power the pump doesn't work. Ergo, no water flowing from the taps.'

'Or filling the toilet.'

'You've got it.'

'I will bear that in mind,' he said with a laugh.

They faced each other from either end of the sofa, the fire before them, the glow from the trio of candles barely reaching where they sat. She put out cheese and crackers, then without even asking if he was staying, she headed back to the kitchen, torch in hand, to rustle up something for dinner. Luckily the stove was gas, not electric.

After moving Brian from his lap, Tom followed, proving himself to be more than capable. A tub of store-bought tomato soup was jazzed up with chorizo, capsicum and some herbs from her limited selection. Paired with some butter-soaked sourdough, it made the perfect meal for a miserable night. A fire, red wine, good company and a simple rustic meal—yes, the evening was the most enjoyable thing to happen in her life for a very, very long time.

As the hours passed in easy, uncomplicated conversation, there was a tightening in her stomach, like how it felt right before the drop on a rollercoaster. The pleasure came from the wine, the fact Tom was a funny, self-deprecating, good-looking guy, and the sheer joy contained in the moment. When was the last time she'd felt joy? When was the last time she'd felt so *normal*? There'd been the thrill and excitement of Hayden, but nothing about their eight-month relationship had been normal. There'd been too much sneaking about, and the constant awareness she was doing something morally wrong and that he was no mere mortal.

After Hayden there had been only one guy, an ambitious young banker. For her, the relationship was based on a desperate craving for reassurance and contact with others. For him, it was based on an unashamed desire to savour something—someone—illicit. Hayden Carlyle was top-shelf famous, desired by thousands, extolled for his clean-cut, happily married lifestyle. Having sex with Hayden's infamous ex-lover was a significant notch on his belt, or bedhead, or Instagram.

But Tom gave zero indication of knowing who she was, and she easily steered most of the talk away from her and towards him. It was easy enough to do, because she'd never met a game producer or director before.

'I have a company that oversees the publishing of new indie games. We're not up there with one of the triple-A studios, but we've produced some great titles. We're big enough to get plenty of good exposure on Steam. Not as big as Devolver, of course, but in the last few years we've had a pretty solid presence at E3. And I act as director on some of our own commissioned games as well.'

'Okay.' She pretended that made sense.

He read her lack of comprehension and dumbed down his explanation. A game director, she learnt, was to videogame development what a director was to a movie. He was a tech guy, but a creative one. His passion for his career and enthusiasm for sharing the details made her laugh.

Then they talked about London, exploring a shared love for BBC property shows and an interest in Scandi-noir thrillers. She briefly touched on her work in exclusive hotels, which reminded her what she had loved about the career she had chosen—and from which she had retreated.

There were moments when the conversation paused and their eyes caught and held. Fleeting instances of connection. And maybe—if she wasn't misreading the atmosphere—appreciation and interest?

It was a disappointment when the lights snapped back on at eight. Even the corner lamp seemed harsh after the soft glow they'd been held within.

'I guess I should be going,' said Tom as he carried their dishes to the kitchen.

Olivia was aware that in this moment, things between them had the chance to go one way or the other. Or was she kidding herself? She was so out of practice. She barely spoke to anyone these days, let alone shared space with them—her last conversation with a man had been the discussion of anti-venom with the firewood bloke. Plus, she had drunk several glasses of wine, more than Tom had. Her rational mind was skewed a little by the pinot noir. She could be reading it all wrong.

Then, of course, there was the question of whether she'd ever had any skill at judging people. Her recent track record wasn't encouraging.

'Okay.' She finished stacking the last bowl into the dish-washer and turned to smile at Tom, keeping a steadying hand on the bench. *Best to play it safe.* She imagined stepping forward, kissing him—and more. But she couldn't bring herself to close the space between them. Her body both yearned for his touch and retreated from the idea of making herself vulnerable. Did she trust him? She'd known him for only a few hours. Did she trust herself? Not particularly.

'Thank you for dinner,' he said softly, then cleared his throat. In a swift movement he pulled his hands from his pockets, rocked back on his heels and folded his arms. Then, just as quickly, he unfolded them and let his hands hang by his sides as though he couldn't decide where to put them. 'And thanks for sheltering me in such cosy comfort.'

He's nervous, she thought and almost laughed. She found it reassuring, even charming. His insecurity bolstered her confidence more than any sweet words or smooth moves could have.

She walked to the table and picked up her phone, but there was still no reception. Making a snap decision, she found a pen and pulled an envelope from the untidy stack of mail at the edge of the table. She wrote on the back of the envelope. 'Here,' she said, handing it to him, wanting to show she trusted him. 'Eloise's number. Mine too.'

He took it from her. 'Are you sure?'

'Mm-hmm.' She nodded while immediately thinking she shouldn't have done it. *Too late now.* 'If Eloise doesn't want to talk to you, she can tell you so herself.'

He folded the envelope in half, pushed it into a pocket of his jeans, then pulled out a chair and sat to put on his shoes. 'I'll have to let you know how I go.'

'I'd like that,' she said. *Don't leave* was what she thought.

She held the door as he stepped into the cold. As she watched him walk to his car, the bubble of momentary happiness began to deflate. In minutes she would, once again, be alone. The contrast between comfortable companionship—and all the warm, fuzzy feelings that had come with it—and her solitary existence was overwhelming. 'Drive carefully, there's likely to be debris on the road,' was all she said.

He lifted his hand as he slipped into the driver's seat. 'Talk to you soon,' he called before he shut the door.

Although she was shivering, she stayed on the step and watched him pull away. Then she shut the door and moved back to the lounge to pick up her unfinished wine. She walked to her bedroom and collected the remnants of the postcards that she'd dropped there earlier. Back in the lounge she opened the door to the fire, dropping the pieces into the flames. It was as easy as that. Any more letters from her psycho ex-friend would be going the same way. It was time for her to concentrate on getting some joy back in her life. Tom wouldn't be in Tasmania for long. He hadn't said when he was due to leave, but she presumed that as soon as he'd achieved his goal he'd need to return to his job. But he had her number, and she had his. Maybe she could call him if he didn't call her by tomorrow evening.

'What do you think, Brian? Is Tom a decent guy?'

She was testing this thought, imagining herself having the courage to make contact, as she headed back towards the kitchen. She glanced at the stack of mail on the table and stopped. 'Oh shit,' she breathed. The envelope, the one she'd written on ... Eloise's number and her number were scribbled on the back, *Olivia Haymers* on the front.

Tom probably wouldn't know her by name—the story had been big, but she thought her notoriety was less widespread outside of Australia. Tom, surely, would be far too busy to be concerned with celebrity gossip. But wouldn't he be curious? She imagined him sitting in his hotel room, checking emails, updating his Instagram, typing her name into the search bar. He'd be interested in seeing what he could find, wouldn't he? Didn't everyone Google-stalk new friends? She lowered herself into a chair and covered her face with her hands. She felt so stupid.

Tom was about to plunge into a smorgasbord of content about her. He would find not only *the* video, the one at the centre of the court case, the one that would never be fully stripped from the internet, but also snippets, teasers and memes. There would be footage of her leaving court, at work before she was fired, and even jogging in the park. There would be photos, mostly unflattering. And there would be the words. He would read the allegations, the exaggerations, and the vicious commentary spewed by the press and public.

She groaned as the familiar slurry of shame rose within her. The past few hours had been the best in a long, long time. Tom had been wonderful, and she wanted more, but she doubted he would ever be back.

CHAPTER TWELVE

Saturday, 24 June 2017

It was Olivia's first visit to the one and only restaurant in the village. It was a surprisingly glamorous establishment on the edge of the water that still managed to feel casual despite the soaring glass construction and award-winning chef. She'd found a table outside, and now the winter sun was on her face, even if the breeze coming off the water made her nose and cheeks tingle. Her freshly washed hair was stuffed back under her beanie, her favourite rollneck jumper sitting above her chin, and sunglasses were in place to cut the glare. *Hidden in plain sight*, she thought as she sipped from a mug of hot chocolate, the cinnamon-scented steam warming her face. Only someone who knew her would recognise her, which was her intention.

The temptation to wallow had been pressing, especially after a sad, sleepless night, but she'd hauled herself out of bed and forced herself to shower and dress. She may have only had one evening with Tom, but he'd made her feel normal, and for that she was thankful. Now it was up to her to take the next tentative step. She couldn't wait around for another nice stranger to turn up on her doorstep—she had to make herself move towards a real life.

She glanced around, trying to be subtle in her perusal of the other diners. This restaurant, perched on the edge of Devils Bay, had a reputation worthy of a special trip. The out-of-towners were easy to identify, with their expensive coats, soft scarfs draped with care, and stylish boots. Then there were the locals, who were perfectly comfortable wandering in from their gardens wearing shabby polar-fleece jumpers, baggy workhorse jeans, and even gumboots or mud-crusted Blundstones. Some had dropped in while walking their dogs, their charges tied to table legs, bowls of water at their feet. There was chatter and laughter, children played on the lawn, and the view over the channel was stunning. A few small yachts sat off from the shore. Seagulls flapped in lazy circles above calm water that sparkled with blinding, dancing light.

A young waitress in a chambray shirt and black apron stopped beside Olivia's table. 'Your risotto?'

Olivia nodded, thanked her, and accepted the plate. The first mouthful almost made her groan with delight. It had been close to a year since she'd gone out to eat.

The trial had finished, and the banker had taken her to one of those upmarket restaurants in Sydney where the celebrity status of the chef ensured there was never an empty table. The meal was divine, the champagne French, and the glances and whispers of the other diners were discreet. But her date seemed to revel in the attention, even going so far as to smile at the trash photographer when they were leaving. The photo made the gossip pages of *The Sydney Morning Herald*, showing the banker looking smug, proud to be seen with a disreputable woman, while Olivia looked like she was being hunted, her head down, her hair—which had still been long—covering her face, her arms crossed. When she refused to go out with him again, he became irritated, telling her that infamy was better than anonymity. 'Revel in the moment,' he said, his fingers darting over his phone. She suspected he was circulating the picture through his network—probably with a note boasting of his date. 'People know who you are, and that's a *good* thing.' She left his apartment and never went back.

Since then she'd avoided running the gauntlet of public dining. But now here she was, and so far, so good. No one was watching her, and no phones were raised in her direction, no heads huddled together madly whispering. She was out in the world, enjoying simple food cooked to perfection. She was living like a regular person—almost.

She imagined how things could have been if the night before had gone differently. If she had asked Tom to stay. If she'd kissed him. If he had spent the night. They could have been sharing this lunch together. Right now, they could have been laughing and holding hands like the couples around her.

At least last night had shown her that moments of joy were still possible. There was hope in that knowledge.

A voice yanked her from her thoughts. 'Hello, Olivia. Having a good lunch?'

She snapped her head around, her heart giving a thud that she felt in her throat. Wendy's friendly face was smiling down at her. Another woman stood close by, watching with an undisguised curiosity.

'Sorry, love,' said Wendy. 'Didn't mean to make you jump.'

Olivia put a hand over her heart and gave a shaky laugh. 'Sorry, I was in my own little world.'

'Don't blame you! Perfect day for dreaming a little. Have you met Tilly?' Wendy flicked a hand towards her companion. 'Tilly lives in the old schoolhouse. You know the one on the hill road, with the fabulous garden? Anyway, she's been there forever.'

The woman was dressed in a long red skirt, black lace-up boots and a vivid purple jacket. Her grey hair was swept up in a high bun, and earrings dangled to her shoulders, their coloured glass catching the light. *A character*, Olivia thought. One of those women who made middle-age look like fun.

Tilly waved a hand in the air, her other hand grasping the lead of a very old border collie. 'Hardly forever—only forty years or so,' she protested, then laughed.

Wendy rolled her eyes and carried on as if she hadn't been interrupted. 'And Olivia here, she's living down in Eloise's old place.'

'Oh, how fabulous for you. Marvellous house. How are you finding it?'

Olivia looked from one woman to the other, the speed of their chatter putting her off guard. 'The house is great, thanks. Gorgeous.'

'I never thought Eloise would move to the city, but there you go,' said Tilly. 'Still, she hasn't sold the house, has she? Don't think she can bear to let it go. Too much history in the place.'

Olivia didn't know what to say to that, so she smiled and fell back on the basics. 'Beautiful day, isn't it?'

Tilly replied quickly. 'Another stunner. Have to say we do winter rather well down here. How did you fare in the storm last night?'

An image of Tom on her sofa came to mind, his smiling face illuminated by soft candlelight. 'I coped,' she said.

'No trees down?'

'A few branches, but nothing I couldn't move.'

'Excellent,' said Wendy. 'Well, we'll leave you to your lunch. See you soon.'

'Okay.' Olivia lifted her hand in farewell. 'Nice to meet you, Tilly.'

Normal friendly conversation with normal friendly people— it was so much better than stewing in angst and fear at home. Olivia returned to her meal, revived by the interaction.

Her plate had been cleared and she was debating the wisdom of dessert—sticky date pudding, how could she possibly say no—when her phone rang. So few people had her number that it took her a while to realise the ringtone was coming from her bag. She had to scramble to find it in time.

Eloise's name was on the screen, dousing the nascent hope the call was from Tom before it could take hold.

'Hello?'

'Olivia. It's Eloise. Where are you?' she asked in the same direct way of all their limited conversations.

'Eloise, hello. Umm, I'm out having lunch.'

'Right. Well, I'm coming down that way today and thought I'd pop in for a visit. You don't mind, do you?' It was a state- ment rather than a question. 'I know it's not quite the way things are done, but I'd like to meet you.'

Olivia considered the usual rules for tenant and landlord rela- tionships, confident there was meant to be more notice given before visits to the property. But there was nothing to be gained by pointing this out. They had an informal arrangement, with the one-page lease covering only the basics. Anyway, she had no objection to Eloise inspecting the house—and she thought that meeting her landlady could be interesting. It might even be a chance to ask some questions about that summer when Tom's father was here, and about Leo the missing boy.

'I can be there in about thirty minutes,' Olivia said.

'Lovely. I'll be there in an hour or so.'

As the call ended, Olivia wondered if Tom had already rung Eloise. Was that what had prompted this visit?

*

Olivia opened the front door as soon as the red Mini Cooper pulled up. It wasn't the car she'd expected a woman in her senior years to be driving. Eloise stepped out and strode energetically towards the house. 'You must be the famous Olivia Haymers.'

'And you must be Eloise.' She shook her outstretched hand.

Eloise was a tall woman of indeterminate years, with a striking face. She had high cheekbones under soft, creased skin, and her sharp eyes were framed by oversized fuchsia-pink frames. Her hair was cropped into a layered silver bob—proper silver that was highlighted, Olivia presumed, in a range of metallic hues. She was wearing folds of cashmere over a long A-line leather skirt and ankle boots, all in black. The ensemble was effortlessly chic.

Olivia realised it was entirely possible to be envious and in awe of a woman who must have been in her seventies.

'You're prettier in person than in those tacky pictures in the magazines,' Eloise said as she entered the house, making Olivia fumble for what to say.

'Would you like tea?' she managed. 'Coffee?'

'Thank you. Coffee, but only if it's not that instant crap.'

While Olivia made plunger coffee, Eloise took a seat at the dining table, one elegant leg crossed over the other. She asked after the house, making sure everything was working as it should. Olivia expressed how delighted she was to be living in this haven.

They took their cups to the lounge, Eloise fobbing off Olivia's concern when Brian made his way onto her lap.

'But you'll be covered in hair,' Olivia said, worried Eloise would leave with thick ginger fur layered over the expensive black fabric.

Eloise gently laid her hand on the back of the purring cat. 'It's fine. Couldn't care less. It'll all come off eventually.' She sipped her coffee, making a face that seemed to indicate satisfaction, and then turned her full scrutiny towards Olivia. 'I think you know why I'm here.'

Shit. Was she cross? 'Not really?' Olivia said tentatively.

'I received an unexpected phone call from someone named Tom. I believe he got the number from you?' It was hard to tell what Eloise thought of this, but there was definitely no enthusiasm.

'Yes, he did,' said Olivia, flustered. 'I was reluctant to hand it out, but I had a long chat with him and he seemed genuine. He didn't seem to have any other options for finding Pippa.'

'Yes. Well. I had thought you, of all people, would appreciate the sanctity of privacy and would've been a little more restrained in handing out my personal details.' The look she gave Olivia was that of a school principal gently chastising a child who had disappointed her greatly. She was still stroking Brian, still sipping her coffee and still smiling, yet the words hit Olivia with a sharpness and accuracy that cut to her core.

'I'm sorry, you're absolutely right. I shouldn't have given him your number.'

'No. You shouldn't have. But what's done is done. There's a complicated history here, one which I feel is better left in the past. This Tom has no real need to be chasing down people he doesn't know.'

'Oh.' Olivia fumbled for a way forward with the conversation. She wanted to defend Tom—his desire to deliver the envelope seemed reasonable to her. 'I believe he's doing it for his father, who has passed away.'

'So he said. For Jeremy, who is no longer with us.' Eloise sipped again, appearing to consider what she would say next. 'Jeremy was my godson, you know. We were close once.'

That was interesting. 'Tom didn't mention that. I don't think he knew.'

'It's irrelevant. Jeremy left here one summer, and then he changed. He didn't come back even when people needed him. We were supposed to meet in London straight after he arrived, but he didn't bother to turn up. And because of his lack of concern for Pippa, for what was happening here ... well, my feelings towards him altered significantly at that point.'

Olivia couldn't help herself. 'Aren't you curious? Don't you want to meet his son and find out what happened to him?'

'Not particularly.' She paused, her hand resting on Brian's head as she smiled down at the contented cat. 'I feel no urge to delve into what he may have done with his life over the last few decades, or to meet his son.' She looked at Olivia again, giving a small shrug to indicate her lack of interest. 'You seem to be rather invested in this little escapade.'

'I'm very sorry. Guess I got a little caught up in Tom's story.'

Eloise turned her attention back to the cat before she leant forward and placed her mug on the coffee table. 'I can understand that. I got the impression he is a very likeable young man. But I will be blunt with you, Olivia ... Pippa does not need to have the past dug up. My priority is keeping her protected, and I don't see how a package from Jeremy will do anything other than drag the hurt and pain of the past into the present. Especially since, with Jeremy dead, there can be no apologies or happy ending.' Eloise stood and moved to the windows, addressing the next statement over her shoulder. 'If you do speak to Tom again, please encourage him to leave this matter alone.'

Frustration edged out the deference Olivia had been feeling towards Eloise. From what the woman was saying, she knew exactly how to contact Pippa. She could, in one breath, give Tom the chance to achieve his goal. What the hell had gone on in this house that after all these years she wouldn't allow this to happen? Was there more to this? Did it have something to do with the disappearance of Leo Clifford?

'But could you, perhaps, just pass on Tom's details to Pippa?' Olivia asked. 'Give her the option?'

'No. I don't think so.' It was obviously her final say on the matter.

Eloise walked to the front door, and Olivia followed her out to her car, unsettled by the tone of her dismissal. They said their goodbyes, Olivia promising to let her know if there were any issues with the house, Eloise thanking her for the coffee.

The landlady was opening her car door when she said, 'Did Tom ask about anyone else?'

'No.' Olivia thought back on their conversation. 'But we did wonder if Pippa and Jeremy were here at the same time as the boy who disappeared.' It was uncomfortable bringing up the case when Eloise had never mentioned it, as though Olivia was voyeuristically preoccupied with other people's dramas.

But Eloise just nodded, as though this question was to be expected. 'One of those sad tales the locals love to natter about. Yes, he was here at that time.' Sorrow drifted across her face.

'You knew Leo too?'

'Not as such.' Eloise cast a shrewd look at Olivia. 'I knew his mother. Both of their mothers, from when we were younger. Leo's mother was the older sister, and we didn't have much to do with each other. Jeremy's mother remained a friend for many years.' Eloise stepped into the car and closed the door, turning on the ignition so she could let the window down.

Olivia struggled to get her head around this. 'Leo and Jeremy were cousins? They knew each other?'

Eloise sighed impatiently. 'Yes. They were cousins.'

'And Leo was house-sitting at the time Jeremy and Pippa were here?'

'No. Jeremy and Pippa were my house-sitters, but I believe Leo was here for much of the time.'

'With his girlfriend?'

'His girlfriend?' Eloise exchanged her pink frames for a pair of dramatic sunglasses. 'Pippa *was* his girlfriend.'

'Leo and Pippa were together? But ...' Olivia trailed off. 'I thought Pippa was with Jeremy. Surely that's why he left a package for her—she's the one who got away or something like that.'

Eloise put the car into gear. With her foot on the brake, she looked up at Olivia. 'They were just friends, and the friendship died when he left. Tell that boy Tom to forget this whole thing. If Jeremy held a candle for Pippa, he shouldn't have treated her so poorly.' With an emphatic nod, she began to roll the car forward.

Olivia couldn't help herself. She trotted beside the car until Eloise stopped. 'Sorry. Can I just ask ... when Leo disappeared, what did Pippa do? Did she stay on here?'

'Yes, for two years. But, Olivia, you need to let this go.' Eloise was terse now. 'It was a terrible time. Something awful happened, we lived through it, and we have no answers. And digging it all up achieves nothing.'

With that, she pulled away. Olivia stood in the driveway, trying to make sense of a story that wasn't hers.

CHAPTER THIRTEEN

Wednesday, 1 January 1986

'Your cousin? Are you serious?' Pippa stared at Jeremy. He nodded, not looking at her. Instead, he studied the empty stubbie in his hand. Tiny curls of paper were accumulating on the table as he methodically picked off the label.

'You've never mentioned having family down here,' she said. 'You don't *have* family. It's just you and your mum.'

In the time they'd been friends there had been many, many hours of conversation. They often had late-night deep-and-meaningful discussions over a bottle of bourbon. They'd shared stories of their pasts, moaned about their families, confessed their greatest regrets, explored their wildest dreams. Jeremy knew the details—sordid, glorious and boring—of her life, and she knew the details of his. She knew his family was a loose unit of two. He had no siblings, no aunts or uncles, no cousins—just Jeremy and his mum, Angela, a serious woman who always seemed a little distracted. According to Jeremy, she had been a dutiful mother, a decent parent who had done her best to bring him up. His absent father's name wasn't even on the birth certificate. He'd filled the gap in his childhood with fantasy figures, until the day he'd realised he didn't need a father. He had done alright without one.

'Mum has a sister,' Jeremy said now. 'Leo's her son.'

Pippa lifted her bare feet, pulling them onto the edge of her chair. The warmth of the day had faded with the light, and the air was cool against her skin. 'That's why you wanted to go and see his boat.'

'Yeah. I guess.' Jeremy still wouldn't look her in the eye.

'You already knew about him?'

A quick shrug. 'The last time Eloise came to Brisbane, she slipped up. I think she'd pretty much been sworn to silence by Mum. But I'd overheard the two of them talking, Eloise saying something like, "Don't you think he deserves to know?" Something about family. Then when we were alone at the pub the next day, I kinda pretended like Mum had said something to me. Acted like I knew more than I did. Eloise said she was glad, that it was about time. That secrets have a way of rotting things from the inside, and that Leo and I might meet one day. That Angus Clifford was a disgrace, but not to judge the son by the father. And that Mum's sister was nothing like Mum. Stuff like that—I didn't dig too hard. Coming across that article about Leo was a coincidence. I saw the name and the picture and guessed it was him.'

'And you didn't think to share any of this with me?'

'It never came up,' Jeremy said.

Bullshit.

'Look, there wasn't anything to say.' He put the bottle down, then rubbed his palms back and forth across the stubble on his cheeks. 'I didn't even know what the story was. I didn't have much to go on.'

'How can you be so sure the Leo I met last night is this long-lost cousin?'

Jeremy gave her a withering look. 'I think the chances of there being more than one Leo Clifford in Hobart are fairly slim, especially one who has a bit of a resemblance to me.'

'He doesn't. Not really.' She wasn't sure why she was denying the obvious—probably because admitting she was attracted to someone who looked like her best friend was awkward. Besides, the longer she'd spent with Leo, the less she'd noticed the similarities. From a distance his smile had reminded her of Jeremy's, but up close, set against his quiet humour and steady presence, it hadn't felt familiar at all. Their eyes, though, were the same.

'Oh, be honest,' said Rebecca. 'He is good-looking in exactly the same way.' Her tone was firm, as though she was having the final word on this. 'It was the first thing I noticed.' She was sitting next to Jeremy, rubbing his back, soothing him as if he was suffering from illness or trauma. The look she shot Pippa was a warning. Was she revelling in the drama? She was certainly enjoying the fact she'd known about Jeremy's secret before Pippa.

Jeremy slumped in his chair. He had none of his usual bounce. The last time Pippa had seen him like this, he'd been accused of sloppy work, of making a serious error that had cost thousands. He was a business analyst in a finance company, whatever that meant. Pippa barely understood what it was he did in his office all day. What she did know was he loved the job. When he'd been hauled before his superiors he'd been mortified, especially since the mistake wasn't his. To prove his innocence, he had been forced to throw another guy under the bus—a bus driven by an aggressive middle manager determined to prove his worth to the bastards higher up the ladder. It hadn't been pretty, and Jeremy had been anxious, chewed by guilt for days. He didn't like conflict, and he didn't like drama. Right now, he looked like he was dealing with both.

Last night, on the drive home, he'd quizzed Pippa about her night with Leo. He'd been judgemental and sanctimonious, and she'd been pissed off. Today he'd said nothing, and Pippa had avoided him. She'd lazed about, reading, eating, and recovering from the excesses of the night before. Rebecca and Jeremy had drifted through the house, whispering together, but she'd ignored them. By evening she'd thought they were back on smooth ground. As they'd sat down to eat, she'd told Jeremy that Leo would be visiting. Prepared for a snide reaction, she'd been relieved when his response had been nothing more than silence and a shrug.

After dinner he'd gone off with Rebecca, then returned to the table with this bombshell.

'The thing is,' Rebecca was saying now, 'Jeremy feels very uncomfortable with this boy coming down here. He feels it would be disrespectful to Angela. Don't you, Jeremy? And, of course, it's very awkward for him. Obviously, there must be a serious reason this other family isn't talked about.'

Pippa wondered when Jeremy had started telling Rebecca more than he told her. She put her feet back on the ground and crossed her legs. 'Is that what you think, Jeremy?' She folded her arms. It was hard to say whether she was more annoyed with Jeremy's feeble demeanour or Rebecca's smug authority. 'Do you think I should ban Leo from your presence?'

'You don't need to be so huffy about the situation,' Rebecca snapped. 'I thought you would be a little more understanding of Jeremy's feelings.'

'Well, perhaps Jeremy could start by giving me a little more information and explaining for himself his actual *feelings* before he dictates who I can and can't have visit. So, Leo's mother is your mum's sister?'

'Yes.'

'And they don't get along?'

'I don't think they've had anything to do with each other since before I was born.'

'Do you know why?'

He shrugged yet again. She itched to grab those twitching shoulders and give him a good shake.

'What happened between them?' she asked.

All of this sounded like the storyline of a daytime soap. A dramatic fallout between sisters. An antagonism that couldn't be overcome. A family ripped apart. Pippa wanted details. Her family was so dull and ordinary that their most sensational drama had happened when her father had changed from Holden to Ford. Her grandfather and Uncle Steve had turned up on the doorstep, angry at such blasphemy. They'd tried to convince her dad to take the new car back to the showroom. Christmas had been a bit tense that year, but by Easter it was all forgotten. 'Was it over a man?'

'I don't know.' Jeremy was obviously irritated with the questions. 'I don't know anything! It's between them. And I didn't want to bring it up with Mum.'

'Perfectly understandable,' said Rebecca.

'Sure,' said Pippa, ignoring Rebecca, 'but this seems somewhat significant, don't you think?'

'No, not really,' Jeremy said. 'Not until now.'

'It's ancient history, Pippa,' Rebecca interrupted. 'Do you think you could maybe move on from the fact he can't give you more information? We need to focus on avoiding an ugly situation.'

'Fine.' *Oh, for god's sake*, thought Pippa, *can't Rebecca leave?* This discussion would be a whole lot easier if she could talk to her friend—alone.

Jeremy looked at her for a moment, then slipped further down in his chair, tilting his head back to contemplate the stars. 'It never occurred to me to bring it up. Obviously it crossed my mind when I knew we were coming to Tasmania, but I wasn't planning to contact the Cliffords. I don't even know if they still live in Hobart. I mean, yeah, I was a bit curious about Leo, especially after reading about his role in the race. But I still had no plans to wrangle a visit with an aunt, uncle and cousin I don't know.'

'Cousins, plural,' murmured Pippa. 'Leo has a younger sister. I think her name is Maggie.' She'd picked up that much from their limited discussion about family. He'd mentioned a sister whom he liked, a father who had his flaws, and a mother who cared very much about appearances and was busy decorating their new house in the Hobart suburb of Sandy Bay.

'Right,' said Jeremy. There was a long silence while he processed this fact. 'All I can guess is Mum must hate her sister—that something unforgivable must've happened. Mum left Tassie and moved to Brisbane, and she's never come back.'

'But isn't that a situation between your mum and her sister?' Pippa asked. 'It's a drama from the dim, dark past. It doesn't involve you, and it certainly doesn't involve me.'

'I think it would be a bit easier if he didn't come here. It's okay if you meet up with him in Hobart—if you need to see him.'

'I don't need to, Jeremy. I want to.' All day she'd been think-ing about the boy with the rough hands and quiet energy. Knowing she was going to see him again had given her a warm curl of anticipation.

'Why?' Rebecca asked. 'You don't know him. It was a meaningless New Year's hook-up. You were drunk. *And* he's younger than you.'

Pippa glared at her. 'Please. Don't try to tell me who I should like.' She forced down the urge to be more expressive. 'I don't appreciate your ridiculous judgement.'

Rebecca huffed. 'I'm just saying, there couldn't have been any sort of real feelings. And now that you know the con-nection to Jeremy and how uncomfortable this makes him, it shouldn't be hard to choose your friend over some fling.'

Pippa took a long breath as she looked out into the dark garden. It would not be helpful to slap the arrogant cow. 'Thank you for that input, Becky.' She couldn't keep the sarcasm from her voice. 'But actually, I don't need to explain or justify my feelings to you. Quite frankly, who I'm attracted to—and why I like them—is none of your business.'

Rebecca tossed her hair, her arms folded tightly across her chest.

Jeremy touched her on the back. 'It's fine,' he said stoically. 'I'm okay with this. We'll say hello, then we'll head out for the day.'

'What?' Rebecca spun to face him. 'Why should *we* leave? Where will we go?'

'We'll go on a picnic or something. And we'll be the ones to go because I'm the one who has an issue. Actually, like Pippa said, it's my mum's problem, not mine. It's certainly not

Pippa's.' He pushed himself upright and put his hands on the table. 'This doesn't need to be a big deal.'

'It won't be any deal at all,' Pippa said. She realised there was something they hadn't considered. 'I don't think he knows anything about you. You didn't know about him until recently—well, he may not know about your mum and you.' Pippa thought back to the brief meeting between the boys and the way Leo had shown no sign of recognition. 'If he doesn't, it can be our secret. We can skip the whole family reunion thing. I won't say anything.'

Jeremy considered this. 'And I don't have to say anything to Mum.'

'Well, if you want my opinion, it would be better to avoid any chance of conflict.' Rebecca displayed the tense resignation of a politician thwarted by an adversary.

'There won't be conflict,' Pippa said with a smile. 'It will be a thoroughly civil and delightful day.' And perhaps a little bit naughty.

CHAPTER FOURTEEN

Thursday, 2 January 1986

Leo arrived trailing a cloud of pale dust and the blurred notes of Van Morrison. The dust hung in the warm air, a weightless cloud drifting high and wide. The music seeped from the open windows even after he'd killed the engine. His dull-red ute sat low to the ground, a faded black tarp over the tray. One corner flapped loose where the rubber loops had been left unhooked.

Pippa waited by the front door, watching as he turned off the stereo and climbed out. There was a metallic groan when he closed the door behind him.

He was as appealing as she remembered. He wore basic tan shorts over strong legs. His white t-shirt had no collar, no logo, and it wasn't new but clean, stretched at the neck and hem in the way of a comfortable favourite. His sun-streaked hair dropped close to his shoulders, with a fringe that was pushed back out of his eyes. He was a little scruffy—in a good way. A guy who wasn't too fussed about the way he looked, who didn't try too hard. This impressed her more than a little.

'Hello, Leo,' she said, unexpected butterflies beating in her stomach. 'I was wondering if you would turn up.'

He walked towards her. 'There was no chance I wouldn't.'

She went to meet him, a hint of unfamiliar shyness seeping through her as he scrutinised her face. 'So,' she said, 'am I what you remembered, or does the harsh light of day have you doubting why you're here?' She held out the hem of her short sundress, twisting from one side to the other. He didn't need to know she was nervous. Her mother had once mucked around with Amway and started spouting odd phrases. 'Fake it till you make it' was one of the better ones and seemed to fit the moment. Pippa fluttered her lashes, doing an exaggerated impersonation of a girl pretending to be both coy and smitten.

Leo stood with his legs braced, hands in his pockets. He gave a slow smile. 'You'll do.' He nodded. 'Although obviously it's easier to hide your age when you're in a dark pub.'

'Hey! I'm twenty-two, not thirty-two.'

'Which makes you the oldest woman I've ever kissed. Might take some getting used to.' His smile dropped, and he looked serious, as though he expected this situation to be a challenge. Then she saw the slight pull at the corner of his mouth and knew he was teasing.

'Kissed many girls, have you?'

'A few.'

They both grinned, both took another step forward. They were nearly touching, their eyes locked. Pippa brushed his hand with hers, their fingers entwining, as their lips met. He dropped her hand to slide his arms around her waist, the space between them vanishing in a way that hadn't happened on New Year's Eve.

When they eased apart, he laughed quietly. 'Right. We might need to do that a few more times. So, you know, I get used to it.'

'I'm okay with that. But I have to say, that was better than the other night. Why didn't you kiss me like that in the pub?'

He paused. 'Well, you were drunk. I was drunk too. And you were getting a bit wobbly.'

'You know, that doesn't stop most people. In fact, I'm fairly confident there's a whole lot of snogging that happens *because* people are drunk.'

'Yep. And I didn't want to think you were kissing me just because you'd sculled a jug of rum and Coke. I didn't want to take advantage of the situation.'

He had integrity, something that was both old-fashioned and intriguing. For a brief moment she considered taking him by the hand and rocking his well-behaved socks. She shoved the idea aside. If he was a gentleman, then she needed to be more than a free-loving, free-spirited, free-with-her-body wild child. Whatever simmered between them deserved a more tender approach.

Still, teasing was acceptable. 'It wasn't only the rum and Coke. The fact it was New Year's, that was a contributing factor as well.'

'Good to know.'

They both laughed.

'Come on,' she said, 'let me show you the house.'

Jeremy and Rebecca had left an hour earlier, and they had the place to themselves. Rebecca had still been acting put out, hissing at Jeremy that she saw the situation as hideously unfair. She wasn't interested in going to Hobart or to Port Arthur. Jeremy had tried to convince her this was the best arrangement, winning her over in the end with promises of stopping somewhere for a nice lunch—somewhere expensive and stylish, which meant she could get dressed up.

Pippa pushed open the door. Honey was sitting inside, wagging her tail fiercely, eager to see who had arrived. Leo dropped down to the dog's level and scratched her behind the ears. 'How ya doing, girl?' He stood up, Honey close to his heels as they walked down to the lounge. 'Very cool house. Who owns it?'

'Eloise, an amazing lady,' Pippa said. 'We're lucky to get to stay here while she's away for two months in London.'

'How do you know her?'

They walked out to the terrace, pulling up chairs to sit at the long table. 'Through my friend Jeremy. You met him the other night? She's his godmother.' Pippa edged around her words, aware of how easy it would be to let slip too much information. At the same time, she was tempted to find out what Leo knew of his family drama.

'And you're all from Brisbane?' he asked.

'Yep. The land of perfect beaches and the Big Pineapple.'

'What the hell is a big pineapple?'

'A world-class tourist attraction, celebrating the king of tropical fruit. When you come to visit me, I'll take you there. Best fruit salad you'll ever have.'

The suggestion was on the table. Maybe they would see each other beyond Pippa's time in Tasmania.

'I might have to take you up on that.'

There was a pause, the idea hanging between them, neither wanting to push it further. It was way too early for them to be making any sort of plan. Pippa broke the mood by moving to the kitchen, returning with beers and a packet of Samboy barbecue chips.

'Are your friends here?' Leo asked, taking a beer.

'Out. Gone for lunch in town. We've got the place to our-
selves for the day.'

With one hand he pushed his hair off his face. The corners
of his mouth tugged into a smile he was clearly trying to hide.

I know what you're thinking, she thought, her mind in the
same place.

But there was no rush.

'So, tell me about the sailing,' she said, deliberately changing
the tone of the conversation. 'Have you always been about the
water and boats?'

He surely knew what she was doing. He grinned, looking
down at his beer for a moment, then started to talk. He told
her about the first time he sailed, about the thrill of the water
rushing beneath the boat and the satisfaction of learning to
read the wind, to tame it and bend it to his own purpose. He
talked about his father encouraging and supporting his chosen sport—and of the costs involved, which meant there were
too many wankers filling out the yacht club members list.
His father was one of those guys who liked the prestige of
being involved in a sport that was, in many ways, restricted
to people who could afford the expense. There were others,
though, who found it almost spiritual. Who had a true connection with the ocean, a love of the freedom and the breathing room that came from being on the water. The beauty
of a curving horizon. The peace. The adrenaline. And the
challenge of being better. Better within himself. Better than
others.

It was obvious Leo was competitive but grounded. Aware of
how lucky he was. Humble.

Pippa watched him talk, his face animated, his hands occasionally moving, emphasising the tilt of a boat, or the motion of
water or wind. Every now and then he'd pause, run his fingers

back through his hair or take a pull from his beer. When he hesitated, she urged him to continue.

'Aren't you bored yet?' he asked.

'No,' she said. And she wasn't.

They were on their second drink when he leant back in his chair and shook his head. 'Okay. Tell me about you. You write? Something to do with travel?'

She laughed. 'Did I say that? To be precise, I *like* to write. Occasionally I can string words into reasonable sentences. And there is a very slim possibility something might be coming up that involves travel writing.'

'Which you love doing? The travelling, as well as the writing.'

'I do. But so far neither have paid the rent.'

She sketched out the story of the arts degree she'd started, then stopped. How she'd realised she was merely killing time. The part-time job she had at the restaurant, which had turned into a full-time gig. The fashion parades she sometimes did for the money, nothing high-end, just at Myer and David Jones. How it was unlikely she would ever be used again, since she may have— accidentally, sort of—come home with a particularly cool denim jacket she'd modelled one Saturday. 'They couldn't prove it was me, but word does get around. And I'm replaceable. There are plenty of girls with the right sort of figure and shoe size.'

'I hope the jacket gets plenty of use.'

'Nope. It hasn't left the house. Turns out it wasn't so fabulous after all.' She leant forward on her arms. 'And there may be the issue of guilt.'

He laughed with her, not seeming to judge her sticky-fingered ways.

Then he asked again about the travel, and it was Pippa's turn to be effusive. She gushed about the thrill of the unknown, about discovering different worlds and like-minded people. About youth hostels, street food and cheap booze. About islands and beaches barely visited by travellers. About tranquillity and soul-searching moments of peace, and parties and camaraderie and friendships made. 'That's how I met Jeremy. Actually, I'd met him a couple of times at uni, but he's a few years older than me and I didn't know him well. Then there he was on Khao San Road in Bangkok.'

'You travelled together?'

'Yes. He only had six weeks, and I'd already been in Thailand on and off for three months. I kind of took him under my wing.'

'Lucky guy.'

'It worked for both of us, I guess. As a girl on my own, I had my share of hairy moments. Usually I'd try and get together with other groups or couples who were heading in the same direction as I was. But when I met Jeremy, I was alone. It was fortuitous.'

'And you've stayed friends.'

'We have. Best friends.' She thought about what the two of them had been through together, wondering how much she should tell Leo. Maybe not the bit about them having sex on a beach one night. The drama of the accident and saving Jeremy was also a story that could wait. 'Until a few weeks ago we shared a house. Now we're both between places, he's heading off to London, and I'm presently undecided about what comes next.'

The question was in the tilt of his head and the crease between his eyes.

'Sharing a house as housemates and friends,' she clarified. 'You met his girlfriend the other night. Rebecca.'

This led to a brief discussion on the perils of having a guy as her closest friend.

When they got hungry, they moved to the kitchen. As they put together sandwiches, the space between them closed again. Standing side by side at the bench, they reached across each other to grab tomatoes, cheese and ham, their forearms brushing. In an effort to keep her mind away from the lure of his body, Pippa listed her pleasantly ordinary family members. Then Leo enthused about his livewire younger sister, Maggie, and glossed over his parents.

Pippa couldn't stop herself. 'Do you have much in the way of extended family?'

'No. Mum and Dad don't have siblings. Well, my mum did have a sister, but she left a long, long time ago, and there's no connection. Makes for a pretty small Christmas dinner.' He picked up his plate and turned towards the open French doors.

So, his knowledge of his family was a fraction greater than Jeremy's had been, but still limited. It would have been harder to deny Angela existed in a small place like Hobart. *Bloody hell*, Pippa thought, *those sisters must have done a number on each other.*

She could feel the secret squirming and twisting, but it wasn't for her to say anything. This had nothing to do with her, not really.

She followed Leo to the outdoor table, knowing that if she were to release the beast of truth, her afternoon would change direction. That thought, more than anything else, quenched her urge to blurt. She let the moment slide away.

*

After lunch they went on a walk, her hand slipping into his. Honey followed them as they made their way down to the water. At the rocky beach they climbed onto a flat-topped boulder, sitting with their feet hanging over the edge. Leo threw sticks for Honey, who bounded into the water, shaking herself vigorously each time she emerged. Finally, exhausted, she wandered into the shade of a tree and flopped to the ground.

Above them the sky seemed especially huge. It was a pale, cloudless blue. A flock of black cockatoos passed overhead, their exuberant screeches echoing off the water.

'Attention seekers,' Pippa said with a laugh, then realised Leo was watching her intently.

'I like you.' He said it quietly.

The words were simple, but they had more emotional punch than any declaration of how hot she was, or how gorgeous, or how sexy—or any of the usual eager comments she received from guys.

A dozen quips sat on the tip of her tongue. Her instinct was to deflect the intensity with flippancy. She said nothing. This moment mattered.

Then she breathed in. 'I like you too.'

The kiss was gentle, for a while. Then it wasn't. The two of them were grabbing, grasping, a more urgent need pushing them together. Pippa climbed to her knees and shifted to straddle his lap. His arms held her fast, a hand in her hair, one on her lower back. Her shins were pressed into the rough rock, a ridge in the surface digging in painfully. She noticed but didn't care, the discomfort pushed out of her mind by overwhelming sensations. She was also ignoring their vulnerable position right at the edge of the water, with a real chance of a boat passing, of them putting on a show for an unsuspecting fisherman. Too bad.

There was an awkward struggle to get to each other, to find a position that worked. Then it was fumbled and quick, clothes mostly staying in place. None of which mattered. They held tight, still facing each other, Pippa's legs now wrapped around Leo's waist, his mouth at her ear. She could feel his heart thudding and pressed herself hard against his chest so the beat reverberated through her skin.

When finally they made their way back up the hill, they moved slowly while Honey raced ahead. There was a languid peace in their bodies. A knowledge that this was a beginning.

CHAPTER FIFTEEN

Saturday, 24 June 2017

After Eloise left, Olivia went down to the rocky beach. She sat on the uneven ground, lowering a single smooth rock onto the stack she had started. It was always at the third stone when things got wobbly—stone stacking was harder than it looked. Apparently you needed to be all calm and Zen and attuned to the weight of each stone, feeling the moment of balance in your fingers. She was failing. Way too much stuff was tumbling around in her head. Her own problems had been causing enough mental havoc, and now she had thoughts of Tom—the idea of him knowing her history, along with her questions about his quest—tossing around as well.

She gave up and threw the stone, hitting a dead tree with a satisfying *thunk*.

She needed to work out what to do next. For a start, she now knew details that could help Tom. But the cold grip of shame froze her hand every time she picked up her phone. She didn't want to hear his voice straining with fake politeness or hear him make leering references to what he'd seen—not that he was likely to do that. He was the sort who'd try to hide that he knew her story. He would be nice, thankful for her help. Then he would say goodbye and block her.

Picking up more stones, she threw them one after another, gleeful when she hit her target, increasing her effort with every attempt until her arm began to ache.

Her phone rang. She pulled it out, shielding the screen from the glare. Tom.

Shit. She wasn't prepared.

'Hello?' Unflattering images of herself flicked rapidly through her mind.

'Olivia?' There was buoyancy in his voice. Delight.

'Hi, Tom.'

'Hi. How are you? I'm glad I caught you. I wanted to say thank you for last night. I had a great time. Lovely. And I made it home okay. Didn't hit a kangaroo.' He laughed. Stopped. 'Not that hitting wildlife is funny. I mean, there are so many dead animals on the roads. Have you noticed?'

Her laugh was small. He was back to being awkward. 'Yes, I have noticed.'

'Yeah, of course you have. Obviously. You live here.' A brief pause, as though he was trying to get back on track. 'Anyway, I talked to Eloise, and it didn't go well. She was no help, I'm afraid.'

'Yes, I heard. She visited me.'

'Oh bloody hell. Really? Was she cross with you? Oh shit, I'm so sorry. I put you in a tricky position with your landlady. I shouldn't have pushed for her number.'

Olivia lowered herself to the ground again and picked up another stone. 'It's fine. Really. In fact I found out some details you might find useful.'

'You did? Odd that she talked to you but had no time for me. But, hey, that's brilliant. Thank you.' She could tell he was smiling. 'Would you like to meet up? I could come down. Or you might feel like a trip to the city. We could have a drink, maybe dinner?'

While he talked, she played with the stone, turning it over, running her fingers across the worn surface. Had he not googled her? Could she be that lucky?

'When were you thinking?' she asked, stalling.

'Um, tonight?'

His tentative tone won her over. 'Okay. I could come in.'

As they arranged a time and place Olivia set her stone atop the two she'd placed earlier, adjusting the position a fraction before gently lifting her fingers away. The stone remained perfectly steady.

*

At quarter to six Olivia was sitting in the sunken bar of Tom's hotel, waiting for him to arrive. The lobby was cavernous, a void rising above her to a mezzanine level where, she presumed, the function rooms would be. The bar was in front of huge sheet-glass windows that looked across the one-way flow of city traffic to the water of the harbour.

She twitched the hem of her dress and smoothed a crease in her tights. After deliberating all afternoon she'd chosen a short red woollen dress over warm tights, ankle boots with a heel, and a white coat, also in wool. The outfit was the nicest one she'd worn since her fling with the banker, because dressing down was a good way to avoid being noticed. Before she'd left Sydney she'd also cut her hair and got rid of the auburn highlights, so she was one-tone dead-leaf brown, and it was barely long enough to scrape into a stubby ponytail. Tonight she was wearing it loose and soft.

She jabbed her straw into her drink, bobbing the lime and swirling the ice cubes. She'd ordered as soon as she arrived, uncomfortable without something in her hands. She tried not to look around and clutched the glass so she wouldn't fidget with her phone, her bag or the little dish of rice-cracker nibbles the bartender had put on the low table.

It was already dark outside. Through the glass wall she watched the slow flow of cars. People wandered along the docks, hunched into puffer jackets or heavy coats, beanies protecting their heads. A trio of young women jostled through the revolving hotel door, clutching each other and shrieking as the cold slapped bare legs beneath their short skirts. Once upon a time Olivia would have done the same. She would venture out determined to flaunt a new outfit, convinced she could handle the cold for a few blocks—after all, you didn't need winter woollies in a hot sweaty club. It had been a long while since she'd done any sort of flaunting.

She sensed eyes on her and turned her head to see Tom striding across the lobby. He was wearing black jeans and a jumper with the same grey jacket he'd worn the other day. His hair appeared to have been brushed before being knotted back. 'Hello, sorry, I had every intention of being down here before you arrived.' He dropped into the seat opposite. 'Was on the phone to work.'

She waved away his apology, aiming to seem casual and at ease despite her nerves. 'Would you like a drink?' she asked, feeling self-conscious about having had a head start. She should have waited.

'Would love one.' He smiled. 'I've heard the whisky is good down here. Would you like to go to a whisky bar before dinner?'

Olivia hated whisky, or rather she had never learnt the art of whisky appreciation. Two years ago, back during the heady days of Leena's friendship, she would have insisted on a cocktail bar where the drinks had a long list of exotic ingredients and took twenty minutes to make, the bartenders were minor celebrities, and the crowd was preened to perfection. She didn't even know if Hobart had places that pretentious—if it did, she didn't want to find them. 'Sure, why not? But I warn you, I know nothing about whisky. I may embarrass you by ordering a G & T.'

'If you prefer, we can stay here or find a pub.'

'No. You're the visitor, and I'm up for the challenge.' If she was lucky the whisky bar would be dimly lit, the clientele sophisticated, and the chances of being recognised slim.

*

An hour later Olivia was well on her way to understanding whisky, even if she had yet to enjoy any of it. Tom had been so determined to get her to like the stuff, she had been unable to say no. 'Okay, okay, I can smell all those things you're saying, but can I be honest?'

'Absolutely.'

'A glass of crisp champagne would be divine right now.'

He burst out laughing. 'You can take a novice to the whisky, but you can't make them appreciate the drink.' He leant back in his leather armchair and raised his glass. 'I have done my best here.' He shook his head, pulling a woeful face.

'If it's any consolation, I know more about whisky than I did yesterday.'

They were ensconced in a corner of the room, the low beams of the ceiling and the subtle mood lighting tucking them out of sight from the world. She smiled. This was good. She'd stopped waiting for the accusing glances from strangers and let herself sink into the pleasure of the experience.

'I'll get you champagne.' He leapt to his feet when she said yes.

Sometimes he was a serious, considered man, she thought, and in other moments he was as unsophisticated as a twenty-year-old. She watched him chat effortlessly with the barman. She couldn't keep him, of course. He would return to England, and she would return to her hideout. The difficulty of her situation and the threat of Leena hadn't been obliterated because she'd met a great guy. But if she kept her mind away from the past—or even the future—she could be happy for a few hours.

'Hey, what's up?' Tom set down her drink as he returned to his chair. 'You look deep in serious thought.'

Could she tell him? Would there be any point? No. Why throw open the cupboards and pull out her filthy laundry?

'All good.' She smiled. 'Now, we've got some things to talk about.' So far, they hadn't even mentioned Eloise or Pippa, or the clues to a thirty-year mystery. Olivia explained how Eloise had been forceful in her insistence on privacy and stubborn in her refusal to divulge any information on Pippa's whereabouts. 'But despite that, she did let slip a few interesting details. Firstly, Eloise confirmed that Leo spent time at the house while Jeremy was there. Jeremy and Pippa were the house-sitters, so I suppose Leo was their guest.'

Tom looked thoughtful. 'I was curious about the missing kid before, in an abstract kind of way, but now he seems so much more important.'

'You're certainly right about that. Leo and Jeremy were cousins.'

'What? That's insane.' He flopped back in the deep chair, dragging his hands down his cheeks, his mouth open.

'And—'

'There's more?'

She nodded. 'According to Eloise, Pippa was Leo's girlfriend, not Jeremy's.'

'Whoa.' His look of surprise almost made her laugh.

Olivia was leaning over the low table towards him, caught up in the drama of her discoveries. 'Yes, but Pippa and Jeremy were friends. Sounds like they were very close.' They must have been, given the impact Jeremy's decision to cut ties seemed to have had on Pippa. It must have been a significant betrayal for the thought of Tom making contact to be so repugnant to Eloise.

'But.' He rubbed his mouth, then dropped his hand to pick up the jacket he'd thrown over the spare chair beside them. He searched through a pocket and pulled out a stiff envelope before sliding out some photos. 'Have a look for yourself. These don't feel like the photos you would take—or keep— of someone who was just a friend. Or even a friend you had a crush on.' He shifted his chair around till it was hard against hers, and they began to look through the photos. 'The house and Eloise,' Tom said as he showed Olivia the first image. He flipped to the back. *Eloise Fowler at her stunning home, Channel Highway, Devils Bay, first driveway after the Trevallyn Rivulet, Tasmania, December 1985.* 'That's all I had to go on to find the house. Street numbers didn't come until later.'

'However did you find it?' she said, poking fun at him.

He chuckled. 'Google Maps.' He sounded quite pleased with himself and oblivious to her sarcasm. 'Oh wait. You mean, there were enough instructions there for me to find the place without street numbers.'

'Yep.'

'Yeah, you're right. But still, it was cool to see it from a satellite view.' He grinned. 'Have to be thorough, you know.'

'Of course.' They both laughed, their eyes locked for a moment. She looked away, picking up the next picture. Eloise was standing on the terrace, dressed in a white summer dress, with bare feet, a number of silver bangles, and long red hair with a blunt-cut fringe. She was stunning, and as commanding then as she was now. Next to her was a pretty girl in shorts and a Hoodoo Gurus t-shirt. The house appeared not to have changed at all.

'Pippa.' Tom tapped the picture. 'Also December 1985.'

A flicker of excitement danced across Olivia's skin. The elusive Pippa—it was like sighting a mythical creature.

'Pippa again.' He showed Olivia the next picture.

Yep, Pippa had been beautiful, and sexy. Long, tousled dark hair fell past her shoulders. She was sitting on the edge of a heavy outdoor table, leaning back on her hands, and she wore a loose white t-shirt pulled into a knot at one hip and a pair of denim shorts. An orange typewriter sat beside her, and she was laughing. Behind her were the open doors of the house, and Olivia could make out the blurred silhouettes of two people standing in the shadows.

Tom flipped it over. *Big plans for me and my typewriter. Pippa. January 1986.*

'And these other two.' He stalled for a few seconds. 'Well, these are the ones that made me think they were a couple. Isn't that the impression you get?'

He laid the last photos on the table. Olivia stared, a twinge of embarrassment making her reluctant to meet his eye. These photos were intimate. Both were of Pippa in bed. In the first she was on her back, dark hair spread around her head, eyes closed, one arm resting above the pillow, the other at her side. A white sheet covered the lower half of her naked body and one breast. The picture had been taken from the side of the bed.

The scene was repeated in the next photo, except now her eyes were open, and this one was taken from above as though someone was standing over her on the bed. She was smiling softly, without any self-consciousness. It was the sort of look one lover gave another.

Tom turned the last one over. 'No date, but I mean, *I will always love you*,' he said, pointing at the words on the back. 'That's a pretty clear message. And it's in my dad's handwriting. See how it's different to the others?'

'A sentimental note for himself?' Olivia mused. 'He might have added that message much later, just for himself. You've got to presume he took these, or else how did he get them?'

'That's what I thought. But there's no date, so they could possibly have been taken at a different time. Or even place. But there's no mistaking the feelings evident here, right? And, anyway, it doesn't alter what I'm trying to achieve.'

Olivia made a noncommittal sound. Eloise remembered Pippa being with Leo. But Tom was right—the intimate details of what could have been a love triangle didn't change anything when it came to his quest. 'Regardless of what their relationship was, your dad still wanted her to have that package at some point.'

'Right.' He slipped the photos back into the envelope and put them in his jacket pocket. 'And I'm still determined to make that happen.' They were close, and when he turned to look at her, the space between them became even smaller. 'Thank you for bringing me this information. I didn't mean to get you involved in this crazy task.'

She shifted slightly in her chair to put a fraction more distance between them. 'I'm glad you did. It takes my mind off the hideousness of my own life.' What the hell was she saying? She was being lulled by his proximity and the moody ambience of their corner.

He frowned. 'Christ. I've been so preoccupied with my own crap that I don't know a thing about what's going on with you.'

She laughed a little. 'I'm not interested in talking about me. It's boring.' She raised her chin and gave a quick nod. 'And it doesn't define me.' *Hallelujah, sister,* sang a voice in her head, praising her show of strength.

'Will you tell me about it?' Tom asked.

'One day,' she said. 'Right now, I'm starving. Let's go and find something to eat.'

A few minutes later they walked away from the bar. Olivia pulled her coat tight, then without any hesitation or awkwardness Tom took her hand, his grip comfortable and firm. She stepped in close to him, their arms brushing, her shoulder coming to a spot well below his. Neither said a word as they walked, their pace so slow they were barely ambling. A light mist had settled, the streetlights taking on an ethereal glow, the noise of the crawling traffic now softened to a gentle, muted *whoosh*.

'Can you imagine loving someone for the entirety of your life?' he asked. 'Someone who wasn't even a part of your everyday existence.'

She thought about it. She had been in love—or she'd thought it was love. Hayden had swept her off her feet into a world of luxury and secrets, of clandestine weekends and acts of devotion. She had felt worshipped. He'd made her feel that she was the only one with whom he could be his true self. He'd made her feel significant and needed. He had made her feel … The words suddenly had clarity: he had *made her feel* what he wanted her to feel. He had set about eliciting a response in her. But how had she truly felt about him, about the person he was? If anyone had asked her why she loved him, she would have said just that … *because of the way he made me feel.* But what had she liked about him? Which of his traits had she admired, had she reacted to, had she loved? She struggled to articulate anything significant. He had wanted her. And that had been enough—enough for her to ignore, then completely discard, her values.

'You're in deep thought about this,' Tom observed, jerking her back to the present.

She glanced up at him. He was watching her, a look of concern etched on his face.

She smiled and widened her eyes. 'Well, you would throw deep questions at me.'

'And after all those deliberations, what is your answer?'

'I like to believe it can happen.'

'It hasn't happened to you?'

'No. Definitely not. And you?'

'Nope.' He held her gaze, the softest smile on his lips. 'But I haven't given up hope.'

*

Later, as they scooped up tzatziki and hummus on pieces of warm pita bread, Tom brought them back to the subject of their search for Pippa. 'I've had a thought. Let's consider this. Jeremy and Pippa and Leo were all at the house together, right?'

'Yes, that's what Eloise confirmed.'

'Okay. And there's information around about Leo?'

'Not a lot, but yes. Bits and pieces about him being an unsolved missing person case.'

'I'm thinking, let's find out about who Leo Clifford was. Didn't you say he was from a good Hobart family? We now know his mother and my dad's mother were sisters. I imagine I could track down his family quite easily, and chances are they'll know something about Pippa. Especially if she was his girlfriend, as Eloise said.'

Tom's enthusiasm was infectious. 'Okay, that makes sense. And I could ask around Devils Bay about Pippa. Eloise said she stayed on with her for two years, so other locals surely knew her too. I know there are residents who have been there for more than thirty years. I met one of them this morning—she seemed very approachable.'

Wait … Had she just volunteered to initiate conversations with people she didn't really know?

Tom held up his hand and waited for her to high-five him. 'What a team,' he said as their hands smacked together. 'You are one brilliant woman, Olivia Haymers.'

'He knows my name.' She feigned shock and awe as her stomach dropped.

'I told you—game master.' He tapped a finger to his chest. 'I have amazing powers of logic and deduction. And I might have an envelope with your name on it.'

'See, you're quite the sleuth. Now let's apply those skills to the hunt for Pippa.' *And please, please don't judge me too harshly when you uncover my sins*, she silently pleaded.

CHAPTER SIXTEEN

Olivia had stuck to one glass of red wine, yet by the time their plates were cleared she was suffused with a mellow, soft-limbed contentment. The feeling was so unfamiliar that a little wave of euphoria washed through her, and she had to quell the urge to giggle. When Tom asked what she was smiling about, she simply shrugged and folded her napkin, biting back the stupid grin.

It was the simplicity that had got to her. There was nothing pretentious—not in Tom, and not in the restaurant. Tucked into an alley between the heritage buildings of Salamanca Place, the Greek restaurant had white walls, unsophisticated furniture, and abundant, delicious food. It was both comfortable and comforting. Every table was taken, with only minutes between one group leaving and another taking their place. A couple of young children had come loose from a large family and were camped in one corner with colouring books. The waitress who looked after Tom and Olivia had a Scottish accent so broad, Olivia had to ask Tom to translate. Their table was in the middle of the room. Noise washed around them, a happy babble of voices, not so loud they had to shout, but not an intimate setting where words could be whispered.

He couldn't have chosen a better place.

Not once did she feel exposed.

They lingered a little longer, neither of them in any rush to leave. When they finally stepped outside, Tom lifted his arm and laid it gently on her shoulders, his hand at the side of her neck. He, too, seemed to be less nervous and unsure. Olivia moved inside his reach, till she was against him, and slipped her arm across the width of his lower back. They walked back towards his hotel at the other end of the waterfront, moving as though they'd spent years walking side by side. Despite the cutting chill of the wind, they didn't hurry.

'Why leave Sydney?' he asked. 'I haven't been there, but I'm guessing it's bigger than this wee city. It must be a bit of a change, coming from there to here.'

'It was a change I wanted. I needed to …' She sought the right words, wanting to avoid flippant platitudes but not wanting to delve too deeply into her circumstances. 'I needed to get away from the intensity of the big city. To be somewhere quieter.'

'A lifestyle change?'

'Yes. You could say that.' Her lifestyle, for want of a better word, had been through more changes in the past few years than she would ever want it to go through again. 'I'd made some bad choices, and I wanted—needed—to start fresh.'

He was watching her. 'A man?' he asked.

'It's not always about a man.' She tried to laugh this aside.

'But it was this time?'

She tucked her chin down into her coat before making a small noise of agreement. 'Yes, alright. But it was more than running from a broken heart. I needed to make a real change.'

'What do they call it ...?' He searched for the words he wanted.

'A tree-change?'

He clicked his fingers loudly, as though he'd solved a great puzzle. 'A midlife crisis!'

'Hey.' She hit him with her free hand, her palm landing against his stomach. She let her hand rest there, her body curving towards his. 'Are you saying I'm middle-aged?'

He trapped her fingers where they rested, his hand completely covering hers. 'Absolutely not. Obviously, I meant to say *quarter*-life crisis. That's a thing, isn't it, for the mid-twenties?'

'I'm about to kiss my twenties goodbye,' she said. Oh, to wind back time and do everything again. Where would her life have taken her if she'd made different choices? Wisdom, it seemed, was something gained through pain and penance.

They had passed the lawns of Parliament House and come to a stop on the wide boardwalk opposite the Customs House Hotel, muted noise from the classic renovated pub reaching them from across the road. The noise from the next pub along was far more raucous. A heritage tall ship was moored behind them alongside one of the developed piers, its hulk barely moving on the still, black water. A cluster of people in matching black puffer jackets, all carrying paper cones of steaming fish and chips, wandered past. Tom and Olivia still had their bodies angled together, his palm gently moving across the back of her hand. Then there were just his fingers tracing over her skin. His eyes were on her, as though he was trying to read her, to assess the woman she was. 'Are you happy?' he asked, his voice soft.

She sucked in a deep breath. 'That's a strange question.' It had been so long since someone had cared enough to ask. Her mother had worried and fretted throughout the court

proceedings but afterwards couldn't understand Olivia's lack
of emotional and mental resilience. They spoke once a week,
with her mum encouraging her to meditate, come and visit her,
and to eat healthy. During those phone calls Olivia faked a
positivity she didn't feel. Her father had a hard time hiding
his disappointment and embarrassment. When the media had
realised Eric was Olivia's father, it added an extra layer of titillation. When they discovered Leena was selling some of his
apartments, the trash papers were even more gleeful in their
reporting. Despite that, he had supplied and funded his legal
team to look after his daughter. But facing him had been difficult, and they hadn't seen each other since the trial. There
hadn't been anyone else close enough to notice how miserable
Olivia had truly been.

'It's just ... sometimes you have a look about you, as though
you're hurting. Or lost.'

Olivia shook her head with quick denial. 'I'm fine.'

'Fine isn't good enough. Fine is holding it together. Fine is
not happy. Trust me, I know the difference.' He dropped his
arm from around her and placed his hands on her shoulders,
shifting so they were face to face. 'We don't really know each
other, not yet. And I don't expect you to spill your deepest
darkest stories.' He slid his hands upwards, his fingers at the
back of her neck, his thumbs along the line of her jaw. 'But I
hate seeing you sad.'

She wanted to look away. His touch, the way he looked at her,
and his words were all connecting with the crumpled, destitute
part of her being. Her shame curled deep inside her, afraid of
being laid bare. And under it all was her physical awareness of
him. His hands were warm where they held her, she'd felt the
strength of his body, and she kept glancing at his mouth.

She gripped the front of his jacket and gave a small tug. '*You* make me feel good,' she said. 'So, I'm thinking you should kiss me.'

His eyes widened. The moment stretched out, almost unbearable as she waited.

Gently, ever so gently, his mouth came down to hers. Their lips touched with the slightest pressure, brushing against each other, restrained, tender, teasing. He dropped one arm to reach behind her lower back, pulling her against him.

Olivia had been kissed too many times to remember. Kisses from strangers in bars and clubs, kisses redolent with the taste of booze and sweat. Illicit kisses, staged and performed for an imaginary audience. Sweet kisses, rough kisses, bad kisses, sloppy kisses. Kisses that evoked no feeling whatsoever.

This was more. So much more.

The rush from tentative to intense sent her spinning. One of his hands was behind her head, and she could feel the rasp of his stubble. He was fierce yet gentle, as though he wanted her desperately but was cautious of getting it all wrong. As though he wanted to savour her, not simply devour.

She wriggled a hand free and reached up to wrap an arm around his neck, lifting herself higher.

'Get a room!' The yell from a passing stranger brought them back to the world.

Tom raised a hand to acknowledge the group of hooting guys as they passed, while Olivia let herself back down onto her feet, glad his arm was still there to support her.

They looked at each other and laughed, finding their balance.

'Anytime you need me to do that again, let me know,' he said. 'I like a woman who knows what she wants and isn't afraid to ask for it.'

'But I'm not usually so sure of what I want.' She touched her mouth without thinking, then dropped her hand when he gave her a look that said, very clearly, *More?* 'These days I haven't a clue what I'm doing most of the time. I don't even know where I'm going to be in a year.'

'But you haven't always been like this?' They untangled from one another and began walking again, his arm keeping her close.

'Good lord, no. I used to have plans. And I worked hard towards the things I wanted to achieve.'

'What happened?'

'Things got out of control. I made mistakes. Big ones. I made choices which were so very wrong.'

'We've all made bad choices,' he said. 'My judgement has been seriously flawed lately.'

'Relationships?' She thought of the pictures of his redheaded ex-wife and held herself back from referring to his short-lived marriage.

He pulled a face and nodded, watching her for a moment as though deciding whether to explain. Then he looked away. 'Let's say that with success comes attention. Sometimes it's the wrong sort of attention—the sort that has more to do with money in the bank and the buzz around someone, and a lot less to do with who you are as a person. At heart I'm still the geeky, awkward, ugly kid who never had a girlfriend. But then I did this magazine thing. "Top Young Tech Titans" or something stupid like that. Turns out financial success transforms tech geeks into hot property. To get attention like that, when you're not used to it … well, it's easy to get caught up in something that isn't real.'

'I think I know what you're talking about. Sometimes our ability to see the real nature of things can get lost behind flash and bling and the *act* of living a life you think you want.'

Tom stopped walking, and she paused beside him. 'That's it exactly,' he said urgently, his eyes on hers again. 'Although ... I can't imagine you getting swept up in something just because someone pretty stroked your ego.'

'You'd be surprised,' she said with a laugh. Before Hayden she'd been confident, capable of flirting, and comfortable enough in the way she looked. But when he'd walked into her hotel and focused his million-dollar smile on her, she'd found it impossible not to confuse the fantasy of the big screen with the reality of him as a person.

'I bet you're not so shallow as to be blinded by a hot bod and some fake add-ons.'

She laughed at his self-deprecating honesty. 'That's a bet you'd lose. I am well acquainted with fake. I bet *you* weren't so stupid as to believe the person on the big screen was the person in the room.'

He gave her a questioning look. 'Interesting. Do tell.'

'Maybe ... one day,' she teased. Yes, she could imagine explaining everything to him. In some ways they had a lot in common. But would he be here long enough for her to get to the point of revelation?

It was his turn again in their litany of silly confessions. 'I bet you didn't fall for someone who only wanted your money.'

'I bet *you* didn't fall for someone who thought they were above and beyond mere mortals.'

'I bet you've never been so stupid as to fall for someone just because they made you feel wanted.' He was trying to keep the tone light, but Olivia could hear the hurt behind the words. His ex-wife had smashed his heart—not only his heart, but his pride and confidence too, by the sound of things. 'And,' he added, 'I bet you didn't marry someone after just three months.'

'Okay, you win.' She said it lightly, wanting to keep the mood from getting too serious. 'I'm presuming you're not still married? You don't have a ring.' She hoped the gossip rags and social media discussions were accurate, but that wasn't a thing to bank on.

'No,' he said. 'No, I'm not. We're divorced, I promise. I wouldn't do that.'

She sensed a shift in his body, a sudden rise in tension.

'I may be many things.' Although he spoke quietly, his tone was more fierce than anything she'd heard from him so far. 'But I wouldn't cheat on someone. Even when she cheated on me—all the times she cheated on me—I didn't do the dirty. I was determined to take the high road. It was bad enough I'd ignored my friends and family and married Nessa against all their tactful advice. I wasn't going to lower myself further. We've been divorced for almost as long as we were married. We didn't even make our second anniversary.' As he talked he shifted back, just a little, and released her from his hold. She let him go. 'Have you ever been cheated on?' he asked, his voice edged with a pain that was obviously still fresh.

A noise escaped her, something between a laugh and a sob. 'Me? Oh no, I wasn't cheated on.'

When he looked at her with his steady, searching gaze, she had to look away. What would he think of her if he knew she'd slept with a married man? Maybe it would be better if she told him. That would stop this—whatever it was—before their emotions became caught up in the rush of attraction.

She turned back to him, gritting her teeth, holding eye contact. 'My last real boyfriend, he was definitely cheating. But not *on* me—*with* me.' She swallowed down the self-loathing and kept going. 'I was the other woman. The seductress. The marriage wrecker.'

A silence fell between them as the magic of the evening fizzled to nothing, like a sparkler sputtering out till it was no more than a scorched wire.

She shoved her clenched fists into her pockets and studied him for a second. His face was inscrutable, the dim light hiding the expression in his eyes. But as he folded his arms across his chest, she could read his body language. It was unmistakable— he had shut himself off, putting a wall between them.

'Look, I have to go. My car's parked back there.' She jerked her chin towards the off-street parking area they'd just passed.

'You don't have to,' he said. She could tell he was only being polite.

'I've got a long drive home.'

'Okay. Drive safely.' He stepped forward, lifting a hand to her shoulder as though he was going to give her a goodnight kiss.

She stepped away. A polite peck would be unbearable.

'I'll let you know how I go with asking locals about Pippa,' she said. 'I'll send you a text if I come across anything.' She wanted to make it clear that it was still her intention to help him with the search for Pippa, but she wouldn't make things awkward with unwanted phone calls. She wouldn't be pursuing him. She certainly wouldn't use his quest as an excuse to cling.

'Olivia,' he called after her. But she had turned away, hurrying back along the footpath, and did not look back.

She told herself she'd done the right thing.

CHAPTER SEVENTEEN

Thursday, 2 January 1986

Jeremy passed Leo another beer. 'I'm guessing you're staying here tonight?'

Leo looked at Pippa, checking. She nodded. 'I'm guessing he might.' She ignored Rebecca's frosty stare.

Leo's smile was one of teasing anticipation, and Pippa put her hand on his thigh, wanting desperately to touch him. She definitely wanted him here.

After they'd recovered from their encounter on the beach, they'd wandered back to the house to find the others had returned. There had been a moment of awkwardness, with Pippa prepared to stave off any confrontation. But Jeremy had reached out to shake Leo's hand and then asked if he'd like a beer, and they'd all settled on the terrace. The conversation had been polite at first, then more relaxed as they discussed the yacht race, but several times Pippa had caught Rebecca staring at Leo, her eyes tight with calculation and judgement.

Each time she'd then flicked her attention back to Jeremy, and her face had eased into calm determination.

Rebecca was always quick to comment on how much Pippa drank, but tonight she was the one who was not holding back, topping up her wine repeatedly and even going to the fridge to get the cask. When she caught Pippa watching, she jutted out her chin and widened her eyes, daring her to say something.

Now she spoke with resentment. 'Well, I guess I'd better do something about dinner.' She got up and turned towards the kitchen, preparing to be the martyr.

'We've got snags, don't we?' Jeremy asked, jumping to his feet. 'And lamb chops. We menfolk can fire up the barbie. You right with that, Leo?'

Leo stood. 'Of course. I'll get the fire going.'

Eloise's barbecue was a chunky brick construction with both a heavy iron plate and an open grill. Set a short distance from the terrace, it had a built-in space with stick kindling and small logs ready to get it fired up.

'Great idea,' said Pippa. What could be more chilled out than two guys shoulder to shoulder over a fire, beer in one hand, tongs in the other? 'Let's go, Rebecca. We can do the salad thing and get them the meat.'

While Pippa found a serving plate for the sausages and chops, Rebecca pulled out the iceberg lettuce and a bag of tomatoes. She slammed the fridge door as she moved to the bench. She hadn't said a word, displeasure evident in every movement.

'It's all fine, Rebecca,' Pippa said, trying to placate her. 'They're getting along and there's no drama.'

'Yet!' Rebecca stuck a short knife into the bottom of the lettuce and wrenched out the hard centre, then tore the leaves apart. 'Sure. It's fine now, at this moment. But secrets don't stay secret, do they? Then what? How are people going to react? You don't know.'

'People?'

'You know, *them*—' She waved an arm in the direction of the boys. 'Or Jeremy's mum. Or even Leo's family. You don't know what you've started here. And it wouldn't have happened if you'd been more considerate.' She thumped the wooden salad bowl onto the bench. 'Just for once.'

'Oh, come on. Don't you think you're being a bit overdramatic?' Pippa was surprised—direct confrontation wasn't Rebecca's usual style. 'And what do you mean I'm not considerate? When have I ever not been considerate?'

Rebecca was throwing the lettuce in the bowl, the odd piece flying off the bench. 'Oh, I don't know. Maybe every time you come home late and then proceed to bang about in the kitchen, not caring whether you wake Jeremy and me. Or worse, whenever you bring some stranger back and get all hot and heavy, knowing how noise carries in that house. Have you any idea how uncomfortable that is for us? And you know Jeremy and I don't always get that much time alone, but you still tag along with us to dinner or the movies. And here! This trip could've been just us, our special time together. But, no, best friend Pippa—third wheel Pippa—didn't think of that. Jeremy will fly off to London in five weeks, and you couldn't even give us this time alone. Couldn't bear for me to be alone with him. And now this—this rat's nest of a drama. You've made it so these last weeks will be all about you, and that boy, and his dirty little family secrets, whatever they are!'

Pippa was stunned. There was so much resentment, so much pent-up anger. There were some uncomfortable truths, but also accusations that were just plain unfair. 'Actually, Rebecca,

Eloise asked both me and Jeremy to house-sit. The three of us coordinated this trip around the end of our lease, Jeremy's flight to London, and Eloise's travel plans. It was a group plan. I didn't tag along.'

'Are you insinuating that I did?'

'God. No! That's not what I'm saying. I'm saying I don't have a home right now, my plans are up in the air, and Eloise invited me here. Besides, Jeremy leaves before Eloise gets back. I need to be here.'

'But you didn't have to come *now*, did you? Do you not see how special, how important, this time would have been for Jeremy and me? I mean, I'm not even here for the whole ten weeks. You know that I have to go back to work on the twentieth of January. You could've come then. Given us time together, alone. Before he heads to the other side of the world. I wanted to make the most of it, because I have no idea when we'll be together again. Now it's not only you here, but some long-lost cousin too. Maybe I should say something, get the whole business out in the open. Then we won't all have to tip-toe around. Maybe when he knows the truth, he'll leave. And maybe you'll go with him.'

Pippa banged the tray of meat on the bench and leant closer to Rebecca, trying to get the woman to look at her. 'You will not say anything. This is none of your bloody business. I'm sorry being here hasn't worked out the way you wanted. Maybe you should've said something before we left. But don't you dare stir up trouble.'

'Don't you talk to me like that.' Rebecca swayed a little as she faced Pippa.

'Hey, what's going on?' It was Jeremy, bouncing up the stairs to the kitchen.

Rebecca turned away and snapped open the bag of tomatoes.

'Nothing.' Pippa wasn't going to let Rebecca spoil the night. 'Just a disagreement over the salad.' She could tell Jeremy wasn't buying it.

He put an arm around his girlfriend. 'You okay, babe?'

She sniffed as she nodded. 'Let's tell Leo. I hate this atmosphere. Keep thinking someone is going to say something wrong.'

'I don't think we need to do that,' he said. 'Not right now.' He kissed her on the cheek. 'Let's enjoy the night. All of that can wait.' He turned to pick up the meat tray. 'Right, let's get this lot sizzling. Thanks, Pip.' He planted a kiss on her temple, an affectionate gesture he made sometimes—usually not in Rebecca's presence. Now was definitely the wrong time.

'This is ridiculous!' Rebecca spat. 'How long are you going to let this go on?' Her face was ugly with anger and inebriation. 'You can't ignore the truth. You can't!'

Jeremy tried to hush her. 'Give it a rest, Bec.'

'Don't call me Bec. I hate Bec. You know that! I'm Rebecca.'

'Fine. I'm sorry, Rebecca.'

'Tell him.'

'No. It's not the right time.'

'Tell him, or I will.'

Jeremy set the tray back on the bench and reached for Rebecca, trying to pull her into his arms for a calming hug. 'Sweetheart, you're being unreasonable.'

'Me? *I'm* being unreasonable? Your *friend* there—' she flung out her arm in Pippa's direction '—she goes against your wishes and brings that boy here, and you think *I'm* being unreasonable. What is it with her? Why do you always let her do whatever she wants? She doesn't even care about you. She doesn't care about how this whole situation makes you feel. *I'm* the one who cares.'

'Rebecca, please stop. I'm fine. This situation is fine.' His voice was quiet and calm.

She turned her head away from him and sniffed again. Swiped at a tear running down her cheek. *Putting on the waterworks,* Pippa thought. Rebecca lifted her eyes to Jeremy's before gazing past him. A scowl settled back on her face.

Pippa turned to look over her shoulder. Leo was standing at the top of the steps, looking into the kitchen. He was watching them, obviously wary. He'd stumbled into an ugly domestic scene and clearly didn't know whether to retreat or step into the tension.

'Tell him,' Rebecca said, loud enough for Leo to hear.

The moment hung there. No one said a word. No one moved.

Finally Pippa walked towards Leo. 'Let's leave these two to hash it out,' she said, taking his hand.

Leo gripped her hand but stood firm. 'What do you need to tell me?' The question was directed at Jeremy. 'Is there something I should know?'

'Yes,' said Rebecca. 'There is. Jeremy?' She had forced them all into a corner.

Jeremy sighed, letting go of his girlfriend as she stepped away. He shoved his hands tight into his armpits—not in a defensive or aggressive gesture, just one of reluctance.

Rebecca wiped her tears with her fingertips and flounced her hair.

Pippa focused back on Leo. 'Let's go and sit down. This might take a while to explain.'

*

In the end, the explanation was less difficult than Pippa had imagined. Sometimes she underestimated Jeremy. As he spoke, she could see the man he must be at work. Professional, collected, succinct in his delivery of information. In this case, he put forward the complex scenario in the simplest terms. His mum, Angela Kearsley, had a sister she hadn't spoken to or seen since 1961. Jeremy didn't know why they had fallen out, but whatever had caused the rift, it had wrought irreparable damage on their relationship. The sister's name was Evelyn. She'd been Evelyn Kearsley originally, but was Evelyn Clifford by marriage.

Leo just listened. Hunched forward in his seat, he held Pippa's hand in both of his as if anchored by the contact. Rebecca, meanwhile, sat silent and still beside Jeremy, her face tight with disapproval.

'Mate, I don't know what else to tell you,' Jeremy concluded. 'I was a bit thrown when I saw you the other night.'

After taking a moment to absorb it all, Leo said, 'This is a pretty big thing.' He didn't sound upset—a bit confused, maybe.

If Pippa had suddenly discovered dramatic secrets about her parents, she'd have been outraged. A revelation like this would have trashed the security she felt in her straightforward family. But Leo was simply thoughtful.

'You know,' he said, sounding almost amused, 'I remember doing family trees in Grade Four or Five. I was a real swot, even back then. I was so disappointed when I realised how limited our tree was, with basically no extended family at all. I thought I'd get marked down, so I bulked out the sheet of cardboard with old family photos. Mum caught me going through boxes I'd found in the garage—boxes of photos from when she was at school. That earned me a smack around the head. She was furious. I guess I was a little too close to uncovering a few secrets.'

'You've got no idea what might have caused the falling-out?' Jeremy asked.

Leo stopped to think. 'None whatsoever.'

'Eloise might know,' said Pippa.

'That would make sense,' said Jeremy. 'She and Mum were at school together, and I'm guessing Evelyn was there too, a grade or two older. Eloise was the one who told me about you.' He nodded towards Leo. 'I'd like to know what happened. Wouldn't you?' He said it with a grin, lightness masking frustration. 'You could always ask your mum.'

Leo shook his head. 'Nah. It's not the kind of discussion I want to have with her. She's not ... She's not the most easygoing of mothers. But what about *your* mum? If you asked, do you think she'd tell you what happened?'

Jeremy grimaced. 'I doubt it. The past is a bit of a no-go zone with her. And I'd rather not open that can of worms before I leave for London.'

'Fair enough. So your godmother would be the easiest option?'

'Probably.'

'Pity you can't have a proper chat with her at the moment,' Pippa said. She couldn't imagine trying to have this discussion over the phone, and long-distance calls were always hard work, with their lags and clunky pauses and awkward moments when you talked over each other, not to mention the limited time and ridiculous cost.

'Yeah,' he said, 'I guess I'll have to wait until I get over there.'

Through the entire conversation, Rebecca had sat beside her boyfriend in silence. Now she stood, wavering a little. 'I'm going to bed,' she announced. 'Are you coming, Jeremy?' Her huffiness reeked of disappointment. She had clearly wanted fireworks. She had wanted Leo turfed out of the house. She'd wanted to win. All of this had nothing to do with Leo and everything to do with how Rebecca felt about Pippa.

After a delayed dinner of burnt sausages and fatty lamb chops, the rest of them headed to bed too. The clever design of the house proved perfect for their needs, with a bedroom and bathroom on each side, the sunken lounge room and the kitchen between them. The two couples separated by the length of the house.

'Let's not talk about my messed-up family anymore,' Leo said as Pippa led him into her room. 'It's complicated and a bit weird, but kind of irrelevant.'

'Irrelevant?'

'It doesn't change my life, not really. Jeremy seems like a cool guy. I've gained a cousin, I guess. I reckon we can be mates, and maybe one day we'll get some answers. Maybe next month when he sees his godmother.' Leo stopped talking when Pippa slid her arms around his neck, her fingers playing in his hair. 'Right now—' he settled his hands on her hips, pulling her gently forward '—right now, let's change the subject.'

In the cool of the night, with the cries of nocturnal creatures coming through the open windows, they found each other. No rush. No misgivings. Only trust and the thrill of discovery.

CHAPTER EIGHTEEN

The next two weeks passed with the unhurried pleasure of sun-toasted holidays and new love. Leo came and went. Mostly he stayed. They swam in the channel and warmed themselves on the rocks. There were barbecues with Jeremy and Rebecca, and games of Cluedo and Trivial Pursuit. Long slow mornings, languid afternoons, and evenings when they wrapped themselves in blankets and lay on the grass gazing at the astonishing sky.

Whenever Leo was in Hobart, Pippa read books, wrote on the typewriter, talked to the chickens, and took long walks with Honey. She daydreamed about her future, seeing endless possibilities. Travel, writing and adventures lay ahead. Her sense of her own potential and her self-belief, which had always been quietly present, unfurled even further. She filled a notebook with places she wanted to see, stories she wanted to write, and ideas of who she could be. In all these dreams Leo kept appearing by her side, a thought that made her both excited and nervous. Was she being ridiculous?

She asked him to read the articles she was writing. He didn't gush about her work or trivialise it, and he was specific about what he liked and why.

He told her she was beautiful. He also told her she was gutsy, intelligent, provocative, generous, stubborn and brave. Being *seen* was the most wonderful feeling in the world.

When a letter arrived from Eloise, he hugged her tight.

'Eloise says that Richard—he's the publisher—she says he likes my pieces. Really likes them! He's asked for more, and given me some guidelines and specific things he's looking for. Eloise says ...' Pippa scanned the thin paper, looking for the exact words. '*Richard is eager to read more of your writing and is considering how you may possibly fit into his new line-up.*'

'Brilliant.' Leo kissed her on the mouth. 'Would you have to move to London?'

'Possibly? I mean, I'd have to travel. God, I'd be paid to travel and write! Can you imagine that?'

They celebrated by falling into bed, their exuberance leaving them sweaty and exultant.

Later they were sprawled across the sheets. 'Pippa?'

'Hmmm,' was all she could manage.

'I'd love to come with you.'

She turned to look at him, and he gave her a timid smile. She reminded herself they had only known each other less than a month. Told herself it was just an intense summer fling. But the thought of sharing her adventures with him sent a giddy swirl of butterflies through her chest and out to her fingertips.

'What about uni? What about your sailing?'

He put his hands behind his head, staring up at the ceiling. 'Well, uni can wait for a bit, and there's plenty of sailing in

England. Or we could end up somewhere else that has open water racing.'

She turned to face him. 'What will your parents say?'

'They won't like it. But that's their problem, not mine.' There was determination in his eyes. 'I want to experience the world, get off this island, get away from this small pond, learn about life by actually living and taking risks. I want to be with you.'

'I'd like that,' she murmured as she reached for his hand, their fingers entwining.

It wasn't too much, or too early. It was real.

*

Jeremy and Leo became friends, enjoying each other's company, and most evenings they cooked dinner side by side at the barbecue. Their questions about family had been put aside for now. Neither of them had any intention of discussing the matter with their respective mothers, Angela and Evelyn.

Pippa knew that in Jeremy's case, asking his mum those questions would be disastrous. Angela would be hurt and angry if she found out that Jeremy was spending time with her sister's son. It had been bad enough when he'd announced he was going to house-sit for Eloise—according to Jeremy, Angela's words had been something along the lines of, 'Why would you want to spend time in that narrow-minded, archaic hole of a state? It's full of stupid, close-minded people. I got out as soon as I could, and I will never, ever go back.' The fact he would go straight to London without returning to Brisbane hadn't helped the situation, but since the international flight left from Sydney, it made sense. Angela had been quiet and sad at his farewell dinner. She was still an attractive woman, but bitterness had given her a tough exterior. Saying goodbye to her only child—her only family—had cracked her hard veneer.

Pippa soon learnt that for Leo there was no possibility of asking Evelyn these questions. He made it clear his parents were difficult people. His childhood had been a privileged one, but his mother was a stickler for doing things 'the right way', and his father was determined to see his children succeed—success being determined by his limited set of values and priorities. A life path had been dictated to Leo for as long as he could remember. First, there'd been the private school, next was a law degree. Then he would join his father in his legal firm.

'Do you want to do law?' Pippa asked one afternoon, when they'd walked the roo track to the top of the hill. They were sitting on the ground, Leo having first checked the area for jack jumper nests. 'Your heart doesn't seem to be in it.'

There was a long pause before he spoke. 'Not really.'

'You only applied because of your parents?'

'Pretty much. Dad has always made a big deal of how important it is to have a professional career.'

'Like being a solicitor.'

'Yeah. He likes the idea of "Clifford and Clifford" on the nameplate,' he said with a touch of sarcasm.

'It's going to be hard to do well in a job you have no interest in. Man, it's going to be hard to do well in a degree you don't care about.'

'I know.'

'So don't do it.'

'It's not that easy.'

'Of course it is.' This was 1986, not 1950. Children weren't beholden to their parents' expectations anymore. When Pippa's mother had suggested she become a teacher like her, Pippa had made it absolutely clear that this would be a total disaster. Her parents had sighed, warbled on for a bit about job security, financial well-being and getting serious about the future, then resigned themselves to observing Pippa live her own life.

'It's not that easy for me,' Leo said.

'Don't be such a wimp. Stand up for what you want! What are they going to do?'

He picked up a small branch and began peeling off strips of grey bark. 'I feel obligated,' he said, sounding resigned. 'My dad recently sorted out a problem for me.'

'You got a girl pregnant?'

'What? No!'

'Then what?'

He started snapping the branch into smaller pieces. 'I hit someone.'

Pippa waited for him to continue, having quickly learnt he liked to find the right words when he spoke about anything remotely serious.

'It could've been really bad. I hit a teacher. I could've been charged with assault.'

'Holy hell. Okay, yes, that is serious.' He'd shown no signs of having a temper, and she was taken aback. 'What happened? I'm guessing something more than being given too much homework.'

Dropping the last of the stick, he rested his arms on his bent knees, staring out over the trees to the water far below them. 'There was this bloke in my year. He was a bit on the small side. Quiet. Not the brightest spark. He struggled a little in class. Got picked on. I found him one day, crying. It's awful when you see an eighteen-year-old bawling his eyes out—you don't know whether to leave him alone or say something.'

Pippa put her arm across Leo's back and leant into his shoulder. She had a gut feeling about where this story was going.

'Turned out a teacher, this arsehole, had been, well, you know ...' He faltered.

When he didn't continue, she suggested a scenario. 'The teacher had spotted a weak student and taken advantage of his authority?' She'd heard rumours about creeps like that being in some schools.

'Yeah,' Leo murmured. 'So, I encouraged this guy to hang out with me and my mates. I didn't tell them why, just said, you know, he was a friend.'

'But it wasn't enough?'

'A few weeks later I'd been in the library after school, stayed there until it closed. I started walking home, and I saw them in a space between two school buildings. The teacher had him by the arm, was right up in his face. The bastard was furious.' Another pause. 'I lost it.'

'What happened?'

'I dropped my bag, walked straight up to him. Didn't say a word. He looked at me. Fuck, that look. Arrogance. Loathing. He let go of my mate's arm, told me to get home. I didn't even hesitate. He didn't expect me to hit him.'

'Did he fight back?'

'No. Gutless prick. He started screaming at me. I grabbed my mate, picked up my bag and got the hell out of there. The next day I was called before the headmaster. My parents were there. I was told I had been expelled. But—given my exemplary record, and since it was nearly the end of the school year—they were going to be generous and let me sit my final exams.'

Injustice always upset Pippa. Right now she was furious at all those gutless, swaggering men who let this happen to Leo and to his friend. She shifted her position so she could face Leo, making him look at her. 'What you did, that was incredible. You know that, right? You stood up for someone who couldn't.'

'Yeah, well, my dad didn't see it that way. Didn't matter what I told him, as far as he was concerned I wasn't responsible for the problems of other students. It wasn't my place to get involved. And, according to him, I only had my mate's word about what had happened, and he was making it up to get attention—what I'd seen, that was probably the teacher reprimanding a bad student.' Leo rested his chin on his arms. 'It wasn't.'

'Of course it wasn't,' she said vehemently. 'That student wouldn't have made up a story like that, and I bet your dad didn't really believe it was a simple reprimand either. It was just easier to sweep it all aside than to truly defend you. I thought a lawyer would've wanted to fight for justice.'

A look of resignation settled on his face. 'Not if it's going to bring gossip and unwanted attention and expose the family in any way.'

Un-bloody-believable. 'And the threat of legal charges?'

'Dad did his important lawyer act and met with the teacher, said the right things to make it go away. Then I had to apologise, in person.'

'You're kidding.' She imagined what she would have said to that disgusting abusive teacher or to Leo's pathetic father. She moved back beside him, reaching both arms around his waist to give him a hug.

'Hardest thing I've ever, ever had to do. I couldn't look at him. Couldn't force myself to meet the eye of that piece of shit. Dad and the headmaster were both there. That smug prick, he knew he had won. I'm pretty sure Dad donated some money to the school too.'

'That is so wrong.' Pippa was rigid with indignation. 'Oh my god, I can't believe you went through that. I wouldn't have had the courage to do what you did. And to be treated as though you were the one at fault! To have to bend down to that creep. That's really, really wrong. I'm so angry.'

Leo turned his face into her hair. 'You would've done something. I know you would've.'

'I wouldn't have had the guts to hit a teacher.'

'No. But you're smarter than me. You'd have figured out a way to get payback and save your mate without getting yourself in trouble.'

She laughed a little. 'Maybe.' Then she asked softly, 'And what happened with your mate?'

'Never came forward.'

'But if he'd substantiated your story, he could've saved you.'

'I don't blame him. How could he have sat in front of our headmaster and spilled details about things he didn't even want to admit to himself?'

'You are *incredible*,' she said forcefully. 'I love that you stand up for others. I love that you have a sense of justice. I love the person you are.' She kissed him. 'I don't love how you feel so beholden to your folks. But I love you.'

She'd said those three words to a man only once before, on the third and last time she'd slept with Jeremy. They'd been at home, both single, tossing back the bourbon and listening to Prince. Lying on the sofa in the dark, they'd turned to each other, letting the mood sweep them along. The sex was quick and fun but not great, the itch scratched but not soothed. As they lay among the sofa cushions and their discarded clothes, they looked at each other. 'You know I love you,' she said, laughing. 'But we should stop doing this.'

He had pretended to be wounded, then agreed. 'Let's not fuck up our friendship, right?' he said after a minute.

She did love Jeremy. But this was nothing like that—this time the words were enormous.

'I love *you*,' Leo said, and she knew it was true.

CHAPTER NINETEEN

Friday, 17 January 1986

Pippa was struggling to find a subject for her next piece when Leo said he would take her out on his friend's boat so she could write about sailing on the Derwent River.

The weather was perfect. Leo showed his skill handling the compact boat before he encouraged Pippa to try her hand at the wheel and to tighten the sails. Mostly, though, she was happy to recline with her face to the sun, her bare legs stretched out on the wooden deck. They'd brought a picnic lunch, Leo surprising her when, instead of beer, he pulled a bottle of champagne from the esky. It was late afternoon when they tied the boat at the yacht club marina. They were off-loading their gear, Pippa kneeling as she retied the laces on her Volleys, when Leo stopped. 'Shit,' he said under his breath, looking at something behind her.

Pippa looked over her shoulder. 'What is it?' Striding confidently towards them was a man dressed in long white shorts and a navy polo shirt.

'You're about to meet my dad.' The quiet words held a warning.

So this was Leo's father. The slippery, truth-dodging, image-obsessed man who'd saved his son from assault charges while refusing to truly stand by and support him. She stood, tugging down her pink singlet top and pushing her sunglasses up on her head to hold back her wind-messed hair. Despite every-thing, she would try to make a decent first impression. Not because she cared what he thought of her, but because winning him over could only help Leo, and telling him exactly what she thought definitely wouldn't.

'Leo.' The heavy voice carried to them. 'I heard you were out on the water today.'

'Hello, Dad.'

He was in his mid-forties. A tall, lean, handsome man like Leo, but with a rigidity to his manner. There was a prominent logo on his shirt, letting the world know how much it had cost, and he wore tan leather deck shoes and a faded green cap over thick, light-brown hair. His look was crisp and expensive, and he carried himself with self-appointed authority.

The distance closed between them, and he stopped. Father and son shook hands as though they were acquaintances. He took off his Wayfarer sunglasses and assessed Pippa, a fast glance from toe to chest, before his smirking blue eyes met hers. 'Hello, I'm Angus Clifford.'

Leo lurched into an introduction. 'Dad, this is Pippa French. Pippa, this is my father.'

She hid a quiver of repulsion as she extended a hand for Angus to shake. His grip was firm and held on for an uncom-fortable length of time. *What a creep.* 'I can understand why we've seen so little of you lately, Leo. She's a beautiful girl.' His leering was less subtle this time. When he met her eye, he was smiling not only as though he liked what he saw but was confident she would be impressed by him. How wrong he was. 'I believe you're staying at Eloise Fowler's house down at Devils Bay. How are you finding that?'

'It's wonderful, thank you. We're very lucky to have had the opportunity to stay there. Tasmania is beautiful.' Pippa could do polite small talk. She could even ignore the rude once-overs and the way he'd talked about her as though she was an object.

He finally broke eye contact to look at his son. 'Come for dinner tonight,' he said. Then to Pippa, 'My wife Evelyn would be delighted to meet you.'

'I think Pippa has to get back,' said Leo firmly. He shifted closer to her, as though he wanted to deflect his dad's attention. 'Maybe another time?'

'Do you, Pippa? Surely you'd like to spend an evening with us. I don't bite.'

Instinct told her Angus Clifford would think nothing of flirting with his son's girlfriend. There was a challenge in his words and questioning gaze. He clearly wanted to see which way she would bend. Would she be impressed or daunted by their affluence? Would she be flattered or scared of his attention? It was likely that if she didn't measure up, the situation for Leo and herself would be made more difficult.

She angled her head and gave him a look, framed with a smile, to let him know she wasn't to be intimidated. 'Actually, I would love to join your family for dinner. It is so lovely of you to invite me.'

'Well then, we'll see you at the house. As soon as you've finished here.'

'Looking forward to it.' Pippa had been leered over, pawed at, and talked down to by men like this for as long as she cared to remember. She'd learnt how best to handle them. *Don't be timid. Call them on their bullshit. Smile to keep them passive. Draw a well-defined line against their behaviour. And sometimes let them mistakenly think you're impressed by them.*

*

An hour later Pippa and Leo arrived at a large double-storey house built in light-brown brick. The long driveway delivered them to a turning circle with a fountain at its centre and a double-width garage to one side. The architect appeared to have been aiming for faux Federation, with bay windows, gables jutting from the second storey, a verandah wrapping from the front door around one side, and white posts and railings. It all felt a little overdone.

The two of them were soon standing on the deck off the kitchen, taking in the property's front-row position along the wide harbour of the Derwent River. In front of them, a dinghy was tied to a jetty that extended from the expanse of lawn. Running along the property boundary were saplings strapped to posts, promising to one day provide privacy.

'This is an amazing house,' Pippa said to Angus when he handed her a glass of wine.

'It is.' He directed her to take a seat with him and Leo at the outdoor table. 'Cost us a pretty penny, but it's a stand-out in this area—in all of Hobart, actually.'

'Hello.' A woman emerged from the house. Elegant and slim, she was wearing a white collared shirt, wide and rounded at the shoulders, and tucked into the cinched waist of her pleated pants. Her perfectly styled hair was bobbed to her collarbone and streaked with blonde and copper. Her make-up was evident but not gaudy. She moved gracefully and looked expensive.

Leo stood, and Pippa followed his lead. 'Mum, this is Pippa. Pippa, this is my mother, Evelyn Clifford.'

'Hello,' said Pippa. She smiled, wanting—for now—to appear deferential.

Evelyn's sharp eyes held Pippa's. 'Hello, Pippa.' There was a beat before she smiled with a measure of polite warmth. 'So, you're the charming girl who's been distracting Leo this summer. Very nice to meet you. I hear you're staying for dinner. It's so nice of you to join us.' She addressed this to her son with the tiniest hint of reproach.

'Yes. If that's alright. Dad ran into us at the yacht club and suggested we come.'

'Well, it's lovely to have you both here.' She sounded sincere, but Pippa wasn't convinced. 'I put dinner in the slow cooker a few hours ago. But I'm sure it will stretch to two more.'

'Great. Thanks, Mum. Is Maggie here?'

'She'll be home soon.'

'Can I help with dinner?' asked Pippa. 'I'm very good at following instructions.'

Another pause—Evelyn was probably weighing up whether she wanted Pippa in her space. Then with a hitch of an arched eyebrow, she gave another of those smiles. 'Thank you, that would be helpful. Lord knows these men don't ever offer to lend a hand.'

Pippa followed Evelyn into the impressive kitchen. A large centre bench had black bar stools lined up on one side and divided the cooking area from the dining room. The unblemished white of the benchtops stood out sharply against the dark wooden cabinetry. There was a built-in wall oven, a large electric stovetop, a stainless-steel rangehood, and even a microwave with its own custom-built nook. On the bench an orange crockpot was simmering.

'That smells good,' Pippa said, not having to fake her sincerity. She'd noticed the aroma as soon as they'd entered the house.

'The family do love my apricot chicken. Do you cook? I can give you the recipe.'

'Thank you, but I'm not the greatest in the kitchen. I can manage the basics. My housemate and I would take turns.'

'Well, I'll give it to you anyway. Between the two of you girls, I'm sure you can put it together. It's very easy.'

Pippa hesitated, deciding not to correct the assumption she had been sharing her home with a girl. That might lead to more questions about whom she lived with. Surely Evelyn wouldn't make the connection just from the name Jeremy, but Pippa wasn't going to paddle this conversation any closer to those dangerous waters.

'You live in Brisbane, I believe?' Evelyn said.

'I have been, yes. I grew up there. But I've been travelling the world a bit as well.'

'How nice. I'll put the rice on. If you could top and tail the beans—they're in the crisper in the fridge.' Pippa did as she was told, Evelyn directing her to a chopping board, a sharp knife and a pyrex bowl. 'The beans can be done in the microwave.'

'You might have to show me how to use it.' She and Jeremy had never bothered to get one.

Evelyn gave her quick instructions on how to set the timer and how long they needed to cook. 'Tell me, Pippa,' Evelyn said as she retrieved wineglasses and plates, 'how old are you?'

'Twenty-two.'

'And have you finished your studies?'

'I didn't go to uni. Well, I did, but I didn't finish my arts degree. I wasn't enjoying it.'

'I see. And what are you doing now?' There was curiosity and perhaps a flicker of judgement in the spaces between her words.

'I've travelled overseas. I do some waitressing. Modelling sometimes. And I write.' Pippa wasn't going to feel ashamed. 'I may have an opportunity to do some travel writing soon, which hopefully will mean new places and new adventures.'

'How interesting. And when are you heading back to Brisbane?'

'I did have a vague plan to head back when my house-sitting duties were done, five weeks from now. But that might change. I have no real reason to return. Who knows, I might head to London instead. I probably should start making some plans.'

'Then this thing you have with my son will be over soon.'

Ouch, Pippa thought. *This thing?*

'We haven't talked about that,' she said.

'Yes. But you're not going to stay here in Hobart.' Evelyn seemed hung up on the detail.

'I'm not sure,' she answered truthfully. After all, that idea had occurred to her—before Leo declared his desire to leave.

'Leo must have told you he's going to university this year. He's received an offer to study law. He's very focused on achieving academically and pursuing a profession.'

'Yes. He's told me that is the plan.'

'He won't have time for a girlfriend.' Evelyn made it a statement of fact. 'And surely you're ready to flit back out into the wider world. It sounds as though you're a free spirit.' She made this seem like one step up from a prostitute. 'What would be the point of staying here? You don't want to be sitting around while he studies—while he focuses on his future. Do you?'

'Well, no. But maybe Leo will do some travelling of his own before he settles down to his future.'

Evelyn laughed, a light tinkle of amusement. 'Oh heavens. No. That won't be happening. If he has let you think that is an option, you will be rather disappointed. Leo is very committed to this next stage of his life.'

Pippa tried to frame a reply but was interrupted when a girl's voice echoed from the front of the house. 'Mum, I'm home! Karen's mum dropped me off. What's for dinner?'

'Maggie, please don't shout. If you want to have a conversation, please enter the room.'

A girl about fifteen or sixteen years old, dressed in an orange-and-black netball uniform, burst into the kitchen. 'Fine. I'm here. What's for dinner? Oh, hello, who are you? I know, let me guess ... You're Pippa, aren't you? I can tell. Leo has described you perfectly.' The girl hoisted herself onto a stool, leant across the bench and grinned at Pippa. 'I love your hair. Is that a perm or is it natural? Gosh you're pretty. I'm Maggie, by the way, Leo's little sister. And I'm way cooler than my brother.'

*

It was late by the time Pippa and Leo were finally on their way back to Devils Bay. Leo drove carefully, ready to brake if a wallaby launched itself from the bush into the path of the car. They passed only the occasional house, the glow from windows like distant gems in the dark. Pippa was in the middle of the ute's bench seat, her hand resting on his thigh, relieved that the ordeal was over. She felt more than a smidgen of satisfaction in knowing she now had Leo all to herself, especially when she recalled Evelyn's rigid, insincere smile when her son had left the house hand in hand with Pippa.

'Thank you,' Leo said.

'For being the epitome of grace and poise and good breeding?' She'd been on her best behaviour all night.

'For not telling my father to go shove his outdated attitudes.'

'Oh, that.' She giggled. She would very much have liked to have cut through Angus Clifford's smarmy charm and less-than-subtle criticisms. But she hadn't. 'Yes, well, it was a struggle. Especially when he suggested my writing would be a fun little thing to keep me busy until I got married.'

'I was thinking more of the other suggestion.'

'That we were welcome to enjoy our holiday fling, but then I should clear out so you can focus on building your illustrious career?' It had been less a suggestion and more a series of assertive comments about what was going to happen, backed up by Evelyn. 'To be fair I am a terrible distraction.'

'True.' Leo glanced at her for a second, smiling. 'In fact, I'd say you're life-changing. But ...'

She waited a few seconds before prompting him. 'But?'

'Well, I might not have any choice about uni—about staying here and doing what they expect. What they want.'

'Because you feel obligated?'

'Yeah.'

'You know, Leo, that sounds an awful lot like manipulation. Your father did this thing for you—which is morally dubious, by the way—and now they're both holding it over you.'

'I guess.'

'So, don't. You're an adult. You are free to make your own choices about your life.'

He was silent again.

She bumped him with her shoulder. 'You'd like to travel a bit, right? Well, if that's what you truly want to do, you can defer uni for a year. It's not hard. Get out and explore the world.' His passive acceptance of his parents' demands was making her a little irritated. She wanted him to show more balls. 'There's no hurry to get on this path they've chosen for you, so push back a little. Negotiate. Stand up to them. What's the worst they can do?'

He gripped the steering wheel, his eyes not leaving the road. 'That's just it,' he said quietly. 'I don't know what they would do. How far they would go.'

*

When Pippa and Leo arrived back at the house, they found Rebecca and Jeremy sitting in the lounge, curled into each other on the sofa. 'Welcome home, lovebirds,' Jeremy called out.

'Good to be home,' Pippa said. Leo took the armchair, and she sank to the floor at his feet, leaning back against his legs. 'I have had the esteemed pleasure of dining with the illustrious Cliffords of Hobart.'

'Leo's family?' Jeremy sat up and leant forward. 'How was that?'

Leo's hand was on her shoulder, and she laced her fingers through his. 'I can say with great confidence, you are not missing out on much by not being invited to Christmas lunch.' She looked up at Leo. 'Sorry, darling, I know this is your family

I'm talking about. But they're not the warmest pair of parrots, are they?'

'It's true.' He shrugged, seemingly unconcerned by her judgement.

'I like Maggie, though. She's cute—and so energetically normal!'

'You know, Pippa,' Rebecca interjected, 'you're the only one of us, besides Eloise, who has met both Angela and Evelyn.'

'Wow. I hadn't thought of that.'

'Do they look alike?' Jeremy asked, his curiosity obvious.

Pippa thought about Evelyn. Her features were less attractive than her sister's, but Angela didn't have her air of wealth and decorum. Angela had lived a harder life and it showed. With the expensive clothes, the obvious pampering and her friendly but direct manner, Evelyn had commanded the dining room. Even while Angus had been throwing out his barbs, he'd continued to glance at his wife, looking for her subtle nods of encouragement and approval.

'Yes,' Pippa said. 'Sort of. I could see similarities. There must only be a year or so between them.'

'It must've been hard not to blurt something out,' said Rebecca.

'Like what?' Pippa laughed. 'Oh by the way, Mrs Clifford, it might come as a surprise to you that in Brisbane I've been living with Jeremy Kearsley. You know him? Your sister's son? The sister you deny even exists. Isn't that the most astonishing coincidence?' Pippa said all this with an exaggerated plummy accent.

Leo groaned. 'Yeah, that would've made the night interesting.'

They were all quiet for a minute before Jeremy changed the subject. 'Hey, two pieces of news. Firstly, we're all going to a party tomorrow night.'

'Are we? Whose?' Pippa decided she could do with a good party. 'We don't know anyone here.'

'*You* don't. But while you two have been making googly eyes at each other and playing about on boats—still pissed you didn't take me, by the way—we've been meeting locals. Had lunch today at the Oyster Cove pub and ran into a group our age. Ended up getting flogged in pool. Anyway, they invited us all to a party tomorrow not far from here—some guy's birthday.'

'Excellent,' said Pippa. 'Let's see how the locals entertain themselves. And the second piece of news?'

Jeremy took Rebecca's hand, and she smiled sadly at him. 'Just a reminder that my lovely girlfriend heads back to Brissie the day after tomorrow.'

This had always been the plan. The three of them would come down to house-sit, then Rebecca would go back to Brisbane for work. Jeremy would stay until it was time for him to leave for London in February. Pippa would be the last one holding the fort until Eloise returned.

'Well, Rebecca,' Pippa said, clapping her hands together, 'we'd better send you off with a bang.' When Rebecca shot her a sharp look, she wondered if maybe she'd sounded a little too gleeful.

CHAPTER TWENTY

Saturday, 18 January 1986

The girl next to Pippa flipped the top of her cigarette packet and held it open. 'Smoke?'

Pippa didn't smoke and had never even bought a packet for herself. But sometimes, when the drinks were flowing and someone offered, she'd take a cigarette. That was what parties were for—letting loose, being a bit naughty, having fun.

'Thanks,' she said.

'No problem.' She was wearing fingerless lace gloves and long strands of fake pearls. Her hair had been teased into a caramel-blonde cloud and was topped off with an oversized pink bow. Madonna had a lot to answer for. 'I'm Tilly,' she said as she held out her lighter. 'You're one of those Brisbanites staying down at Eloise's place, right?'

'Yep. I'm Pippa.'

She lit the cigarette and sucked, holding in the smoke until her throat and lungs burned. Exhaling, she squinted to avoid the sting. A guy in battered workboots and a chambray shirt came out of the house with a huge boom box and carried it across the yard to a ute parked near the paddock fence. He wrestled it onto the open tray as a mate followed him from the house, unravelling a long extension cord. Looked like the party was about to kick up a gear.

'Pippa?' said Tilly. 'Is that short for Philippa or something?'

'Penelope. But, god, don't tell anyone. Nobody calls me that. I hate it.' She picked up the wine cooler at her feet and took a drink.

'Penelope is a pretty name, though. Why not Penny?'

'Don't know. I've always been Pippa.'

Tilly took a drag on her own cigarette and nodded energetically. 'Cool. And is that your boyfriend?' She pointed towards Jeremy.

Pippa laughed. 'No. That's just Jeremy. He's my best friend. Housemate too—or he was. He's sold me his car for next to nothing, packed up his stuff, and is about to ditch me for a new life in London.'

'Right.' Tilly took a swig from her beer. 'I thought he must be your boyfriend. The way you gave him a hug before.'

Pippa shrugged. 'We're like that with each other. We know each other so well.' She pointed to Rebecca. 'See her, next to him? That's his girlfriend.' But they didn't look like a couple. Jeremy was half turned, his back to Rebecca, talking animatedly with the guy on his other side. Rebecca was staring straight ahead. She'd sunk low into her seat, the canvas of the fold-out chair sagging even under her light weight. Her legs and arms were tightly crossed, her dangling foot jerking in a hard, impatient rhythm. Despite being there when the invitation to the party had been made, she'd clearly had a change of heart. She didn't want to be here.

Tilly peered across the yard. 'She's very pretty, isn't she? She's got the whole preppy thing going on. I like her jacket.' Another drag, another swig. 'Does she mind you being so chummy with her boyfriend?'

'Jeremy and I were friends before she came along, so she kind of had to accept our relationship. But, yeah, I think it's sometimes hard for her.'

'Yeah. I might have found it a bit hard if my boyfriend was friends with someone as gorgeous as you. Has there ever been anything more between you two?'

This was the other thing parties were great for—having significant conversations with people she'd only just met.

'Sort of,' Pippa admitted. 'For, like, a minute. We were both travelling, and it's easy to get caught up in the magic of an exotic location. You know, far from home, from ordinary life, feeling like you're conquering the world. No inhibitions.'

'It didn't last after you got back?'

'No.' She put the cigarette to her lips and inhaled. She wasn't going to detail every encounter. 'But we have a really strong connection. One night we were sleeping together in a hut on the beach—the next night I was rescuing him from a ditch and getting him to hospital. Then I sat by him until he was well enough to get his arse back to Brisbane.'

'Seriously?' Tilly looked impressed. 'Wow. What happened?'

'It turns out that driving a crappy little scooter while really drunk, at night, down dirt roads, on a hunt for food, is not smart. No one else even noticed he was gone. I got worried and went looking.'

'And you found him.' Tilly's eyes were wide, a length of ash threatening to fall from her cigarette. 'Holy shit.'

'Yeah, I found him. He was so messed up.' When she thought about that night, she could still feel the fear that had struck her when she found Jeremy's bloody, unconscious body.

'But you got him to a hospital. Got him home. You saved him!'

'Eventually.' Pippa grinned. 'And I've never let him forget it.'

Tilly offered up her words of wisdom. 'You two will be friends forever,' she said, taking a drag and nodding wisely. 'That's an unbreakable bond, right there. No matter what happens in your lives, you will always have each other.' She squished her cigarette butt into the ground, then gave Pippa a sentimental smile. 'That's a beautiful thing you have. You're very lucky.'

She knew she was. She had saved his life, and he had been there for her when she'd needed him. Like when one dickhead hadn't wanted to take no for an answer and expressed his displeasure with a fist. Or the time she'd had a pregnancy scare. Or whenever she needed to get her thoughts straight, and the only way she could do that was to talk for hours and hours, right through the night. Jeremy had listened, given her advice, and stayed up with her even though he had to work the next morning. He was her best friend. He was even prepared to accept Leo.

'And that—' Pippa pointed her bottle to the other side of the crowd '—that beautiful young man there, he's my boyfriend. That's Leo.'

Leo must have sensed them looking because he lifted his head and looked in her direction. He didn't smile at first, but Pippa felt the pull of their connection. Then his mouth spread into a slow grin. A promise for later.

'Goddamn it, I can feel the sizzle from here,' Tilly said with a laugh. 'I can tell that you two are absolutely smitten.'

'Completely and utterly gone.' Pippa gave a small shake of her head and wrenched her focus back to her new friend. 'I'm head over heels,' she confided as she finished with the cigarette.

'He's from Brissie, too?'

Pippa shook her head. 'Met him here.'

'You've nabbed a Tassie boy.' Tilly pulled her mouth into a glum smile. 'And there are so few good ones. So, what happens next? How are you going to make this work? Are you going to stay here, or is he going to move up north?'

There were so many options for them, provided Leo was prepared to stand up to his parents. 'Maybe I'll stay here.' She said it without thinking, but she didn't mean settle down and throw out the anchor, but more like set up a base she could call home. It was certainly an option. Leo would go to uni, if that's what he decided, and she could write and take trips. She had no commitments in Brisbane. She had no home or job holding her in place. There was her family, but they understood her need for change. If her future was going to involve writing and travel, she could be based anywhere. Hobart and London both had airports, although London would be more exciting. Leo wasn't the only thing in her life that mattered, but if they could work out a way to be together it would be wonderful. With him, it was as though she'd turned a corner and could see a future filled with possibility.

'Good plan.' Tilly raised her bottle in salute. 'Next thing you know you'll be raising a tribe of little Tasmanians.'

Pippa snorted. 'Let's not get too carried away.'

Music suddenly burst across the party—the power must have finally been connected to the boom box. There were cheers, someone whistled loudly, then the volume was cranked and the beat was pulling people to their feet.

Tilly bounced up. 'I love this song,' she yelled, skipping over to her boyfriend, who looked as excited as a dog being dragged towards a bath.

Pippa dropped the cigarette butt into her empty bottle, set it on the ground and stood. It was time to shake and shimmy. She raised her arms, her hips moving, a double beat to each side. She had a lovely buzz from the wine cooler and the cigarette, and the music was lifting her, making her move.

The young crowd whooped. Mostly it was the girls who rushed to dance, but the party had picked up speed and a few guys were making an effort. Some had style, while others were happy to get a few laughs.

She caught Leo watching her. She tossed her hair and grinned, then beckoned. When he came to her, she was surprised—getting guys onto the dance floor was usually hard work. Then when they got there, they mostly wanted to grind themselves against her hips or arse. Leo stopped, close but not on top of her, and began to move, not overdoing it, not show-ing off. The boy could dance. Pippa reached out a hand, resting it on his chest, and let him lead.

*

Pippa didn't know how much time had passed, but when Rebecca tapped her on the shoulder, suggesting they should go, she shook her head and flung her arms high. 'No way, this party is just getting started.'

'We've been here for hours,' Rebecca shouted over the music and the noise of the crowd. 'And I'm leaving tomorrow.'

'Then you should be letting your hair down,' Pippa yelled back, grabbing Rebecca's hand and trying to get her to dance. 'It's your last night in Tassie. Go wild!'

Rebecca pulled her hand away. 'I want to be with Jeremy. I'm not going to see him again for god knows how long. He says he'll be away for a year.' Her face was taut with distress until anger took over. 'Why can't you think about someone other than yourself for one fucking night?'

What the hell? Pippa stopped dancing and stared. Rebecca never swore. Occasionally she'd say 'crap' or maybe 'bloody hell', never anything more. 'What have *I* done? If you want to be with Jeremy, go be with him. He's over there.' She pointed to a group sitting at a rickety wooden table. 'Be with him. Have fun. Laugh. Enjoy yourself.' Why wasn't Rebecca making the most of the night? The vibe was good. The people were friendly. Jeremy was right there. Okay, so, they weren't alone, but they were together. And, if they wanted, it wasn't hard to find private space at a party like this, especially one with paddocks next door.

Rebecca opened her mouth, then shut it, shaking her head with slow emphasis as though there was no point in arguing. In her mind, she was a superior woman displaying disappointment and disdain for an idiot beneath her standing. She began to walk away, then spun back around. 'You are such a self-centred bitch, aren't you?' she spat, a rush of fury escaping her tight-lipped control.

'Why are you angry with *me*?' Pippa was confused and annoyed.

Rebecca gave her a withering look, and then she was gone.

Pippa looked at Leo, who had witnessed the whole confrontation. 'Well, that was a bit unfair—I think she's a bit emotional,' she said, but she didn't laugh.

Rebecca's raw feelings were confronting. Her refusal to enjoy her last night in Tassie was silly and only hurt herself. Yet, with Leo now in her life, Pippa could understand her anguish.

'Should we go?' Pippa asked Leo.

He looked over at something. 'Not yet.'

Pippa followed his gaze. Rebecca had pulled Jeremy from his conversation and had him locked in a fierce grip, their mouths pressing together in a frantic kiss.

'Right,' said Pippa. 'Well, I'm sure Jeremy will come and get us when it's time.'

An hour later, as Pat Benatar sang about how they belonged, Leo and Pippa finally stopped dancing and sat down. Many of the partygoers were now shuffling and swaying, leaning against each other, holding each other up, as they howled along to the song. Needing a drink, Pippa headed to where several dented rubbish bins were serving as the help-yourself bar, and Leo followed her there. She peered into the murky soup of melted ice, disintegrating cardboard and half-submerged bottles. Her wine coolers were in there somewhere—or not. At parties like this, it was always a game of trust, hope, and grab-what-you-can.

'My West Coast is all gone,' she told Leo with a laugh. 'But I saw some Malibu in the kitchen.' She pulled out a dripping, half-empty bottle of Coke. 'Let's go fix a drink.'

He pulled a face. 'I'll stick to this.' He dunked his hand in and pulled out a stubbie. The label was long gone, floating somewhere in the grubby water. He picked up the thick twine tied to the handle of the bin and followed it down to the over-sized bottle opener at the other end.

'You don't even know what that is,' she said.

He popped off the top and took a swig. 'It's beer—don't care who made it,' he said, with a satisfied smack of his lips.

As they made their way back to the house, Pippa spotted Jeremy and Rebecca. The couple were near the fence, away from the light. Jeremy was slumped, his hands in his pockets, head down as though listening intently. Rebecca had her arms folded and was leaning towards him. Her chin jutted forward. As Pippa watched, Rebecca lifted a hand to swipe at her cheek, first one side and then the other.

Pippa tugged on Leo's arm and nodded in their direction. 'They don't look happy.'

As they watched, Jeremy pulled Rebecca towards him, her body slumping against his, her head on his shoulder. Her arms went around him, and it was obvious she was crying.

'Come on,' Pippa said to Leo, 'let's say goodnight to our new friends, then we'll leave.'

But it took them some time to get away. Someone had pulled out a camera and was trying to get group shots. Then Tilly had to find a pen and paper to write down her phone number, insisting she and Pippa should hang out again soon.

It was close to two-thirty when they got away. When they arrived at the car, there was a quick discussion about who should drive. In the end, Pippa got behind the wheel, arguing she hadn't drunk all that much. The drive home was slow and cautious, the car quiet, nobody talking much beyond the odd observation. 'It was great to meet locals.' 'The music was awesome.' 'Did everyone see the guy in the green pants throw up on his mate's shoes?'

Pippa was heading up the driveway when Rebecca spoke, her voice quiet. 'It's a long drive to the airport. I'll have to leave early, at eight. I would prefer it if just Jeremy takes me, so I'll say goodbye to you two before you go to bed.'

*

Rebecca and Pippa were in the lounge alone. They'd arrived back to find they'd forgotten to lock up the chickens, so now the boys were stumbling about with a torch and attempting to count wayward hens in a tree. Rebecca had insisted it was pointless, since dawn was only a few hours away. They hadn't listened. Pippa had a suspicion Jeremy was avoiding an emotional confrontation with his distraught girlfriend.

'Are you okay?' Pippa asked Rebecca, hoping to smooth away the spat they'd had at the party.

Rebecca was straightening the cushions on the sofa, stopping only when they were all aligned. 'Not really,' she said, finally looking at Pippa. 'I'm sorry for taking it out on you.'

'That's okay.'

'It wasn't your fault. Jeremy wanted to be there. I was a bit angry. And it's hard to be saying goodbye to him.'

'I get that.'

'The two of you have something that's not always easy for me to deal with. It gets the better of me sometimes.'

Guilt nudged Pippa's conscience. 'I should have given you both more space.'

Had she been a little selfish in wanting Jeremy's company even when he had a girlfriend? Yes, she had been. Unimpressed with Rebecca, she'd also been happy to push the girl's buttons.

'Yeah, a bit more space might have been nice,' Rebecca said quietly.

'Are you all packed?' Pippa asked after a few moments of silence.

'Yes. Of course.'

'Well, I guess I'll say goodbye then. I think I'm ready for bed.' She moved to give Rebecca a quick hug.

As they parted, Rebecca spoke quickly. 'Are you going to London next? Is that your plan, so you can meet up with Jeremy over there?'

'No. Well, I mean, not at the moment. I'm still working out what happens next.'

'Because he said you might, for that writing job.'

'Who knows? It's all up in the air. Leo and I haven't made any decisions.'

Rebecca was staring into the distance, sadness hanging over her like a dripping weight. 'Do you know why I'm not going?'

'To London?' Pippa shook her head. 'Your job?'

'Yes, that … and because Jeremy asked me not to. Not right now. He says he loves me but isn't ready to settle down. He needs to do this on his own. Then maybe, later …'

'Oh.' That would have hurt to hear.

'I've never been able to compete with you. But you know that, don't you?' Rebecca had returned to her issues with Pippa.

'What?' Pippa sighed and rubbed her eyes. 'No. That's not true.' She was tired, wanted a shower, and didn't need further admonishment from Rebecca.

'Saving his life, that's too big a thing. And he thinks you're so exciting. In his eyes you're some kind of wild-child goddess, all freedom and energy and sexiness.' Tears slid down her face. 'Most of the time, I do believe you only slept together the once, but even that was a big thing for him. For you it was just another night of fun. I can't compete with the myth of who you are. He compares every other woman to you, and it's not fair that you have that hold over him and are always right there. Right *there*. In the house. Together. Here. Together. I never stood a chance. I think you enjoy having that position in his life. You get off on it.'

Pippa could only stare at her for a moment. *Shit*. Rebecca was finally saying all the things she'd kept bottled up. 'Rebecca. I'm sorry I didn't make more room for you. Maybe you're right about that. But the rest of what you're saying? I don't have a hold over him. We have a history, that's all. And I definitely don't "get off" on having that relationship with him. None of that is true. We're friends, best friends, but that's all. I know he loves you. I'm sure you'll be together again.' There was no way Pippa was ever going to confess to the other occasions they'd got down and dirty.

'Ha.' Rebecca shook her head. 'The way things are going, you'll be with him again long before I am. You don't understand how it feels to know you're not enough—that I don't measure up to some idealised version of a pretty basic slut. And because of that I'm going to lose the person I love.'

Whoa. Rebecca had gone from an apology to name-calling in five minutes flat. Pippa's temper flared, but she knew Rebecca was hurting and just lashing out, venting all her long-held grudges. Nothing was going to be achieved by fighting back. 'Goodbye, Rebecca. I do hope you and Jeremy survive the long-distance thing. And I hope you get to see him again soon.' She turned to leave, catching the look of pain on the girl's face. Despite everything, Pippa's heart ached for her.

Pippa stood in the shower, the hot water easing some of her emotions. Slipping into bed, she waited for Leo to return from his chicken rescue mission.

Later the two of them lay wound together. Leo slid his fingers into her hair, getting them snagged in the tangles and then carefully easing them through before he started again, combing out the knots. 'I guess we'd better start thinking about what we'll do next,' he murmured.

'Big plans or little plans?' she asked, fighting sleep.

'The big ones.'

She smiled into her pillow, their future spreading out before them, their worlds settling into a single orbit. Unlike Jeremy and Rebecca, who were spinning away from each other.

'If you were leaving,' Pippa said, 'heading off on an adventure without me, I'd be pretty distraught too.'

'Would you?'

'You know I would. Don't ever abandon me and go running off to the other side of the world.' She wriggled against him, pulling his body over hers.

He propped himself up on his elbows. 'I promise,' he said, his face solemn. He sealed his commitment with a kiss.

Pippa softened under his weight, a sudden thought halting her progress towards passion. She pushed him up. 'You know, I wonder if Rebecca's anger has been made worse because she is losing Jeremy while I still have you. It's hard to see other people in love when the love of your life is leaving. Truthfully, I think she'd be happy if you were to throw me to the kerb. She'd like to see me hurting like she is.'

'That's not going to happen.' His mouth returned to hers, erasing all thoughts of Rebecca.

CHAPTER TWENTY-ONE

Sunday, 25 June 2017

Tom woke with his determination refreshed. Sure, the day before had been a bit of a ride, but he'd more or less got his head around the situation.

Thanks to Olivia, the easy part was planning how to move forward with the quest. With the information she'd got from Eloise, they had a new thread—one that had been easy to grasp and follow even late at night in his hotel room. Half an hour of dredging through the limited content about Leo Clifford's missing person case had finally delivered an old newspaper article with details about his family. Further digging revealed his parents were still active in the Hobart community, particularly the yacht club, and Tom had quickly compiled relevant contact details for Mr Angus Clifford. A photo in the newspaper article showed Leo had been a good-looking kid, and Tom could see there would have been a resemblance to his cousin, Jeremy. Tom had also confirmed the date of Leo's disappearance—last seen on the ninth of February 1986, at approximately 9 pm—a whole day after his dad had flown to Sydney. The unspoken, niggling worry he'd been keeping to himself was swept away. Jeremy had not been involved in whatever had happened.

A less straightforward task was working out how he felt about Olivia Indigo Haymers. He couldn't deny that her revelation had been a shock, one he'd been unable to hide. After he'd finished researching Leo's family, he'd looked her up. What he'd found made his experience with the dirt-digging gossip media seem like a sweet love fest.

He left the hotel early for a run, a habit he'd forced himself to develop to compensate for his long hours in front of screens. He crossed the main road and cut down closer to the water, pounding down the same boardwalks and small streets that he and Olivia had walked the night before. Even with the sky a moody grey, and the roads slick from overnight rain, he quickly warmed up. He passed over two moveable bridges that he presumed lifted to allow the trawlers and yachts on one side access to the open water on the other. A bit further along there were dozens of small yachts moored, a few larger boats for day tours, and the tall rigged ship he and Olivia had stood next to the night before. The same spot where he'd kissed her and where she had left him.

He didn't blame her for taking off. Her confession had surprised him, and he hadn't responded all that well. But any feelings he might have about her affair were quickly outweighed by his fury over what she'd been put through. Christ, no wonder she was holed up alone in an isolated country house. It wasn't only the vicious judgement and denigration of her by that actor's legions of fans, but the violation of her privacy by the woman who had pretended to be her friend. What kind of crazy person sets up cameras to film a friend having sex and then tries to use the footage for financial gain? He couldn't get his head around this betrayal of friendship. He'd come across the video and seen less than five seconds, scrambling to close the tab the moment it started to play—he did not need to see that.

Diving deeper, he had found voices raised in her defence, mainly the voices of feminists who pointed out the obvious. Why were the women always blamed in these cases? Why was the married man always cast as the hapless fool, lured astray by the conniving seductress? Put the focus back on the man, they argued. Hayden Carlyle had been more than capable of controlling his actions, of making choices around what was right and wrong. And Hayden Carlyle had held the position of power—not the assistant hotel manager.

Tom wondered if Olivia had listened to these arguments. It seemed more likely she had been completely overwhelmed by the negative commentary. Thinking of her initial reaction to him, and of her wariness around talking about her own life, he suspected the whole thing had crushed her confidence and trust in others. That would be completely understandable. Hell, after the drama of his mistake of a marriage, and the intrusion of the gutter-dwelling press, he had his own troubles with trust and confidence.

His run took him to the fringe of the inner city, to an old suburb of narrow streets and tightly packed cottages. A sign told him that if he kept going down the main road, he'd reach Sandy Bay. He stopped, hands on hips, as he caught his breath. Leo's parents lived in Sandy Bay, but Tom discarded the idea of turning up unannounced. He would ring them first, and he would ask Olivia to come along. She was the reason his search was progressing. It was only fair he offered her the chance to continue.

Who was he kidding? He wanted her with him.

But was she wanting to spend time with him? If he told her he'd dug around in her past, would that make her more or less comfortable with his company? Less, he imagined. He didn't think she'd moved to Tasmania for the scenery alone, as lovely as it was. And if she'd wanted him to know what had happened to her, she could have brought it up.

Tom would honour that and pretend he knew nothing. He would show her, indirectly, that he didn't think less of her for having been with Hayden Carlyle. Well, not such that he didn't want to see her again. Because, at the end of the day, Olivia had impressed him greatly.

CHAPTER TWENTY-TWO

Monday, 26 June 2017

The post office was busy, or as busy as Olivia imagined a rural post office could be. Five customers chatted among themselves while they waited their turn at the counter. Olivia stood to one side, ostensibly browsing the shelves as she battled the urge to flee.

Since Saturday night her head had spun on its never-ending cycle of *what if* and regret. Last night, tossing and turning in bed, she'd grown fed up with her insomnia and got up to half-heartedly do some yoga. It must have helped, because on climbing back into bed she'd finally fallen asleep. Her last thoughts had been a determination to follow through on her offer to help Tom. The kiss was a one-off, a delicious reminder that there was life to be had beyond her dramas. She would consider it the encouragement she needed and leave it at that. Only a week ago she'd screamed at the fumbling stranger at her door to leave her alone. It was ridiculous to be letting herself get caught up in the pleasant buzz he had since brought her. He was lovely, but she didn't know him and didn't need him—despite how her body reacted to his proximity.

She'd said she would help find Pippa, and she would. Getting involved in the quest was good for her, and she was enjoying being useful again. It was confirmation she still had worth.

'Hello, love, sorry to keep you waiting.' Wendy was beaming at her while waving a hand to cut through her distraction.

She looked around. She was the only customer left. Her ruse of flicking through a book on raising happy chickens had worked too well. 'Hi, Wendy, how are you?' She stepped up to the counter, took her mail from the postmistress's outstretched hand and shoved it in her bag.

'Good, good. How are you coping with winter?' Wendy picked up a cup of tea that must have been quite cold, given how long she'd been serving the folk of Devils Bay.

They chatted for a bit about the weather, gumboots, and the benefits of merino wool thermals. Then, realising she had a brief window before other residents wandered in, Olivia put on a smile. 'Can I ask you about some local history?'

'Of course! What would you like to know?' Wendy's still-beaming face was encouraging.

'After you mentioned him, I became quite curious about the missing boy. It must've been a significant thing when he—was it Leo?—when he disappeared.'

'My goodness, was it ever. I wasn't living here back then, but I've heard all about it, many times. It's a bit hard to tell what's truth and myth and guesswork. Are you going to try and solve the mystery?' She raised a sceptical eyebrow.

'No. Well, not the mystery of Leo. That man, the one who turned up at the house … he's sort of connected to that story.'

'Is he?' Wendy sounded dubious. 'How's that then?'

'His father was house-sitting for Eloise at that same time. He was there with a good friend, a girl called Pippa.'

Wendy pondered this, appearing to think back over the stories she'd heard. 'Pippa? I haven't heard of a Pippa, but that sounds about right. Leo was from Hobart, I believe. His girlfriend was staying at the house, and there were a couple of others who were house-sitting for Eloise—they were relatives or friends or some such of hers, I think, in their late teens or early twenties. And they weren't from Tassie. You're saying one of those kids was this Tom fellow's father?' When Olivia nodded, Wendy's expression went from being doubtful to alive with interest. 'Isn't that interesting. What's he hoping to find out?'

'His father recently passed away. Turns out the man left something to be delivered to this girl Pippa. They'd lost contact over the years. Tom's just trying to honour his father's wish.'

Olivia had noticed a little knowing smile on Wendy's face at the mention of Tom's name. Had Olivia's tone given her feelings away?

'It sounds like this friend of Tom's father might have been Leo's girlfriend, the one who saw him last.'

Olivia nodded. 'Eloise told me she stuck around for two years after he vanished, waiting for him to come back.'

'Actually, yes, that does ring a bell. I think someone told me she stayed here until she had the baby, then for a year or so after that.'

What the hell?

'A baby?' That hadn't been reported anywhere. Why hadn't Eloise mentioned it?

'Yep. That's what makes the story so tragic. Not that a boy disappearing isn't tragic—of course it is. But when there's a love story *and* a baby, I don't know, it seems all the more poignant, don't you think?'

'Yes, it does.' Was this an important detail? Did it give them a new lead? Was the baby definitely Leo's?

'I tell you what, if you want to get a first-hand account, go and pop in on Tilly—you met her the other day. I think she'll be happy to talk to you about all this, given the connection with your new friend, and that you're living in the house and all that. She'd be home now at the old schoolhouse, and she's always open to visitors. I even think she knew the girlfriend … She'll know something about this Pippa you're looking for. Might even have met Leo, come to think of it.'

Biting down on her grin as she left the post office, Olivia had a sense that the mystery was untangling.

*

Olivia sat at the well-worn wooden table and dug a fork into her second slice of lemon syrup cake. A pot-belly fire was keeping the kitchen toasty, and a speaker, hidden somewhere among the piles of books and magazines and half-finished knitting, was softly playing Janis Joplin.

'You'd never know it was gluten-free, would you?' Tilly poured tea from a pot and slid the pottery cup across the table. 'And the eggs are from my chooks, the lemons from my own tree.'

'It's really, really good,' Olivia said. And it was—the moist, tangy cake was divine.

'Thanks. I do love to get into the kitchen.' She hooted with amusement. 'As you can see.' She waved an arm to indicate the wire rack where fresh biscuits were cooling, the stacks of cooking books, and the large glass jars of ingredients still sitting on the bench. It was a charming, chaotic mess. *Tom would've loved this*, Olivia thought. This was exactly what he'd been expecting, right down to the crocheted chicken that covered the teapot. She wished now she'd invited him along.

'So, anyway, as I was saying,' Tilly said, 'Pippa and I became proper friends. Two waddling knocked-up girls with nothing in common besides morning sickness and backache and being stuck in this tiny place. I had my new hubby, Steve, but she was pretty much on her own.'

'She must've been a bit lost,' Olivia said. 'With her boyfriend missing and being away from home.'

'And pregnant. Wasn't that a story!' Tilly rolled her eyes. 'She was quite the talk of the village. I mean, who was she? This girl from Brisbane who nobody knew. She became the centre of the action when Leo disappeared, and it wasn't like the locals knew him either. Anyway, the police kept wanting to talk to her.'

'Did they believe she'd had something to do with whatever happened to him?'

'No, I don't think they did. But she was the last one to report seeing him, so I guess they wanted to get as much detail as they could.'

'Did she talk about it with you?'

'Eventually. I'd met her and Leo and Jeremy and the other girl—what's-her-name—right before it all happened. They came to a local birthday party—it was quite a bash. Then I didn't see her again until a while after Leo went missing.' Tilly stopped to take a mouthful of cake. 'There's more there if you want.' She nudged the cake stand towards Olivia.

'I think two pieces might be enough. Who was this other girl?' Olivia was trying to keep track of who was who in this story.

'Jeremy's girlfriend. I'm pretty sure she'd come down from Brisbane with him and Pippa. The three of them had been looking after Eloise's place, then Pippa had met Leo.'

So, Jeremy *had* been at the house with a girlfriend, but she hadn't been Pippa. Olivia was impatient to fill Tom in, regardless of what he might be thinking of her.

'Anyway,' Tilly continued, 'I think Pippa hid there for a while after Leo vanished—at the house, I mean, with Eloise. But about three months later we crossed paths. Honestly, I was surprised she was still here. We started hanging out a bit. She did talk about him and about what had happened, but not a lot, and I didn't want to probe too much. You could see it had really affected her. I tell you what, she loved that boy. And in all the time I knew her, she never gave up believing he would come back. Amazing, isn't it, how people can go on keeping faith, even when there's nothing to support their hope?'

'I guess letting go of that hope would be to admit the worst possible scenario.'

'It was so sad. Leo was a gorgeous guy. Good-looking in a rugged, fresh-air and open-sea kind of way. Came from a solid family, we were told. He was a bit intense, a bit quiet—not like Jeremy at all, from what little I saw. But then Pippa seemed to be able to make him lighten up. You should have seen them dancing at that party. In among all these uncoordinated kids, who were jumping and bumping and showing off, those two were brilliant. I know it's strange that detail has stuck in my mind, but I remember sitting there watching them, wishing my guy could dance with me like that. They were so good together.'

'Did you know Leo and Jeremy were cousins?'

'I don't remember it being mentioned at the party. I think I found out later. But you could tell they were related.'

'They looked alike?'

'Sure did.' Tilly sat up straighter, delight on her face. 'I tell you what, I think I've got some photos around somewhere. Do you want to see them?'

A thrill whipped through Olivia. 'Yes, please!'

'Okay. Stay put, eat some more cake, and I'll see if I can get my hands on them.'

As Olivia waited, she went to the window to look at a garden that wouldn't have been out of place in *Country Style*. There were raised garden beds with weathered timber edges, willow teepees waiting for the next planting of tomatoes, and a chicken house with a noticeable lean and a red door. A tiny blue-chested bird bounced across the worn red bricks of the garden path, getting ever closer to the border collie sprawled in the sun.

'Found them!' Tilly came back into the room, a sagging shoebox under her arm and a bunch of photos in one hand. She put everything on the table. 'I've been meaning to stick all the old photos in albums.' She laughed, spreading out half a dozen prints. 'Been meaning to do it for fifteen years. Still, I found what I was looking for, so my system must be working.'

Olivia sat next to the woman and peered at the picture she was holding. It showed a group of young people, all facing the camera. Those on the outside were leaning towards the centre, making sure they were in frame. Most had their arms lifted, big smiles on their faces. Everyone had a drink. There were eight in the shot.

Tilly tapped a finger on one boy. 'Jeremy,' she said.

Nice guy, was the first thing Olivia thought. Tom's father had been a good-looking young man, neat and wholesome in his collared shirt, even with a beer held high and his mouth wide open as though he'd been caught yelling out to the photographer. She could see hints of Tom in his features. Beside him was a blonde girl with a pink polo shirt and a classic eighties perm. She didn't look happy.

'That's his girlfriend. Damn, still can't remember her name. Rachel? Rita? No, Rebecca! I remember now. She introduced herself, and I called her Bec. She corrected me and said Rebecca, not Bec or Becca. She was a little stuck up. I mean, nice and all, but wound a bit tight. Come to think of it, she and Pippa had an argument that night.' Tilly glanced over the other photos. 'Haven't looked at these pictures in ages. Amazing how the details start to come back. Anyway. Jeremy. Rebecca.' She tapped as she spoke. 'And that's Leo. And that's Pippa.'

Olivia had already picked Pippa from the line-up and guessed the boy with her was Leo. He looked a little like Jeremy, but he was blonder, his hair messier and longer, and he seemed taller. He was staring straight at the photographer, a small blissful smile on his face. His arms were wrapped around Pippa, who was leaning back against his chest, one arm lifted up, her hand behind his neck. Her head was tilted to rest on his collarbone. Her smile made her seem as though she was the holder of some exquisite secret. She was wearing a black tank top, a red bandana around one wrist, and large hoop earrings but no other jewellery. *A woman who knew the power of her looks*, Olivia thought, *and was with the man she wanted*.

While everyone else in the photo whooped it up, Leo and Pippa seemed to be in their own world, a space only big enough for two. But there had been four people living in Eloise's house.

Had there been an uncomfortable dynamic? How had Jeremy come to have photos of Pippa naked in bed, pictures he'd held on to for the rest of his life?

'Jeremy left for England, didn't he?' Olivia asked. 'Must have been after this party.'

Tilly made a contemplative sound. 'I can't remember when he left. It was before Leo vanished, and that was about two or three weeks after the party. I remember Rebecca left first—or she was going to. She had to get back to Brissie. I think it was one of the things she and Pippa fought about, not that I can remember the details.'

'But Jeremy wasn't here when Leo disappeared?' Hadn't Tom said there was the itinerary for his father's trip in with the photos and letter? Had he brought it with him?

'No. I remember that, because of course everyone was talking about what had happened. It was mentioned quite a bit that Leo's cousin Jeremy was in London, and the question was whether the police would talk to him over there or whether he would come back.'

'But he didn't come back.'

'Nope. Pippa talked about it once or twice, how she couldn't believe he didn't return when he heard what was going on. They'd been friends for a long time, you see. They were really close. They'd been flatmates in Brisbane. And she'd once saved his life when they were travelling, got him to a hospital or something like that. Anyway, I think that was one of the reasons she stopped writing to him, because he wouldn't cut his trip short to be with her when she needed him. She was terribly hurt and angry.'

Olivia picked up another photo. 'Then she found out she was pregnant.' With Leo's baby, or could it have been Jeremy's? Was his absence an avoidance of a responsibility he didn't want? Or was she just letting her imagination run a bit wild?

The picture was dated *20 August '86* and showed Tilly and Pippa, their stomachs rounded, sitting together outside the Devils Bay general store. Tilly was beaming, and she had on a bright pink beanie with a pompom and a matching knitted scarf, her hands resting over her belly. Pippa was much less effusive, her eyes sad. She had no hat but was wearing a rather ugly corduroy jacket over a large sweatshirt and tracksuit pants. She was staring at a point beyond the photographer, as though she'd been asked to smile but couldn't quite make it happen.

'Did you keep in touch with Pippa when she left here?' Olivia knew it was a long shot.

'I did for a bit. But we were both so busy with bubs and life and stuff. And it wasn't like we had email in those days. Finding time to write and post a letter was hard, and long-distance phone calls cost a mint. Then we moved to a new house. She was back in Brisbane, and the connection faded. I tried looking her up on Facebook once—there was nothing under Pippa French, or Penelope French for that matter.'

'Penelope French?' Excitement sparked through Olivia's body.

'Yep, not that anyone ever used anything but Pippa.'

*

Olivia let herself into her house, Brian nearly tripping her as he wound his way around and between her legs. She scooped him up for a quick smooch before searching out her laptop.

As always when she went online, she thought fleetingly of checking up on Hayden. In the beginning she couldn't help herself. There had been pictures of him with his gorgeous, apparently forgiving wife—she had stuck by him for the first year after the affair was outed, then dumped him after the trial had finished. Oh, how the masses had wept. 'Poor, sweet woman,' they'd clamoured, 'her marriage destroyed by that hideous slut.' 'Hayden, you fool,' they'd cried, 'you were led astray. How *could* you? Especially with *that*, with *her*.'

Olivia had become an expert in self-discipline. No Instagram-stalking. No googling. No going anywhere near the *Daily Mail* in case Hayden was featured in their endless parades of celebrity sightings.

Her mobile rang as she began her search. It was Tom, but she wasn't ready to take his call. He could be ringing to add his commentary to the mess she'd made of her life—or he could just be wanting to know if she'd found any information about his quest. Either way, he would have to wait a little longer. She had so much to share, but first she wanted one more detail.

She wanted to be able to tell him how to find Penelope French.

CHAPTER TWENTY-THREE

Olivia's phone rang, Tom's name on the screen for the third time in an hour. He was certainly persistent.

Two hours of searching, and she was no closer to Penelope 'Pippa' French. The internet was meant to be a bottomless pit of information where anyone could be found—which obviously wasn't true. Penelope French did not exist online, or not the Penelope French who had once lived in this house. There was a florist in New York who was fifteen years too young, an academic specialising in Scottish myths who was ten years too old, and a five-year-old beauty pageant queen from Illinois.

The phone kept ringing, but she wasn't ready to speak with him. If she was going to hear condemnation in his voice, she wanted the conversation to focus on what she'd achieved.

The ringing stopped. Thirty seconds later her phone pinged.

Hope you got home ok. Thanks for a great night!!! We should do it again soon. Btw I've found Leo's family here in Hobart! Would really like you to come meet them with me tomorrow, think I need moral support. These people are family, aren't they? Great-aunt and great-uncle I guess. Please come. Tom x

Flopping back in her chair, Olivia read the message twice. The jaunty, enthusiastic tone was not at all what she'd been expecting. And signing off with a kiss? Had he not looked her up? Was he not freaked out by what she'd told him?

Okay. *You can do this,* she thought. *You've been through worse.*

After grabbing the phone, she pushed the chair back, walked down to the lounge and stood at the windows. A sea eagle glided upwards on a current of air. The Bruny ferry crossed to the island. A dozen tiny birds bounced on the terrace.

She tapped the screen. He answered immediately. 'Olivia. Hi. How are you?'

Breathe out, breathe in. 'Sorry, I was out walking.' The white lie made her grimace. 'I just got your message. That's great news.'

'In the end, it wasn't that hard. Leo's father Mr Angus Clifford is on a yacht club committee, and they kindly post PDFs of their meeting minutes, including committee members' mobile numbers.' He sounded jubilant, without a hint of judgement.

'That's fabulous.' It seemed that if they concentrated on the quest, they would be fine. 'I've got something for you too.' The thrill of discovery kicked back in. 'I found out Pippa had a baby in 1986.'

There was a pause, then he exhaled loudly. 'A baby?'

Olivia turned from the view and sank to the floor, her back against the glass. 'Yes. I was speaking to a woman who met

Pippa and Leo at a party, and she stayed friends with Pippa after Leo disappeared. According to her, Leo and Pippa were very much in love.'

'Did she say Leo was the father?'

Did he have the same thoughts she'd had? 'Not exactly, but from what she was saying about Pippa and how the two of them were as a couple, we could assume that he was.'

'But it could have been Dad's baby. Right? I mean, it's a possibility. They obviously had an intimate relationship.'

Olivia thought back over Tilly's recollection of Pippa. She had been emphatic about the baby being Leo's. But that wasn't enough. They couldn't be certain one way or the other. 'Yes, it's possible.'

'So, the three of them were at the house, and Pippa got pregnant—'

Olivia interrupted. 'Actually, there were four of them here. Your dad had a girlfriend who was also staying at the house that summer. Did he ever mention a Rebecca?'

'No.' Tom seemed to be thinking it over. 'Never. Are you sure?'

'Yes. I even saw a photo of the four of them at the party. Leo and Pippa. Jeremy and Rebecca. Apparently, Rebecca left to return to Brisbane a day or so afterwards. Also, while they were at this party, the two girls had a bit of an argument. I have no idea what it was about.'

Two couples. But Jeremy had kept photos—including intimate photos—of Pippa, not Rebecca. Throw in a pregnancy and a missing person, and it was clear something complicated had happened that summer.

'Did you get a copy of the photo?' Tom asked. 'I'd love to see it.'

'Shit. Sorry, I didn't. But I'm sure I can go back to Tilly and get one.' Damn. She really should've thought of that. Of course Tom would want to see the picture.

'You know, I've never actually seen a photo of my dad as a young man or even as a kid.'

'That's never struck you as odd?'

'Never really thought about it. He told me he didn't bring any when he came across.'

'But he had those photos of Eloise and Pippa?'

Tom contemplated this for a moment. 'They were taken— and developed—right before he moved. I guess he had them when he flew over.'

'Makes sense.'

'I wonder what this all means,' Tom said thoughtfully. 'What the hell happened? I don't know how all these details fit together, or how it's going to help me find Pippa, but it does feel kind of important. Don't you think?'

'I agree. But I do have another detail that might just help. Pippa's full name was Penelope French. I'd assumed Pippa was short for Phillipa, but apparently she was a Penelope.'

'You absolutely brilliant woman.' His enthusiasm made her smile. 'You'd think Dad could've added that wee detail to the envelope he wanted delivered,' he added drily.

'You'd think so. But before you get too excited, I've searched online and come up with zilch.'

He sighed. 'Of course, that would've been too easy, wouldn't it? Still, I'm sure it will help, knowing exactly who we're looking for. Can I say, Olivia, you are a godsend. I mean that. I don't know where I'd be without your help. Thank you. Sincerely, thank you.'

Her fingers traced her mouth. 'I'm happy to help. It's actually sort of … fun.'

'I agree. A bit frustrating, but I think we're up for the challenge.'

We? Olivia liked the way he automatically included her in his plans.

'Hey, you said the two girls argued at the party. Any idea what about?' He had returned to musing about the dramas of the mysterious foursome.

Olivia thought it through. 'Jealousy? Maybe Rebecca had issues with the relationship between Jeremy and Pippa. Or maybe Pippa was the jealous one. Or maybe it had nothing to do with the boys and was something trivial, like who'd borrowed clothes without asking.'

'Don't you have the feeling we're being sucked into a bigger story?' he said, with both excitement and trepidation in his voice. 'I mean, the priority is delivering the envelope, but I'd love to discover how it all fits together …'

'And to know what happened to Leo,' she finished for him. 'Me too.'

'So, you'll come tomorrow?'

Olivia was well and truly entangled in Tom's quest. She hesitated for only a second. 'Yes, okay, I will. Text me the details.'

'Excellent. And, also, I feel I should thank you properly.' There was an undercurrent of suggestion. 'But I promise I won't kiss you inappropriately … not unless you want me to.'

She gave a short, breathy laugh. This was nuts—he wanted to kiss her? Even if, by some amazing chance, he still didn't know the full story, she had admitted to being an adulteress. For someone with strong feelings and bad experiences around infidelity, he was being incredibly non-judgemental. 'Well, let's see if we get anywhere first,' she said lightly, not knowing how to respond to his suggestion.

'I have a good feeling about tomorrow,' he said. 'Although, it might not be all smooth sailing. The Cliffords did lose their son, and talking to us might not be easy for them. Still, I do think we're going to make progress.'

'Well, fingers crossed they're helpful,' she said. 'They hopefully know where she is—I mean, chances are Pippa's baby is their grandchild.'

'Or my half-sibling.' His energy had dimmed a little, as though he was starting to realise that the answers he got might not be a sweet ending to a sad love story.

*

The stack of split logs beside the fireplace was getting low, so Olivia made a couple of trips out into the cold to fill her arms with wood, then stoked the fire till it was burning fiercely. She headed to the kitchen to see if there was anything even slightly appetising, settling for one of her last frozen meals. While she waited for the microwave to work its magic, she fed Brian and poured a small glass of wine. Then she took her dinner and drink to the table.

The laptop was still there, and for a moment she contemplated going online. Was she still number one in the scandal department? Probably not. In the way of these things, there was likely some fresh victim being sacrificed to public outrage. Scandals erupted and faded, and maybe hers was fading from people's memories. She patted the closed lid of the laptop. 'Time will heal,' she murmured, almost convinced it was possible.

Her bag sat beside the laptop, and as she finished off the edible but uninspiring salmon and rice, she pulled out the mail she'd collected that morning. There was an update from one of the animal protection groups she supported and a statement from her insurance company. Then she pulled out a small but weighty padded bag, redirected from Sydney. She opened it and slid out a folded sheet of white paper and what looked like a black box. But it wasn't a box. The rectangular chunk of plastic fit in her hand but was heavy for its size.

There was a small logo on one side, which told her nothing. At one end there was a USB charging port and what looked like a SIM card slot. She turned it over. A tiny white note with red writing and a sprinkle of glued-on glitter was stuck on with clear tape.

Found you!

Fear surged from her gut to her head. She pushed back the chair and stood up before she even processed what was happening.

What was this thing? A bomb? Had Leena sent her a mail bomb?

Olivia dashed from the table down into the lounge, the thing in one hand. Ominous. Threatening. The French doors were locked. She yanked at the bolts, top and bottom, and wrestled them free. Pushed open the doors and ran to the edge of the terrace.

She threw the device, her shoulder wrenching with the effort. It bounced on the grass, twice. Tumbled further down the slope. Sent two wallabies loping into the bush.

She waited, breathing hard. Nausea sat at the back of her throat.

Blackbird song trilled through the darkening dusk. There were snaps and thuds in the bush as the wildlife stirred. The air was cold. Her socks were wet. White puffs of breath escaped her mouth as she panted, her body shivering from the inside out.

She could see the thing where it had come to rest. She didn't want to go near it. Instead, she crept back inside, locking the doors behind her. She peeled off her socks as she huddled in front of the fire. After waiting till she had regained feeling in her fingers and the trembling had stopped, she retrieved the letter that had come with the parcel.

Here is my gift to you. Or to me, really.

This is a tracker. Activated. And I know exactly where it is. Where you are. I want you to remember that I'm smarter than you.

This will be a very interesting piece of information to have. Sadly, though, I may not be able to come visit—there are conditions with this so-called suspended sentence. And you know how much I hate rules. Oh, don't worry, I'm not going to send someone to negotiate on my behalf. Not yet.

Instead, here is a little incentive for you to visit me. I have a video of you and lover-boy. No, it's not the version they fussed about in court. This is take 2. Same place, different time, different angle. Personally, I think it's a much better performance all round. The viewer gets to see sooo much more. Not of him. But of you. Girl, you need to get yourself in shape!

If you don't want this out there in the world, then you'd better get back to Sydney. Before the end of June. You have my number. And you'd better have the money you owe me—the money you were paid.

And if you don't do what you're told …
Well, I know where you are.
Leena xx
PS. Take this to the police and I WILL send out the video.
One touch of a button and BOOM … you're back in the spot-
light for all the wrong reasons.

*

It was well after 7 am when pink and orange finally seeped into the grey sky. Olivia watched with the desperate appreciation of someone emerging from an underground bunker. She hadn't slept—well, not much. And when she had, it had been shallow and short, doing nothing to refresh or ease her mind. Every word of Leena's threat was stabbing into her brain.

There were things Olivia could do to defend herself. There were laws against revenge porn and secretly filming someone in an intimate act. Leena was risking a return to jail. But only after the release of the video, and by then it would be too late.

Asking her dad to line up his lawyers again was out of the question. His acute disappointment and ensuing distance from her had been too painful. But if she did nothing, Olivia Haymers would once again be bouncing naked on the screens of Australia, and probably the rest of the world. She couldn't live with that again. She *couldn't*. It was all well and good for a celebrity to leak a carefully choreographed sex tape, but raw footage of unsuspecting participants was completely different. Olivia's default presumption was that everyone she met had seen her at her most exposed. That level of humiliation and shame was corrosive. It ate away at her ability to interact, to make eye contact, to exist in the world with confidence.

In the hour before dawn, she'd given up trying to sleep and come out to curl up on the sofa. Now she dropped the blanket from around her shoulders and shifted Brian off her lap. She needed a shower—and coffee. In two hours she was meant to be meeting Tom. Not going with him to the Cliffords wasn't an option, even though the weight of dread made every move an effort. A headache pressed at her temples and behind her eyes.

She needed a friendly face and based on their conversation yesterday, against all odds it seemed Tom would deliver. Perhaps he would open his arms and offer his personal space and warmth. A great hug would be sublime. His solid chest would be the perfect place to nestle. Then again, the connection they'd experienced the other night would likely disperse in the light of day and the absence of whisky, in which case she would happily settle for a non-judgemental, welcoming smile and a conversation that would take her away from her troubles.

Under the hot water her body went limp. Her mind was sluggish after hours of tramping over the past and present. There was a certain irony to being on the receiving end of one of Leena's schemes. Obviously, blackmail was her favourite strategy. Her attempt to extort money from Hayden had certainly been slick and audacious.

He'd been in Thailand filming an action blockbuster. Something big and international that would push his star even higher. He'd persuaded Olivia to take time off work to fly to Bangkok. Having her waiting in a hotel suited him. Not his hotel, of course, but something accessible. The situation was discreet. His wife was at home in Byron Bay.

For the first couple of days Olivia hadn't seen him. She'd wandered the shops, swum in the pool, and generally swanned. It was always a pleasurable change to be the guest and not the staff. Lying in the enormous bed at night, a panorama of city lights wrapping around her, she'd been exhilarated. Weeks earlier she'd come so close to ending it with Hayden. But, ensconced in exotic luxury, she was glad Leena had convinced her to continue the affair.

On the third morning, the in-room phone rang. She danced across the carpet, sure it would be Hayden planning when and how they'd meet. *Here,* she thought. *Right here, with room service and champagne. Let's make the most of this suite!*

'Olivia, lovely girl, guess who!'

'Leena!' She didn't stop to think why Leena was ringing her at the hotel—she was just glad to hear the voice of the one person she could talk to about her lover. 'You won't *believe* this place. He's truly outdone himself this time.' Olivia sank into the sofa cushions and put her feet on the coffee table.

'What floor are you on?'

'Thirty! The views are incredible.'

'Well then, you'll have to come down and get me, because my little ol' key card won't get me all the way up there.'

Olivia stopped, suddenly confused. 'Are you here?'

'Indeed I am. I've come to your rescue, you poor deprived thing. I've booked a room, although mine sounds a lot less fabulous.'

'Rescue?' Olivia laughed. 'Oh honey, I *do not* need rescuing.'

'Then I'll hang out with you until his royal highness gives you the pleasure of his company.'

Olivia rushed down to the foyer, Leena throwing her arms around her in greeting. They chatted and laughed as they rode the lift up, planning cocktails and shopping trips.

Leena was suitably impressed with the room. She inspected the lounge, bedroom and bathroom, marvelling at the decor and view. 'This will do,' she said.

'Yes, it will do just fine.' Olivia sighed from where she'd thrown herself on the bed.

In hindsight Leena's comment was obvious, but at the time it had meant nothing. Olivia had honestly thought her friend was there to keep her company and have some fun.

At the trial an expert had talked about surveillance cameras. They were tiny. Remotely activated. Easy to install when Olivia was in the shower or down at the day spa. The footage was remarkably clear, despite the low lights and the participants being oblivious to their roles.

Leena's scheme had been dependent on Olivia's trust, but also on Hayden's wealth and his need to keep his exploits secret. Image was everything to that man.

This time, however, Olivia wasn't simply the means to an end, she was the end itself. She had no choice. Tomorrow she would go to Sydney.

CHAPTER TWENTY-FOUR

Wednesday, 22 January 1986

'Do you miss her?' Pippa asked.

A soft rain was falling, the day grey and cool, and she and Jeremy were stuck inside. She was sprawled on the sofa with Honey. Jeremy was on the floor, propped up on a comfortable pile of cushions. For the first time in weeks, it was only the two of them. Leo had left that morning, summoned home for an important family lunch. He had wanted Pippa to go with him, but his parents had insisted that their wedding anniversary was an occasion for family and close friends only. Leo had been quietly furious but hadn't wanted to challenge their position. Pippa had calmed him, saying it wasn't her scene, that it would be easier for him without her there. Truthfully, she was relieved not to be spending a day on her best behaviour trying to impress unpleasant people who had a seriously limited opinion of her abilities and value.

'Jeremy?' she prompted. In the three days since Rebecca had left, he'd been quieter, more introspective.

'Yeah. I guess so.' He had a bowl of chips balanced on his stomach and was methodically eating them one by one. 'It's strange not having her here.'

'You "guess so"?' Not heartbroken then.

'No, that didn't come out right. I do miss her, very much. But it's more than that. Saying goodbye meant things have changed.' He picked up another chip, considered it, and dropped it back in the bowl. 'And things are going to change even more, in a big way. Rebecca leaving, me being on my own, has brought home how close I am to altering my whole life.'

'You don't think you altered your life when you, I don't know, quit your job, sold most of what you owned, packed a bag and came down here? Because all of that feels like a significant life change.'

'Yeah, of course. But being down here has given me a brilliant bit of breathing space before the big leap, a lovely chunk of limbo. Over the last few weeks I haven't actually given much thought to what will come next—living for today and all that. It's been a great summer. Now it's about to get serious. Seeing how upset Rebecca was, it made everything more real. Make sense?'

It did. 'Another step closer to a whole new life in a different country. A new job. A life without me hogging the bathroom. A life without your girlfriend there ... wait, is she still your girlfriend?'

'Yes! I mean, technically, yes.'

'They say long distance is hard work.'

'Yeah. She's talking about coming over for a holiday in June.'

'Great, that gives you something to look forward to.' Pippa carefully shifted Honey to one side and sat up. 'Do you want a drink?'

'Can of Coke, if there's some left. Thanks.'

She moved to the kitchen. 'Geez, it's cold. We might have to put the fire on. So much for summer.' Leo had given her one of his sweatshirts. She'd had to roll up the cuffs, but it was snuggly warm with a faint smell of his body and salt water. He wasn't getting it back.

She took two cans from the fridge. As she was tugging off the ring pull, the phone rang.

'That'll be lover-boy saying he's escaped the family asylum,' called Jeremy as he headed towards his bathroom.

Pippa picked up the receiver. The phone was on the wall next to the kitchen, and she was able to stretch the curled cord till she was sitting at the dining table. 'Hello, this is the Devils Bay Den of Ill-Repute,' she answered. 'How may we corrupt you today?'

She'd sung out her greeting before she registered the long-distance beeps. Not Leo, then. Oops.

'Hello,' she said again, normally this time.

'Is that Pippa?' A clipped voice. A woman with a purpose.

'Yes.'

'This is Angela, Jeremy's mother.'

'Hello. Sorry about the greeting, I was expecting someone else.'

There was a pause. 'Is Jeremy with you?'

'He's in the bathroom … Shall I get him to call you back or are you happy to wait?'

'No.' Her answer was abrupt. 'I wanted to speak to you. And I need you to not tell Jeremy I've called. Do you think you can do that?' Angela had never been the most vivacious person, but today she sounded anxious—and angry, as though she was about to launch into a lecture.

'Okay. Can you hold on?' When Jeremy wandered back into the lounge, Pippa walked as far as the cord would stretch and put her hand over the mouthpiece. 'Hey, Jeremy?'

'Yeah? How's Leo?'

'Leo? Oh, he's great. Look, could you do me a favour? It's stopped raining, and Honey needs to go for a walk ...'

He put his hands on his hips and gave her a reprimanding look mixed with raised eyebrows. 'When did you get so bossy? Next you'll be expecting me to make you dinner. You're with me, Honey. Let's go, girl.' He pushed open the doors to the terrace, Honey trotting after him. 'Wait.' He sprinted back up to where Pippa was standing and grabbed one of the cans. 'You want me out of here just so you can talk sexy,' he called as he headed out the door.

Pippa took her hand from the phone. 'What's going on?' she asked.

There was a huff of air before Angela spoke. 'I've had a visit from Rebecca.' This wasn't a surprise: Jeremy had given his girlfriend some things to take back to Brisbane, including a gift for his mother. 'She said you're hanging around with my sister's son. Is that right?' The word 'sister' came out half choked.

Bloody Rebecca. She couldn't leave it alone, could she?

Pippa sat down, her back rigid, her fingers tight around the hard plastic of the phone. Her guard was up, the accusatory tone making her wary. 'Yes. His name is Leo, and—'

'Stop seeing him. Right now.'

'What?'

'You should never have brought him anywhere near Jeremy. Rebecca told you not to, didn't she? But you did.'

Pippa closed her eyes. Rebecca was an interfering, self-righteous cow. 'I met a guy who turned out to be Jeremy's cousin. There is no harm done here, Angela. The two of them get along great. They're friends.'

'You don't know what you've done. But I'm asking you to please remove that boy from your life, at least until Jeremy leaves.' Her voice was rising, agitated, as though she was afraid. 'Actually, you can't see him again. At all. Ever. Because Jeremy will come back eventually, and if that boy is still around … well, he can't be. You and Jeremy are so close, if that boy is in your life then he will be in Jeremy's life too. And that can't, *can't* happen. It will end in disaster—'

'Angela!' Pippa had to be loud to cut through the anguished, confusing words. 'What are you talking about? What's wrong?'

The woman didn't answer the question, continuing with barely a pause for breath. 'It's too late to undo. But those boys should not be together. Do you understand?'

'No. I don't. You aren't making sense.' Pippa's heart was racing—the panic in Angela's voice and her rapid, illogical demands were scaring her.

There was a sob. Shuddery, gulping breaths.

'Angela?' Pippa needed to make the woman explain what she was trying to say. Keeping her own voice calm, she tried again. 'Angela, can you please tell me what this is about? Does this have something to do with the fight with your sister?'

'Fight?' She spat out the word. 'Is that what *she* calls it?'

'If you mean Mrs Clifford, then no, she hasn't said anything about it at all. She doesn't know about Leo meeting Jeremy.' Should Pippa mention Leo's former lack of knowledge of his extended family? That his mum had barely acknowledged Angela's existence? If Pippa said the wrong thing, she knew there would be another explosion of words. She needed answers, not a confusing tirade.

'You met them?' Angela asked. She sounded like she'd bitten into something foul.

'Yes. I did.'

'You don't want to be involved with them, Pippa. You don't want to be anywhere near them, do you hear me?' This was more understandable.

'I don't have a very high opinion of the Cliffords, to be honest. I'm quite happy to steer clear of them. But I'm not about to end my relationship with Leo. He is a good guy. A *great* guy. And he's part of my life now.'

'You'd choose that boy over Jeremy? You value him more? Someone you've known for ... what, how long? It can't be more than a couple of months. He's more important than my son? You know, I thought it was strange when you two came back from Thailand, the way you were with each other. I could tell he was besotted with you, but you kept him by your side— friends only, you said. And I was worried for him, thought you were stringing him along. But then I saw how you were together. And I came to like you, Pippa. I did. Then Rebecca came along, and I was so happy for him. I realised you two were just good friends. Jeremy mattered to you. Does he still matter? Do you still care enough about my son to do the right thing? Do you?'

Pippa was staring out the window, seeing nothing. What the hell was this about? Something was seriously not right. Either Angela had flipped a gear or there was a real and significant issue behind her words. But she was clinging to her reasons like a growling cat with a dead mouse.

'Angela, do you think you can give me a bit more detail? I'm listening to what you're saying, but it's not making much sense to me.'

Pippa heard the *click, click, click* of a cigarette lighter, then the sucking inhalation as Angela drew smoke deep into her lungs. 'You won't take my word?' The nicotine must have pacified her a little, because she sounded calmer. 'You can't simply believe me when I say there's a good reason?'

'No. Not when you're asking so much of me.'

Pippa waited.

'Do they look alike?' Angela asked quietly.

Presumably the woman was asking about the two boys. 'I guess so. There are differences, but when they're together you can tell they're cousins.'

'Cousins?' A laugh was strangled at the back of Angela's throat. Pippa listened as she inhaled deeply. The exhale came in a rush, forced out so she could quickly speak. 'They're not cousins, Pippa,' she said wearily.

Of course they were cousins, one born to each sister. 'I don't understand.'

'Well, they're not just cousins.' The words were squeezed from a locked mouth. 'They're brothers.' A hiccup of laughter. 'My son. Her son. They're brothers. Half-brothers.'

Holy shit, Pippa thought. *That's what this is about.*

'Mr Clifford is Jeremy's dad?' she said. 'Angus Clifford?'

Pippa could barely hear the answer, the word a scraping whisper.

'Yes ...?' she prompted.

'Yes,' Angela said, louder this time but flat and dull. A forced confession.

What could Pippa say? She wanted to know what had happened. She wanted to know who and how, and why and when—all the details that would fill in the picture.

'I don't want Jeremy to know,' said Angela. 'Do you see now?'

'Doesn't he have a right to know?'

'No.'

'And your sister knows about … about this situation?'

'Oh, yes. She knows. She knew. She knew what happened. But she didn't want to know, didn't want to rethink her perfectly laid plans.'

Pippa pictured two young women both wanting the same man. Who had him first? Was he Angela's boyfriend and then Evelyn stole him away, or did he get Angela pregnant after he was married? No, wait—at the lunch today, the Cliffords were celebrating their twenty-fifth wedding anniversary. Jeremy was twenty-four, turning twenty-five in April. Angela had got pregnant before Evelyn married Angus. And back then, an unmarried pregnant girl would have had few options. If the guy didn't want to marry her—wanted to marry someone else, like her sister—then what would the girl have done? Perhaps been sent to an unmarried mothers' home.

'Angela, when you got pregnant, did your family make you leave? Did Angus know you were pregnant?'

Click, click, click. Another cigarette to replace the one she must have finished. 'That's what happened to unwed mothers if their families didn't want to support them.' Her voice was rigid, the pain still evident after all these years. 'And that bastard, he didn't have a right to know. No right to claim his son.'

Pippa's heart ached for the desperate girl Angela would have been. 'Did you love him?' The story was coming together in her head, a tale of foolish love, of family estrangement, of a cruel, selfish older sister who wanted the man, the marriage, the perfect family. Pippa disliked Evelyn Clifford and her veneer of welcome, which didn't hide her snobbish ways. It was easy enough to cast her in the role of villain. And what about the parents? What had Angela's mother done for her unmarried daughter?

'No!' Angela snapped out the word. 'I did *not* love that man. I did not even like him. He was an arrogant beast, full of his own importance. He was nasty, manipulative, so sure he could have anything he wanted. He wanted it all. And what he wanted he took.'

Horror trickled across Pippa's skin. 'He wanted both of you?'

'Oh yes, of course. He certainly wanted Evelyn—she was perfect for him, would make the perfect wife. She was as conceited and ambitious and narrow-minded as he was.'

'And you. He wanted you too.' Angela was determined for Jeremy to have no contact with the Cliffords because of the fear that her son would be exposed to the truth of his conception. 'You didn't want Angus. But that didn't stop him, did it?'

Pippa could hear nothing but the rasping inhale and exhale of smoke. She pictured Angela sitting in the immaculate kitchen of her neat little weatherboard cottage, a modest, simple home that she had been renting for the past ten years. She had wanted to buy it, had worked hard to save, but couldn't, of course, since banks wouldn't lend to a woman without a man to go guarantor.

'No,' said Angela. 'It didn't. It didn't stop him. *I* couldn't stop him. He took what he wanted at their stupid engagement party. He took *me*.' Bitterness hung from every word.

Pippa stood. She walked back to the kitchen and rested her head against the wall next to the phone. 'Oh, Angela.' She wanted to put her arms around the woman, to comfort her. To do whatever she could to take away a pain that had barely lessened over the years. 'And Evelyn? You told her?'

Angela gave a dry, barking laugh. 'She told me I was a jealous, lying child. That I was trying to ruin her future. That if anything had happened between me and her fiancé, it was all my doing and all my fault. I was a poisonous, scheming hussy. And she hated me.'

'What about Eloise? She was your friend. Did she believe you?'

There was a long pause. Not even the sound of smoke being drawn.

'She knows who Jeremy's father is. That's all. I never told her. My sister didn't believe me. My mother didn't believe me. I couldn't face the thought of Eloise not believing me.'

CHAPTER TWENTY-FIVE

The phone call ended as it had begun, with Angela increasingly agitated. She remained insistent that she did not want Jeremy to know that Angus Clifford was his father, let alone how he had been conceived. She said she couldn't bear the shame. She begged Pippa to be done with Leo, paranoid that through their connection the truth would be discovered.

There were tears. Angela begged, saying that if Pippa cared about Jeremy then she had to protect him. 'I haven't been the best mother,' Angela said, 'but I have done what I could to give him a happy life, to not let his life be defined by what happened to me.'

What could Pippa say? Angela's anguish had left her shaken. How would Jeremy react if he knew the whole truth? Pippa didn't want to do anything to hurt him or upend his world, but she wasn't going to end things with Leo.

Now she stood at the terrace doors, watching as Jeremy made his way up the hill with a wet and grubby Honey. Pippa went to fetch the old towel used to dry the dog. 'Looks like

Honey enjoyed herself,' she said when they arrived, dropping to her knees.

'Crazy dog. Likes to bite the water. And when the itty-bitty waves keep coming, she jumps on them. Great game.' Jeremy laughed. 'When I settle down—wherever, whenever that may be—I'm going to get myself a Honey dog.'

'Good plan.' Pippa rubbed Honey's shaggy coat, finding everything easier without eye contact.

'How's Leo? Is he coming back down tonight?'

'Not sure.'

'Didn't he say?'

Generally Pippa could pull together a quick little lie. There had been a few. A sudden bout of the flu had kept her from work. Yes, she remembered hanging the jacket back on the rack at the end of the show, and no, she hadn't seen it since. Yes, she liked Rebecca, the perfect girl for Jeremy. But at that moment Pippa went blank.

'He might not be able to get away,' she said vaguely.

'Is he having fun with the family?'

Loathing swept through her as she imagined the Cliffords celebrating with their friends. How had such vile people brought up such a balanced son, one with integrity? Maggie seemed unscarred too. Yet their father was a rapist, their mother an unfeeling, spiteful woman who had chosen to throw her sister away rather than admit her fiancé was a piece of shit.

'Pip?'

'Sorry, what?' Honey was dry, so Pippa couldn't stay on the floor any longer.

'You're out of it.' Jeremy had one shoulder against the door-frame. He looked relaxed. 'Everything okay? Did you two have an argument or something?'

'No, no, I'm just missing him. I wish he could get away.' She headed to the laundry, using the dirty towel as an excuse to leave the room.

When she returned she found Jeremy with his head in the fridge. 'Hungry? 'Cos I'm starving. We didn't have lunch, did we? What do you reckon? Toasted sandwich?' He began assembling ingredients on the bench. 'You want me to make you one?'

Leo and Jeremy. Half-brothers.

And Maggie. A half-sister.

A shared father.

This secret, so enormous it cast a shadow over everything.

'Hey, earth to Pip, do you want a sandwich?' He was waving his hand back and forth, trying to drag her from her thoughts.

'No. No. All good.' She forced a smile. 'Might go and have a nap.'

His gaze was penetrating. 'Okay.' A moment passed as he waited for an explanation that she couldn't give. 'You'd tell me if something was wrong, wouldn't you?'

Shit, he could read her so well. 'Maybe.' She heaved her shoulders in an exaggerated display of nonchalance. 'Depends what it is. There are some things a girl doesn't share.' She rolled her eyes, sighed loudly and then inspected her nails, the picture of moody feminine reticence. Being over the top was easier than trying to fake being at ease.

'I'm always here, princess, if you need advice or want to vent.'

'Well, maybe you could help.' She put her hands on her hips and faced him. 'Leo wants to do this thing, and it's a bit out there, and I wondered if you've ever—'

'Okay. Nope.' He stuck his fingers in his ears. 'Too much information.'

She pouted. 'You said you could give me advice.'

'Yeah. Well, that wasn't the sort of thing I had in mind. Way, way too personal. Off you go.' He waved her away.

'Chicken,' she called over her shoulder as she left the room.

She knew this guy. Knew him so well. They had laughed and danced, teased and talked, lain tangled together with sand in every crevice and the waves nearly at their feet. She had held him as he lay unconscious in a reeking ditch. Had sat beside his hospital bed as he babbled incoherently, drugs taking his mind on a happy adventure. Had brought him cold drinks and mopped his face when the overhead fan did little more than wobble and creak. Her heart had ached for him, fear nearly suffocating her when she'd thought he might not wake up.

As a couple they wouldn't have lasted. She didn't fit him, not as a lover or a girlfriend. But as friends bound by the highs and lows of their shared history, they were perfect.

He was her anchor. She loved him.

And now she knew more about him than he knew about himself. It was very, very wrong.

She could not keep this secret. It was too much for her to carry.

Except the truth would surely bring chaos. She couldn't do that to him—couldn't be the one to rip apart his understanding of himself.

*

For dinner they heated a can of tomato soup on the stove and served it with buttery toast. The burnt bits were scraped off with the edge of the butter knife. They were both quiet. Having shared a house for so long, they didn't need to entertain each other. Pippa pretended to be engrossed in a book from Eloise's extensive collection, and Jeremy watched *Neighbours*, then a movie.

When Leo pushed open the door, Jeremy greeted him. 'Hey, mate, how was the lunch?'

Pippa's heart lurched. Seeing them together was almost too much. The similarities she'd first noticed now seemed more obvious, more significant—especially their eyes, that soft blue with the dark rim. When they both turned to face her, she had to look away.

'You okay?' Leo was asking this time, while Jeremy returned his focus to the TV.

'Yeah. Yeah. Just tired.' She walked to him and gave him a kiss.

He wrapped his arms tight around her, the kiss turning into a long hug. Leo buried his face in the unbrushed mess of her hair. 'I am so glad to be here,' he murmured.

'Tough day?'

'You know, I love my sister. She's an awesome girl. But my parents can go to hell.'

Yes, they could. And they would.

A deep groan caught in her throat. She wasn't only keeping the truth from Jeremy—she was also keeping it from Leo. He hadn't been worried by the news he had a cousin, but how would he react to the discovery of a half-brother?

And then there was the truth about his father. She couldn't be the one to tell him.

He pulled away, inspecting her face. 'Are you sure you're okay? You seem upset. Has something happened?'

She shook her head. 'Let's go to bed. You can tell me all about what your diabolical parents have done this time.'

'Oh, they tried to set me up with a friend's daughter, then got all cranky with me when I pointed out I have a girlfriend. One I am madly in love with, and who will be a major fixture in my life going forward.'

She wished she hadn't asked—she did not want to talk about the Cliffords. 'They probably think I'm going to lead you astray. Divert you from the grand plan.'

'You are.' He took her hand. 'Which is a very, very good thing, because that plan sucked.'

They both said goodnight to Jeremy as they walked towards their bedroom.

'Do you have a new one?' asked Pippa. 'A new plan.'

'It's starting to take shape,' he said with a teasing smile. 'I'll tell you about it when I have some details worked out.'

Passion and need shut down the storm in Pippa's mind for the next hour. Afterwards, she lay on her stomach, Leo on his side, his fingers tracing long loops across her back. They hadn't closed the curtains, and pale moonlight gave the room a soft grey glow. She tried to hold on to the feeling of calm.

Jeremy was leaving in less than two weeks, which would remove the danger of secrets being accidentally revealed. But she and Leo were planning a future together. How would it be possible for her to keep this knowledge hidden from him? Could they not share the burden of the truth? Maybe not all of it, not yet, but the truth about his connection to Jeremy—he could handle that. She couldn't carry this alone.

'Leo?' she whispered.

'Mmmmm?'

'I had a phone call today.'

His hand stilled, then resumed its path over her skin. 'Who was it?'

'Angela. Jeremy's mum. She was upset.'

'Does this have to do with me and him? About what happened between our mums?'

'Yes.' Pippa needed to tread carefully. Choose her words. Not say too much.

This time his hand halted. His voice was calm. 'My dad is Jeremy's dad, right? We're brothers? Is that what his mum told you?'

CHAPTER TWENTY-SIX

'How do you know that? Did your mum tell you? Your dad?' Pippa flipped over and sat cross-legged, dragging the sheet to cover herself. 'How long have you known?'

Leo pulled himself up, positioning himself so they were facing each other. 'I didn't know. It was a guess.'

'Nobody in your family has said anything?'

'Are you kidding? My parents avoid discussing anything unpleasant.'

'I don't understand. What made you think Jeremy might be your brother?'

He shrugged. 'I kept thinking about why my mother would cut her sister out of her life. About what could've happened back when they were girls that would've been so completely shocking or devastating or unforgivable. There are only a few options. I didn't think either of them had murdered anyone, and back in those days the biggest scandal was being pregnant and not married. Then there was the thing about me and Jeremy looking a bit alike—and some other similarities, like how we both hate vinegar.'

'Seriously? You guessed Jeremy was your brother because he doesn't like vinegar on his chips?'

'It was *one* small clue.'

A strangled laugh burst from Pippa. Leo grinned, then the two of them descended into manic giggles, collapsing back onto the pillows. Relief rushed through Pippa, and it took her a few minutes to calm down. 'What else?' she asked, wiping her eyes. 'What other clues were there?'

He stretched out and pulled the covers back over them, then turned onto his side again to face her. 'Obviously our good looks, intelligence, and all-round decency.'

'Yes to all of that.' She trailed her fingers through his hair, pushing it back from his face. 'Although, you can't thank Angus Clifford for the decency part,' she said sombrely.

'No. You're right.' Leo's mouth tightened. 'The hard thing for me is that he hasn't always been an entirely crap parent. You might not believe it, but as a kid he was a pretty good dad,' he said, then added quietly, 'just not so much in the last few years.'

'Or maybe you've come to see him flaws and all as you've got older. Sometimes horrible things are done by men who everyone thinks are "great guys".'

He exhaled slowly, and even in the shadows she could see his eyes were grim. 'You're probably right.'

'How do you feel about it?' Pippa asked. 'About the thing with Jeremy?'

'A bit strange right now.' He flopped onto his back, staring at the ceiling. 'I mean, this has been at the back of my mind for the last few weeks. Like, one of those things you take out and mull over when everything is quiet. Something I thought I might find an answer for, one day. To be honest, it didn't seem like that big a deal. He was either my cousin or my half-brother. Finding out for sure doesn't change how we get along.' He seemed philosophical about having his suspicions confirmed.

Leo, it seemed, was both pragmatic and forgiving. Pippa realised she would inevitably be the more fiery one in their relationship. 'But doesn't it change how you think about your dad?'

He was quiet for a beat. 'It's not like I've got any illusions about him. I've known for ages that Dad has played around on Mum. That's the other reason I thought he and Jeremy's mum might have been together. He's a bit of a player now—wouldn't be a surprise if he was back then as well.' Leo had made this declaration with barely a hint of emotion, no outrage or distress, but she could feel his body tensing. A muscle flickered in the edge of his jaw as he gritted his teeth. She sensed he was cutting himself off from how he truly felt.

'How do you know all this about your dad? Please don't tell me he confides in you.' Nothing about Angus would surprise her now.

Leo made a noncommittal noise at the back of his throat. 'I saw him once, at a party at our family friend's house. I must've been about fifteen. Found him snogging someone else's wife in the laundry. He saw me. Didn't stop at first. Then the woman got all upset about being caught. Dad got me by the arm, led me away and said I was never to tell Mum—that some things had to stay secret between men. And that if she found out it would upset her, and she'd be cross with me for telling her something she didn't want to know. She'd blame me. She'd punish me for ruining the family.'

'That's horrible. What a wicked thing to say to a kid. Seriously, your father is a real piece of shit.' Not to mention a leering, arrogant rapist. How on earth was she ever going to be able to deal with Leo's parents without showing her revulsion?

'I know that now. Back then I still worshipped him. My dad. The guy every other kid wanted as their father. Up until that moment, I'd thought he was cool, and generous, and fun.'

'It must've been hard to realise he wasn't so great.'

'To realise he was a total wanker?' Leo laughed without any humour. 'And I've heard stories since then. Recently I over-heard two men talking at the yacht club, two friends of Dad's. They were making some rude comments about a pretty girl. This girl was only a few years older than me. And the two of them were laughing about how my dad had slept with her on the boat. Three times, they said. Then he'd had to get rid of her because she got all clingy and made lovey-dovey eyes. They made it sound like he was some sort of hero for getting away with it. They were envious of his so-called success, thought he was a stud. When they realised I was standing right there, they just laughed into their beers and gave each other a look, like, "Oops, might have said the wrong thing." Then one of them winked at me and said something like, "You're a good-looking kid, bet you're a chip off the old block." And they laughed again. I wanted to smash them in the face. I am *nothing* like my father.' He spat out the last words with fierce intensity.

Pippa reached for his hand where it lay on his chest. 'I would not love you the way I do if you had anything in common with your father. You are a hundred times the man he is.'

Leo closed his eyes, as though bracing himself. Then he opened them, looking at her intently. 'Which is why I need to stand up to him. I need to pick my own path.'

At last, Pippa thought. It was hard for a son to pull away from family expectations, especially when they had been drummed into him since he was a toddler and, more recently, amplified with a sense of obligation. 'Okay. What do you have in mind?'

'I'll tell you tomorrow.'

'Why not now?' She wriggled closer, till their faces were only a breath apart. 'You know I hate waiting.'

He brushed his nose against hers. 'You'll have to wait. It's big … well, biggish. And I want to talk it through with you. Now, though, you need to sleep.'

'Should I be nervous?'

'No. Absolutely not. I just think we should make major decisions together. My plans are going to include your plans.'

'Now I really want to know.' What *did* he have in mind?

'It can wait. We have a more important question to answer before sleep.'

She brushed a kiss over his mouth. 'More important than the rest of our lives. What could that possibly be?'

'The big question.' He pulled back a little so he could give her a questioning look. 'Do we tell Jeremy who his father is, or do we leave him in happy ignorance?'

'Ignorance?' she suggested, feeling a twist of guilt at keeping the more brutal truth from Leo. He didn't fully understand what might come from revealing Jeremy's paternity. But then she was no longer confident that silence was the best idea. Would they be protecting Jeremy by not telling him, or would they be hiding something he had a right to know no matter the consequences?

'Maybe,' Leo answered. 'I can't imagine he would really want my dad as his own.' There was a new resentment in the way Leo talked about his father, as though he was pushing aside the loyalty of a child to a parent and seeing the man as a deeply flawed person.

She had made the right choice to tell him about the phone call—or, at least, to tell him about the bits she'd mentioned. This outcome had been far better and easier than she had expected.

And the deeper, uglier truth? That could wait, for now. Maybe forever. She wasn't going to deliver that blow. Leo wouldn't be so calm if he heard the full story.

CHAPTER TWENTY-SEVEN

Tuesday, 27 June 2017

Tom was waiting for Olivia to pick him up outside his hotel. Too nervous to stand still, he walked to the end of the drive, turned and headed back. He couldn't decide whether he was more worried about being with Olivia again or speaking with Leo's parents.

He was hoping Olivia would be the less stressful interaction. Which it would be, if he could keep things easy between them by not mentioning her recent dramas. It wasn't the right time or place to admit he'd read what he had—or seen what he had. That would make things horribly awkward, and he was wanting to rekindle the connection they'd had on Saturday night.

The Cliffords, on the other hand, weren't likely to be easy at all. He hadn't mentioned this to Olivia, but his phone call to Mr Angus Clifford had received a mixed response. Tom had needed to explain himself several times, with Leo's father demanding to know who he was and what he wanted. The call had ended abruptly when Angus had said he wanted to confer with his wife. Tom had waited three hours for the man to call back, and the message had been terse: yes, they were prepared to meet Tom, but only out of courtesy, and he wasn't to expect any information that was likely to help him find Pippa.

He was on his second lap of the hotel drive when Olivia arrived. He strode to her silver car, opening the door as soon as it came to a stop. 'Good morning,' he said brightly as he climbed into the passenger seat and turned to face her.

Her caramel-coloured hair was soft and straight today, her fringe swept back and to one side, held in place with pins. A pale pink scarf was wrapped loosely around her neck, and she was dressed in dark denim jeans and a large white jumper. She looked gorgeous but tired. Her eyes met his, but her expression told him she wasn't entirely at ease. 'Hello.' Her smile was tentative. He had the urge to kiss her on the cheek, but he hesitated too long, and the sweet moment when it would have been natural passed. Bloody hell, why did he have to make things so hard?

Her warm, gentle scent made him want to burrow his face into her neck and breathe deeply. 'Your perfume smells marvellous,' he blurted out.

Her laugh was small but felt genuine. 'Thank you. You smell pretty good too.'

He did? He was trying a new cologne. He knew his grin was big and stupid.

'Shall we get going?' she asked, and he nodded.

It had been her idea to pick him up. He'd texted her the Cliffords' address, and he could see it was already in her GPS system. In the same text, he'd suggested meeting for breakfast—sadly, she'd said no. Having a chance to smooth over their abrupt parting the other night would have been good, but he hadn't pushed. Now her proximity was accentuated by the limited space of the smallish SUV. He tried to keep his thigh from drifting too close to the centre when she released the handbrake.

'So, tell me about Leo's family,' she said. 'Are you ready to tackle his parents? What are they like?' She talked quickly as she busied herself with checking the rear-view and side mirrors and looking over her shoulder when they moved forward and into the traffic.

'I only spoke to Angus, Leo's father. He was willing to see me, but honestly, I'm not too sure how things will go. He didn't sound enthused.'

'It must be hard talking about his son.'

It had felt like it was more than that. 'When I told him who I was, he became very abrupt. Wanted to know why I was looking for Pippa but barely let me finish my explanation. Then he asked if my dad was here with me and seemed shocked when I said he had passed away. At that point Angus hung up while he went to speak to Evelyn.'

'Reasonable enough questions, I guess,' Olivia said distractedly.

'Yes, I suppose.' Tom thought back through the conversation. 'But there was an underlying tone of … I don't know, maybe anger? Bitterness? I was surprised Angus said yes to our visit. I guess their curiosity won.'

'We're not expecting a warm welcome, then?'

'Unlikely—although he did ring back this morning to confirm the time. If he and his wife don't want to talk about Leo, he could've said no.'

Olivia negotiated the weekday traffic, taking them from the city, through a shopping strip, then along a main road that followed the curve of the water, until the GPS showed them they'd reached their destination. The drive had taken all of ten minutes.

'You're kidding,' Tom said. 'We're here already?'

'Yep. Sandy Bay. Inner-city living at its best.' She parked on the road, a discreet numbered letterbox the only indication they were at the right place. 'Do we go down?' she asked as she stared at the entrance to the drive, which dropped dramatically towards the bay. The road had the high ground, the houses in this stretch all tucked away from the traffic noise, hidden down a slope behind walls and trees and long, long driveways. Tom and Olivia could see down to the water over the tops of roofs and gardens.

'I guess so,' he said. 'We're expected.'

Olivia turned the car in and edged forward. There was a perfect line of silver birch trees on the right side, the impressive fence of a neighbouring property on the left. 'Not short of money,' she said. 'I did pick up they weren't poor. Leo had gone to a private school and was big into sailing.'

'That's definitely not a cheap sport,' Tom said.

'And this is definitely not a cheap house,' Olivia murmured as they came into an open turning space, a large inactive fountain at its centre. The two-storey house was impressive, with a number of peaks and gables on the roof adding architectural interest. Large bay windows broke the line of the solid brick walls, and a low verandah ran around the side from the front door. The trees were well established, the gardens immaculate. It was a definite display of wealth.

'Wait,' Olivia said, putting her hand on Tom's arm as they made their way towards the front door. 'I've already forgotten their names.'

'Evelyn and Angus Clifford.'

'Right. Okay. That helps.'

'Here goes,' he said, hesitating before he pressed the door-bell. 'All going well, we will leave here with everything we need to solve this puzzle. If I don't make a mess of it.' There was always a good chance he would say exactly the wrong thing and they'd be thrown out.

Olivia laid her hand on his arm again. 'You've got this, Tom.' Her smile was reassuring. '*We've* got this.'

'You're right,' he said. 'We've definitely got this.' He was going to pretend this was a business negotiation. He had no problem being fierce when it came to his company. Plus, he wasn't on his own. He rang the bell. When there was no response, he used the polished brass lion's head knocker to rap on the glossy dark door.

They were giving each other a look of doubt when the door was pulled open.

Tom's first impression of Angus Clifford was that the man was a fierce, well-preserved snob. He glanced between them, then his gaze ran over Olivia from top to toe, almost lazily. A fierce snob and a fucking misogynistic old perve. Tom tensed, reaching for Olivia's hand. He wanted to grab her and get the hell out of there. The squeeze she gave told him to calm down.

'Yes?' The man turned his attention to Tom, a hint of a smirk twitching his mouth.

'Angus Clifford?'

'Yes.'

'I'm Tom Kearsley.' He swallowed, the acceptable pleasant-ries getting a little stuck in his throat. 'Thanks for speaking with me on the phone and agreeing to meet at such short notice.' Tom couldn't put warmth in his voice. 'As I said, I'm Jeremy

Kearsley's son. My father left something he wanted delivered to Pippa French, and I'm hoping you can help.' Angus's focus had drifted back to Olivia. Tom's jaw tightened. 'This is Olivia Haymers, a close friend of mine who has been helping me with some missing details.'

The man looked at Tom again, silent for an uncomfortably long time. Then he sighed heavily. 'I guess you'd better come in.' He opened the door wide and stepped back, indicating for them to move inside. They followed him through a spacious foyer with a sweeping staircase, then down a short, wide hall-way. They glimpsed a cosy lounge with French doors leading onto the side verandah and fat upholstered sofas facing each other over a polished coffee table large enough to dance on. At the end of the hall they emerged into a huge open kitchen saturated with natural light. The cooking part of the space was dominated by an enormous black marble island bench. Pendant lights hung down over the surface, and slate-grey upholstered stools were tucked in on the open side. A hefty wooden din-ing table was flanked by ten chairs, and at the other end of the room stood a group of wicker sofas and armchairs filled with colour-coordinated cushions. All of it was arranged to take in the stunning outlook of garden, beach, and water through the wall of bi-fold doors.

Angus nodded towards the dining table. 'Take a seat.'

They did as they were told. 'You have a beautiful home,' Olivia said.

Tom appreciated her attempt to initiate polite small talk. He was still swallowing the urge to say something more caustic.

'Thank you. My wife Evelyn will be down shortly.' Angus took the chair at the head of the table. 'But why don't you tell me what it is you are after?'

'Okay,' said Tom, mimicking the body language of their host, placing his hands together, forearms on the table, and leaning forward. 'Can I ask, though, if you knew my father?'

Angus took his time answering as his eyes shifted away from Tom. He was looking out the window when he spoke. 'No. I never met him.' The tone was clipped, a statement of fact. 'His mother and my wife were sisters, but it was a family connection in name only. The two women did not speak. Hadn't for years.'

'And the boys didn't know each other before the summer of 1986?'

'Absolutely not. Even then, it was a chance encounter. They met through that girl, Penelope.'

Tom could hear the bitterness. Pippa was clearly not a part of this family, despite the child. He just nodded as though this all made sense. 'My father never talked much about his life before he migrated to England. In fact, the first I heard of Leo was after I arrived in Hobart.'

'Didn't he?' The look on Angus's face was odd. He saw a wistfulness quickly obliterated by a dark frown. 'You said your father died ... What happened to him? Was he sick?'

The question took Tom by surprise. He looked down at his hands. 'It was an accidental death. He fell.'

'Fell? From what?'

Tom did not want to discuss the incident with this man. 'From a path—one of the cliff walks in Cornwall, where he lived,' he said abruptly.

Angus recoiled, his head jerking back, and gave a sharp intake of breath. 'I see. And the authorities are sure it was an accident?'

Seriously? What the hell sort of question was that? As Angus had said, he didn't know his father, and what had happened to

Jeremy wasn't relevant to the current situation. This stranger had no right to ask such a thing. 'Yes, absolutely certain,' Tom snapped. Of course, this was not entirely true.

'Tom's father left something for Pippa.' Thankfully Olivia spoke up, working to redirect the conversation. 'It was important to him. Tom would very much like to honour those wishes, and we're hoping you can help.'

'Help in what way?' The question came not from Angus but the woman who had just entered the room. 'Help you find that woman?'

They all turned. She was well into her seventies but carried herself with the grace and vitality of someone much younger. She wore a navy shirt under a soft grey cardigan with crisp, slim white pants. Her grey hair was pulled into a low bun, not a whisper out of place. She looked like a long-retired ballerina.

Tom stood as she approached. 'Tom Kearsley.' He leaned forward and offered his hand when she neared the table. She looked at it as if it were something contagious, finally placing her fingers limply in his for the briefest moment. Her expression looked pained.

'You're Jeremy Kearsley's son.' It was a sharp statement, not a question. She looked him over, openly appraising him. 'Interesting,' she said quietly, before turning away. 'Jeremy—' she said the name as though it was sour on her tongue '—is not someone we hold in any regard.'

What? Hadn't Angus just said the Cliffords didn't even know Jeremy? Tom tried to stay polite. 'Why is that?'

'Why?' Evelyn gave a small huff of disdain. 'Because he got to live his life and—' she indicated towards Tom '—have a family. And Leo did not.' She folded her arms loosely, long fingers gripping her elbows. Her chin went up a fraction. 'That is an injustice beyond my comprehension.'

Tom looked quickly down at Olivia, confused as to how to respond. Her eyes widened in surprise as they met his.

'I was sorry to hear about what happened to Leo,' he said at last. 'I'm sure it must be very hard, even after all these years.'

'Hard?' The woman barked a small sharp laugh. 'It is insurmountable. Our loss has shaped our lives. And you—' she breathed in as her gaze swept over Tom again, her thin lips twitching in distaste '—you now stand here in my home. Oblivious, I imagine.'

'I'm sorry?' he said, trying to grasp her meaning. 'Oblivious to what?'

'That your existence is only possible because your father got away with what he did.'

CHAPTER TWENTY-EIGHT

The room was silent. Tom stared at Evelyn, who in turn hadn't taken her eyes off him. Her chin was still raised, defiant, but there was a quiver about her as well, as though she were only just holding herself together. Or maybe she had wanted to shock and hurt Tom, and now she was gloating in her success. Her accusation hung suspended in the room.

'What he did? Are you suggesting my dad was involved in what happened to Leo?'

'I know he was.' She lifted a hand. 'Don't worry, no one ever took me seriously. There was no evidence. But I knew.'

What the hell was Tom supposed to say to that? Did she truly believe that Jeremy—his father—had somehow been involved in the disappearance of Leo Clifford? That didn't make sense on any level. Not if you looked at the facts, and not if you knew the calm, gentle man who had been his father.

Olivia got up from her seat. 'Mrs Clifford, I'm Olivia Haymers.' She didn't put out her hand. 'Is there a chance you could sit with us and share what you believe happened to Leo?'

Cold blue eyes turned towards her, the older woman's thin lips twisting into a sneer. Olivia didn't flinch. 'And we were hoping to find out how to contact Pippa. We understand she is the mother of your grandchild.'

Evelyn inclined her head a fraction. 'Olivia Haymers?'

'Yes.'

'I know that name.'

Damn. Tom couldn't imagine a moneyed, mature-age Hobartian following the trials and tribulations of some over-rated actor—but anything was possible. *Please don't say anything*, he mentally begged. He didn't want Olivia to feel exposed and humiliated in front of these people.

Olivia simply smiled politely. 'Do you? I can't think why. I'm relatively new to Tasmania.'

Evelyn considered her as though she were a mess in the pristine house.

'My father can't have been involved,' Tom said, bringing the attention back to him. 'I didn't know about Leo till a few days ago, but I can say emphatically that Dad—Jeremy—had left Tasmania before Leo went missing. Among his things was a travel itinerary from that time. It shows he flew out of Hobart on the eighth of February 1986, then to London from Sydney on the tenth. Leo was last seen on the night of the ninth. So, you're wrong.'

Olivia turned her head, giving him a pleased look. He realised he had forgotten to explain this detail. He gave a quick smile and a small nod.

Evelyn, meanwhile, had shifted to stand beside her husband, while Angus looked from her to Tom, his eyebrows raised slightly like he was waiting to see how things proceeded.

Evelyn grimaced. 'For heaven's sake, do sit down.'

Tom and Olivia both sat as Evelyn finally deigned to take a seat. A mean smile crossed her face. 'You know that Pippa had a child, but you're wrong if you think it was Leo's.'

Tom's head snapped back to her. 'We were told it *was* Leo's.'

'Were you?' Evelyn smoothed her flawless hair and continued talking with exaggerated calm. 'That would be wrong. Jeremy would have been like his mother. My sister Angela was an extremely proficient liar. And, when it suited her, she was also excellent at keeping her dirty little secrets. She was manipulative and cunning. I presume Jeremy didn't fall far from that tree.'

'Hold on. You're talking about my father. About my grandmother, too.'

Evelyn flicked her fingers as if she were waving aside a point of no consequence.

This was truly becoming ridiculous. 'I'm sorry, I strongly object. My father was many things, but he was neither nasty nor manipulative. And while he was reluctant to talk about his childhood or life in Australia, he was always honest and open about the things that mattered.'

Evelyn stared out the window towards the water. 'Was he?' she asked. 'Do you truly believe your father was an honest man, one who valued family?' Was there genuine curiosity in her question, or was he imagining it?

'Yes. I do believe that.'

Olivia rested her hand on Tom's thigh, and he covered it with his own. Thank god she was here.

'Why are you so sure,' Olivia asked quietly, 'that Jeremy was the father of Pippa's baby?'

With a sniff, Evelyn turned her head a fraction. 'When Penelope determined there was no place in her life for us, we realised the truth.' She enunciated the words with tight-lipped precision. 'She didn't want us around the child because the child wasn't Leo's.'

'What exactly did Pippa say?' asked Tom.

'She denied it. But then she would, wouldn't she? There are advantages to being part of this family.'

'Advantages?' Tom asked cynically. He could see no advantage to being associated with the Cliffords.

Angus spoke up. 'Wealth, security, respectability.' He ticked through the list with pride. 'She was a knocked-up twenty-two-year-old with no job and no money. She'd played around with Leo, a boy several years younger I might add, while keeping her *friend* Jeremy on a string. Her options were limited, weren't they? Jeremy had run off overseas, and Leo was gone.'

Tom gave a snap of hard laughter. *Honestly?* Did Angus and Evelyn not see the contradiction in what they were saying? On the one hand, Pippa apparently didn't want the Cliffords to be involved with her child. On the other, she had supposedly claimed that the child was Leo's in order to access the benefits of being part of the family. It didn't add up. These two were quite possibly delusional.

'She stayed at Eloise's house for two years,' Olivia said calmly. 'Why do you think she did that?'

'Eloise Fowler was always gullible. She'd been fooled by my sister as well. Pippa got a free ride. There's a chance she knows what happened to our son and was staying there to ensure no evidence was ever found. After all, who reported Leo missing? Pippa! She could have delayed that call by a day—or more.' Evelyn delivered the words with contained bitterness. The sourness of curdled emotions was visible in her curled lip and narrowed eyes. 'Who's to say something didn't happen before your father ran away?'

There was silence. Under the table Olivia's fingers entwined with Tom's, and he turned to her. She shook her head slightly, telling him to ignore what Evelyn was saying. But uncertainty was squirming through his thoughts. Overall the Cliffords' version of events was preposterous, yet there could possibly be some truth in what they were suggesting.

'Jeremy had the gall to write to us.' Evelyn was still venting. 'Can you imagine that? He wrote from London, after we realised Leo had been taken from us, attempting to engage us in some sort of familial connection. We refused to respond. And then—' her voice shook '—and *then* he refused to attend the coronial inquest. It took us years to have that inquest called. We knew Leo was dead. And Jeremy couldn't be here. That fact only speaks of his guilt and of what a weak man he was. He should have done the right thing.'

Tom had no idea how to respond to an accusation of such magnitude, especially when he could see no way of proving it to be false.

Olivia spoke, her voice now clipped but steady. 'Are you able to help us find Pippa or not?'

'What makes you think we'd know where Pippa is?' Angus asked.

The slam of the front door startled everyone. A voice called out, followed by the boisterous entrance of a pleasant-looking woman probably in her forties. Her curvy figure was wrapped in expensive work-out gear, her well-tended blonde hair pulled up in a messy but healthy ponytail. 'Oh, hello. Didn't realise you had company—except that would, of course, explain the car out front. Christ, I'd never be good as a detective, would I? Can only put things together when they're all spelled out.' She crossed the room towards the four of them, bending to brush a quick kiss on Angus's forehead first, then place a cheek against Evelyn's. 'Mum. Dad.' She turned to look at the visitors. 'Hello, I'm Maggie.'

'Hi, I'm Olivia. This is Tom.'

'Gosh, you look familiar. Do I know you from somewhere? No? It'll come to me. I'm terrible with names, but I always remember a face. Can be a problem, though—I say hello to everyone. Then hours later I'll realise it was the guy who makes my coffee or someone off TV. Usually takes me a while to place people.' She considered Tom. 'You I don't know. I'd definitely remember your face.'

'He's Jeremy's son,' muttered Evelyn.

'Jeremy? As in the cousin who shall not be spoken of? That Jeremy?' Maggie looked at each of them, nobody speaking. 'Right, well that explains the slight frostiness we've got going on in this room.'

'I think we're finished here, actually.' Angus stood as he spoke, while Evelyn turned fully towards the window, effectively cutting herself off from any further interaction.

Maggie ignored her father. 'What brings you here?' she asked Tom and Olivia.

'Pippa French,' said Olivia. 'We were hoping to get her contact details.'

'Ah, I see.' Maggie flicked an assessing glance at her parents. 'I'm afraid Pippa hasn't been here for many, many years. I'll show you out. Dad, you stay here. I know talking about this stuff gets you a bit worked up.'

Tom and Olivia made restrained sounds of thanks. The meeting had been a painful waste of time, and all they had gained were insults and accusations.

As they followed Maggie to the front door he reclaimed Olivia's hand, needing her touch. She squeezed tight and didn't let go.

Maggie bounced down the stairs and walked with them to the car. 'Sorry, needed to get you out of there. Those two are ... well, let's say they've held on to a lot of anger. You're not going to find out anything from them, unless you want to hear their various conspiracy theories.'

Tom went around to the passenger side and opened the door, desperate to get away from there, then stopped and rested his arms on the roof, looking back at Maggie. 'Why did they even agree to meet me?'

'Oh, I should think good ol' curiosity. And a chance to spit venom on Jeremy's son. Look, I can't talk now, but are you free this afternoon?'

Olivia and Tom looked at each other over the car, and she gave an emphatic nod.

'Yes, we're free,' he said. 'Absolutely. Do you know something that might help?'

'Of course! I know where Pippa and Paige are. We are very much in contact, always have been.'

'Paige?' asked Olivia.

'Pippa's daughter. My goddaughter, not that we ever made it into an official thing—there was no christening or any of that hoo-ha. Anyway, how about we meet in the botanical gardens?' Maggie looked at her watch. 'Let's say two o'clock. I can get the kids from school when we're done chatting. Yep. Perfect. At the conservatory?' She did a little bounce from foot to foot as though the excitement of meeting them was hard to contain. Maggie had the unbridled exuberance of a teenager.

'Yes, sure,' said Olivia. 'I know where that is.'

'Excellent, let's do that. You know what? Pippa would love to meet you. She lost both her best friend and her boyfriend that summer. It was horrible.' For a moment Maggie grew still, her eyes sad. She shook her head as if to clear those thoughts away, and her wide smile came back. 'Okay, got to run! They'll be hunting me down in a moment. But I'll see you in a bit, yes?'

Olivia and Tom nodded. Apparently satisfied, Maggie gave a little wave, turned and jogged back towards the house. Tom felt slightly knocked about by both her energy and the sudden offer of information.

Back in the car they were silent. As Olivia turned into the traffic, Tom couldn't help giving a burst of laughter. 'I'm having trouble processing what just happened.' He shifted in his seat so he could face her. 'This might be it, Olivia. This afternoon we might know how to find Pippa.'

'You thought the same thing this morning before we met the Cliffords,' she said with a hint of amusement.

'I know. But this feels different.' He wasn't going to let the Cliffords' warped accusations dampen his optimism.

'Yes, I hope you're right. Fingers crossed Maggie shows up.'

His stomach sank. 'We didn't get her number, did we?'

'No. If she doesn't turn up, we have no way of contacting her.'

'Unless we come back here.'

They pulled up at a red light, and Olivia looked at him, her scepticism obvious. 'Let's hope it doesn't come to that, because I don't think Evelyn and Angus would give us even that scrap of information.'

He dragged his hands down his face, then checked his watch. 'We've got nearly three hours. Damn, I hate waiting.'

'Let's find some lunch. I need to eat, and a walk in the fresh air would be good.' There was exhaustion in her voice.

'You okay?'

He saw her struggle to smile. 'Didn't sleep well.'

'Something on your mind?'

'You could say that.'

'Right, let's find lunch and you can tell me what's bothering you. You've dealt with all my dramas—the least I can do is repay the favour.'

Will she? he wondered. *Does she trust me enough to share more of herself?*

CHAPTER TWENTY-NINE

Tuesday, 28 January 1986

Pippa knew she would have to force herself to step into the Cliffords' house. Before Leo had a chance to get his key in the lock, Evelyn threw open the door, eager to welcome her son back to the family fold—or to expunge the tatty girlfriend from his life. The curl in the woman's lip was fleeting, replaced by a bright fake smile. 'How lovely to see you again, Pippa. Do come in.' Her voice held no real warmth.

She all but pushed Pippa through the foyer and down the hallway towards the kitchen. Pippa glanced back over her shoulder and saw the woman grasp Leo's arm with one hand, while the other was clenched in a fist at her side. She hissed in his ear, yet his face remained passive. He met Pippa's eye, his expression letting her know that he was determined not to be intimidated by his mother, or his father.

If greeting Evelyn was unpleasant, being in Angus's presence was nearly impossible. Pippa's skin tightened, rejecting his touch as he put out his hand to shake hers. She had to pull her fingers free, and her reluctance was noticed, one eyebrow rising in an amused query. He scrutinised her. *What's wrong with you, girl?* he seemed to be saying.

Then he shifted his focus to his son. 'Hello, Leo. You'd better come in and get comfortable. Your mother has been playing a nervous guessing game since you rang yesterday. You made it sound like you have something important to share.'

'I do.' Leo had moved to Pippa's side. 'Why don't we sit down?'

Nobody moved. Evelyn and Angus exchanged looks.

'Alright. If that's what you want.' Angus took the lead, moving to the table and pulling out a chair. 'Evelyn,' he said, indicating for his wife to sit. Leo and Pippa took chairs on the other side and waited for Angus, who remained standing a moment longer, asserting his dominance. He obviously didn't like being told what to do by his son, even if it was about something as small as sitting at the table. The arrogant wanker wanted the upper hand.

'Why don't you tell us what's going on?' asked Evelyn. 'I'm presuming this is something that involves Pippa. That *is* why she's here?'

'She's here because she's my girlfriend. But, yeah, this is about the both of us.'

Evelyn gazed at Pippa, breathing deeply, a glimmer of fear in her eyes. 'You're pregnant,' she said. It wasn't a question.

'No, I'm not.' Pippa was surprised her voice stayed steady and calm. What she truly wanted to tell them was that she knew exactly what they'd done to Angela. Nope—tonight she was here for Leo. The day after the Cliffords' anniversary lunch he'd explained his plans, the two of them getting increasingly excited the more they'd talked. They'd waited a few days, but now he needed to tell his parents. He'd asked her to do this with him, and she couldn't refuse. They were in it together.

'Well. That's a relief.' But Evelyn looked almost disappointed, as though Pippa had failed to live down to her expectations. She must have spent the night convinced Pippa was a manipulative tramp who'd entrapped her precious son.

'We're not ready for children.' Pippa squeezed Leo's hand and smiled sweetly at his mother. 'Not yet.'

The wide-eyed outrage on Evelyn's face was immensely satisfying.

Leo cut in. 'I have decided I will not be studying this year.'

Silence. Seagulls outside. The tick of the oversized wall clock. The vibrating hum of the fridge.

Then restrained fury. 'That is not your call to make,' Angus gritted out.

'Actually, it is. I am an adult. It is my life, and I will make my own decisions.' Leo sounded thoughtful and mature, while his hand crushed hers.

'Don't give me that trite bullshit,' Angus spat. 'You don't know what's right or what's best. How could you? You have zero life experience.'

'You're right about that, my life experience is very limited. Which is why I want to get off this island. For a while, at least.'

'What? You're leaving us?' Evelyn's veneer of manners dissipated. Her anger was shrill, a vicious wasp to Angus's snarling dog.

'Not leaving, travelling. Seeing something of the world.'

'Is this your doing?' Evelyn directed her question at Pippa.

She swallowed, wavering under the older woman's glare. 'This is Leo's decision.'

'You've put these ideas in his head, haven't you? You've told him what fun it is, wandering aimlessly through life. What fun it is living without responsibilities. You want to flit away somewhere else? Well go, nobody's stopping you. But you're not taking Leo with you. You're not! You don't need him. You'll pick up some other boy as soon as you find somewhere new to flaunt yourself.'

'Don't talk to her like that.' Leo had never sounded so cold.

Pippa placed her free hand on his arm, urging restraint, easing him back from the edge. She could handle Evelyn's spite. 'It's okay. Your mum is upset. I can't imagine it's easy to hear what you're saying.'

'Oh, please. Don't patronise me, girl. Honestly—' her head whipped around to face her husband '—didn't I tell you she'd be trouble? You said it was a bit of summer fun. You thought she'd be nothing but an easy distraction for a few weeks. Christ, is it only women who can see the danger when a young girl with a pretty face and long legs comes wriggling about? You men are so easily destroyed. Haven't you learnt anything? Well, now you know. Again.'

The emphasis on the last word spoke volumes. Evelyn considered herself to be the saint, her husband the sinner—and other women were always to blame. According to Angela, this was exactly the view Evelyn had held towards her younger sister.

Pippa let go of Leo, put her hands flat on the table and leant forward. 'Mrs Clifford, your view of me is irrelevant. I'm not going to try and get you to like me, or even to get to know me. It's enough that Leo knows me. Your son is intelligent. He has a strong moral compass. He knows his own mind. No—' she raised a hand as Evelyn opened her mouth '—I haven't finished. It wasn't my suggestion for him to travel. I'd decided I would be happy staying here with him while he began his studies. The only thing I've done is talk about my life, about the things I've done and seen, the adventures I've had and how they've shaped me. What Leo is suggesting isn't the end of the world. So what if he takes a year off, or even two? If he decides to then study law, he'll be better at understanding the people he defends. You aren't going to lose your son.'

She sat back, putting her hands in her lap, and braced herself. Leo was turned towards her. She dared to glance sideways and saw his soft smile, full of admiration.

How could silence come in so many different tones? This silence wasn't peaceful—it screeched with indignation.

'You plead an eloquent case.' Angus was clearly aiming for a smooth, pacifying tone. 'However, I have to object. Leo is my son. I know him better than anyone, certainly better than you do. And I sincerely feel this is the wrong decision. Leo,' he said with gravity, 'we had a plan, you and I. You're coming to work with me, making the firm a true *family* business. All those times on the boat, when we talked about your future, about the wonderful things that lay ahead of you, you saw the brilliance of what your life could be. Didn't you?'

'I saw what you wanted me to see. But now I see things differently, I—'

'Yes, I know. Pippa has shown you an alternate life, one that's easier. And I understand how appealing that seems. But if you knuckle down and get on with your studies—'

'I need to take time away from here, before—'

'—then you can travel later.' They were talking over each other, and Angus was louder, with the authority of a father who'd never been questioned. 'Travel now and you'll be slumming it, living rough. Wait, then do it in style and comfort, when you have money. You can do anything when you have money and a respected position in society.' His laugh made Pippa cringe. The bastard truly believed what he was saying. 'I want what's best for you.' He leant back in his chair, a smarmy smile on his tanned face. 'You have to do me proud.'

'Why?' Leo asked.

'*Why?*' The question seemed to floor him. 'Well. Because you are important to me. You're my only son. You will follow my path of success.'

Pippa looked at Leo again. He was sitting perfectly still, his features calm, his gaze locked on his father across the table. But he was simmering. The stillness was only on the surface.

Pippa realised they had to get out of there. 'Leo.' She tugged at his arm. 'Maybe we should leave this for today. Let everyone digest what's been said.'

He looked at her, his mouth moving into a sad smile. No, not sad—resolved, as though he knew what was coming but had already accepted the outcome. He leant towards her, kissing her delicately on the forehead. Then he turned back to his father.

No! She couldn't stop him.

'But I'm not your *only* son, am I?'

Pippa let out the breath she'd been holding.

The air was heavy, like the atmosphere half an hour before a tropical thunderstorm burst open. The clouds building on the horizon, promising devastation. The stillness as creatures hid from what was coming. The intense pressure in the air. Then the first rumble, quiet before it increased in intensity.

'What are you talking about?' asked Evelyn.

'Your sister's son.'

'I don't have a sister.' Sharp, clipped words. Evelyn seemed determined to deny the facts.

'You do. Her name is Angela. Her son's name is Jeremy. I've met him, and I know we're more than cousins.' Leo looked at Angus, who hadn't moved. 'I think, Dad, you've always known about him.'

Angus sat back in his chair, his mouth pulled downwards, his eyebrows disappearing into his hair. 'Interesting.'

'I tell you I know about my brother, the one you've kept a secret, and all you can say is "interesting"?'

'What would you like me to say?'

'I don't know. I don't *know*.' Leo suddenly looked distraught, the fight leaving his body. Despite his fierce determination, Pippa could see that this was confusing and difficult.

Evelyn interrupted. 'Where is he? Where did you meet him? What lies has he told you?'

'Actually,' Pippa spoke up, 'Jeremy—his name is Jeremy—hasn't said anything. He doesn't know who his father is.'

'Angus is not his father.' Evelyn shoved her chair backwards and stood, striding away from the table. Then she returned, standing rigid beside her husband.

Angus gave a tight chuckle. 'Of course I am. You can't have it both ways, darling. You can't banish your sister for climbing into my bed, then deny her child is mine.' He looked back to Leo. 'Now, tell me about this kid. What's he like? What does he do?'

His change of mood had Pippa off balance. There was no way she was going to get into a discussion about her friend with his biological father when he himself knew nothing of his parentage. She needed to end this conversation.

Evelyn had the same idea. 'I think you should leave, the both of you. You have brought enough upset into this house tonight.' She was an impenetrable figure, her face blank, her chin lifted, her mouth quivering ever so slightly. Her fingers gripped the back of the chair. 'Please, if you would give us the courtesy, I need to be alone with my husband. I'm very sorry, Leo, but you have disappointed me greatly, and I can no longer continue with this visit.'

Evelyn led the way out, holding the door as Pippa and Leo stepped out of the house. Leo was ahead of Pippa. He did not look back. Pippa paused on the doorstep, trying to find words to make things right for Leo, to calm his mother.

'Don't bother,' the woman hissed. 'You've done enough. You do not get to prance in here and lure my son away. And our family is none of your business. It is for me to fix this.'

As the door shut, Pippa saw a look of undisguised malevolence twist Evelyn Clifford's elegant face.

CHAPTER THIRTY

Tuesday, 27 June 2017

The botanical gardens were quiet. The blurred noise of traffic was held at a distance by the original high red-brick walls, wide lawns, and groves of thick-limbed trees planted by Europeans desperate for a reminder of home. Olivia had only been there once before, on a Sunday in autumn when the lawns and paths had been cluttered with running children and parents with fancy prams. Families and friends had sat on blankets, loved-up couples walked hand in hand, and avid gardeners reverently stroked leaves and noted complicated botanical names. Olivia had been alone, the movement and clamour of others heightening her isolation. She hadn't stayed long.

But today she had someone at her side. A very appealing someone who had taken her hand as soon as they left the car and stood with his body close.

'There's a restaurant, or we could get takeaway,' she suggested as they headed down the path towards the visitor centre.

He took in the sloping stretches of clipped grass and the thick garden beds. 'Let's eat outside,' he said decisively. 'It's nice out here.' He turned his attention back to her, lifting her hand and rubbing the back of her cold fingers. 'If you're warm enough, that is.' It was a small considerate action, and Olivia's heart soared.

The lack of sleep was making her sensitive and soppy, she told herself. The tingle of joy in her chest was an overreaction. But, dammit, this moment was precious and she was going to enjoy it. 'I'm warm enough.' She smiled at him.

Twenty minutes later they settled onto a bench with a view over the gardens, the day grey but not wet. They settled on a simple, comforting lunch of hot chips and sausage rolls and were quiet as they ate. Her stress seeped away, washed aside by the pleasure of comfort food, the presence of Tom, and the sheer normality of what they were doing. They were a couple on a seat eating lunch in the gardens—they were utterly and blissfully normal.

How long since she'd been in a scene like this? Certainly not with Hayden. Their time together had been almost entirely behind closed doors. He'd never walked with her anywhere, or held her hand in public, or arranged a picnic. They had never even eaten together in a restaurant. How could she have been so blind as to think they were in a genuine relationship? She'd been deluded. And how long had it been before Hayden? She'd been so busy with her career, so determined not to get caught in the emotional trap of becoming half of a couple, that she'd avoided any sort of commitment. Then the Year of Leena—as she had taken to calling 2014—had been purely hedonistic.

Olivia tilted her face to the sun and closed her eyes, tears tickling behind the lids. She tried to smooth down the jagged spikes of emotion. Ups and downs. Highs and lows. No sleep. It had been a challenging week.

'You feeling alright?' Tom asked gently.

She nodded twice but kept her eyes shut—if she looked at him, she would come undone. His arm reached around her shoulders, tugging her closer, enclosing her in his strength and warmth. She turned her head into his shoulder.

'You don't have to tell me if you don't want to. But I'm here if you need to talk.'

She managed a muffled 'okay'.

They sat like that for a while. Tom played with her hair, twirling a piece round and round his finger before letting it slide off, then starting again. 'You're not falling asleep on me, are you?' he whispered, just when the rhythm of his touch was lulling her into the floaty state of being not quite awake.

She smiled into the warmth of his solid shoulder. 'Maybe.'

'Good.' He brushed a kiss over her temple.

After a few more minutes, she lifted her head. His face was turned to hers, leaving little space between them. His kiss was cautious, barely touching her, with an exquisite gentleness. Then their mouths pressed together a little more, lingering before they slowly pulled apart.

'You're so beautiful,' he murmured.

'Thank you,' Olivia managed. 'So are you.' *So are you?* 'I mean, you're very attractive. And lovely.' She groaned inwardly.

He laughed lightly. 'And we make a pretty amazing team, don't you think?'

She returned his smile. 'Yes, I think we do.'

'But it doesn't have to be all about the quest, you know. If you want me to help *you* with anything, you just have to ask. I'm here for you.'

The urge to explain her life was pressing, words pushing upwards before jamming hard and sharp in her throat. Once she talked, there would be no taking back the knowledge he would have. He would think differently—it was inevitable. This perfect moment of connection would be washed away. 'I'll keep that in mind,' was all she said.

She didn't want to think about Hayden and Leena, blackmail or sex tapes. She wanted, desperately, for Tom to remain separate from all of that. He would eventually learn about her, but she hoped it would be after they parted. Because that was the other thing—he was leaving. This thing between them, it couldn't last. The best—the *very* best—she could hope for was a little bubble of pleasure while he was here. A joyous, sexy interlude from reality. She could live on the memories of these few days.

'Do you want to walk?' she asked, needing to break the confessional mood.

'Sure.'

They meandered hand in hand along one of the wide avenues as a few ducks ambled out of their way. A lithe runner sped past them in a blur of lycra. 'I have to go to Sydney,' Olivia said as they passed the rough white trunks of the birch grove.

'When?'

'Tomorrow.' It was fine, she told herself. Tom wouldn't be staying in Hobart much beyond then anyway. If Maggie turned up today with the contact details for Pippa, he would be off on the next stage of his search. The confrontation with Leena could not be put off or avoided.

'Oh,' he said, as though the news was disappointing. 'How long will you be gone?'

'Only a day. Maybe two.'

He was quiet for a bit, then asked carefully, 'What will you be doing in Sydney?'

She aimed for flippant to divert the conversation. 'Have to get off the island every now and then, otherwise I'd go nuts. One of my favourite five-star hotels has refurbished recently, so I thought I'd give it a quick visit.'

'Okay. Right then. Sounds … nice,' he said despondently. He probably thought she was ditching him for an indulgent city break.

She rushed to add, 'And there's someone I need to see. She's asked me to visit. Something urgent has come up.'

'A social trip, then?'

Olivia couldn't bring herself to answer straight away. 'It's important,' was all she could manage. 'And I guess you'll be heading off to find Pippa?'

'I guess so. All going well.'

They were both quiet as they contemplated the reality of their short-lived romance—could she even call it that?

He gently tugged Olivia to a stop. 'Thank you for being here, for coming this morning and doing this with me. And thank you for helping me with this insane search. I had not expected to meet someone so lovely when I started out on this.' He kissed her tenderly. 'Thank you.'

She slid her arms under his jacket and around him, leaning her head against his chest. 'You're welcome,' she said, the words muffled. Chances were, this would be their last day together.

*

They made it to the sandstone conservatory twenty minutes before Maggie was due. The building was long and narrow, with a door at each end, filled on both sides with plants.

Halfway along was a circular fountain, the noise of the tinkling, dancing water amplified under the curved roof. After
walking the length a couple of times, they sat on one of the
benches.

Maggie arrived a little after two. She'd changed out of her
workout gear but still bounced with pent-up energy. 'Hi!
You're here. Fabulous. As soon as you left the house I thought,
Oh my god, I don't have their number. I had this sudden mad
thought that something would happen, you wouldn't be able
to make it and then we'd never be in contact. But, hey, you're
here! I'm so glad. Do you feel like an ice-cream?'

'An ice-cream?' Olivia almost laughed. 'But it's the middle
of winter.'

'It's one of those bizarre connection things for me. When
I was a kid, we'd come here with our babysitter, and there'd
always be an ice-cream for Leo and me. Then I got older, and
I'd come with my girlfriends, and I'd still want the ice-cream.
Doesn't feel right if I'm not chomping down a Maxibon while
I'm here.'

'Yeah, sure.' Tom grinned. 'We've had chips and a sausage
roll. Let's top off our lunch with ice-cream. Sounds good.
Olivia?'

'Why not.'

Maggie didn't stop talking as they headed back to the takeaway counter at the visitor centre. She asked what Tom thought
of Hobart, what he did for a job, where he lived in London.

When he went up to order, she linked her arm through
Olivia's and said in a quiet voice, 'Mum pointed out why I
recognised you. Can I say, I think Hayden Carlyle is a piece
of shit. An absolute shit! I can't stand the way it's always supposed to be the woman's fault in these things. That's absolute

bullshit. And that friend of yours, whatever her name is, she did a very, very bad thing. You, on the other hand, have dignity. I even said that to Mum back when the story was all over everything. I said, "That woman is being harassed from here to hell and back, but she carries herself with such dignity!" Oh yay, is that for me?' Her voice jumped back to normal as she took her treat from Tom. 'Thank you.'

Olivia had no chance to respond, not that she could think of anything to say. Since the trial the occasional person had gone out of their way to offer support, and every time she'd been ridiculously grateful and teary. When it felt like the whole world hated her, it was overwhelming when someone stepped through the dark clouds of hostility to put warmth in her day.

She watched Maggie peel back the ice-cream wrapper and, with a total lack of self-consciousness, make noises of intense satisfaction as she took a bite and began to stroll away. 'Let's find a spot to sit, and I'll fill you in,' she said.

Tom and Olivia followed, tearing open their own ice-creams. They settled on a wooden bench beside the large stone-edged pond with its covering of lily pads. Maggie sat in the middle. Tall ornamental grasses and small dormant trees surrounded them. A sign advised visitors not to feed the wildlife, and the ducks seemed to have got the memo, ignoring them completely.

Maggie's exuberance had been replaced by a subdued gravity. 'Now, first and foremost, I need to say I definitely do not agree with the brouhaha my parents carry on with. I do not think Jeremy was involved in Leo's death. And yes, before you ask, I do think he died.' She finished her ice-cream, scrunched up the wrapper and shoved it in her handbag. 'Leo would not have left of his own accord—he just wouldn't have. And, yes, I know the families of missing people often say the same thing, but it's true. There was absolutely nothing that would've made him leave. I accepted that very early on.'

'How old were you when it happened?' asked Tom.

'I was sixteen. Leo was my big brother.'

'That must've been hard,' said Olivia. She took another bite of her ice-cream.

'God, it was horrible. Not only did I miss him, but there was so much drama around it.' She'd extracted a tissue to wipe her hands. 'Mum and Dad, they'd never been easy people, but they were definitely nicer, more relaxed, more fun, before it happened. Life had been pretty good for us as a family, especially me. They put a bit of pressure on Leo, but I had a great childhood. Afterwards they became more constrained. Angry, of course, and, I don't know … determined? Yes. They were determined to find someone to blame. Determined not to look like bad parents. Determined for me to pick up the slack and become the star of the family. Which was never going to happen,' she scoffed. 'After I finished school I immediately moved to Melbourne with some girlfriends and had a brilliant time there. I couldn't be in that house any longer. But Mum and Dad have always been focused on being successful, and they have a tight definition of what that means. Sometimes it felt like Leo's loss was this huge inconvenience to them.' Maggie must have seen the shock on Olivia's face. 'Oh, don't get me wrong, they loved him. Of course they did. And there was a lot of grief. But Dad was seriously pissed off too—nothing like a massive family tragedy to make the slog up the social ladder a tad more precarious.'

'And they didn't want to know Pippa or her child?' Tom asked. He'd finished his ice-cream and was smoothing the wrapper between his fingers, folding it over and flattening it. Olivia noticed he didn't refer to the baby as being Leo's.

'At first Mum did. I mean, Pippa was a connection to Leo, and she was pregnant with his baby! It was absolutely Leo's, by the way. And Mum kept trying to get Pip to come and live at the house. They'd only recently built that place then.'

Maggie was adamant about the child's parentage, as Tilly had been. It was only the Cliffords who had cast serious doubt. Olivia imagined Pippa being coerced by them. They might have been nicer people back then—if Maggie was right—but Pippa apparently hadn't felt comfortable being in their house. 'She stayed with Eloise,' Olivia said.

'Yep. Pippa isn't stupid. She had met my parents, and Leo had talked to her about how unhappy they'd made him—not unhappy enough to run away, mind you, but enough to not want to live with them. Anyway, Pip is a smart girl. She didn't move in, Mum threw a bit of a hissy fit about not getting her way, and the next thing they're suggesting that Leo isn't the father. If they couldn't have Paige on their terms, then they didn't want her or Pippa at all. Things deteriorated from there.'

'But you and Pippa stayed in contact?' Tom asked, and Olivia could hear his nervous anticipation.

Maggie nodded, looking first at Tom, then Olivia. 'You've got to understand, Leo was not a foolish kid. He put thought into everything he did. He was also good-looking. The girls at school all wanted to meet my big brother. If he'd wanted to, he could've been a bit of a player, but he wasn't. Then he met Pippa, and he absolutely fell for her, and she for him. You had to see them together—it was the real deal. I was so envious of what they had. To a romantic sixteen-year-old, it looked like some fated love story. And I liked Pippa. She was so bloody cool.'

Olivia's heart broke as she thought of the young couple. What a terrible thing for Pippa to have gone through. They still didn't know how Jeremy fit into this love story, but the relationship between Leo and Pippa rang true. 'Your dad said she was older than Leo.'

'Only by a couple of years! And Leo always seemed older than he was. I mean, when he and Pippa met, he'd just finished the Sydney to Hobart.' She turned to Tom. 'Have you heard about that? It's an open ocean yacht race. Seriously challenging stuff.'

Tom nodded. 'Yeah, I know it.'

'Well, Leo did it at nineteen. It's a gruelling event—you need to know what you're doing out there. My brother had been around the boats since he was about ten, and he was well respected by the older yachties. Anyway, what was my point?'

'You were saying you and Pippa were friends and have kept in touch,' Olivia prompted.

'Yes. Right. My point was Leo was mature, Pippa was fun and cool and exciting, and they were absolutely besotted with each other. I wanted to be her friend. First because of how she was, then later because she was a connection with my brother. And then there was Paige. I would get down to Devils Bay whenever I could. Eloise always invited me to stay, and I'd help out any way I could. Mum absolutely hated me being there, but I didn't care. It was so good to get away from them. I even gave Pippa money—which, of course, she didn't want to take. So I'd stuff it in Paige's nappy bag. Then after Pip left we would write, talk on the phone. These days we video chat, and I visit her from time to time.'

'Where is she living?' asked Tom nervously.

'Her home town, Brisbane. Her mum and dad got over the shock and stepped up to the role of grandparents, and Pippa finally let go of the idea that Leo would come back.'

Olivia thought of Pippa pregnant and forlorn outside the general store with Tilly. 'She waited for him, until there was no hope,' she said quietly.

'Yes. Pip didn't want to believe he'd died. She held strong to the belief he was still out there somewhere.' Maggie lifted her handbag onto her lap and stuffed in her used tissue, then pulled out a piece of paper. 'Tom, can I ask you something?'

'Of course.' Olivia could hear his restrained excitement.

'Why didn't Jeremy keep in touch with Pippa? Did he ever say anything to you about his reasons? They'd had years of a close friendship that shouldn't have been obliterated so easily.'

'I wish I could answer that, but the first time I heard of Pippa was when I came across an envelope addressed to her.' Tom was staring out over the pond, his face serious. 'Dad relegated the years before he moved to England to a locked-up section of his memories. There was the time before his big move, and there was the time after.'

'I have to admit, if it was me, I might have opened that envelope,' Maggie said, then chuckled. 'No. I *definitely* would have.'

He gave her a cheeky look, the smile he was smothering making it clear he'd come close to doing the same. 'Don't worry, I've been tempted.' He stretched out his legs and folded his arms. 'But I told myself I had to at least make a solid effort to deliver it before I gave in to that temptation. I have no idea what it's about and, yeah, the more we've found out, the more nervous I am about what's in there.' He lifted his shoulders, let them drop. 'Maybe he has regrets. Maybe he wants to apologise? I don't know.' He didn't mention the photographs, which Olivia thought was tactful.

Maggie was watching him closely. 'You actually remind me of Leo a bit, you know. That same seriousness when you speak. Same eyes, of course. But then Jeremy and Leo looked a lot alike, so I guess it's the whole family gene pool thing. Or, of course, I could be seeing things I want to see. Did he have a good life over there?'

Tom nodded. 'I think so. He was successful with his business—he started out working in pubs, then not long after I came along he bought one. Renovated it, built it up. Sold it, bought a few more nice places. He was married only once, to my mum, which didn't last. I still got to spend a lot of time with him. He was a great dad.'

'Was?' Maggie asked.

'He passed away at the start of last year,' Tom said.

He was still mourning the loss of his father, thought Olivia. He was doing all this for his dad—but what would happen if, at the end, there was a revelation that didn't measure up with the man he'd known?

'He must have had you pretty soon after he settled there,' said Maggie. 'When were you born?'

'Nineteen eighty-nine. He and Mum were married in early eighty-eight. Whirlwind romance, I've been told. Then they had me.'

'So, he went over there and instantly put everything in Australia behind him, including his best friend. And he never looked back?' Maggie sounded critical.

'Doesn't sound great, does it?' Tom replied, exhaling deeply. 'But people who knew him liked and respected him. He was a good boss to his staff. Ran his pubs well. Was kind and thoughtful. Looked after people who needed a hand. I don't know why he blanked out his early life. But there were times when he would be quiet—sad, even. In hindsight, I wonder if there wasn't huge regret. Maybe he did have a longing for Australia. But I guess I might never know.'

'Have you asked your mum about what he was like when she met him?' asked Olivia. The more she heard of Jeremy, the less his story made sense. 'Does she know about this trip and why you're here?'

He shook his head. 'She says he was quite closed off back then too. It was one of the things that affected their marriage. She described him as a good man with locked doors in his life. She knows I'm here, but not why.'

Maggie rested a hand on Tom's shoulder. 'Maybe there'll be answers in the envelope,' she said. 'Although I suppose it'll be up to Pippa to share them with you. I checked with her, and she's happy for you to reach out.' Maggie handed Tom the piece of paper. 'Her email address and mobile number.'

'I can't tell you how much I appreciate your help,' Tom said as he took the note. 'Eloise had been ... somewhat reluctant to share these details or to let Pippa know about me.'

'Yes, well, as much as I adore Eloise, she has always been a guard dog for Pippa and Paige. Probably thought a delivery from Jeremy would hurt Pippa, bring back all the emotions around him cutting her off. After that summer she was brutally scathing towards him, took his actions quite personally.' Maggie looked at her watch. 'Crap. Sorry, I'm going to be late. Again. The kids get so stroppy when they have to wait. Not that it hurts them, precious little darlings that they are.' They all stood, Maggie pulling first Olivia then Tom into a heartfelt hug. 'Wait. Wait. Before I dash, I need your numbers. Tom, you're family after all. Twice removed or second cousins, or something. I can never remember how it works.' Maggie dug

around in her bag. When she found her phone, her fingers
tapped the screen. 'Here—you first, Olivia, pop your num-
ber in.' Olivia did as she was asked, then passed the phone to
Tom, who typed in his number and handed it back to Maggie.
'Anyway, Tom, I hope you get resolution and enjoy meeting
Pip. And Olivia, good luck with everything. You deserve some
fabulous things in your life. Well, that's my opinion, anyway.'
She grinned and fluttered her fingers in a wave. 'Bye. Bye. Bye.'
And she trotted off.

They watched her go, then sank back against the bench.
Tom sat forward, arms on his thighs, and unfolded the piece
of paper, reading the contents several times. This was a big
moment for him. Her own buzzing anticipation was making it
hard to sit still. Tom must be just as excited, but he was taking
his time. Was he worried about what would happen next?

'I have to say, I rather like Maggie,' Olivia mused while she
waited.

He leaned back and met her eye, smiling vaguely. 'I think
she's brilliant. Hard to imagine she's related to her parents.'

Olivia laughed. 'Tell me about it!'

'We've been lucky.' It was almost like he couldn't believe he
had what he needed. 'Without her we wouldn't have this.' He
held up the note.

'Now what?'

'I guess we call.' He held her gaze until she nodded.

'No point waiting,' she said, letting her hand rest on his arm.

'Right.' He pulled his phone from his jacket and carefully
entered the number, looking intently at Olivia as he lifted it
to his ear. Fear and hope were written in his expression, and
his chest was rising in slow, deep breaths. She reached over
to wrap his free hand in both of hers. He returned her grip

tightly. This was the beginning of the end, thought Olivia. The last run towards the finish line for Tom. She was happy for him—a feeling outweighed by the dread of seeing Leena and saying goodbye to this gorgeous man.

She could hear the call ringing, then the sound of a woman answering.

'Hello,' said Tom, not taking his eyes from her. 'Is that Pippa French? My name is Tom Kearsley. I'm Jeremy Kearsley's son.'

CHAPTER THIRTY-ONE

Thursday, 6 February 1986

Pippa took Leo's outstretched hand, letting him haul her onto the back of the ute. The canvas cover was off, and they sat with their backs to the cab. They were in the carpark on top of Mount Wellington, a landscape of rock and stunted alpine growth spread before them. The view beyond was even more spectacular. Hobart sat tight against the base of the mountain, the Derwent River opening wide at the edge of the city. Up on the mountain they were in another world—a world 10 degrees colder than the one down below. Leo unfolded an old tartan blanket and pulled it over their laps, reaching across to tuck it in around her.

She opened the paper bag in her hand and passed out the meat pies. 'Not steaming hot but still good,' she said, taking a bite.

As a glob of filling fell onto her sweatshirt, Leo laughed. 'Doing it in style, babe.'

Since the evening with his parents, it had become something of a catchphrase for them.

'With or without money,' Pippa added.

They grinned. Humour had become the best way to deal with the situation. A week had passed, and Leo had yet to return to his parents' house. There had been no phone calls, no contact at all.

Secure within the sanctuary of Eloise's home, Leo and Pippa had talked. About his family. About Jeremy. About their plans. Whenever the topic of his parents became difficult, they'd pull the atlas from the bookshelf and start planning itineraries. Pippa was going to write about their travels. Maybe she'd have a contract with Eloise's publishing friend, or maybe she wouldn't. Leo had suggested she could go freelance. He had some money put aside, could keep them going for a while. There had been a generous Year Twelve graduation gift from his father, and he'd saved his wages from part-time jobs on other people's boats. He could sell his car.

When Jeremy had heard their plans, he'd been excited for them, insisting they visit him in London. He still didn't know that Angus was his biological father.

'Jeremy's flight to Sydney is on Saturday,' Pippa said as they ate their pies. 'We've got less than two days.'

'Do you want to tell him?'

Did she? Perhaps it would be the best thing to do, definitely better than if her friend found out from the Cliffords—not that she expected Leo's parents to drop in for a session of family confessions. But if the positions had been reversed, she'd want to know. And keeping secrets from Jeremy was all wrong ... or mostly wrong. There were valid reasons for staying quiet, mostly to do with what would happen next. Predicting

Jeremy's reaction was difficult, and she didn't want either of the brothers to learn about Angela's rape. Pippa was protecting her friend—protecting both of them. Wasn't she?

'My gut feeling says this is the wrong time,' she said. 'What if we tell him and it gets ugly? He's about to kick off a huge, exciting chapter in his life. Does he need to know about this right now?'

'You think we could tell him when we catch up over there?' Going to London was high on their wish list. It wasn't a bad idea to delay the drama until whenever that might be.

'Damn, it's freezing up here.' Pippa pulled the tartan blanket higher and snuggled into Leo's warmth.

'Bloody Queenslanders.' He laughed, wrapping his arms around her. 'Can't handle a bit of fresh air.'

*

The road down from the mountain merged into the inner-city suburbs of Hobart. It was the closest they'd been to the city for a week, and Pippa asked Leo if he wanted to go by his parents' house. His answer was simple. Why would they want to ruin a lovely day? He knew he'd have to return eventually, but there was no hurry—he had enough clothes stashed in Pippa's room. First they'd lock in their plan and book some tickets. Then he could visit a few times before they left. That would be some-time after Eloise came home in a bit over two weeks.

'Well, don't make me go with you,' Pippa groaned. 'I may not be able to be nice if your mother starts in with her charm-ing comments.'

'That's probably for the best,' Leo said with mock serious-ness. 'I may need someone on the outside to raise the alarm. If

I don't return after three hours, you'll have to come and save me. My father will be determined to get his way. God knows what he'll do.'

'I'll kick in the door and rescue you from the basement.'

'We don't have a basement. There is, however, a shed at the bottom of the garden.'

'Good to know.'

They were still making jokes about Pippa's ninja breaking-and-entering skills when they turned off the highway and through the gates of home. They drove up the hill, the ute jolting and rocking over the potholes. Coming around the bend, Leo braked sharply, the dust rising and drifting through their open windows.

Pippa looked ahead. 'Whose car is that?'

'Dad's.'

Not good. Really, really not good. 'Where's Jeremy? Was he going out today?' she asked before realising the pale blue Laser was sitting in the carport.

Leo nudged his car forward, parking beside the black BMW, then killed the engine. Neither of them spoke. Pippa could hear the melodic notes of magpie song. The rough caw of a crow. A softer chorus of chirpy whistles.

A minute passed. They were avoiding the inevitable like two children covering their eyes and thinking no one could see them. But they had to go into the house.

They held hands as they walked to the door.

'This could get ugly,' Pippa whispered. There was something repugnant about having Angus anywhere near her personal things.

Leo didn't answer as they stepped inside. At first they couldn't hear anything unusual. Honey came trotting up from the lounge, sniffing at their legs to see if they'd been anywhere interesting. Then she turned and headed back through the house to the open French doors. They followed.

Jeremy and Angus were facing each other at the outside table, two beers sitting between them. Angus was speaking, at ease with what was happening or even enjoying himself. Jeremy was staring out towards the water. He nodded once. Then he turned his head, noticing Leo and Pippa. There was a flicker of anguish on his face before he looked away again.

Angus twisted around in his seat. 'Hello, Leo, Pippa,' he said loudly. 'You had better come and join us.'

If not for Jeremy, Pippa would have walked away. Being summoned by this man made her cringe. How satisfying it would be to give him the finger, to ignore his commands—to, in some small way, retaliate. Holding the idea in her head, she let Leo lead them forward.

He stopped at the end of the table. 'Dad, what are you doing here?'

'Thought we should have a chat. Your mother is worried about you. She's very upset. And since you don't seem to be coming home anytime soon, I had to come to you.' He picked up his beer, tilting it in Jeremy's direction. 'And, I have to say, I'm very glad I did. I got to meet Jeremy.'

Leo's grip on her hand tightened and she could feel the tension in his body. He didn't say anything, as though trying to read the situation before he spoke. Jeremy was now staring at Angus, his features slack. Angus looked first at one then the other of his sons, his eyes amused as though he found this entertaining. He was revelling in the shock and upheaval he'd just delivered—Pippa had absolutely no doubt that was what he'd done.

She focused on her friend. 'Jeremy, are you okay?'

He looked at her, frowning. 'Hard to say.'

Pippa let go of Leo and pulled out the chair next to Jeremy, angling herself so she was facing him. 'What has he told you?'

Angus answered before Jeremy had a chance to speak. 'I've told him the truth. I thought it was well past time someone did.'

'You knew, didn't you?' Jeremy asked Pippa with a sigh. 'And you.' He turned to Leo, who looked wary. 'Jeez, guys, it might've been good if you'd talked to me about this.'

'We didn't know if it was the right time—with you leaving and everything ...' Pippa trailed off. It was a pathetic excuse. Seeing the hurt in his eyes, she knew she'd made the wrong call. 'I'm sorry.'

She reached for his hand, relieved when he took it and squeezed. 'Yeah. This is up there as far as big news.'

'We only found out a week ago,' said Leo, who finally took a seat to the other side of Jeremy. 'Bit of a shock for us. For me.'

Jeremy choked out a small laugh. 'Mate. Brothers. Fuck.'

'Yeah, fuck, what the hell are we going to do with that?' Leo said, the two of them ignoring Angus.

'Well, good to see you two boys getting along.' Angus clapped his hands together, rubbing one palm against the other, drawing the attention back to himself. 'Jeremy was just telling me about his job. A business analyst—impressive. With an economics degree. I'm already proud of you. Guess you got your brains and ambition from me.'

Jeremy's face shifted, the slightly stunned look hardening. He moved his gaze from Pippa and sat a little taller. Behind the shock, he was still there, and the Jeremy she knew could recognise a smug prick from a mile off. He worked with enough of them and had made it clear he didn't have time for those arseholes. 'Sorry, Angus, I didn't get anything from you. You have had no input into my life. Please don't think you can take any credit for who I am.'

Leo suppressed a noise that seemed to be both a laugh and a splutter of surprise.

Angus jerked his chin in an abrupt nod, not used to being put in his place. 'Alright. Fair enough.'

'Look, Dad, it might be best if you left,' Leo said. The three of them were facing the older man, their show of unity impossible to ignore.

Angus, however, wasn't finished. He pulled a folded envelope out of his pocket and laid it on the table. 'Your uni offer, Leo. I wanted to remind you what you're throwing away.' The Cliffords were obviously a long way from accepting Leo's choices.

'Thank you, but you didn't need to bring that here.' He was being polite but not submissive.

'I'm presuming you've changed your mind about walking away from this?' Angus slapped the letter with his hand. 'You've come to your senses? Stopped wasting time on pointless fantasies?'

'No. I have not changed my mind.'

'Then we need to talk. If you could excuse us—' he looked at Jeremy and Pippa, motioning that they should leave '—this is between my son and me.' He chuckled. 'My *youngest* son. Sorry, Jeremy, that's going to take some getting used to.'

Pippa let out a shuddering huff and shook her head. His audacity was unbelievable.

'Please, go,' Leo said, equally unimpressed. He got to his feet. 'I'm not going to talk about this right now. You've come in here and dropped a bombshell, and now you want to tell everyone what to do. That's not how it works.'

Angus pushed back his chair and stood. Leo was a fraction taller, but Angus's bearing had the weight of authority. 'Actually, that's precisely how it works. You do not talk to me like that.' His words were stones, hard and heavy, aimed to flatten dissent.

Leo held his ground but wavered. 'It doesn't have to be like this. I'm nineteen. You could treat me like an adult.'

'You don't deserve it.' Angus braced his arms on the table and leant forward. 'You're a spoiled kid who's fucked a sexy piece of arse and let it go to his head. Get over it. There's plenty more of that around—don't throw away your future because you're pussy-whipped.'

Pippa gasped. Despite everything she knew of this man, his denigration of her was a slap in the face. 'You are really something,' she spluttered, as Jeremy surged to his feet.

'Don't you *ever* talk about her like that!' Leo shouted.

'Get out!' Jeremy was just as fierce in his anger, clearly holding no fear of this man. 'Get the fuck out.' He said each word with force.

Angus held up his hands. 'Sorry, did I go too far?'

'Dad, go.' Leo folded his arms.

'Sure—as soon as you promise you'll come home to talk.'

'Fine.' The word was forced out through his clenched jaw. 'When?'

Leo folded his arms and looked at the ground. 'Next week.'

'If you don't turn up, I'll come down here to find you.' Angus finally stepped towards the French doors. 'By the way, don't think you can just take off. I've got your passport.' He raised his hand in a stiff wave and laughed as though they had amused him. 'Look at you two! I've made some good-looking kids. Come and see me anytime you want, Jeremy.'

Angus sauntered into the house. Pippa watched him leave, the intensity of her loathing and the anger at the stunt he'd just pulled making her hands tremble. No one moved. A few seconds later they heard the front door close, then the muted rev of his BMW.

Pippa let out a growling scream of rage. 'That man! That entitled, smug, revolting man.'

Leo came around to crouch beside her chair, concern and anger in his eyes. 'Are you okay? I'm so sorry he said that.'

'I'm fine.' She pressed her hands against her face, then rubbed her eyes hard. 'But I never want to see him again.' She looked at Leo, making sure he understood. 'Not ever.'

'Understood,' he said with gravity.

Still standing, Jeremy took a long drink from his beer before he sat. 'Well, folks,' he said, apparently trying to break the tension, 'this has been an interesting afternoon.' He rested a hand on Pippa's shoulder. 'And I think I speak for Pippa as well when I say that your father is a complete tosser.'

CHAPTER THIRTY-TWO

Friday, 7 February 1986

The three of them sat on the step at the edge of the terrace, Jeremy in the middle. The morning was crisp, the sun yet to warm the ground. 'What if I drive myself tomorrow, and you can come and pick up the car from the airport the next time you're in town? You've still got the spare key, don't you, Pip?'

'Yes. Are you sure it's okay if I sell it? I know it wasn't the original plan.' Jeremy had sold his car to her for next to nothing before they left Queensland. It felt wrong to be ditching it so soon.

'It's your car now—you've got the paperwork. If it helps fund your escape from Tassie, then that's a good thing.'

'Thank you.' Pippa had an arm around Jeremy's back. She gave him a squeeze. While his attempt to save her from an early morning start was appreciated, it seemed wrong to say their goodbyes at the house, like they were getting rid of him early. 'It's okay, though. I don't mind driving you there. You're heading off to the other side of the world. Two days of hellish travelling. It doesn't seem right you should have to drive over an hour to the airport as well, especially at sparrow's fart.'

Jeremy bumped her shoulder with his. 'You know what, I've got a better idea. I could leave here today instead and stay the night in town at a backpackers. I can book into that one on Liverpool Street. Then it won't be such an early wake-up. I'll still take the car, and you can collect it from the hostel whenever it suits.'

'Today? But we were going to have a special dinner. A proper send-off.'

'Oh yeah? What was on the menu?'

Leo answered. 'Sausages with black bits, barbecued the way you like them. Might be a while before you get a good overcooked snag again.'

Jeremy laughed. 'Aw, the things you do for me. I'm going to miss you. Both of you.'

Pippa's eyes filled with tears. 'Fine.' She sniffed. 'I hate goodbyes anyway. Why don't I go for a nice long walk? While I'm gone you can slip away. That way there'll be no big, emotional scene.'

'How about a small scene. Can you handle that?'

She shook her head and rubbed her face against his shoulder. The night had been long, and she was exhausted, her body demanding sleep, her heart and mind needing a break from the intensity of the past day.

Yesterday, after Angus had left, each of them had explained what they knew and how they'd come to know it. First Pippa, then Leo, and finally Jeremy. Pippa had, of course, still held back the ugliest slice of the truth, saying only that Angela had rung. 'I got the feeling she despises Angus. That she didn't want him in your life,' Pippa had said.

Leo had talked of how, throughout his life, there had been things that didn't quite add up. The awareness of family secrets.

Jeremy told how Angus had arrived, introducing himself, saying he was looking for Leo. How Jeremy had invited him inside, offered him a beer, Angus showing great interest in what Jeremy did for work, his degree, his prospects, the job he had lined up in London. 'Do you know who I am?' Angus had asked.

'Ah, yeah. You said you were Leo's father.'

'I am. How's your mother, by the way?'

'You know my mum?'

'Haven't seen her for about twenty-five years, if I remember correctly. The last time I saw her was a few months before my wedding to her sister. I think Angela was quite jealous of Evelyn. I think she wanted what her sister had. I'm guessing you were born in '61, right? Around about April, by my calculation.'

Jeremy had read between the lines.

While he'd absorbed the words, the man had kept talking as if recounting a happy memory. 'Your mum was so pretty—the prettier of the two sisters, I have to admit. But she wasn't quite the woman for me. I think I made the right choice. Although—' and he laughed '—Evelyn can be a bit of a ballbreaker.'

'What are you getting at?' Jeremy had asked. 'What is it you're trying to say to me?'

'Haven't you ever wondered who your father is? What did Angela tell you?'

'Are you saying you're my father?'

'Come on, Jeremy. You know I am.'

Recounting the conversation, Jeremy veered from cynical amusement to outrage. 'Fuck him,' he said when he'd finished, saying it softly as though he refused to react with anything more than scorn. But then he raised his voice. 'No, seriously, fuck him! What sort of fuckwit just saunters in and throws that sort of shit around?'

'An arrogant cockhead, I'd say,' said Leo mildly.

'You'd know,' said Jeremy, his laugh caught somewhere between hysteria and tears.

'Yep. I'd know.'

The night slid over them as they talked. There were accusations and excuses when Jeremy explained how pissed off he was that neither of them had told him. He was furious to have learnt about it from his biological father rather than from friends who had held on to the secret for a week. But he forgave them, because that was the man he was. He wasn't going to hold a grudge, not when he could direct his disgust at Angus Clifford.

'Are you going to talk to your mum?' Pippa asked at one point, dreading where that might lead.

'Not yet. She obviously thought she was doing the right thing by not telling me. From what you're saying, she was a young girl forced to go it alone with a new baby and no support. I totally understand her disdain for her family—and for that arsehole. She did the best she could, and she didn't want anything to do with her parents or sister. If I'd known about him earlier, I might have insisted on a meeting. She thought she was protecting me. Let's face it, Evelyn wouldn't have welcomed me or my mum.'

'On the bright side, you now have a brother,' said Pippa.

'And a sister,' added Leo. 'Don't forget Maggie.'

They discussed how to let Maggie know about Jeremy and when he might meet her. They all decided to put it aside until she was older, perhaps when he came back from London.

They'd all fallen asleep in the lounge, reluctant to leave each other after such an important night, the three of them connected by the strong silken threads of history, love, and friendship.

*

In the end Pippa did go for a walk, deciding that hovering about while Jeremy finished packing was too difficult. He promised her he'd still be there when she got back.

She and Honey returned to find the brothers back on the terrace. She stood at a distance and watched, her heart burning with a mess of emotion. She was sad for the upcoming absence of her friend, felt the choking weight of the unspeakable secret, but also the love she had for both of them.

Then it was time. They all walked through to the other side of the house. Standing beside the Laser, the boys hugged, slapping each other on the back.

'It's been a ride,' said Jeremy. 'One hell of a ride. But I'm glad our paths crossed. Look after this girl, she means the world to me.'

'I promise.'

'And good luck with sorting out your old man,' said Jeremy. 'Get out of here, get to London soon. The beers will be on me, okay?'

'It's a deal.'

Then Jeremy faced Pippa.

'No riding on scooters,' she said. 'I won't be there to save your arse.'

He pulled her into a fierce hug. 'Don't play strip poker with card sharks. I won't be there to lend you a shirt.'

She laughed. Then sobbed. Then laughed again when Leo said, 'It's alright if she teaches me how to play, though. I mean that's okay, right?'

'Yeah, I can live with that.'

Jeremy let her go, opened the driver's door, then stopped. 'This has been a great summer, despite the dramatic moments. Leo, mate, you're alright. If anyone deserves this girl, then it's you.' He gave his widest grin. 'After all, you're my brother. You're the best there is. Next to me, of course.'

Then he was gone.

CHAPTER THIRTY-THREE

Tuesday, 27 June 2017

Tom's gaze stayed locked on Olivia as he lifted his phone. This was it. He was within reach of the prize.

The call was answered mid-ring. A woman spoke. 'Hello?'

'Hello,' he answered. 'Is that Pippa French?'

'Yes, it is.' A pleasant voice, throaty and moderated. In a few words she had evoked the image of a newsreader with her careful, well-articulated pronunciation and warmth. The beautiful girl in the photo was now a mature woman.

'My name is Tom Kearsley. I'm Jeremy Kearsley's son.'

Silence for a few beats. 'Yes. I was expecting to hear from you, Tom. Maggie rang me earlier. How can I help you?'

He spelt out his quest in a few simple sentences, breaking the news of Jeremy's death but deciding not to mention the photos yet.

'I'm truly sorry to hear that Jeremy died,' she said, and Tom sensed the truth of her sadness. 'I've always had a tiny hope that one day he'd turn up and explain himself. I guess this is as close to that moment as I'm ever going to get.'

'I wish I had more answers for you. Maybe he did try to reach out. I don't know.'

'He could've done. I have moved a few times, and I haven't been Pippa French for a very long time, not since well before the digital age. These days I'm Penelope Braden, divorced mother of one, Penny to friends and family.'

'Well, it's a great relief to speak to you, Penelope. I was hoping I could come and visit you, if that's alright?'

'I'd like that. And please, I'm happy for you to call me Pippa. I quite like hearing it, and that is the name on the envelope, right?'

'Pippa, then. I should be able to get up there tomorrow,' he said. 'Is that too soon?'

'Not at all. Let's meet the day after that, on Thursday.'

They exchanged a few more details, then she rang off with plans for him to contact her when he arrived in Brisbane. As easy as that, it was done.

'We did it!' Tom's laugh was light with relief. 'We actually did it.' He drew Olivia into a hug, the feeling of her in his arms accentuating the rush of the win. They drew apart and he kissed her quickly. 'We make an awesome team.'

She sat back, her face flushed. 'I've enjoyed myself.'

God, she was beautiful. He had to go to Brisbane, but he could spare a few days after that—he could come back here before he had to return home. 'I'll make the booking now.'

'How exciting,' she said, but her eyes showed more despair than delight.

'I could come back here for a few days after I'm finished in Brisbane, before I have to head back home. If you want.' His stomach knotted as he waited for her to say yes.

She looked away. 'That's okay, it is what it is,' she said before giving him a quick smile. 'It's fine. This—' she waved a hand between them '—whatever this is, it can't go any further. I know that.' She sounded stoic. Practical. But there was a waver in her voice.

'The tyranny of distance,' he said, trying to lighten the mood.

They looked at each other, fully aware there would be no chance for them to explore things further.

He slid a hand behind her head and pulled her gently towards him. This kiss was as wonderful as their first, their looming separation making them both desperate for the contact. 'I don't want to say goodbye,' he breathed when they eventually moved apart.

'Then we won't—not yet,' she said. 'We have the rest of the afternoon and a good chunk of the night. And it's getting too cold to sit here any longer.'

They walked back to her car with their arms around each other. Every now and then he'd lean down and brush his lips across her hair or forehead. Her Honda seemed to have shrunk even further, and the drive was excruciatingly slow despite the short distance from the gardens to the hotel. He rested his hand on her thigh as she drove, her hand dropping to his every time they came to a standstill. They pulled into the hotel drive, where Olivia handed the keys to the parking attendant and put the car under Tom's room number.

Walking into the lobby, he took her hand again and headed towards the lifts. But before he could push the call button, she tugged him to a standstill. He saw the wariness in her face and mentally kicked himself. 'I'm so sorry,' he said, mortified. 'I don't know what I was thinking.'

She raised her eyebrows and gave a small smile. 'I have some idea of what you might have been thinking.'

'Yeah. And now *you're* thinking what a complete tosser I am,' he said, trying to make a joke about the situation. 'Olivia, we do not have to go up. In fact, let's just go and get a drink.'

'It's a little early, isn't it?'

'Not when we have something to celebrate. We found Pippa—that means we deserve some champagne.'

She took both his hands and moved closer, tipping her head back to look at him. 'Tom, it's not that I don't want to, you know, go up with you. I do. I really do. But let's not rush just because we're on a deadline.'

'I'm okay with that.' Which he was, of course. But boy, he did not want to say goodbye to this woman. They needed more time.

'I don't trust myself to make good choices at the moment,' she said firmly, her eyes still on his.

Of course she didn't. He was a complete moron. Olivia surely had serious trust issues. Could he be more oblivious? 'That's totally fine,' he said, turning for the hotel entrance. 'Let's go find somewhere warm and friendly.'

Once again, they walked along the waterfront. The air was cold and fresh, the sky a pale grey, with no rain falling. They stopped first to watch a small yacht manoeuvre away from its moorings, then the arrival of the large catamaran ferry, painted in camouflage greys, that carried visitors to and from the MONA art gallery further up the river. They skirted around a mob of seagulls fighting over hot chips thrown by a tradesman in a high-vis vest, while ahead of them sat Mount Wellington, the snow-capped peak a soft contrast against the rocky outcrops.

Tom kept his arm around Olivia, savouring her presence at his side. All they had was this precious time, and he was not going to mess it up.

CHAPTER THIRTY-FOUR

Olivia's head was spinning, her emotions and responses affected by the lack of sleep. During the meeting with the Cliffords it had taken all her self-control to contain her anger. Baseless accusations enraged her, reminding her of her own inability to be heard against a barrage of unjust commentary. Watching Tom flinch with every attack on his father, she'd only just managed to hold back the words she wanted to hurl at those two horrible people.

Then there had been the calm of being with Tom in the gardens and the reignition of their attraction. It was almost too much, her emotions overshadowing the thrill of Tom being so close to his goal.

Now she led him into a waterfront bar on the ground floor of a particularly ugly building that must have been built in the 1980s. While the red-brick monstrosity was an eyesore, the space inside was dark and atmospheric. It was also warm and nearly empty. There was a long table-height bench running the length of the window, and they took a seat looking out over the boats. Olivia went to get drinks, returning with a whisky for him and a sparkling water for herself.

He took a short sip then stopped to hold up his glass. 'We should toast to our success.'

'Congratulations and well done,' Olivia said with all the enthusiasm she could find. 'Here's to the completion of your quest.'

'Cheers!' he said as they clinked glasses. 'To excellent team-work. And can I say, you have been the best thing about this trip.'

She laughed a little. 'I think that's a bit of a stretch. Fulfilling your father's wish might come first.'

'True. But then meeting you is a very close second.' His grin was wide and infectious. 'Promise me that you and I will stay in contact.' He touched her knee.

Impossible declarations stuck to her tongue. She played with the paper straw in her drink and looked out the window. 'We could,' she said. 'I'm not on social media these days, but we could email, send Christmas cards, that sort of thing.'

'Would you consider a holiday in England?' His question was a surprise.

'Maybe. I don't know what direction I'm heading in at the moment,' she said at last. 'But a bit of travel could be a good idea.' Away from Australia, meeting his friends, spending weeks together … Could she do that? Yes. She could.

He grinned. 'I'd really, really—*really*—like to see you again. I think we could fit together well. Not that I'm rushing. Just, you know, I'd like to spend more time with you. Properly.'

'Tom.' She kept her voice gentle. 'You don't know me. You might think differently once you know more about me.'

He looked away and took a sip, then another. 'I have a con-fession to make,' he said carefully.

Wariness made her straighten up. 'What sort of confession?'

He was having trouble looking at her—his gaze kept flicking away. He took another sip before setting his glass down. He twisted it around.

He was gathering his courage, she realised, and instinctively braced herself.

At last he spoke. 'I know about the things you've been through in the last couple of years.'

He knew. Which meant he'd seen, read, and watched. She sagged inwardly. It had been inevitable. The clammy grip of shame tightened around her body, her defences putting up a protective steel wall.

She slipped her hand from his. Not a quick snatch, but a careful extraction. She laced her fingers together tightly, resting them on the table. 'You read about me?'

'Yes.'

'When?'

'What do you mean?'

'I mean, how long have you known about me?'

'Umm, I looked online the night after you came into town for dinner. When was that? Friday?'

'Saturday,' she corrected. She looked straight ahead, staring out towards the boats. Why hadn't he said something earlier? Did it matter?

'Olivia, I think what happened to you was horrible. You were taken advantage of, and you were blamed for things that weren't your fault.'

Yes, that much was true. But what about the rest? The things she *had* done. Was he going to ignore all that? He couldn't. She couldn't.

She sat perfectly still, unable to look at him. A void widened between them. He touched her hands, and she flinched. She couldn't deal with this right now. Couldn't process how she was feeling. She needed to leave.

'Olivia?'

'I'd rather not talk about it.' Her voice was pinched.

'Your trip to Sydney tomorrow ... does it have something to do with what happened?'

He waited for her to answer. She watched a young couple walk past. Wondered at the simplicity and easiness of their lives.

'I know you're curious,' she said, speaking carefully. 'I know you'd like to hear some details. But I can't go there.'

'No, it's not like that. I'm not asking out of some morbid fascination with gossip.' He turned in his seat, trying to catch her eye. She didn't move at all. 'Olivia, I wanted only to say all the stuff that happened to you, it doesn't matter to me.'

'Well, it should.' Her throat was tight, her voice strained. 'Because it does matter. All of it ... *matters*. And it didn't happen *to* me. I was an active participant. I had choices. And the fact I made such bad choices says a hell of a lot about the person I am.'

'That's being a bit harsh on yourself.' He placed his hand gently over hers. 'I'm sorry, Olivia. I've handled this all wrong. I didn't mean to. I've enjoyed every minute we've had together, and I don't want to say goodbye. I want to see you again. I wanted you to know that I know about ... things, and that my opinion of you hasn't changed. If anything, I see you even more as a strong, resilient woman. I admire you.'

She turned her head sharply towards him. 'You've got to be kidding. Admire *me*? Why?' She didn't need hollow flattery that came from pity.

'I don't know.' He was trying to find the words. 'Partly because you stood up in court and told them everything. After you were a victim of the most insane breach of privacy, you were brave enough to go in there and relive it. And you were brutally cross-examined by that other woman's defence lawyer.'

Olivia sighed. 'I didn't have much choice.' Tom was clearly waiting for more, but she had nothing to give. This was too hard. She didn't have the emotional strength to go any further. 'I'm sorry. I shouldn't be so defensive. But shame is so hard to put aside. Knowing that you, that you've—' she sputtered to a halt, the thought of him watching that scene choking her voice '—that you've seen *that*. It's too hard for me.'

'Let's put it aside for now, shall we?'

Not possible. 'I can't. Not today.'

'We could talk about something else—'

'I think I might head home,' she said. 'I'm operating on very little sleep, which always makes everything far more dramatic than it ought to be.'

'No. Please. Stay a while longer. I don't want to end it like this.' There was panic in his eyes.

'It's okay, Tom.' She bent to pick up her handbag. 'I really have enjoyed spending time with you. And I'm glad you found Pippa. It's a good result. It's enough.'

As she stood and walked towards the door, he followed. 'It doesn't feel *enough*.'

'It is, though. Isn't it? We had dinner. Shared some lovely kisses. We worked well together. It's been good, and I appreciate that.' She couldn't hold eye contact so kept her focus on a point over his shoulder.

'I don't know what to say.'

She recognised that he was desperate to find the words to make things right between them. They stood facing each other, not touching. Fuck, this hurt. She looked past him to the back of the bar, trying to keep it together. 'Okay then. Well, good-bye, Tom. I hope it goes well in Brisbane. And it was very nice to meet you.'

'*Olivia*,' he pleaded, 'don't be like that.'

She refused to meet his gaze. If she did, she would shatter. 'I have to go.'

'Please.' He put a hand on her arm, then dropped it when she remained immovable. 'Thank you for everything.' He had clearly realised she wasn't going to soften. 'You've truly made this trip so much more ...' He seemed to struggle to find a word to sum up his feelings.

'Dramatic?'

'Wonderful.'

He reached for her then. She stepped back. 'Bye.' She walked away before he could respond, leaving him standing on his own.

CHAPTER THIRTY-FIVE

Sunday, 9 February 1986

Pippa was floating through time. It was only the two of them in the house, Leo and her. Well, Honey too.

Rebecca was nothing but a distant memory, barely missed. Jeremy, on the other hand, had been gone for less than two days and Pippa yearned to hear his laugh. She expected him to wander out from his bedroom, to come up behind her, to criticise her cooking, to tease her about her hair. She wanted him to cajole her, harass her, until she gave in and sat down at her typewriter. His absence was profound, and from tomorrow afternoon he would be even further away.

Her time in Tasmania was nearing an end. Eloise would be back in two weeks. Pippa and Leo needed to come up with arrangements for what would happen next, yet it seemed neither of them wanted to make decisions. They hadn't even managed to coordinate themselves enough to collect Jeremy's car from the city. Mostly they lazed about, disconnected from the rest of the world. Leo would have to face his family eventually but continued to put off what he knew would be a nasty confrontation.

'We have to go to town,' Pippa said without enthusiasm. They were lying on their backs on the grass in front of the terrace, the sun warming their bodies after a quick plunge into the chilly waters of the channel. 'Tomorrow?' she suggested.

'I guess so,' Leo said.

'I don't want to see your parents.'

'Coward.'

'Yep.'

In the end Leo decided he'd do what had to be done and see his family that night. He would deal with them, explain his plans again, collect his passport and return to Devils Bay. He expected it could be a lengthy night. He might stay at the family house, or if that was too uncomfortable, he'd drive back. Either way he intended to be back with Pippa the next morning. Jeremy's car could wait another day.

That afternoon was spent in bed, moving together to a slow rhythm, skin on skin.

'I love you,' Leo whispered in her ear, his weight pressing her down, his touch making her yearn for more.

They fell asleep as dusk fell. Opened their eyes to darkness.

'Are you still going?' she asked as she watched him pull on his t-shirt.

'I don't want to. But I have to.'

'It's after nine.'

'My folks stay up late.' He pulled on his clothes. 'Stay there.' He bent down to kiss her again. 'I've got to get this over with. I'll be back tomorrow morning, before lunch.'

'With your passport.'

'With my passport. With my freedom.'

'I miss you already,' she called out as he let himself out of the house.

She listened as he drove away.

CHAPTER THIRTY-SIX

Wednesday, 28 June 2017

Sydney had changed. Or rather, the city was the same, and it was Olivia who was different.

She'd loved this place once, truly loved it. From the moment she'd crossed the Harbour Bridge in her little yellow car, she'd been hooked. The pushing, pressing traffic had been terrifying. The street signs had been confusing, changing lanes had made her heart race, and she'd got lost over and over as she tried to find the backpackers she had booked for her first week. But overriding all the fear had been exhilaration. She was really, truly there. In Sydney. Her *life*—the life she planned and was willing to chase—was beginning.

She'd rushed into the fray with her head up, her eyes wide, and a false confidence pushing her forward, determined to become a part of the city. Determined to achieve.

Today, she sat in the back of a taxi. She looked out and saw crowded footpaths, roads choked with traffic, brightly lit shopwindows, and cooler-than-cool coffee shops. It looked

grubby. The streets were grimy, the shops were gaudy, the endless enticements to spend, spend, spend were an assault.

Sydney had been good to her for many years. Then cruel.
Now it was a foreign world. There was no connection. No
sense of homecoming, no excitement at the familiar sights.
Only sadness. A nostalgia for who she had once been. Especially when the taxi pulled off the freeway and into the more
interesting streets of Surry Hills.

This inner-city locale, with its rows of tight terrace houses
and narrow, dead-end side streets, was a quirky blend of boho,
genuine hardship, and monied gentrification. It had once been
home. There had been four of them altogether, in a three-
bedroom, one-bathroom share house. Random people she'd
met when she'd answered an ad. The rent had been high, her
bedroom tiny, and the location fantastic.

Most days she'd walked to work, partly to save money but
mostly because she liked the feeling of being out on the city
streets. She hadn't been a party girl. Hadn't spent money on
designer clothes. Hadn't even had many friends. Her focus had
been on *making something of herself.*

That drive and focus were gone. This was her greatest loss—
not the loss of her dignity, privacy or job, but that of the person
she had been. She'd been more than optimistic. She'd had an
unwavering belief in herself and in her worth. She wanted to
feel that again.

The taxi pulled up in front of the hotel, the Harbour Bridge
sweeping up and away from the prime waterfront position.
She'd stayed there once before, at a time when spending hundreds of dollars on one night's accommodation had been a
truly crazy thing to do. She'd wanted to experience life as a
guest, to see things through the eyes of the consumer. She'd

loved every minute and hadn't left the hotel between check-in and check-out.

This stay was likely to be far less enjoyable.

She paid the driver and stepped out of the taxi, pulling her small suitcase behind her. As she walked into the lobby, the usual fears skittered over her, and she kept her focus on the floor in front of her feet, vaguely aware of the vaulted lobby with its dark timber beams and sleek honey-coloured marble. It didn't help that the flight up had involved several occasions of accidental eye contact with people who had either identified her or been trying to fathom why she looked familiar. Or was it all her imagination? She understood there was a possibility that nobody recognised her. It had probably been a long while since her face—or her arse—had been featured in the trash media. But fear of public humiliation was a hard thing to shake.

Her room was lovely, with leather trim, soft grey flannel upholstery and floor-to-ceiling glass doors that opened onto a harbourside balcony. But Olivia didn't waste any time admiring her surroundings. She sat on the bed and opened her phone to swap the SIM card for a prepaid version she'd bought that morning, then set it down. Beside the phone she laid the bank cheque. Two hundred thousand dollars.

After the court case, one of Hayden's lawyers had contacted her, apparently polite, sincere and concerned. He claimed to sympathise with what she'd been through, his voice stroking her in such a way as to leave her skin crawling. He emphasised how much Hayden appreciated her discretion, and how her ex-lover would like to offer her an apology … well, a financial expression of regret, if she would simply sign a non-disclosure agreement. There were to be no interviews. No intimate details of her affair with the great and talented Hayden Carlyle, dedicated family man, were to be shared in any form with anyone. She had to remain silent, and to sign here and here and here. The cash transfer would be made right away.

She had been paid for nothing. She would never have sold her story to a salivating press. She'd been offered a much larger sum by *60 Minutes*, and she'd said no—and then no again, every time they'd upped their offer. Instead, she accepted Hayden's money, signed the papers, and walked away from that meeting wondering what was left of her life. She was still wondering.

She wasn't the one who leaked the story of this hush money to the press. She certainly didn't tell anyone she'd received half a million dollars, because she hadn't. The cash transfer had been half of that, most of which had been sitting in her bank account till this morning.

Olivia dropped her head into her hands and let out a small moan. Her stomach twisted in apprehension whenever she thought of Leena's threat of another sex tape. There would be more crass exposure, more humiliation, right when she was daring to hope that people had forgotten her. More naked, writhing images of herself would be viewed by hundreds of thousands of people. Her body on show, a physical, intimate act being watched over and over and over by the creeps, the commentators, the judges. Her parents. People she had once known.

Tom. Oh god, Tom.

Olivia picked up the phone and typed a message. *I'm in Sydney. I can meet you today. Olivia.*

The response was quick. *How exciting! Be here in an hour. Hope you've got everything I need.* It was followed by the address of a serviced apartment on Pitt Street.

Olivia walked to the window and stared out at the expensive harbour view. Ferries busied themselves, cruisers took sightseers on tours, and a few sleek yachts gracefully slid towards the bridge. A magnificent scene. A place where she had once played.

With Leena, she had spent many evenings on the waterfront, immersed in the vivid life of the city. They'd always had fun, sometimes at another's expense. Leena could be so caustic, so critical of those she deemed lesser, snide and scathing towards those who were less attractive, less stylish, less young and free. She would play with men, taking what she wanted and tossing them away without a thought. On more than one occasion Olivia had been cornered by the confused discards of these short-lived flings. What could she say? Leena was a bitch. A self-centred, narcissistic bitch. Something Olivia had known but, caught in the whirlwind of the good times, had chosen to ignore. If only she hadn't.

Beneath her shame and fear, her anger unfurled. Something forceful. Something with heat. It was aimed at herself—her weaknesses, her failings, her mistakes and bad choices—but aimed at Leena as well.

CHAPTER THIRTY-SEVEN

Seventy minutes later Olivia stood in the small bland foyer of the serviced apartments where Leena was staying. Her hair was tied back, her make-up carefully applied. Her bold dark lipstick had last slicked her mouth at the trial. Looking better than she felt was the best mental defence she could manage. Leena would, of course, be nothing less than magnificent.

Olivia felt like a tethered sacrifice waiting for the dragon to emerge. She'd sent a text when she'd arrived twenty minutes ago. Making her wait was another little mind game from the queen of manipulation. Every time the lift pinged, Olivia's stomach heaved.

Then she was there. The doors opened, a pause for impact, and Leena was marching towards Olivia, heels clacking on the tiled floor. Leena wore expensive-looking wide-legged pants and a casual tailored wool blazer over an immaculate white collared shirt. Her lush hair was swinging with every step. The stodgy, high-fat prison food had filled her out, softening her face and adding curves, none of which looked bad. Her mouth was pulled into a mean smile, her gaze raking over Olivia, a single eyebrow rising in disdain.

Olivia didn't move. She let the beast come to her.

'Olivia.' Leena said her name as though she was greeting a long-lost acquaintance, with a hint of delight, a touch of enquiry. Then she leant in and pressed her cheek against Olivia's, the puckering smack of the air kiss loud in her ear. 'How lovely to see you. It's been too long.' There was no lightness or joy in the words.

'Hello, Leena. You look good.'

'I do, don't I. I've spent a small fortune on fixing the more obvious effects of that hideous place. Can't tell you how divine it feels to be out of those vile clothes. Trust me, I am never, ever going to wear green again. And you—' she sighed dramatically, then gave another slow assessment '—well, I hate to say this, but you seem to have let yourself go.' She held up her manicured hands as though asking for forgiveness. 'Sorry, just being honest.'

It was about as close to honesty as Leena was ever going to get.

'Shall we go up to your apartment?' Olivia asked.

'What? Why?'

'You want to talk?'

Leena scoffed and tossed her hair. 'No. I think we can conduct our business somewhere far more pleasant. What about drinks at some fabulous bar? Like we used to. Before you betrayed me.'

'Don't you think we might get noticed—'

'I should hope so! What's the point of notoriety if you can't get some mileage from it?' Leena gave a huge smile as she slid her hand under her hair on one side, lifted it, then let the length drop back onto her shoulder.

'I'm not having this meeting with you in a public place.' Olivia looked around the foyer, aware of the receptionist casting glances at them.

'Oh, for heaven's sake, why on earth not?' Leena seemed genuinely puzzled.

Did the woman imagine them perched on bar stools while catching up on old times over cocktails and champagne? Or was she intent on humiliating Olivia in as public a fashion as possible? 'Because I *don't* want to be noticed.'

'Oh, that's right. You're the little mouse who skedaddled away to some hole in the middle of nowhere—or should that be rat, not mouse? Couldn't you handle the heat in the city, little rat?' She gave a laugh that tinkled with spite. 'I must admit, after I got over the surprise and disappointment, I did get a small degree of pleasure in discovering you'd scurried away. I hadn't liked the idea of your life continuing in style while I rotted.' She leant in closer, her eyes wide and unblinking. 'Are you happy down there, Olivia Indigo Haymers? Or are you miserable? You do sort of look like someone with a pathetic life.'

'Leena, please, let's go up and get this over with.'

'Fine.' She stalked back to the lift.

Olivia followed, then waited in uncomfortable silence until the doors opened.

'I don't want to be seen with you anyway,' Leena said as they travelled upwards, her jaw lifting in defiance. 'You're not in my league, are you? Never were, to be honest. I befriended you out of sympathy, you know, and look where that got me.'

There was no response worth making. Olivia doubted it was sympathy that had prompted Leena to offer friendship—it seemed more likely the woman had instigated their friendship in order to meet Eric Haymers. A connection that had, for a period of time, delivered financial and career rewards to Leena. Olivia fixed her eyes straight ahead, her hands shoved deep into the pockets of her jacket. She was aware of Leena watching her, calculating. Wanting to lash out.

It was sort of understandable. Leena was a meticulous strategist who'd thought she had conceived a clever—if entirely unethical, immoral and illegal—plan. She must have had such confidence to try something so audacious and been shocked when it all failed.

As the lift stopped, in the moment before the doors opened, their eyes met in the mirrored surface. Leena gave a triumphant smile. Then she was stepping past Olivia, leading the way. 'This is somewhere temporary to park myself till everything is sorted out.'

She put her key in the lock and swung open the door to reveal the generic interior of the serviced apartment. The carpets were slate-grey, and there was a tiny dark grey square-edged sofa with two matching chairs and red cushions to lift the drab, durable colour scheme. At least the windows offered good views of the CBD. In one corner there were a couple of packing boxes surrounded by scattered heels and boots. On the small square dining table, several handbags sat beside piles of accessories and scarfs.

'As you can see, this hideous box doesn't even begin to accommodate me. But I'm a patient girl. I've already started house-hunting. It's going to take me a while to rebuild my position, but I'll get there.'

'What happened to your old place?' Olivia asked.

Until she'd been locked away, Leena had lived in a gorgeous art deco apartment in the beach-side suburb of Clovelly. She'd

bought it for what had been a reasonable price by Sydney stan-
dards, then renovated it to create a stunning modern home.
Leena was many things, but she couldn't be faulted on her style.
Of course, the style she wanted cost money. Lots of money.

'Sold it.' Leena sat in one of the chairs, crossing her long
legs and resting her arms languidly on each side. 'When you
sent me to jail, I lost my income. It's hard to sell other people's
property from prison, so I had to either rent it out or off-load
it, and I decided to sell. I did make a nice profit. More than
you did, I see. Although, unlike you, I had all those horrendous
legal bills.' She sighed dramatically, the weight of the perceived
injustice written all over her face. 'I guess it was worth it. If I
hadn't paid for the best lawyers, I would still be in that hell-
hole. That nasty little prosecutor would very much have liked
to nail me for blackmail as well. Completely ridiculous—I was
simply negotiating a business transaction.'

It had been a good defence. Leena had kept herself anonymous in her approaches to Hayden's people. She'd also been
savvy enough to limit her interactions with Hayden and his
manager to discussions of the value of a video—which she
claimed had come into her possession—and how the transaction would take place. She hadn't made any direct threats as
such, leaving unsaid the implication the video could go public.

What Leena hadn't expected was for Hayden to pre-
emptively throw himself at the mercy of the public. When he
outed himself as an adulterer, he diminished the value of the
video. Still, Leena continued to negotiate the sale of the incrim-
inating footage, failing to get the result she wanted. That was
when the snippet went viral, an attempt to apply pressure: *Pay
up or the full clip will be uploaded* was the indirect message.
In her negotiations she never admitted to releasing it, even

suggesting Hayden's team had put it out there. They refused her demands, at which point she should have walked away. But she didn't. The full video hit the internet and the legal situation quickly escalated.

Hayden's people set out on a mission to hunt and destroy. When Hayden had eventually recognised the setting of the illicit film, he'd come to the seemingly logical conclusion that it must have been captured by Olivia, a conclusion bolstered by the fact she had recently ended their affair. She had been convinced that she would be charged for both the filming and the blackmail. It was horrible. After lengthy questioning by the police and a brutal assessment of the situation by her father's lawyer, she gave in to the pressure and named Leena as possibly being behind the filming. Leena had been her friend, but Olivia hadn't been prepared to go to jail to protect her.

In the end, Leena was only charged with filming a person engaged in a private act. There was evidence of her purchasing several micro-cameras. And, of course, there was Olivia's testimony.

'Anyway, I had the packers go in and move all my things into storage. I must tell you, though, it is seriously inconvenient trying to organise your affairs when you're stuck in a stinking cell for most of the day. Did you know, all *inmates*,' she said the word as though it caused her physical pain, 'everyone, even those in low security, must be processed. I spent my first five days in a holding cell at Surry Hills. For those uninitiated in the ways of jail—like you, little rat—that means I was locked away in a basic cell, without fresh air, with five other women.' Leena leant forward, resting her arms on her knees. Her eyes appeared to fill with tears. 'You, my friend, put me in a place where I had to share a revolting cell with fat, foul creatures from the outer suburbs. There was a rubber mattress on a concrete bench and a pathetic limp blanket. It was freezing, and I had to wear a hideous green sweatshirt and pants. Did you know the toilet is right there in that confined space? You shit and pee in front of everyone else. And they're shitting and peeing while you're lying on your bed, trying to sleep, trying to pretend you're not there. Can you imagine how foul that is? Can you?' Manicured fingers wiped under her eyes. She took a long breath and tilted her head back, shaking out her hair and closing her eyes as though she was trying to calm herself. It was a convincing performance. Then her chin jerked down, and her eyes opened. 'My career was destroyed. I spent nine months in jail. Jail! Do you even care, Olivia? Because it sure as hell felt like you'd fucked up my life and walked away without looking back.'

Olivia watched her with a trickle of sympathy and a tidal wave of contempt. Did Leena believe her own bullshit, or did she cry victim in an effort to manipulate Olivia's feelings? The accusation that Olivia was responsible for her downfall was ridiculous.

'I had everything under control, Olly-Indy.' Leena's voice was quiet now, sad. 'You would've been fine, if you'd been smart and kept quiet.'

Olivia wished that were true.

Leena was silent for a moment, probably waiting for Olivia to crumple and confess her culpability, to beg for forgiveness. When she did neither, Leena tossed her hair back and sat up straighter. 'Well, I hope your life is shit. Because you owe me. Only money will fix things. You stuffed up my plan and ruined my life. Then to kick me in the guts, you profited from what I'd done. It's time to pay up.'

'I didn't ruin your life. You did.' Olivia was still standing, reluctant to settle and risk staying longer than necessary.

Leena gave a snort of derisive laughter. 'Oh please. What did I do? Filmed a film star? Christ, I even got him from a good angle. Commenced a negotiation for the ownership of that film? He could afford it. That preening, over-hyped douchebag earned over twenty million last year. Twenty million! For a couple of crap movies where he wiggled his arse and flexed some muscle. What I suggested as a reasonable purchase price wouldn't have made a dent. Trust me, he could've paid it easily and that airbrushed idiot wife of his wouldn't even have noticed. He made it into a big deal. Probably appreciated the free publicity. Instead he got all high and mighty about the situation. And then *you*—' her pointed finger jabbed at the air '—had to go and get involved. I'm the victim in all this.'

Leena's take on the events would have been laughable if her craziness hadn't come with consequences.

'He thought it was me.' Olivia had been determined to stay calm, but her voice came out stridently defensive. 'Hayden thought the anonymous blackmailer was *me*. He thought I'd made the film.'

'Oh my god! It wasn't blackmail. You know what, in America there's a guy who specialises in negotiating deals for sex tapes—it's not blackmail, and it's not a big deal. And as for you getting questioned, well, that's your own fault. You were stupid to break up with lover-boy after Bangkok. That was bad timing. And, besides, they couldn't have proved anything. You were weak.'

Olivia pushed aside the need to defend herself. 'Why did you do it, Leena?'

Leena's brow creased as she considered the question. 'There's a saying: "luck is when opportunity meets preparation".' She shook her head slightly, a knowing smile on her filler-softened lips. 'That's true, but opportunities aren't always obvious. There are moments of potential that don't come with a neon sign saying, "Look here! Here's a situation that will be to your benefit." Most people don't see the hidden opportunities or recognise the chance to create an opportunity.' Leena looked back at Olivia. 'I do. I saw the opportunity you presented me with, especially when you fell into bed with that idiot. I saw the right set of circumstances and crafted them into something worth pursuing.'

'You used me.'

Leena laughed. 'Seriously? What are you, fifteen? Grow up. Get over yourself and have a good look at the world. Look at those who get to the top—successful people always recognise how to make the most of those around them. And that, by the way, includes your father.'

Was she right? Maybe. But however she justified her behaviour, friends didn't secretly film their friends having sex and use the video as a tool for making money.

'Let's get this over with,' Olivia said.

'Sure. I should think the money is burning a guilty hole in your pocket.' Leena held out a hand as though she expected immediate delivery of the bank cheque.

'First, I need to see what you have. Do you honestly have a second film?' The video Leena had used for leverage against Hayden was already out there. There was no longer any power in that particular recording.

'Oh, I most certainly do. At the time I thought, *The more footage the better.* Then I realised how important it was to keep a little something back for myself—an insurance policy.

Thank goodness for the cloud, I say. You can upload and hide things quite easily.'

'Can I see it?' Not that Olivia had any desire to see herself in such a demeaning excerpt.

Leena considered her for a few moments, her eyes narrowed, her head tilted as though she was assessing Olivia's worth. 'Fine.' After pushing up from the chair, she walked to the table, flicked open her laptop, tapped a few keys, then turned it towards Olivia as murmurs and groans filled the room.

Olivia put her bag on the table and forced herself to watch, needing to make sure it was real. Humiliation crawled over her skin, yet she managed to pull out her phone and take a video of what was playing.

'Aww, do you want a copy? Don't worry, I'll send you the full version.' Leena was apparently too confident to be concerned by Olivia filming.

'Enough.' Olivia crossed to the other side of the room, wanting to get as far as possible from those burning images.

'I know, sweetie. It's a bit confronting, isn't it?' Leena sighed. The soundtrack of passion was still coming from the computer. 'I know it's unflattering in parts ... Look, here in this section we get to see you from behind. Definitely not your best angle. There's a bit of cellulite banging about on your thighs, isn't there? Anyway, I don't think Hayden's fans will mind, do you? They get a good view of all his masculine glory.'

Nausea curled upwards. 'You can't release it,' Olivia begged. 'You wouldn't do that. Everyone would know it was you. Hayden's lawyers would come after you, and you'd go back to jail.'

Leena shook her head. 'I don't think so. I've already been charged with illicitly filming Hayden without his knowledge, so I couldn't be charged with that again. And it's not like I'm asking him for money. Oh, no. I'm asking you.'

'What about the laws against revenge porn?'

'They won't be able to prove it was me. I've got some new, very useful contacts—smart people who can get this out there without it being traced back to me. No, this is between you and me. Without any danger for me, and with a whole lot of worry for you. This, my little fat rat, is your chance to save yourself more pain.' Leena finally slapped the laptop shut. 'Don't want your arse and boobs and groans and gasps and fake orgasm going viral? All you need to do is hand over the five hundred thousand. You can buy this one-and-only copy for the bargain basement price of half a million dollars. And before you start complaining about how unfair you think this is, can I remind you that you wouldn't have received a cent if I hadn't done what I did. You benefited from my strategy, and I was punished. That's unfair.'

Oh god. Olivia stared at Leena. 'I don't have half a million.'

'Really? I beg to differ. You were paid to keep your mouth shut.'

'But not that much. Half of that.'

'That's not true.' Leena stood and walked towards Olivia, her face calm, her stance relaxed. 'It was clearly reported that he bought your silence, and half a million would be an appropriate amount to keep intimate details of Hayden Carlyle's sexual prowess—or lack thereof—out of the public domain.'

Olivia stepped back, pressing against the window, wanting to get away. 'I swear, he offered two fifty. And I accepted that.'

'Even you are not that stupid. He may have started with a low-ball amount, but it wouldn't have taken much to negotiate upwards.'

Olivia shook her head.

Leena's eyes darkened. She gripped Olivia's jaw tightly, fingers digging into her cheeks. 'Stop lying.' She pushed, Olivia's head smacking against the glass, before she let go.

Until now Olivia's only fear had been another round of public humiliation. But the adrenaline pumping through her system was warning her of other dangers. Would—could—Leena hurt her? She held up her hands, palms outward, an attempt to placate. 'Leena, I have a bank cheque for you. I can only give you what I've got. I promise you, I did not get half a million. It was half of that. I'm not lying. I can show you my bank account.'

The slap was quick and fierce.

Olivia's head snapped to the side, her hands quickly pressing against the burn and sting in her cheek. Tears came, the shock and pain making her cower. 'I'm not lying, I'm not lying, I wouldn't lie about this.'

'I wouldn't trust you if my life depended on it,' Leena said, her face rigid with fury. 'You have no morals. You have no shame. You lie and cheat and con. You sent me, your best friend, to jail to save your own skin. You betrayed me and destroyed my life. And you're going to pay. Now give me the money. I know how much you got from the sale of your apartment—you can afford it. And you owe me.'

Olivia had to move. She couldn't stay pinned against the window. 'The bank cheque is in my bag.'

Leena shifted to let her pass, then followed so close that Olivia nearly tripped. At the table she extracted her wallet, her hands shaking. As she pulled out the cheque Leena snatched it away. 'You bitch,' Leena said quietly. 'Do you honestly think a year in jail is worth only two hundred thousand dollars?'

Olivia backed up a little, putting space between the two of them and getting herself closer to the door. *Calm everything down*, she thought. *Reason. Explain. Prove the truth.* If Leena would let her. *Get the video and get out.* She was breathing hard, her face aching, tears drying on her skin.

'This—' Leena held the cheque up high '—is not enough. It is simply not enough compensation. It is not enough retribution. It. Is. Not. Enough.' Rage underpinned each word. 'You are *not* going to screw me over again.'

'That is almost everything he gave me.'

'Where's the rest of it?'

'I spent a little. I travelled for a bit. And I need something to live on. I don't have a job.'

'You travelled?' Leena gave a nasty laugh. 'I had someone shitting next to my head, and you were fucking travelling? Unbelievable. Seriously, I cannot believe how selfish you are.'

'Your life wasn't the only one messed up.'

'Oh, don't! Don't even try to tell me how hard you've had it.'

'Leena, I wasn't the one who committed a crime.'

'Don't act like you're so innocent. You seduced a married man. You screwed him over and over, knowing he had a wife. You *used* him.' Leena was pacing now, short, angry steps, turning on her heel, retracing her path. 'You liked the high life he gave you. French champagne. Five-star resorts. Gifts. Jewellery. You loved the buzz of being with someone so famous. Then when he wouldn't leave his wife, when he realised how pitiful you are, how useless and ugly and average you are, when you could see the end coming, you dumped him. How pathetic. If he'd been with me, it would've all been different.'

What could Olivia say? If she hadn't been watching Leena unravel, she might have laughed at her assertion that Olivia was the greedy one. At the same time, the part of her that had been accused and abused by thousands of observers wanted to scream out her innocence. She *hadn't* seduced Hayden—he'd chased *her*. He'd repeatedly tried to win her over. And yes, he had succeeded, but he wasn't a virtuous husband lured away from his vows.

And Leena knew that. She'd been there, listening to Olivia as she confided her confusion, her battle with what was right and wrong. Leena had *encouraged* her to get involved with him. She'd told Olivia how lucky she was. Had pushed her for details. Had argued against her every time she'd contemplated ending a relationship she knew was going nowhere. Had Leena been jealous? Had she wanted to be in Olivia's shoes? It didn't matter now. Things had unfolded the way they had. Olivia *wasn't* an innocent, but she certainly wasn't a criminal—or a conniving, scheming bitch.

Leena held up the cheque again. 'This is most definitely not enough. This is just for starters. If you don't want the world to watch your wobbly arse, if you don't want Hayden dragged back into the gutter with you, then you'd better deliver the rest. Tomorrow.'

Olivia thought of the money she still had tucked away. She had no job. No prospects. She lived in a rented house she couldn't afford indefinitely. Her life was at a standstill. Without the money she would literally have nothing, not even hope.

Leena waved the cheque back and forth. 'Not. Enough.' Her cheeks flared red, her eyes widened, and her mouth tightened, appearing to almost spark with anger.

It would never end, would it? This part of Olivia's life was out of her control. With this video Leena had the upper hand. She could pull the strings and make Olivia jump. And if Olivia handed over every cent she had, would it be enough? Would Leena ever relinquish or delete the video? No—she would always keep her piece of insurance tucked away. Even if Olivia began to pull a life back together, there would always be the threat. At any point Leena could re-emerge, demanding more, saying 'not enough'.

Leena was laughing at her. 'Oh, you are so pathetic. What on earth did he ever see in you? What did *I* ever see in you? I never actually liked you. You're so weak and needy and so, so boring. I despise you.'

Something snapped. Olivia's flimsy thread of hope had been stretched too far.

She could never return to her old life or be the person she once was. Whether she wanted it or not, her mistakes were going to go on shaping her life.

A rush of heat surged upwards. Her hand whipped out, grabbing the cheque from Leena's fingers. 'You are deranged, Leena.'

'What are you doing?' Leena screeched. 'Give that back.'

'No.' Olivia shoved the cheque in the back pocket of her jeans and grabbed her bag.

'Give it back! Have you any idea how screwed up your life will be when I release that video?'

'Quite frankly, Leena, I've gone past caring.'

'Oh my god. You're crazy. I *will* put it online. I *will* do it. Don't think I won't.'

'I'm sure you will. You're vindictive enough to do that. It's unavoidable. Although I still think you're going to be dealing with Hayden's legal team—and the police—if you do.'

'Give me the money.' Leena grabbed Olivia's upper arm, her fingers digging deep, jerking her forward. 'You *owe* me.'

'I owe you nothing.' Olivia sensed she should return to trying to calm the situation, that Leena was physically dangerous, but her own anger was refusing to let her back down. 'I'm not even going to attempt to defend myself anymore. You are crazy, and you are wrong. Now, let me go.' She tried to twist away.

'No!' The scream was savage.

Olivia shoved Leena with all her strength, her desperation to get away making her act on instinct. Leena's fingers loosened as she was propelled backwards, then she was falling. One foot snagged on a gold stiletto sandal lying behind her on the floor. She grabbed at one of the chairs. Missed. Hit the ground awkwardly, landing on her bum, the chair going with her.

For a second there was silence. Leena looked stunned, apparently unable to comprehend Olivia's retaliation. As Leena started to pull herself up, Olivia moved to the door, the sound of Leena's threats seeming to push her out of the apartment. 'You're going to pay for this, you crazy, stupid bitch. You're going to pay! Give me the fucking money—'

The door shut behind Olivia. She punched the lift call button. *Come on, come on.* Leena was going to follow her. Was going to attack her again. Was going to wrestle her to the ground and rip the cheque from her pocket.

The apartment door remained closed. The lift arrived.

Olivia imagined Leena rushing to her laptop, tapping the keys, sending the video out into the world. By the time Olivia got back to her hotel, thousands of people would have copied and shared and liked and commented.

What had she done?

CHAPTER THIRTY-EIGHT

Olivia didn't stop. Her jaw was rigid, her breathing short and shallow, but she walked fast. She raised a shaking hand, touching her cheek where the skin still stung, then pressed at the corner of her eyes. She wasn't going to cry, even if all she wanted to do was sit on the ground and howl with fury and fear and shock.

She gave a sharp gasp as fragments of the scene with Leena twisted through her head. The images and sounds from the laptop, Leena's gloating, gleeful face, her own hand snatching back the cheque, Leena stumbling, hitting the ground.

Was Olivia crazy? What had she done?

She had said 'enough'. She'd fought back, and it had felt great. Even though it wouldn't stop what was coming.

In Hyde Park she sat on a bench. She pulled out her phone and sent a message to a number she knew by heart.

Hayden, this is Olivia. I have just met with Leena. She has a second video, also taken in Bangkok. She is threatening to release it. I can't stop her. I wanted you to know.

He deserved to know what was coming, especially as it would affect him more than her. He was still a star, a hot asset. A man, now divorced, who still had to control his image. She, on the other hand, had no career to lose. She could return to Devils Bay, to her hermit-like existence with Brian. Life would crawl along as it had before. She'd ignore the wider world, let time flow. The cheque in her back pocket meant she had enough money to hide for a few years.

The whoosh of the message being sent reminded her that the alternative SIM was still in her phone. It didn't matter—if he needed to verify what she was saying, his solicitor had her email address and her usual number.

A quick taxi ride later, the shock had eased while the dread lingered. She slipped into the foyer of her hotel, where nothing had changed. Her life had been pushed back into the sucking mud of shame and guilt, but this scene of subtle, elegant opulence continued uninterrupted. She half expected everyone to turn and stare at her with curiosity, amusement, or hostility. Which was ridiculous. It would take hours, even days, before that happened.

Lifting her chin, she walked towards the lifts. The doors opened, but her feet didn't move, resisting her march back to safety. Someone stepped around her. The doors closed. Still, she waited.

She was so tired of hiding. She didn't want to retreat, to sit in a room looking out at the city, and there was a plush bar adjacent to the lobby. The woman serving there smiled, poured Olivia a drink and asked after her day. She moved through the interaction with her head up, keeping eye contact and smiling even though her mouth was so stiff and resistant that a tremor began in one corner.

Instinctively she braced for the moment of recognition. But there was nothing except professional, personable service, even when she paid by card, her name right there to be seen. She took her glass to a table facing the lobby, challenging the world to see this wicked woman.

Two hours later, Olivia was still invisible. Hayden's solicitor had rung to verify who had sent the message and then asked for a run-down of the situation. And Leena had sent two texts.

I'm not joking. The video goes live at 5 pm. You want this to stop? Get back here now.

An hour later: *You'll regret this. You're making the biggest mistake of your life.*

Clarity came to Olivia as though a blurred low-resolution picture was suddenly shown in crisp high definition. The thing with blackmail, she realised, was it hung entirely upon the need for the victim to keep something hidden. Hayden had outed himself as an adulterer to remove the leverage Leena had over him. He'd taken control of the revelations. If the impact of the secret or threat was denied, then the blackmailer had nothing.

Leena was screaming into the silence. Olivia had denied her the power she needed. God, that was satisfying.

Her horror at what was coming was still there, shoved to one side, buried under an unfamiliar sense of resolve and a serious measure of delight. What could she do? Nothing she could say would change Leena's intentions.

What she could control was how she chose to respond. For a start, there were laws around distributing non-consensual explicit images, and around using a service to harass and intimidate and cause harm. Leena had said her involvement would be untraceable, but Olivia had evidence. She checked the video she'd taken of Leena's laptop. Olivia's face was clearly identifiable in the clip playing on the screen, and Leena could be seen beside the table, her laugh and voice audible. It had been a spontaneous action, and she'd only expected to catch a few seconds of the clip, but this was even better.

'Excuse me.'

Olivia slammed the phone to her chest and whipped around.

The server from the bar was beside her. 'Sorry, didn't mean to make you jump. Can I get you another drink?'

Heart thumping, Olivia nodded. 'Yes. Please. That would be lovely.'

'Another glass of the rosé?'

As Olivia waited for her drink to arrive, she made a decision. It was time to fight back with more than a quick shove. She was tired of hiding, of flinching, of bracing for ugly criticism and humiliation. Tired of cowering in fear of what Leena might do next. Completely over both being a victim and being consumed by guilt.

Her message to Leena was brief, devoid of theatrics, threats or emotions. Distributing that video was illegal. Olivia would be making a report to the police. Hayden's solicitor had been informed.

Then she took the SIM out of her phone. Maybe the thought of consequences would be enough to stop Leena. Maybe it wouldn't.

Olivia sipped her wine, sitting straight, head up, resolute. Being with Tom had shown her how life could be good again. He'd known her story and apparently hadn't cared. No—he had acted as though she wasn't defined by what she had done. He'd seen right past the mess. As had Wendy in the post office. And Maggie.

Olivia had to start trusting the intentions of those who were kind.

*

Back in her room she took a long bath, then wrapped herself in the hotel robe. She sat in the armchair by the window, her phone in her lap with its usual SIM restored. It was now six, an hour after Leena's deadline. The video might be out there, but Olivia wasn't going to look yet. She had more important things to do.

Tom answered immediately. 'Olivia. Hello. Hi.'

Olivia put her fingers to her mouth. Closed her eyes. The simple relief in hearing his voice cradled her fragile heart. 'Hi.'

'Are you okay? Is everything alright?'

'Yes and no.'

'Do you want to tell me? You don't have to. We can talk about anything. But if you want to talk or, you know, tell me what a cockhead I am, I'm listening.'

She stood, closed the curtains, then moved to the bed, where she pulled the covers over her legs. 'Have you got time?'

'Yes. Yes! I'm in Brisbane. In a room. Waiting on room service. You've got me for as long as you need.'

'Then there are some things I'd like to explain. But firstly—' she took a deep breath '—I want to say, you did nothing wrong.' Another breath. 'I think you're lovely. While I, on the other hand, am a bit messed up.'

'I'd like to help.'

'It's okay, I think I might be sorting myself out.'

They talked for over three hours. His meal arrived, and she ordered hers. They ate and listened and talked. Olivia summed up her life over the past few years, Tom becoming angry on her behalf when she explained how horrible things had become. Then she told him about Leena's latest antics, and he cheered when she described their fight and her intention to get the police involved. By the end she was spent. 'Tell me,' she said, needing to change the subject, 'are you excited about meeting Pippa tomorrow?'

'I am. A little nervous, but mostly excited and relieved.'

'A big moment, I guess. You'll have to tell me what she's like, this elusive mystery woman.'

'You should come. Get on a plane. I'm not meeting her until the afternoon. You're as responsible for finding her as I am. And, actually, I'd love you here, to see you again. Before, you know, I have to leave.'

Could she? 'I've left Brian on his own. I only planned on being gone for twenty-four hours.'

'Could someone visit? Call in and check on him, top up his food?'

Wendy had a key to the house. Was Olivia comfortable asking for such a favour? Not really. But she could try.

The next morning, after a surprisingly deep sleep, Olivia found out how easy it was to ask for help. Wendy was working all day, but Tilly was happily dispatched to care for Brian.

By eleven Olivia had made a statement to the e-safety division of the police, who could find no evidence of the new video but took Leena's threats very seriously. They downloaded a copy of the clip from Olivia's phone, then noted Leena's current address and advised they would be paying her a pre-emptive visit. Throughout the meeting Olivia managed to keep it together, even when the short excerpt was viewed and humiliation scorched her face.

By midday she was at the airport, and two hours after that she was shocked to find Tom waiting for her as she disembarked. The flutter of nerves was stilled when he opened his arms and she stepped into his hug.

CHAPTER THIRTY-NINE

Thursday, 29 June 2017

Tom parked the rental car outside Pippa's house and looked around. He needed a minute to get himself together. The street was straight and wide, with generous footpaths flanked by grass verges and plenty of space between the homes. Trees lined the road, and flowering gardens spilled past boundary fences, adding colour. The high-set weatherboard houses were similar to one another but far from identical. Most had spacious verandahs that in many cases wrapped around the front and sides, and there were character details in curving wooden posts and fretwork. French doors opened outwards, showing glimpses within the homes.

'Nervous?' Olivia asked, squeezing his hand.

'Excited. And pretty bloody pleased with myself. And, yeah, a little nervous about this big reveal.'

'Oh I see,' she said with a teasing smile, 'you're thinking you did this on your own?'

'Yep. Of course.' He considered her lovely face with an appropriate level of seriousness. 'Although you make a perfectly acceptable sidekick.'

She punched him lightly on the arm. 'You are seriously walking on dangerous ground.'

'Okay. Fine. You know I couldn't have done this without you.'

'And you'll give me half of the credit.'

'Absolutely. But you have to come to London to claim it.'

'Hmm. That could be arranged.'

'Really? That would be brilliant.' A silly burst of joy left him grinning like a cat that got the canary *and* the cream.

'Maybe. Let's focus on this first.'

They got out of the car, Tom swinging his work satchel across his body. Jeremy's package and photos were inside, ready to be delivered. 'Right,' he said. 'Let's do this.' He pushed open the gate, and they walked down the path across the clipped lawn to a wide set of stairs that turned at a landing to bring them up one end of the verandah.

A woman appeared, her hands resting on the railing as she looked down at them. 'Hello, you must be Tom,' she said with a welcoming smile. Her curly dark hair, threaded with silver, sat above her shoulders. She didn't wear make-up, or none that was obvious, and her glowing skin had fanned lines around the eyes and mouth. She had on a loose blue-and-white dress with puffed sleeves and a flounced hem that sat above her knees. Silver bangles glinted on one wrist. 'I'm Pippa.'

Tom answered. 'Hi, Pippa. This is Olivia.'

Pippa nodded to her, then swung open the lattice door at the top of the stairs and stood back to let them onto the verandah. 'Nice to meet you. Come in.'

They followed the woman through the main front door, positioned between two flanking sets of French doors, and down a hallway to a living area at the back. Bi-fold doors were pushed open so there was little demarcation between the inside of the house and the expansive deck. The space must have been six yards deep and ran the whole width of the house. It was furnished like a room, with a hardwood dining table, all-weather lounge chairs, potted plants, and a fan set in the high white ceiling. He wondered what happened when the rain came or a storm hit before noticing the rolled-up canvas blinds at the outer edge of the roof, ready to unfurl and be tied down to the railing when needed.

'You have a gorgeous home,' said Olivia as they looked around.

'Amazing,' Tom agreed. 'This must be brilliant to live in.'

'Thank you, it's a great home. I had been about to downsize, but then Paige moved back in. She's thirty-one this year, but she's just returned from four years working in Thailand. Plus she's broken up with her long-term girlfriend and trying to save for her own home,' Pippa said. 'So, it's back to the two of us, which I have to admit, I do quite like. Now, can I offer you a coffee? Or do you prefer tea? A cold drink?'

'A cold drink would be great,' said Tom. Olivia asked for the same. It was warm, and he'd already had to strip down to his t-shirt. He and Olivia looked down over the railing into the back-yard, where the pool, palms and lush growth made him think of a tropical island resort. All that was missing were staff in white shorts and loud shirts, serving pina coladas and margaritas.

Pippa returned with tall glasses clinking with ice and a plate of home-baked biscuits. Her feet were bare, and she was relaxed and at ease in herself, the sort of person who could make anyone feel comfortable—even the son of a long-lost friend who had absconded from her life.

'What was Paige doing in Thailand?' he asked as they sat. It was fascinating to hear what had become of Pippa's child. He dropped his bag at his feet.

'Teaching at an international school. Her partner, who is from New Zealand, was the swim coach. They met there, but unfortunately the relationship didn't last, and Paige felt she wanted to come home. Anyway, I must've done okay as a mum because she's amazing. Or maybe it's just her fabulous genes. She got Leo's looks and my reckless thirst for adventure. I wish more than anything Leo could've known her.'

This seemed to answer the question Tom hadn't wanted to ask—who was Paige's father? It was a relief to know he wouldn't need to negotiate that awkward discussion.

For about twenty minutes they chatted about Pippa's home, her work as a brand manager for a large travel corporation, and how she'd started out as a travel agent and worked her way up. Then she asked about Tom's job in London and what he thought of Tasmania.

Pippa expressed delight when she realised Olivia was living in Eloise's house. 'I love that place,' she enthused. 'I haven't been there for many years.' She laughed softly. 'Actually, I've only been down a couple of times since I moved back here with Paige. Maggie comes up quite regularly, and Eloise visits us at least once a year—they're two of my favourite people in the whole world.'

'Did Eloise let you know we'd spoken to her?' Tom asked, wondering if Pippa had been warned about their search. 'I had originally hoped she would be the one to put us in contact with you.'

Pippa shook her head. 'I take it she didn't help?'

'She was not particularly forthcoming,' Tom replied lightly. He didn't want to sound like he was complaining. 'She gave Olivia slightly more information, but she was fairly adamant we shouldn't contact you.'

'Oh dear,' Pippa said with a knowing look. 'I'm sorry she made it so hard for you. I am, in fact, very happy to have you here. But Eloise has always been protective towards me, some would say over-protective. She was furious at Jeremy for not returning that summer. Still is, it seems. I imagine she thinks letting him back into my life—even posthumously—is a very bad move. Eloise does not forgive easily.' She took a sip from her glass. 'I'm really very sorry to hear Jeremy passed away. He is still the closest friend I've ever had. It's heart-breaking to know we'll never have a chance to reconnect.' Pippa sounded wistful. 'Did he ever tell you how I saved his life?'

'Wow,' said Tom. 'No, Dad didn't mention that. He was always … well, very reluctant to talk about his life before he came to England.'

Reluctant—or secretive? Not for the first time, Tom wondered why his dad had kept his youth a no-go zone.

'Was he?' Pippa sounded curious, not judgemental. 'I wonder why. There are some great stories. It was so hard to say goodbye to him when he left for London. We'd been sharing a house for two years by then and had been through a lot together. There'd been a lot of fun, and we supported each other. I loved Jeremy, though I wasn't *in* love with him. It was the love you have for someone who means everything to you.'

Tom thought of the intimate pictures his father had kept. Perhaps Jeremy hadn't felt *quite* the same as Pippa had.

'When he cut me off it was brutal,' Pippa continued. 'I never knew why he did it, and I was really, really hurt. Especially when I was dealing with so much. I gather from Maggie that you know about my boyfriend Leo vanishing?'

'We do,' said Olivia, and they both nodded.

'At the time it was terrifying. I was on my own for a week before Eloise made it back from London, with the police questioning me repeatedly. Leo's parents were an absolute nightmare.' Pippa's gaze shifted, drifting away from them to a point in the distance, her mouth tightening, turning down at the corners. 'It was a terrible thing,' she said softly. There was so much sadness in the simple statement. In the quiet that followed, the sounds of the suburb drifted through the air. A lawnmower, a short burst of barking, the screech of a bird he didn't recognise.

'Not knowing what happened must be horrible,' Olivia said after a moment, true empathy in her voice. 'First Leo and then Jeremy. I can't imagine how that feels.'

Pippa brought her focus back to them, her smile sad and small. 'Absolutely gut-wrenching.' She looked down at her hands, hesitating before she spoke again. 'I cannot describe the loss I experienced when Leo went missing, the days of fading hope, of confusion and pain. And, yes, it's so hard to never have an answer, only unanswered questions. Every now and then a stupid flicker of hope rises up inside me—that maybe, somehow, Leo's out there somewhere. But, of course, I don't believe that. He's not going to suddenly reappear with a story of amnesia. That doesn't happen in real life.' She shrugged, giving a flicker of a brighter smile. 'And now I'll never get to tell Jeremy how pissed off I was with him. Or hear his excuses. And he'll never get to meet his niece.'

'Niece?' Tom was confused. 'Dad had siblings?'

'Ah, I see, he didn't tell you?' Pippa leaned back in her chair. 'About him and Leo.'

'I'd never even heard of Leo until we started looking for you.' Where was this leading? What else hadn't his father explained?

'Eloise said they were cousins,' Olivia added.

Pippa gave them a strange look. 'That had been the general understanding.'

Tom looked between the two women, saw Olivia open her mouth, her eyes widen, as though she'd made a connection. 'They were more than cousins, weren't they?' she said.

'*More* than cousins?' Tom wasn't following.

'Yes. They were cousins and brothers. Or rather half-brothers. We found out right before Jeremy left that he and Leo had the same father.'

'Angus Clifford?' Tom frowned, looking first at Olivia—who seemed astonished—then at Pippa, trying to get his head around this revelation. The hand he had resting on the table tightened into a fist, until Olivia reached out to cover it with her own. He uncurled his fingers to hold hers tightly, aware of how much he liked her being beside him. 'Hold on.' He ran his free hand across his face. 'That would mean Angus is my grandfather. Right? And Maggie is, what, my aunt?' His family situation suddenly felt complicated and problematic. How had this quest become about him?

'Do the Cliffords know?' Olivia asked.

Pippa's laugh was hard. 'Oh, yes, absolutely. *That* detail was well and truly swept under a rug.'

Tom was incredulous. 'Do you mean to say I sat in their house, and all the time they knew I was Angus's grandson? I mean, I knew Evelyn was my great-aunt, but this is different.' Grandfather was a far closer connection. He flopped back in his chair, bringing Olivia's hand onto his thigh. 'They said nothing. They weren't even welcoming. In fact, they were bloody rude.'

'Of course they were. They're vile people who somehow produced two wonderful children. It is best to completely avoid them. They are both poisonous.'

Tom tried to recall anything in their meeting with the Cliffords that gave a hint of their awareness of the relationship, or of Angus being Jeremy's father. There'd been nothing.

When the silence stretched out again, Olivia spoke up. 'This is a ridiculous question, but Angus and Evelyn believe Jeremy was somehow responsible for Leo's disappearance. You don't believe that, do you?'

'No, absolutely not! Not for a minute.' Pippa was emphatic. 'They are bitter and twisted, and they were like that even before Leo disappeared. Jeremy was *not* involved—the police verified that. He boarded a plane to Sydney on the morning of the eighth of February, leaving his car in the city for me to collect, which was where it was found. I was with Leo for the last time on the night of the ninth. Jeremy wasn't even in the state.'

'That's what we thought, too,' Olivia continued, then turned to Tom. 'You okay?'

'Yes … just trying to get my head around it.'

Pippa gave him a thoughtful look, her eyes filled with compassion. 'This must be hard to take in. And if you're trying to work out the intricacies of your family tree, don't forget Paige is actually a first cousin. She'll be fascinated to hear about this, by the way. It's a pity she's not here today; she'd love to meet you.'

An aunt, a grandfather and a cousin had suddenly appeared in his life. What the hell else had his father been hiding? Had he even really known the man? 'Why didn't Dad tell me any of this?' Tom asked, knowing that Pippa didn't have the answer.

Pippa shrugged. 'Who knows. It seems your father changed after he left Australia. Didn't want anything to do with us anymore. He quite literally cut himself free from us. I can only guess he wanted to focus on forging a whole new life. I got one letter. No return address. Then nothing more.'

'Did he stay in contact with anyone?' Olivia asked.

'No, he didn't. Not even Rebecca—who was his girlfriend before he left.'

'We've heard her name mentioned,' said Olivia.

'We were never particularly close, and I didn't speak to her for almost five years after that summer. Then one day we ran into each other. She still lives in Brisbane too. I think she heads up a marketing company now. Anyway, we spent quite a nice afternoon talking. Your dad had written a very clear letter to her, not long after his arrival in London, saying it was over between them. He was sorry, but his life was moving on and there was no space for her. She was very surprised when I said he'd abandoned me as well. She was always a bit threatened by our friendship and had presumed we were still as thick as thieves. Jeremy also cut contact with Angela, your grandmother. According to her, they'd had an ugly phone call just before he left the country. He'd found out who his father was and rang her the day before he flew to London. Unfortunately, she alluded to an even more serious secret, and I think it messed with his head.'

'What secret?' Olivia asked the obvious question while Tom tried to drag his thoughts together.

Pippa paused, a grim expression crossing her face. 'You'll have to ask Angela—your grandmother—about that. I don't think it's my place to say.'

Tom opened his mouth, but there were no words. His grandmother was alive? There were more secrets? What the actual fuck was going on?

Pippa gave a knowing nod, then asked gently, 'I'm guessing Jeremy didn't tell you about his mother either?'

'He told me she died before he left Australia. It was one of the reasons he didn't make trips back. He said he had no family here.'

'Angela is still very much alive. She's living in a townhouse in a retirement village a couple of suburbs away. I think he wrote her a few letters, then dropped all contact. It broke her heart. We did try to track him down a few times over the years, but we had nothing to go on. And there has never been any sign of him online.'

'How ironic,' Tom muttered without a scrap of humour. 'He couldn't find you. You couldn't find him.' Right now, he was finding it hard to feel sorry for his father. From the moment he'd found the package addressed to Pippa, he'd romanticised his father's motivations and story. But this was starting to feel much less like a love story and more like the amends of a man who knew he'd done wrong. 'Does she know I'm here? Does she know Dad died?'

'No. I haven't spoken to her about any of this. I thought I'd meet you first, see how you felt about it.'

Tom had no idea how he felt. He drained what remained of his drink, the gentle tropical warmth abruptly oppressive. His role in this quest was messenger. His job had been to follow the clues. He'd been horrendously naive. Finding a package addressed to an unknown woman in the possessions of your enigmatic father was bound to lead to revelations—he just hadn't expected this impact. His gaze settled on a fat grey-green lizard wandering across the white ceiling. Finally, he found his voice. 'Can I have a think?'

Pippa nodded. 'Of course. Bringing you and Angela together would be wonderful, but it is your decision to make.' She reached for her glass but didn't drink, twisting it around several times before continuing, her voice hinting at a long-held resentment. 'Jeremy's actions, the choices he made, were unforgivable. They have affected all of us.'

So far she hadn't been overtly critical of Jeremy, but Tom could now hear judgement in her words. His father had left people hurt and bewildered. Surely he must have had a reason. Despite the resentment Tom was feeling towards his father, he wanted Pippa to know Jeremy had been a good person. Tom had loved his father greatly. His death had shattered him. 'I know he's hurt people here, and kept me in the dark about so much, but I do want you to know that he was a great dad, a decent man, generous and considerate, and liked by everyone.'

Pippa seemed to recognise his dismay. 'Oh, Tom, of course he was.' She reached forward, placing her hand partway across the table. It was a conciliatory gesture. 'He couldn't have changed completely. I don't know why he did what he did, but I'm glad to hear that he remained the man I knew and loved. How was his life over there? I haven't even asked.'

'He lived fairly simply. But he did quite well.' Tom briefly gave her the same details of his dad's life that he'd given Maggie.

'A publican—I wouldn't have picked that for his career,' Pippa said when Tom had finished. 'I truly am heartbroken that we'll never have the chance to mend bridges.'

Or maybe she would, at least. Tom reached for his satchel. 'That could be what he intended this to be.' He pulled out the large, thick envelope and handed it to Pippa.

'The mystery package,' she said, taking it.

'I found it when I was clearing out his home office. It's what brought me here to find you.'

She looked at the writing on the front, then turned it over and ran her fingers over the sealed flap. 'What do you think is inside?' she said with almost childlike curiosity. She was being remarkably restrained and calm.

An apology? A love letter? The deeds to a mysterious castle? He was starting to think that anything was possible. 'I don't know.' He tried to sound equally unconcerned. 'But I must admit, I'd love to find out.' Now, more than ever.

'This could be very interesting,' she said thoughtfully, leaving the package on the table. 'If you don't mind, Tom, I will wait till I'm alone to read this. But I will tell you. You deserve answers too. I won't leave you with the gaping hole of not knowing.'

'Thank you, I appreciate that.'

The quest was over, the package delivered into the right hands. Yet there was no feeling of triumph or even success. For a fleeting second he wished he'd never come here. Nothing was resolved, his life messier than it had been before he started this thing.

Olivia rested a hand on his arm reassuringly, and they looked at each other. She seemed to sense his inner conflict. And there it was, the unexpected reward for his effort and achievement: Olivia. On a hero's quest, the prize wasn't always what the hero expected. Their gaze held, and he knew he was going to find a way to make it work.

'We should get going, anyway.' He pushed back his chair, preparing to leave, then had second thoughts. 'There's one other thing.' He had been undecided about whether to give Pippa the photos—it was a little awkward to admit he'd seen pictures of her half naked—but now he knew it was the right thing to do. He pulled them from his satchel. 'These were with the package. They made me believe that you and Dad were ... well, that Dad loved you. I thought this was a love story.'

Pippa took them from him and glanced at each picture. She spoke without lifting her gaze. 'Jeremy had these?'

'Yes. They were all kept together. With that package.'

'This doesn't make sense.' She was still looking at the photos, apparently not the slightest bit concerned about the body of her younger self being exposed. 'These—' she held up the pictures of her and Eloise, the house, and her typewriter '— were taken by me at the start of that summer. These others weren't taken by Jeremy. They were taken by Leo.' She looked up, a deep frown of confusion on her face. 'They were all taken with my camera. I gave Leo these—and quite a few others of us together—a few days before he vanished. The last time I saw them, they were on the front seat of Leo's ute.'

A sense of foreboding rose around Tom, dark and heavy and squeezing out all thoughts of love and light.

What did this mean? What had his father done?

CHAPTER FORTY

Pippa watched from her front verandah as Tom and Olivia drove off. She didn't move, one hand gripping the railing, the other still holding those photos—the captured moments from a perfect summer.

She looked down at the picture on top. It was of her, asleep. Leo had taken it one morning at the house—the click of the camera had woken her. He'd climbed on the bed to take the next one, standing over her, telling her she was beautiful. They'd wrestled for the camera, and she'd taken a shot of him kneeling among the sheets and pillows, his chest bare, his hair tousled. She'd kept that one, still knew exactly where it was in her house. The three other pictures in her hand were of herself with her beloved typewriter, one with Eloise, and one of just Eloise that showed the house clearly. But what about the ones of Leo and her together? Where were they? The ones taken by others on their behalf, the camera handed to Jeremy or Rebecca or to Tilly at that party? Pippa had kept several of them, but she'd given some to Leo. There were no photos of Leo in her hand, or even of the four of them. She was absolutely certain there had been. She remembered seeing them in the ute on that last day. She'd even asked the police to return them to her. They'd told her there were no photos to be found.

Now some of them were back with her, delivered by Jeremy's son. Except there was no way Jeremy could have had them.

The ground was crumbling beneath her feet. There had to be answers in that envelope, but she knew—absolutely knew— the knowledge would be delivered with pain.

She had come so far after those years of grief, despite the endless, bitter state of not knowing: not knowing what had happened to Leo, not knowing why Jeremy would not come home. She had raised Paige, who she loved more than anything. She had built a career, married a lovely man who remained a friend even after the divorce, bought a beautiful home, and gradually accepted the direction her life had taken. But always, always, she had been living with the absence of knowledge.

After all this time, the answers were within reach. Putting it off was not an option—her fear of what was coming wasn't enough to make her stop. She rushed through the house, picked up the package from the table and took it to the kitchen. Grabbing a knife, she slit open the flap as she returned to the table and tipped out the contents.

An Australian passport.

Three photos of herself and Leo.

A thick handwritten document.

She unfolded the pages and began to read.

As she finished the last page her body hunched in on itself. She tried to breathe, a burning rush of pain rising, threatening to knock her to the ground. This was too much. She moved her hands to her chest, sucked in air, and let out a cry of absolute despair.

CHAPTER FORTY-ONE

Sunday, 9 February 1986

Leo didn't want to leave the house. He wanted to climb back into bed with Pippa, to pull her close, to sleep. To wake to another beautiful day.

He hesitated on the front step. What did he think he was going to achieve tonight? By the time he arrived in Sandy Bay it would be getting on to ten. His parents may not even be home. They could be out at a function—wasn't there something at the yacht club this week?

He moved to go back inside. Stopped. *Get a grip*, he told himself, heading quickly to his ute. It had to be done. If he wanted a different life, he had to face his parents. The conversation wouldn't be friendly or even civil. Things were going to be said. It would hurt. But he had to get his passport from them.

He turned the engine over and eased his way down the drive and around the bend. A wallaby hurtled from the bush and then stopped, blinded by his headlights. Leo braked, waiting till it bounded clear.

There was always the option to sneak home when his father was at work, he thought. *Nah.* His father would be expecting that. Leo's passport would be stashed somewhere secret. Angus was smart like that—some would call it cunning or manipulative. Either way, Leo was often forced to negotiate for anything he wanted. This would be no different.

He drove forward carefully, not wanting to kill anything.

Then he braked. *What the hell?*

A car was parked in the middle of the track. Driver's door open. No headlights. Interior light glowing dimly. Engine off. Empty. No sign of the driver.

A local, maybe, someone who'd pulled in and parked there to sleep off a heavy night. It was possible, even though they were some distance from the road, hidden by the bulk of the hill.

Wait, Leo thought. He knew the car. A blue Laser with Queensland number plates. The car he and Pippa were meant to be picking up from the city. Had someone delivered it to them?

Putting his ute into park, he switched off the motor and got out, then circled the small hatchback. Looked inside. The keys were still in the ignition.

'Hello, brother.' A slurred, dull voice from the darkness near the car.

Leo turned. 'Jeremy? Shit, mate, is that you?'

'Have any other brothers? Ha.' There was the sound of movement, a branch snapping, heavy, uneven footsteps. 'Maybe you do. Busy man, your father.' He came into view, unsteady, slipping a little as he made his way towards Leo.

'What are you doing here, mate? You're meant to be in Sydney. Aren't you flying to London tomorrow night?'

'Yeah, well, had a change of plans.' He wouldn't look at Leo. His eyes slid about, not fixing on any one thing, and his head jerked as though it was an effort to hold still.

'Okay.' The guy was rotten drunk. 'What are you doing out here? Come up to the house.'

'Deciding.' The word came out soft and slurry. Jeremy swung his right arm up in a wide arc. There was a square bottle in his hand. With difficulty he brought it to his mouth, took a swig and grimaced, shuddering at the burn of the booze. 'Me and my mate, my mate Bundy Rum. We're thinking through … thinking through stuff.'

'What stuff?'

'Big fuckin' stuff.'

Leo had never seen him like this. Jeremy liked beer, drank with some degree of control, and rarely touched spirits. At least, that was what Leo had noticed in the weeks they'd known each other. 'Come on, I'll drive us up. Leave your car here. Pippa and I can help you with your big stuff.'

'Pip.' Jeremy reared back. 'Yeah. Pippa *knows*. Should've told me. Fuck. I hate secrets. Too many bloody secrets.' He was mumbling, his chin down.

Short of dragging him into the car, Leo had little choice but to wait him out. They could be here for a while, Leo thought, resting against the bonnet of his ute. 'Secrets suck,' he agreed.

Jeremy bent down, put his free hand on the ground and lowered himself to the dirt. 'This is *another* secret.' He chuckled, then took a swig. 'You don't know this one. Not this secret. Not this time. I know something you don't know. *Brother*.' He made the word vile and bitter.

'Okay. Want to tell me?'

'Nup.' A pause. '*I* know. *Pip-Pip* knows. My *mum* knows. Of course she knows—she was there. When I asked about what happened ... she wouldn't tell me. She was still hiding things.' He sounded wounded. He was hurting. For himself, or for someone else?

Leo slid down to sit on the ground, his back against the tyre. The glow from the car gave them just enough light. He could more clearly see the pain and confusion on Jeremy's face. 'Is this about Dad?'

'Your dad. *Not* my dad.' He spat the words, lifting his head to glare at Leo, angry now. 'That man is not my dad.'

'He's not?' What the hell? Had Jeremy's mum told him a different story?

'Sure, he's genetic ... genetically—' he fumbled the word '—his DNA is here.' Jeremy slapped his chest. 'But he's not my *father*. I refuse to be that bastard's son. I refuse.' A burst of breath, half yell, half sob. 'I talked to him, your father. Went to his house. And no, I don't give a shit that you got the comfortable life. And Mum and me, we didn't. Don't care about that. This is not about money. I've got money now, making my own money.' He was swerving from one line of thought to another, becoming incoherent, and Leo struggled to follow. 'Met her. Evelyn. He, that bastard, he wanted me to come inside, he wanted to *talk*. But no.' Jeremy gave his head an exaggerated shake.

Leo was trying to understand what had happened, and when. 'You went to my parents' house? Weren't you getting on a plane to Sydney?'

'Ha, made some dude's day.' He gave a wild chuckle. 'A backpacker—gave him my ticket. He was me for that flight, 'cos I needed to talk. I couldn't leave without talking.'

'To my dad?'

'He wanted to talk. She wouldn't let me.'

So, at the last minute, Jeremy had decided he couldn't leave without speaking to the man who claimed to be his father. That was understandable. Leo had thought Jeremy was way too calm about the bombshell. He must have decided to abandon or postpone his travel plans, then he'd rocked up to the Sandy Bay home of the Cliffords, where Angus had been welcoming and Evelyn had not.

'She kicked me out. Got angry. Christ, she's cold. Said some horrible, horrible things about Mum. Said—' a sob burst from him '—she said Mum was a liar. That what she'd said about Angus was bullshit. That she'd been willing, had seduced him, had wanted it. That she'd made up a story about what happened. Ha. Mum didn't say it clearly, but I can read between the lines. Now I know about him. About how he ...' Another half sob, his head down, his shoulders heaving. A guttural growl of pain. 'He *raped* my mum. She was seventeen.' He lifted his gaze. The disgust was there in his eyes, the twist of his mouth. 'That's how I was put together, through violence. And she knew. Her. Evelyn. Mum's sister, she knew, and wouldn't admit the truth. Had her kicked out of home.' He pushed up to his feet, swayed, stumbled on a rock, then planted his feet wide to steady himself, the bottle still gripped tightly in his hand. He focused on Leo, taking a step closer. 'Your fuckin' dad, he raped my mum. That's how I was made. That's why my mum didn't love me.'

Leo got up slowly. This was crazy. Jeremy was drunk, deluded, raging against the less than perfect childhood he must have had. He had to be wrong about this. His father was many things, and there were no excuses for Angus's flaws. God knew Leo had fought against the man's demands, his warped priorities, his dictatorial approach to Leo's life. Yes, he turned a blind eye to Angus's sleazy conduct, but it wasn't his place to interfere in his parents' marriage or to confront his father over his embarrassing behaviour. Despite all of that, Leo did love him. Leo's childhood had been great. He'd wanted for nothing. His father taught him to sail, and their shared passion for the boats had given them many happy, memorable experiences.

'Jeremy, mate, let's go up to the house. You can crash. Sleep off the booze.'

'I'm not going anywhere with you. You shouldn't be there. 'Cos, mate,' he uttered the word with lashings of sarcasm, 'I don't want anything to do with you. Ever. Get out of here. Piss off. Leave us alone.' He threw his arms wide, the rum bottle swinging like a club. 'Go on. Go back to your revolting family. Go on. Fuck off.'

Leo stepped back, coming up hard against the bonnet of his ute. He put his hands up, the universal sign of surrender, showing he had no fight with his friend. 'Calm down.'

'Don't tell me to calm down. You have no idea, no idea how this *feels*.' Saliva sprayed from between his lips. He took another stumbling step forward, the bottle still swinging.

When he lifted his other hand, Leo was ready. The slow arc of the clenched fist was easy to judge. Leo blocked, keeping the punch from connecting. 'Back off, Jeremy.' He tried to sound calm, but his body recognised the threat and was flooding with adrenaline. 'Seriously, back off.' He gripped Jeremy's wrist and put his other hand on his chest to propel him backwards.

Even with a height and strength advantage, and the benefit of being sober, Leo had to struggle to gain space. Jeremy was fuelled by anger and a sense of injustice—he clearly wanted to inflict damage, needing to lash out against someone. He came back harder, snarling, trying to grab with one hand, holding the bottle as a weapon in the other.

Leo defended himself. The boys were wrestling, shoving. Jeremy hit out. Leo retaliated. His fist connected with the side of Jeremy's face, his fingers crunching on impact, pain shooting through his hand.

Jeremy's head snapped back. The bottle fell but didn't smash, dark rum spilling across the ground. Jeremy wavered on his feet, stumbled back. His heel caught, one hand rising to his damaged face, the other reaching out to stop his fall. He hit the dirt hard, his head smacking into the ground. A low groan sounded from his mouth, fading to nothing.

Leo shook out his hand, flexing his fingers, wincing. His breathing was ragged as though he'd been running, yet the fight had lasted less than a minute.

He waited for Jeremy to move, hoping he would give it a rest. The guy needed to sober up, then they could talk—work out what had happened, what had been said.

Jeremy didn't move. Leo waited.

Then he knelt, put his hand on his shoulder, shook him. 'Jeremy.'

Nothing.

Leo bent closer, a hand on Jeremy's chest. 'Come on, Jeremy, can you move?'

Why wasn't he moving? Was he breathing? Leo hadn't hit him hard.

He groped for Jeremy's wrist, putting his fingers where he expected to feel a beat, then against his neck. Wasn't there a spot under the chin? Why couldn't he find it?

'Come on, come on, Jeremy, come on.'

It couldn't happen. People didn't just die like that. There wasn't much blood, only a smear under his nose, and it wasn't flowing. There was a rock under his head—round, not sharp, sticking out of the ground. He'd fallen hard and knocked his head. But where was the injury? There was nothing to see. No blood—there was no blood.

And no breathing.

Panic surged. Leo had to do something. Had to stop this from happening.

He tilted Jeremy's head back and pinched his nose. Blew two breaths into his mouth. Then again, and again. Tried to remember where to put his hands on his chest. How fast was he supposed to pump? How hard?

Oh fuck. Jeremy. Come on. We'll sort this out. I'm sorry I got mad. Come on. Please. Please.

He breathed into him. Pushed at his chest.

Again.

Again.

Until his arms ached and shook.

Then he was sitting in the dirt, hands over his own face, shaking. Groaning. Then sobbing.

*

He had no idea how much time had passed. It could have been hours. It didn't matter.

At some point he realised he had to move. He needed help.

The walk back to the house was slow. He stumbled several times, barely able to see where he was going.

He silently opened the front door. Honey came padding over to greet him, sniffing around him as he stood in the kitchen as though she could read the night's story in the smells layered into his legs and hands.

Without making a sound he moved through the house. He stood in the doorway of Pippa's room. She was on her side, one leg flung over a pillow, her dark hair tangled against the sheets.

He should never have left this bed. If only he had stayed, he would be there beside her, his world unchanged.

He imagined waking her, clinging to her, wrapping himself in the love and warmth of her body, having her erase the nightmare he was living.

It wouldn't happen. To wake her would be to confess. As soon as she saw him, she would know something dreadful had happened. He wouldn't be able to keep it from her. Then her life would be shattered. Her friend was gone. He had done that to her.

She would hate him. To see that loathing on her face would be too much to bear.

Could he explain? Even if he could make her understand, things would never, ever be the same. She would not want him in her life.

Only one person could help. He pulled the bedroom door closed and crept back to the kitchen. He dialled the number, then stretched the long cord as far as it would go, till he was out on the step, the front door nearly closed behind him.

'Dad?'

*

Leo was sitting in his ute when the headlights swung around the bend. His father pulled up behind Jeremy's car. The three vehicles lined up, one in front of the other.

Leo got out and walked forward, confused when he saw the two figures. 'Mum?'

She moved straight to him, pulling him into a long hug. 'It's going to be okay,' she said, in the soothing voice of a mother easing the fears of a child. 'We're going to make this right.' Gripping him by the arms, she peered into his face.

In the dark he couldn't see her clearly, but he recognised the capable set to her shoulders, the firmness of her grasp.

'It was an accident?' said Angus. Leo wasn't sure whether his father was asking a question or making a statement.

'And you haven't said anything to Pippa?' his mother asked, letting him go and taking a small torch from the pocket of her pants. She moved to where Jeremy lay on the ground.

'No. She's up at the house. I left her asleep. She thinks I'm in Hobart, talking with you.'

'You were coming to see us tonight?' his father asked.

He nodded, then realised they couldn't see him. 'Yes. I needed my passport.'

His mother had crouched down. Leo could see the small circle of light moving over Jeremy's body as she picked up his wrist. There was a brief pause as she felt for a pulse at his neck. She stood and came back to Leo and Angus, giving a grim but firm shake of her head, confirming what he already knew.

'Your mother and I think it's best not to get the authorities involved.'

'But—'

'There is nothing to be gained by you going to jail. Because, you can be certain, that's what will happen.' His father sounded restrained and tense, but also determined. 'Especially with your record of assault.'

'I wasn't charged.'

'It will all be dug up.' His was the voice of certainty.

Leo's mother had come to stand beside him. 'This is a tragedy. But a greater tragedy would take place if two young lives were thrown away tonight. Do you understand, darling?'

He couldn't answer. The guilt was suffocating—surely he couldn't just walk away from this. He deserved to be punished. But ... jail? He couldn't go to jail. It had been self-defence. A terrible accident. There was such relief at having his parents decide what to do. They were going to fix this, make everything okay.

'First, we have to get home.' In her crisp, decisive tone, his mother was taking charge. 'Now, listen. I want you to get in your ute and follow your father. Are you listening? Leo?' She snapped her fingers in front of his face. 'We have a plan, but we need you to do exactly as we ask. Leo? Can you do that? You're in shock, and we will explain everything when we get home. But for now, do what I tell you. You are not in a fit state for making decisions. Yes?'

It was too much. He stopped fighting and let himself be swept along by their authority, their promise of safety. The pressure inside him eased as he let his parents take charge.

Leo and his father carried Jeremy to the back seat of the Laser, then got into their cars. There was a brief manoeuvring as they turned them around, then Angus drove down the hill, Leo following in his ute. Looking in his rear-view mirror, he could see torchlight as his mother checked the ground—searching for evidence, he guessed. Then he lost sight of her as he dropped down towards the main road. He drove on autopilot, following the red tail-lights of his father, and blocked from his mind the picture of his mother in Jeremy's car, the body lying on the back seat. Leo hadn't asked what she was going to do. He was afraid. Didn't want the details. They'd tell him soon enough, if they decided he needed to know. He hoped they wouldn't.

*

His father had left Leo slumped on the sofa while he and his mother went to deal with the situation. It was four in the morning when they arrived home.

Jeremy was gone, and so was his car. They were somewhere out there.

His parents were handling things, almost terrifying in their calm, pragmatic control. There had been no wailing, no outbursts of horror. His mum had never been one for histrionics or wild emotions. His dad could be more dramatic, but he was a lawyer. He knew about these sorts of crimes—these accidents—didn't he?

Leo buried his head into the cushions. Where had they taken Jeremy?

His brother. Dead, cold, hidden. He'd done that.

None of this was right. Leo wanted Pippa.

Then his parents came into the room. His mother was outwardly calm, but her hair was a mess, her jeans dirty at the knees. Her face, without her usual make-up, seemed pale, her eyes wide, mouth clenched into a stiff line. She had done what needed to be done, no matter how distasteful the act had been. His father went straight to the liquor cabinet, poured a glass of whisky, downed it in one hit. Then he poured one for his wife and handed it to her.

She took it and sank into an armchair. 'Maggie is at a sleepover,' she said. 'She will be home at midday. This will need to be finalised by then.' She spoke as though thinking out loud.

'What do we do next?' Leo asked. He was exhausted. He couldn't think, couldn't fully understand what was happening.

'You will give us a precise account of what happened tonight—what Jeremy said to you. But we don't have much time. Wasn't he supposed to be going overseas?'

'He was … His ticket to Sydney, he told me he gave it to someone else. He was due to fly to London from there. He leaves on Monday evening … tomorrow evening.' Except he wouldn't. He wouldn't be going anywhere.

'Why did he have his car?' she asked.

'He drove to town the night before he was going to Sydney. It's Pippa's car now. He was going to leave the car near the hostel, the one on Liverpool Street. We were going to pick it up tomorrow.'

Leo's parents looked at each other. Evelyn nodded slightly, looking almost pleased, as though what he'd said was good news, while Angus shrugged then tossed back the contents of his glass. From her handbag Evelyn extracted a passport. She flicked it open and held it up, looking from the picture on the page to Leo and back, like an immigration official. She handed the passport to Angus, who did the same. After a minute he closed it, holding it tight in his hand.

He glanced at his wife. Leo had never seen his father in such distress. Anguish was clear in the deep lines of his face, a muscle in his jaw jumping, his mouth clamped tight like he was struggling not to cry. He muttered, 'Is there no other way? Christ, I'm a lawyer, we can find a way around this.'

Evelyn showed nothing but resolve and unflinching determination. She was holding it together for all of them. 'For Christ's sake, Angus, you're an expert on tax law, not criminal. This isn't one of your mates and their tax avoidance schemes. This is your son, and he *killed* someone … your *other* son. No. There is no alternative.'

'But what happens when—'

'No!' She cut her husband off, silencing him with her sharp rebuke. 'There is nothing more to discuss. I am the only one thinking clearly, so you will both listen to me.' Her hardened eyes found Leo. 'Are you listening, Leo? Are you paying attention? Because your ability to have a life comes down to this. Do you understand?'

What could he say? He nodded, numb from shock and grief. The world had tilted, and everything he knew was sliding past him, dropping over the edge into oblivion. He was following, unable to stop.

Evelyn stood and crossed the room to where he was sitting. 'In a few hours you will be on a plane to Sydney, travelling under another name. You don't need identification on domestic flights, unlike international travel.'

She handed him the passport. He opened it. Saw the name, and the face that wasn't his.

'Then you will go to London. You will be Jeremy. No one can accuse you of killing that boy if that boy isn't dead. Besides, the greater mystery will be what happened to Leo Clifford.'

CHAPTER FORTY-TWO

Friday, 7 July 2017

Pippa stood at the window, her back to Angela. She tried to focus on the pretty garden beds flanking the paths between the neat villas that made up the retirement village—or retirement *resort*, according to the marketing material. Angela had decided last year that being in a gated community like this would suit her well, and Pippa had helped, working with her through the seemingly endless paperwork and legalities. She'd been happy to do it, their relationship having been cemented in the years after Jeremy left. Pippa had been dealing with the loss of Leo, the absence of Jeremy, and the needs of her baby, and Angela had been struggling with the estrangement of her son, torn apart by his refusal to have her in his life.

Except that wasn't what had happened.

Pippa had sat with Leo's words for a week, drinking far too much as she read them over and over. The waves of grief and pain had started drowning her, then retreated a little, only to wash over her again and again. She'd texted Tom and told him it wasn't the right time for him to meet Jeremy's mother, and to give her a little more time before she gave him answers. She'd called in sick to work and told Paige she had received some bad news. Her daughter hovered around the house, obviously concerned, preparing meals Pippa could barely eat.

'Talk to me, Mum,' she said, gripping Pippa's hand. 'What's happened?'

'I found out some truths. Nothing is what it seemed.' She would explain it all to Paige—just not yet. Before she could share this reality, she needed to come to terms with this knowledge.

Leo had been there, all this time, on the other side of the world. He could have told her, could have explained, could have confessed before he went and died. The stupid, stupid man. Why had he let her suffer? Why hadn't he come back?

The anger had come then. Anger at his foolishness, his gutlessness, his harmful actions.

She couldn't get the horror of that scene out of her head. She could picture the driveway to Eloise's house, the way it twisted around the hill, how dark the nights could be. She saw Jeremy lying on the ground, Leo kneeling beside him, his hands on his brother's chest. Trying to save his life. Failing.

One punch, thrown in a fight Leo hadn't started. Jeremy drunk, unbalanced, unable to break his fall. Head whipping back. Crashing to the ground. Slamming into a rock.

She'd known Leo. In that moment when he knew what he'd done, he would have been in agony. The panic. Fear. Grief. Guilt. The desperation for the reality to be different.

She'd heard the stories of life taken with one blow, a coward punch. Boys and men dying in a gutter or on the footpath. And in the dirt while she slept.

Now she could hear the quiet sobs of Jeremy's mother as she read the letter and came to know the truth. Angela deserved to know—*needed* to know—that her son hadn't chosen to abandon her.

'Thank you.' The older woman's voice cracked. 'Thank you.'

Pippa moved to kneel beside her chair. 'Jeremy loved you, Angela. He didn't leave you by choice.'

Tears flowed down the crevices of Angela's weathered cheeks. 'He was taken.'

'Yes, he was.' Pippa didn't try to stop herself from crying.

'An accident.'

'An accident.' She nodded in agreement.

'I had a feeling when he told me they were all going down to Eloise's house. I had a feeling, an instinct, that something bad would happen.' Her sobs came louder. 'Where is he, Pippa?' Angela reached out a shaking hand to grip Pippa's arm. 'What did they do with my son? What did those monsters do with my boy?'

'I don't know.'

'Can you find him? Can you make them tell you?'

'Yes,' Pippa said fiercely. 'I will.'

But she was going to do more than that. She was going to make Angus and Evelyn Clifford pay for what they did.

*

Tom and Olivia were waiting for her at Hobart Airport. She hadn't told them much, only that she was coming down, that she wanted to share the details of the package Tom had delivered, and that she had to tie up some loose ends. Tom had seemed happy enough to postpone his return to London to meet with her, and Olivia had offered her a room at Eloise's house. She'd accepted.

Seeing Tom again delivered a sharp pang of bittersweet emotion. He was Leo's son and a half-brother to her daughter, and Pippa was about to upend his world. She would explain everything to Paige when she had finished what she needed to do.

'I'd forgotten how fresh the air is down here,' she said, making conversation as Olivia drove them through Hobart.

'Has the place changed much?' Olivia asked.

Pippa looked at the waterfront, studying the buildings that had been new when she was last here, the sandstone heritage facades that had been old then and were older now, the few taller buildings recently added to the skyline. 'Not much,' she said.

They passed the turn-off to Sandy Bay Road. Those people were down there, living their comfortable lives, clutching their secrets. She wanted to see their faces when they realised they were going to be held accountable for their sins.

Angus and Evelyn had controlled the situation—Leo had made that clear. He'd been shunted forward by his mother, told to leave, to run. He'd done what he was told. In his letter—his confession—he'd written of his panic at the time.

My parents put me on a plane to Sydney that morning. I hadn't slept. Was doing what I was told. Not fighting, not thinking. I don't even remember what the name was on the ticket. Back then there were no identity checks on domestic flights. You could swap tickets, make up a name, be anyone. From there I travelled on Jeremy's ticket and passport.

Leaving Sydney, I was numb to the world around me. I had killed my brother, and now I was pretending to be him.

I was running away, leaving you. At any minute I expected a hand on my shoulder. To be dragged aside. But no one stopped me.

The Cliffords had been diligent in creating an alternate reality. They'd given their son money and instructions, kept tabs on him, and told him what to do and when to do it.

At first I was just doing what my parents told me. I was scared, and relieved for them to make the decisions, to take control of the mess I had made. I had to ring them daily.

They told me when I needed to go into Australia House in London to make a statement, as Jeremy. I'd been pretending to be him for two weeks by then. I told them his story as though it was mine and said that I had no idea what could've happened to Leo Clifford. That he was happy and in love, had plans for the future, but he had fought with his parents. They were controlling, hadn't wanted him to leave. They'd been unhappy about what he was doing. This was my one bit of rebellion, to cast a shadow on Angus and Evelyn. I hoped the police would question them and make them uncomfortable.

Then I went to Edinburgh. Time passed, and life began to take shape around me. I got a job in a pub. Rented a flat. And I stopped ringing home—stopped doing what they wanted. I cut them out of my life.

By the time I could think clearly, think for myself, it felt too late. Too much time had passed. I was selfish. I didn't want to go to jail, and I convinced myself that confessing then would've been even worse. I would've been charged not only with manslaughter but also with running away, impersonating Jeremy.

I have been a coward. I do not ask for forgiveness, but I am sorry beyond words. For everything.

And Jeremy? What had those people done with his body? It wasn't only punishment Pippa wanted for the Cliffords. She wanted all the answers, to all the questions.

CHAPTER FORTY-THREE

Monday, 10 February 1986

Evelyn was seething. Other people may have experienced a more delicate emotion, but for her the events of this evening were beyond infuriating. Her stupid, selfish sister was to blame, and her vile stories. Yes, Evelyn had always believed what Angela had said about her husband—that he'd been a little too forceful. But, for heaven's sake, why couldn't the miserable girl simply have dealt with the situation? Why did she have to go and make such a fuss about everything? No wonder Mother had made her leave. The marriage between Evelyn and Angus was far too beneficial to put aside.

Now here Angela was, all these years later, still causing trouble.

What woman tells her child he was the product of such a union? No wonder the idiot boy had gone crazy, turning up at their house with his accusations and questions. What an ugly, unnecessary scene. Thank goodness Maggie had been staying with a friend.

Look where this had all led—look at the mess Evelyn had to clean up.

Well, it was a good thing the boy was dead. She knew that was a harsh position to take, but she wasn't going to lie to herself. It was better this way. If he'd come thrashing further into the lives of the Cliffords, there would have been some unacceptable consequences. She shuddered to think of the gossip once it became known that her successful, handsome husband had fathered a child by his wife's sister. And that ugly word: rape. It could not be associated with her family. What a pathetic mess. At least with the boy gone, the chances of revelation were significantly diminished.

Angus parked the BMW behind the two cars in Eloise's driveway. She could see her son crumpled on the ground, the body beside him.

'Oh Christ,' Angus moaned. 'This is bad.'

She turned in her seat. 'Listen to me, Angus. Don't you dare be weak. You are going to pull it together—we will deal with this. There are some details we need to work out, but I think my plan is a good one. If you want your son to stay out of jail, you will work with me. Do you understand?'

His nod was small and reluctant.

'We don't have time for you to fall to pieces. If we act quickly and efficiently this can all be dealt with before the sun comes up. Life will go on. Alright?'

'Fine, whatever you say,' he muttered, his words filled with hostility. 'I always said you were a cold bitch, and this certainly proves it.'

'Well, one of us has to have balls, Angus.' She pushed open the door and got out, went to Leo, hugged and reassured him, then crouched on the ground. It had been years since her nursing days, but she still knew how to check a body properly. Not expecting anything, she waited for a sign of life.

There it was. A flutter under the skin. The faintest echo of a pulse.

She didn't react. Kept her fingers in place, then shook her head and lifted her hand.

This was not acceptable. When Leo had called to say Jeremy was dead, she had quickly accepted the situation and even found the silver lining. A solution had started to take shape, and she had mentally accepted what would be the outcome. There would be some loss, but no mess, no fallout to tarnish her tidy life. But this ... this would change everything. This boy in the dirt would wreak havoc in her world.

No. She stood. Turned to her husband and son, and told Leo exactly what to do. He nodded and obeyed.

There was a moment when they were carrying the body to the boy's car when she thought it would all come unstuck. The kid would move, moan, breathe. They would notice he was alive.

She didn't relax until Leo and Angus had climbed into their cars and driven away. With the torch she checked the ground, picking up the rum bottle, wiping it down and putting it in the front passenger seat of Jeremy's Laser.

Then she opened the back door wide. His head lolled lifelessly on the seat, but she knew he wasn't quite dead, probably could be saved.

No. Evelyn put her hands on his face, pinching his nose hard, clamping her palm over his mouth. She pressed down, putting her weight over her arms. And waited.

She gazed out the window into the darkness. A night bird screeched—a plover, she thought, or to be precise a masked lapwing. Things ought to be called by their proper names. Turbo chook was another misnomer, a silly name for the Tasmanian native hen. It bothered her, not enough to make a fuss but enough to correct people when they used the incorrect name.

Beneath her hands Jeremy twitched. There was a shudder as if somewhere deep inside he was struggling. Then he was still.

She waited. To be certain.

*

The drive was uneventful, giving her time put together the last pieces of the plan, to turn it over and around in her mind, checking for weaknesses or holes. It felt sound, but she was no fool. There was significant risk. It wouldn't be easy. For his part, Leo would have to be strong, and there would be a cost for them all. But exposure of her family's flaws would be far worse.

On the outskirts of Hobart she pulled over and got out to check the boot for the boy's bags. In his backpack she found what she needed. A one-way ticket to London and his passport. She took a moment to look at the picture. Yes, this would work—they were very similar. The fact that Jeremy was organised enough to also have his birth certificate with him was a surprise bonus.

When Evelyn arrived home, she found Angus sitting in his BMW. Leo's ute was parked behind it in the drive, empty. *Good.* He would be inside, waiting. The less he saw, the better.

Angus was holding it together, more or less. She kept her instructions simple, the details of the plan succinct. It was hard work, but together they managed to carry the boy down the side path to the shed at the bottom of the garden. Later they would take the dinghy out to their yacht. Then it would be Angus's turn to step up. He knew the tides, the currents, the depths. He would know how far out to sail, the best place to dispose of this inconvenience. Sometimes she hated him, but she had faith in his knowledge.

They still had to deal with the cars. Angus drove the ute and Evelyn followed in the blue Laser. At the deserted yacht club carpark Angus parked Leo's ute, then climbed in with his wife. Tomorrow they would leave Jeremy's car outside the backpacker's, as had been planned.

They returned home in silence.

'Are you really willing to let him leave?' Angus asked as they pulled up.

'Willing? You stupid man, it's not about being willing, it's about doing what has to be done.'

'It may be years before you see him again.'

'So be it. That's the price he must pay. But he will be free, our name will not be dragged through the muck, and nobody will know what a despicable creature you truly are.'

As usual her insults slid over him like mud on oil. 'You really think Leo will be able to waltz back into our lives at some point?'

'Of course. He may never be able to *be* Leo Clifford again, but he can still have a brilliant life. And I intend to be there to see his success. He will still be a part of our lives, but quietly, from a distance.'

'And what about Maggie?'

She thought of the pain and loss Maggie was about to experience, her resolve wilting for just a moment. No. It was unavoidable. Knowing the truth would be just as traumatic.

'Obviously she can never know.' She spoke firmly, daring him to disagree.

'Leo's disappearance will be hard on her.' Angus was getting too emotional.

'She'll be fine. Better than being the daughter of a rapist or the sister of a killer.'

That shut him up for a moment.

'You hope he'll do what he's told,' he said quietly before they entered their beautiful home.

'Oh, he will. He always has.'

CHAPTER FORTY-FOUR

Friday, 7 July 2017

Tom took the passport from Pippa's hand, Olivia leaning over to look as he opened it to the photo. They were in the lounge, the fire warming them on a day with a snow forecast for the higher hills. Olivia and Tom sat side by side, with Pippa facing them from where she perched on the edge of the·chaise section of the L-shaped modular sofa. The photo was a typically expressionless picture of a young man with neat, short, dark blond hair and familiar eyes. Tom could see the features of his father as he had known him—older, of course, and subtly changed.

'I've never seen him this young in pictures. He's so clean-cut. I only saw him with longer hair.' He opened the camera roll on his phone, jumped back a couple of years and scrolled till he found something clear. 'He hated being in photos, always facing away a bit. This was taken at a lunch at one of his pubs.'

Pippa gave a gentle smile as she looked at the picture. 'Do you think, maybe later, you could shoot me over some photos of your dad?'

'Absolutely.' Tom immediately sent the picture to her phone.

'You've seen pictures of Leo Clifford, haven't you?' she asked them.

'Yes,' answered Olivia. 'There were a couple of images used with the missing person stories. And Tilly showed me one taken at a party you were all at. I keep meaning to go and copy it to show Tom.'

'We keep getting distracted,' said Tom, thinking of the days of 'distraction' they'd had since he'd arrived.

Pippa nodded, a knowing glimmer in her eyes. 'Tom, did you see the photos online?'

'Yes.' Why was she asking? 'I can definitely see the resemblance between Leo and Dad at this age.'

She handed over several printed photos. 'This is Leo and me, here in January 1986. And here's one of all of us—I remember I had to use a self-timer for this. I think we set up the camera on the barbecue.' She pointed out towards the ancient brick construction.

In the photo, four young people were sitting on the edge of the outdoor table. Pippa, the girl Tom presumed was Rebecca, and the two half-brothers. Seeing them together made Tom uneasy. If he'd been shown this picture a few weeks ago, he wouldn't have known which of the boys was his father, or he would have picked the blonder guy, the one holding Pippa. 'Distinct family resemblance,' he said, suddenly wary of where Pippa was leading him.

'Yes—which was how Leo slipped away.' Pippa was watching him intently.

He felt Olivia put a hand on his leg and heard her quick intake of breath. 'I don't understand ... You know what happened to Leo?' His heart hammered as adrenaline rushed through his body.

'Yes, I do,' Pippa said simply. 'And also what happened to Jeremy. And it does affect you.'

'Okay.' Tom gripped Olivia's hand. 'Alright. Tell me everything.'

Pippa took a stack of pages from the bag at her feet and handed them to him. They were covered in his father's writing.

'Do you want to read this on your own?' Olivia asked him. 'I can leave, if you prefer.'

'No.' His eyes met hers, pleading. 'I need you here.'

He held the letter between them as he read, his world shifting and buckling with every line.

CHAPTER FORTY-FIVE

Sunday, 9 July 2017

The detective sergeant had been clear. She did not want
Pippa to visit the Cliffords. If Pippa were to pre-emptively
divulge the information contained in Leo's written confession
it could jeopardise the investigation. Angus and Evelyn would
have an opportunity to hide evidence or concoct a viable story.
At the very least they would be warned and prepared before
the arrival of the police.

She had promised to stay away. But it was almost impossible to obey. She'd returned to Eloise's house, explaining how
the interview had progressed to Olivia and Tom—who still
appeared to be in a fluctuating state of shock. She'd taken a
call that night, the detective sergeant informing her the investi-
gating team would be visiting the Cliffords the next morning.

Now she had been sitting at the bus stop on Sandy Bay Road,
directly opposite the entrance to the Cliffords' driveway, for
three hours. Watching as Angus drove out at eight-thirty and

returned forty minutes later (with the papers and takeaway coffee, she guessed), and then when two cars arrived an hour later—one marked as police, the other a plain blue. They were yet to leave.

Pippa couldn't wait any longer. She crossed the road and walked down towards the house, then entered the turning circle just as the front door opened.

Evelyn Clifford was escorted out first, not handcuffed but held by one arm. She was being led to the unmarked car when she saw Pippa. 'You!'

'Hello, Evelyn.'

'I should've known you were involved in this pathetic attempt to lay blame. Don't for a second think you've achieved anything.'

'All I did, Evelyn, was bring Leo's story to the right people. Your son is the one delivering well-deserved, long-overdue consequences to you and your husband.'

'My son's fate was sealed the minute you put your filthy whore hands on him and whispered your poison in his ear. I hope you spend the rest of your life consumed with guilt. This all started with you.' The woman was struggling to maintain her well-groomed facade.

'You know that's not true. It all started with him—' Pippa nodded towards Angus as he was brought out from the house '—and what he did to Angela. It was made worse by your despicable treatment of your sister.' Pippa spoke loudly, making sure the woman heard every word, but kept her tone calm and precise. 'The consequences of those actions—of *your* actions—led to a horrible tragedy, a tragedy made worse because neither of you could bear to let go of your pathetic need to maintain your so-called social standing. I hope that one day you have the courage to take a good hard look at yourself, and you recognise the damage you have done, the lives you have ruined. I want to see you crushed. I want to see you curled in a corner catatonic from shame.'

'Shame? *I'm* not the one who should be ashamed. I'm not—' Evelyn's furious response was cut off as she was helped into the back seat of the car.

The detective approached Pippa.

'Did they admit anything?' Pippa asked. 'Did they tell you what they did with Jeremy?'

'At this stage they're denying everything, but they've shown a complete lack of surprise over Leo having been alive all this time. They will be interviewed separately, and I am very hopeful we will get answers.'

'What will they be charged with?'

'I'm afraid I can't answer that now, but we will be in touch at some point, Ms Braden.'

'Has anyone spoken to Maggie?'

'The daughter? No, not yet.'

'Can I be the one to tell her what's happened?' Poor, poor Maggie. Darling Maggie. This was going to hurt her in so many ways. Pippa's already damaged heart ached anew for what her friend would suffer.

The detective nodded. 'But she may have to be interviewed at some stage—she may know something, even if she doesn't realise it.'

They said their goodbyes. As the two cars turned to leave, Pippa stood to one side. Angus Clifford's eyes met hers through the window. He had the look of a man intent on scrabbling to save himself. She suspected he would be the first to make a deal, to secure leverage for himself even at his wife's expense.

Then Pippa was alone. She didn't move. She could hear the muted rush of traffic. A dog barked. A soft shower, more mist than rainfall, eddied around her, and she closed her eyes, tilted her head back and let it settle on her face. They had brought him here in the back seat of his own car. Plans had quickly been made to solve the inconvenient problem. Leo had been sent away, doing as he was told, abandoning his new-found autonomy in the maelstrom of shock and fear.

Leo, why didn't you come to me? I was right there, waiting.

She opened her eyes and looked at the house, then stepped up to the verandah and followed it around to the back, where the garden stretched out to meet the bay. There was a low hedge dividing the property from the narrow beach. Beyond that lay the waters of the Derwent River, a few yachts moored offshore.

She knew Jeremy's remains would never be found. She was convinced that at the hands of his father, he had been thrown away, discarded into the sea. Her heart tore open, the tears falling hard and fast, the sobs wrenching her body till her chest and stomach ached.

She didn't need to read the last page of Leo's letter again. She knew what it said.

Thirty years.

I've lived a life between then and now.

It has passed with fleeting moments of joy and happiness, and long, long days when the guilt and regret have been suffocating. Always I have missed you. Missed us.

You saved me and, in turn, I gave you pain and loss. I lie awake dreaming that your life has been the spectacular, exhilarating adventure you deserve. That your spirit was not crushed beyond repair.

I know you must want answers, but I'm too much a coward. I don't have the courage to face you—I can't be the one to give you the truth.

I have done my best.

It was not enough.

I am sorry, my love.

Always,

Leo.

CHAPTER FORTY-SIX

Tuesday, 3 October 2017

Olivia slotted the envelopes into the postboxes, one by one. 'James Henley?' she asked.

Wendy was beside her, sorting the mail at a far greater speed. She answered without hesitation. 'Two hundred and fifty.'

'Marisa Duffy?'

'One hundred and seventy-eight.'

The next twenty or so were addressed to their PO Box number—they were easy. It was the letters with only street addresses that Olivia had to check with Wendy, whose memory for who went where was infallible.

'Oh no.' Olivia held up a green envelope. 'Poppa Bear, Hill Road, Devils Bay.' She laughed. 'Who is this for, do you think?'

Wendy took the envelope, flipped it over. 'From Max and Bertie. Hmm. If I remember correctly, Sophia Drake's kids are Max and Albert, which I'm guessing gets shortened to Bertie. Sophia's dad is Hamish Wooley, who's up on Hill Road. So, box seventeen.'

'I'll never be able to do that,' said Olivia, shaking her head.

'You would if you spent years at this job, nattering with everyone.'

Olivia wasn't so sure. She'd been doing this for a few months and still kept getting all the various Edwards families mixed up—not that anyone seemed to mind. And she was getting faster at the mail sort. Better, too, at facing customers and having conversations. The trick was to be interested in them or, at the very least, the life of the village. And to not imagine what they might be thinking about her.

One day recently, with the sort finished and no customers at the counter, Olivia had found herself asking Wendy a serious question. 'Do people know about me? About, you know, the whole Hayden thing? The video? Is there gossip?'

Wendy set down her coffee. 'Early on there were a few locals who thought you were the most scintillating thing to happen here in years. More recently, some who were titillated, a bit sniggery. But, honestly, that's only a handful. Most don't know you from a bar of soap, or don't care. And besides, you're old news these days. There're better things to talk about, more pressing matters. Like, haven't you heard, one of Eddie's rams got in with the Mulhollands' pretty little ewes, and now they're asking for money to cover the costs of his offspring. And there's an argument down the road a bit about whose side of the boundary the little creek is on. And there's a bloke from the mainland who's bought up old Arthur's property and wants to build a whopping big palace. Sweetie, you're just the chick who sorts the mail now.'

Olivia smiled. She could live with that level of invisibility.

It helped that Leena's attempt at retaliation had been squashed. The police had acted within a day of her nasty little video being uploaded. Although their warning visit hadn't stopped her from acting, the take-down had been swift. Leena had claimed that Olivia had done it—a woman scorned who wanted to hurt her ex-lover, who wanted more attention. Nobody had bought it, and the cyber experts had worked their magic to gather clear evidence. Leena had been sent back to jail for breaching conditions, with a few new charges stuck on for good measure.

This time around Olivia had focused on the positive responses from the media—social and otherwise—which had been significantly in her favour. She was a victim and a survivor. Revenge porn was a heinous crime. Hayden Carlyle was a cheating bastard, a claim backed up by his latest scandal, and Leena was wicked.

After finishing the mail sort, Olivia helped Wendy to scan all the parcels and tidy the shelves, then she trotted over to the general store, returning with their coffees.

'I'm going to miss this,' she said as she and Wendy sipped lattes.

The woman let out a theatrical sigh. 'Abandoning me when I need you most! It's crazy in here as we get closer to Christmas. I call it the parcel tsunami.' She pulled Olivia into a hug. 'I still don't see why you have to leave. We'd always look after you.'

'I know, but I'd always be a bit worried. Leena will be out before you know it, and then I'd always be looking over my shoulder.' The letters had already started again, sent to Olivia at Eloise's address. Wendy had given her the first one and from then on had taken to binning them the second she saw the Correctional Facility mark on the envelope. 'I know it looks like I'm running away, but I'm not—just having a change of scene.'

'And spending time with your lovely bloke.' Wendy gave a suggestive grin. 'You must be excited.'

'Yup. That too.' Olivia smiled, the silly, giddy feeling impossible to hide. 'And nervous.'

'About seeing Tom? Why?'

Yes, why? Not because she had secrets. Because over the past few months they'd covered all the big stuff—and there had been plenty of big stuff for both of them—plus a whole lot of not-so-big stuff and oodles of day-to-day, insignificant, precious little snippets about themselves. 'I don't know. Maybe because he's so great and we work so well together. I don't want to stuff it up.'

'You won't.' Wendy said this with the confidence of someone who could see the future.

'Or he could be too good to be true. Maybe I'm caught up in the romance and misreading him. What if he's not actually as great as I think he is?'

'Then you'll come home, wiser and with the knowledge that you put yourself out there—that you took a risk, opened your heart a little. That you moved on from that arsehole Hayden Carlyle, and from all that bullshit.'

Wendy was an astute woman and a good friend. Later, when she wrapped Olivia in another wonderful hug, Olivia squeezed her back. 'Thank you. For everything.'

'You're welcome, love. Now go and see that man. Grand gestures deserve happy endings. It doesn't always happen like in the movies, and the happy ending may not be what you expect, and it may not even be an ending but the start of a new chapter.' Wendy laughed. 'Listen to me, I'm making this stuff up! But, believe me, you deserve the next chapter to be a good one.'

It already is, Olivia thought, exchanging several waves as she drove through the village.

At Tilly's house she sat with Brian in her lap and carrot cake on the table.

'Don't worry, lovely,' the woman told her, 'he'll be well loved here.'

'I know.' Olivia rubbed the top of his head with her nose. 'I'm going to miss him. He's my buddy, and I'm abandoning him—for a guy!'

'Well, maybe if you decide to settle over there, we can book him on a flight.'

'I'm sorry I can't be more definite about my plans. I could be back here in a month, or it could be three months, or six. I might end up staying in London. I just don't know.'

'Stop worrying about it. Brian and I get along fabulously. You've got to go and see how things work out. We'll figure it out as we go along. Brian could end up jet-setting across the world to be with you, or he could live splendidly here with us.'

'Thank you.' Olivia pressed her face against Brian's side, quiet tears soaking into his fur.

*

It took her thirty-one hours of travel to get from Devils Bay to Heathrow, counting the hop across the ditch to Melbourne, the easy-ish flight to Bangkok, the horrendously boring five-hour stopover in the airport there, and finally the flight to London. Three hours into the twelve-hour last leg, Olivia was exhausted, grotty, and vehemently wishing she'd put her pride aside and accepted Tom's offer of a business class ticket.

He'd told her it would be his way of saying thank you for being a perfect sidekick on his quest. She'd told him he would have to find some other way of rewarding her for solving the mystery on his behalf. What she didn't tell him was that she was never again going to be wooed or blinded by indulgent offerings.

But when the jostling of her seat woke her from a cramped, uncomfortable sleep, she started to think she'd been too hasty, or even that she should have splurged and used some of her own money.

All the pain of travel was forgotten, though, when she stepped into the arrivals hall at Heathrow and Tom scooped her up and kissed her hard. How they were going to make this work was still a mystery, but this was a good start.

ACKNOWLEDGEMENTS

A tiny spark for this story came to me in 2015. A version of the manuscript was first sent out (with all my hopes and dreams) into the hands of publishers in 2017. It wasn't until September 2021 that Harlequin offered me a contract. The finished copy you're holding was released in January 2022.

That's seven years of writing, rewriting, learning, improving, receiving feedback, and making changes. Sometimes I gave up, but I always came back.

In those seven years there were so many people who helped—who read and critiqued, who gave workshops, who provided advice, who kept me going. I wish I had kept a list.

I will do my best to thank those who've been involved most recently.

Thank you to the wonderful Nicola Robinson. It was an absolute joy to work with you—from that first three-minute Zoom pitch to the moment three weeks later when you rang to offer me a contract, through edits, and right up to the day you left to take a new path.

Thank you to Rachael Donovan for taking me on and including me in your list of amazing authors, and for answering all my questions and getting me through the publishing process. To Julia Knapman and Kate Goldsworthy for your comprehensive edits. This book is better because of what you do. Your commitment to making sure all the intricacies of this story fitted together made all the difference. Thank you to the design team, you gave me a fabulous cover that was so much more than I expected. And books wouldn't go anywhere without the efforts of the sales team. Thank you for putting this book on the shelves.

A special thanks to Fiona McIntosh, your tough but fair assessment of my synopsis was just what I needed. I don't think I would've got over the line without you! Thank you also for running one of your magical masterclasses in Hobart—from that class has come an amazing group of writers. Their friendship and support have been incredible, and our lunches are a monthly highlight.

To all the residents of my own little village. I've never felt more at home anywhere. Woodbridge inspired the setting for this story and so many locals helped answer my strange little questions. A special shout-out to Kelly Eckel for being the best postmistress ever! And for coming up with a very cunning way to find someone who doesn't want to be found.

To Rebecca Le Roy, who has become a much loved member of our family, and who laughed and said she didn't mind that I have a character also named Rebecca who wasn't always the most likeable person.

A special thank you to the RWA. The conferences you run offer writers a space filled with encouragement, learning, inspiration, and friendship. Thanks also to the Australian Society of Authors, your advocacy for writers is so important, and your Literary Speed Dating sessions are an incredible opportunity for aspiring authors.

A special thanks to Kate and Ian and the amazing team at Dymocks Hobart. From the first time I proudly mentioned I had a manuscript through to the day (years later) when I could tell you I was going to be published, you have always cheered me on and answered my questions. Thank you!

Huge hugs and thanks to my darling boys. To my wonderful husband, Damien, who has given nothing but endless encouragement and support. This book wouldn't exist without you. And to Jack and Ben, my two amazing teenagers—who think it's funny to tell people they're not allowed to read Mum's book because it's X-rated—I'm so proud of both of you.

And finally, to you, the reader. Thank you. Thank you for taking a chance on a new author and for choosing to read this story. It means so much to me that this book is in your hands. Without readers, writing would be a lonely place.

talk about it

Let's talk about books.

Join the conversation:

 facebook.com/harlequinaustralia

 @harlequinaus

 @harlequinaus

harpercollins.com.au/hq

If you love reading and want to know about our authors and titles, then let's talk about it.